CLAIMING THE CURSE

CHELLE CYPRESS

CHELLE CYPRESS BOOKS

Cover by Jaqueline Kropmanns

Edited by:
Brittany Mack (Developmental Editing), K.T Wishert (Line Editing) & Beth Lawton
(Copy Edit/Proofread)

ISBN: 979-8-9891185-4-0

TRIGGER WARNING

Anxiety, Blood & Gore Depictions, Captivity & Confinement, Child Abuse, Chronic Illness, Coma, Cults, Death of Loved One, Depression, Disappearance of a Loved One, Explosions, Grief & Loss Depictions, Imprisonment, Kidnapping/Ransom, Knife/Sword Violence, Medical Treatment/Medical Procedures, Physical Assault, Physical Illness, Poisoning, Post Traumatic Stress Disorder, Sexual Assault (Implied attempted rape, dubious consent due to power dynamics), Suicidal Ideation, Terminal Illness, Weight loss

DEDICATION

To my resilient readers, who know that inner strength often comes with a steep price—the sacrificing of softness to harden. I wish you'd been given a safe place to land instead of being forced to grow in barren soil. This book is for you, an ode to the darkness you had to cultivate to survive. In all this, never forget that you matter.

MAP

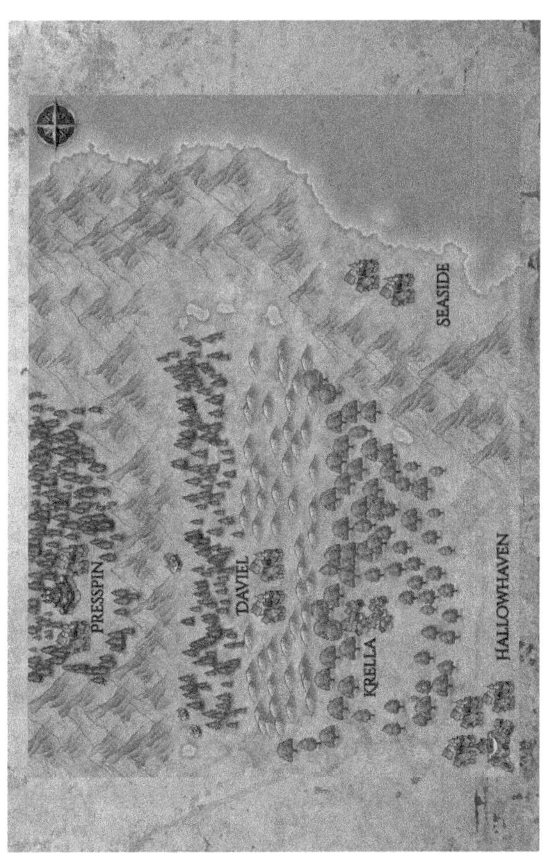

FORWARD

Last time on the Aralian Series

Unmasking the Curse Summary:

Arianna Park is bound to an enchanted porcelain mask to keep her deadly blight at bay. Betrothed to the vicious Theo Terrell, she resigns herself to her fate. However, everything changes when the brooding Silas Belmont strides into town.

Inexplicably drawn to Arianna, Silas reveals his greatest secret—that he too carries the curse—and begins training her to control her inner darkness. However, everything goes awry when their lessons take an unexpected turn, leaving Arianna incapacitated within Archer Estate.

Once well enough to return home, her brutish betrothed punishes her for her impropriety. Though Silas is ready to leave Krella to return to Belmont Manor, he proposes a marriage of convenience to the wounded lady.

After eloping and consummating their marriage, the once fleeting connection between them deepens as if it has a mind of its own. Despite Silas's avoidance, and Arianna's resignation to a loveless life, the pair develop a friendship that sparks into more. However, Silas is hiding a dark secret about the origins of their curse.

Spurred on by the feisty Brielle, Arianna notices inconsistencies between her hometown Krella and Presspin. Why has no one mentioned the Goddess Aralia within the town? Forced to confront Silas, he finally divulges the truth—that Aralia is the Goddess of Darkness who placed the curse upon those who'd once followed the God of Light. The Aralians were not simply containing her darkness with the wards but draining the blighted of their vitality and power. Both gods have disappeared from this world.

Overwhelmed, Arianna scours for any information about the truth. Yet, she becomes sidetracked as word from his sister arrives that her once betrothed's family is seeking retribution and threatening her family with debtors' prison. Silas, unwilling to allow her to run headlong into danger, concocts a plan—secure a solicitor to pay the debt of her bride price.

Uneasy, Arianna has little choice and turns her attention to preparing for the harvest festival, Kesere. Once again, she's accosted by Brielle, who informs Arianna of a lesser-known piece of Aralian lore—that cursed beings who are mates form a unique bond. Arianna, overwhelmed by the information, confronts Silas, who is flabbergasted by the possibility.

However, the bubbling emotions, endless yearning and the revelation lead to a head as passion ignites. The meek Arianna stands her ground against the taciturn Silas, who finally acknowledges his undying love for her. Their union and bond are fully consummated in a night of smoldering passion.

With their connection established and a solicitor within the town to resolve Arianna's familial issues, all is right with the world. Until Silas's brother-in-law, Duncan Archer, who was in cahoots with the Terrells, betrays the pair. Silas is incapacitated, and Arianna kidnapped and whisked back to the Terrells. Silas awakens hours later and dashes off to rescue his beloved.

As Arianna awakens, she's forced to confront the dastardly Fletcher Terrell, who's made a deal with the Aralians to give over Arianna Park, but not before claiming his revenge. On the brink of enduring an assault, Arianna senses her love's presence growing closer through their shared connection. With the joint power of their darkness she's able to burst through the wards, dispatch Mr. Terrell and search for her relations held captive within the manor.

With her mother and sister secured, she rushes to reunite with her beloved but is faced with a troop of Aralian Disciples. Spurred on by her blight, she battles the unit as Silas approaches to offer aid. However, with their onyx armor repelling the dark power of the pair, escape seems hopeless. As Arianna instructs her family members to flee, an arrow pierces her mother's heart, killing her. Enraged, Arianna's blight takes a greater hold, muddling her ties to reality. Overwhelmed by the likelihood that they would either die or be captured Silas makes the ultimate sacrifice to unleash his power in a blast harsh enough to destroy the platoon but likely also kill him as well.

When Arianna awakens, Silas is unconscious and trapped within his darkness. Her sister is alive, and the platoon of Aralians was dispatched. Silas's resourceful sister, Beatrix had rescued them. After days of trying to breach through his mental walls, Arianna finally saves Silas from the darkness, and he awakens.

Though the pair are safe for now, there are ramifications from these events. Silas has contracted the wasting sickness from expelling too much life force and energy in the blast at Terrell Estate; the events at Terrell Estate haunt Arianna; Beatrix is stricken from her husband's betrayal; and Naomi faces a deep depression from the tribulations she endured.

CHARMING THE CURSE'S CONSORT SUMMARY:

Memories of her soulmate, Wren, haunt Brielle. Desperate for relief, she searches for a new paramour during the Kesere festival, only to find the town paired off except for the charming, Mateo Reed. However, there is one issue: Mateo isn't searching for a casual interlude. He promised his deceased betrothed he would remain celibate until he fell in love again. Mateo's pursuit of Brielle is cut short by the unconscious Lord Belmont arriving in Presspin under the guise of having contracted pneumonia, taking most Brielle's time (in tangent with the last chapter of Unmasking the Curse). However, once the Belmonts appear settled Brielle thwarts the young man's pursuit, offering friendship while she waits for an opportunity to find another casual paramour.

As the winter proceeds, Mateo and Brielle form a companionship. However, an underlying attraction bubbles between them, and Brielle finds herself slowly opening up emotionally to the easy-mannered man. All the while, the herbalist is thrust into more of the Belmont's chaos from tending to the depressed Naomi, comforting Arianna and bearing witness to the wasting sickness taking hold of Silas (in tangent with the epilogue in Unmasking the Curse).

Brielle, facing memories of Wren, Silas's ailment and the weight of the past, is offered what she's wanted all winter, a no-strings interlude with the tightly wound Rosalind Collins. However, she rejects the offer and finds herself in Mateo's arms, seeking comfort and a single kiss.

With her feelings blossoming, Brielle's deepest fears rise to the surface. Is she strong enough to accept love after experiencing so much loss? Under Mateo's tender care, Brielle finds herself drawn to the sweet man, which softens her outer shell, allowing her to share the loss she's carried for years. Everything comes to a boiling point when Brielle's longings can no longer be ignored. The pair, finally ready to step fully into a relationship, consummate their connection.

We end the novella with Silas dealing with the wasting sickness, Arianna searching for a cure, Naomi opening up a fraction and working at the herbalist shop with Brielle. Brielle and Mateo are in a committed relationship filled with love and possibility.

The novella serves as a bridge between the beginning of winter and the end of Unmasking the Curse, and the looming spring where we start our story in Claiming the Curse.

See Appendix at the end of the book for further character reminders, if needed.

CHAPTER 1

SILAS

DEATH LURKED IN THE shadows, haunting me. She had tried to take me months ago, but she wouldn't claim me today. Despite my determination to remain in the world of the living, a chill slithered along my spine and settled at its base. Goose bumps rose on my flesh, and a perpetual looming dread curled in my gut. Even the air in the study held a stale tang that coated my nostrils. Certain my demise neared, my gaze trailed from the mahogany desk. I scanned the leather sofa, the dying embers in the hearth, and the bookcase, then shifted on the empty corner, as if the wraith waited. To my relief, only the late winter sunlight glimmered against the bronze flecks in the paisley wallpaper. My palm dragged down my face, anchoring me to reality and away from these macabre hallucinations.

Steadying my focus toward securing Arianna's future, I inhaled. The breath caught in my throat, gargling through my lungs. My chest constricted. A rough, watery cough sputtered from me, causing my spine to curl in on itself. My fingers dug into the polished edge of the desk. Eventually, a harsh bark left me, and a speckling of blood coated the desktop. Agitated, I scrubbed the sleeve of my wool robe against my lips. My teeth clenched at the crimson staining the pristine white fabric and the once shining wood.

I fished the fresh linen handkerchief from my housecoat and cleaned the spittle. I couldn't leave a trace of my presence in the place. Not when I needed to update my will in secret and replace the testament crafted months ago, when this wasting sickness first took hold. Over the past few weeks, as I'd convalesced, watching the snow dwindle, a sense of impending doom had loomed within me. My original declaration had not provided the protection my beloved would need once the spring came, and I...

My hands balled into fists. I pushed the thought of my impending demise away, then tucked the soiled handkerchief into my pocket. I reached for the bronze knob on the drawer. To my surprise, the leaves of paper no longer lay in this compartment. Instead, the leather ledger sat amongst the writing utensils.

Apparently, Beatrix and Vincent had rearranged the drawers. Despite the urgency, I tugged the notebook out. The once crisp pages were worn, with dog-eared tabs throughout, denoting the tallies on the updated food stores. I thumbed through the contents that now held Beatrix's handwriting. Her elegant scroll covered every page in the book. A hint of pride swelled. She had done well, working in my stead as my ailment kept me from my duties. Beatrix would become an excellent overseer of Presspin if Arianna had her way.

I placed the ledger on the desk with a soft thunk. Why were these ominous thoughts leaching within me? Needing to free myself from this heaviness, my gaze drifted to the window.

Gray clouds blotted out the blue sky, casting shadows over the snow-covered mountain range. Despite the gloom, the icy storms were more sporadic, indicating that spring neared. My heart ached. Would I succumb to this illness before the prescar flowers bloomed?

As if in answer, a chill coursed through me, causing me to shake with trembling shivers. My teeth chattered. Despite my blazing skin, I felt as if I'd plunged into the snow. I'd spent weeks battling the fevers lurking beneath my flesh akin to a furnace burning me alive. My fingers wrapped around the cool bronze knob and pulled the next drawer open. A trove of blank sheets lay before me.

I'd just yanked out a sheet and pen when the click of the doorknob drew my attention to the entrance. My shoulders tensed. Had Arianna returned from training with Peter earlier than I expected and come seeking me out? Perhaps Beatrix had risen early to work on the mound of requests submitted by the townsfolk. If they found me here, they'd fetch Roger, our burly footman, to haul me to bed like a sack of flour. To my relief, a swishing of black skirts preceded the mousy features of a maid.

"My lord! What are you doing here?" A gasp escaped from Hannah.

I flicked my gaze to the clock, taking in that seven approached. Since being bedridden, I'd forgotten that a staff member often cleaned the space in the early morning hours.

"We must get you to your quarters before my lady, or worse, Mrs. Potter, sees you in here." Her eyes bulged in genuine fear of the matron who ran the manor's inner workings.

I straightened in my seat and pulled against my waning mantle as Lord Belmont. However, the gesture lacked the authority it once possessed. I'd shriveled under this all-consuming, wasting sickness, becoming a shell of my former self.

In spite of my frailty, command laced my tone. "That shall be all, Hannah. You can clean after breakfast." I waved my hand, shooing the mousy maid away.

She remained rooted to the spot. She bowed low in reverence, then stared at her polished black shoes.

"My apologies, my lord, but if I may warn you, Lady Belmont is expected back from her morning walk with Peter any minute now. Mrs. Potter instructed her that she must eat breakfast under her watchful eye. Your sister, Lady Beatrix..." A crimson tint crawled over the shell of her ears. "She is in an important meeting with your steward. In her suites. They shall be returning here within the hour. Though it might be longer."

With nothing to do but eavesdrop on the maids' gossip, I'd discovered that over the winter, my sister and Vincent had kindled some sort of casual arrangement. I didn't approve but couldn't blame her for seeking comfort in the arms of another after what Duncan had done.

Unaware of my drifting thoughts, Hannah continued. "You are still the lord of this manor, but whatever you are doing here, make haste." Without awaiting my answer, she slipped out the door.

With no time to waste, I picked up the pen and wrote my wishes.

Minutes ticked by as my desires for Arianna's safety were ratified on the page and sealed with my signet. With my will updated, I breathed out a sigh of relief while I waited for the wax to dry. The three pines lined in front of a mountain range gleamed in the crimson. The Belmont crest was the perfect depiction of Presspin—my home. My aching form relaxed into the leather chair I'd occupied for a decade as the Lord of Belmont Manor and overseer of Presspin. The familiar scent of ink curled in my nostrils. My thumb traced along the desk where my uncle, too, had sat before this same ailment claimed him.

Would I be strong enough to revisit this study, or would my body be bedbound? The questions lay heavy on my shoulders, similar to a knoll stone. But given Hannah's warning, I couldn't linger in these sentimental quandaries.

Akin to an octogenarian, I braced against the smooth armrests of the chair and forced myself to my feet. My palm closed around the lacquered crook of the cane I'd left leaning against the edge. With a whisper of foreboding, I shuffled through the office. As I reached the door, the hairs on my nape rose. In my periphery, a shadowy figure lounged on the sofa, my uncle waiting for me to join him in the Great Beyond. My forehead pressed against the doorframe. He's not there. Yet the ghosts of my past, like me, lingered between the living and the dead. Without a glance back, I left.

My feet trudged down the hallway at a snail's pace. Hopefully, since Hannah had scurried off, I'd make it to the master suites unnoticed while the staff were either serving breakfast or partaking of it themselves. To my dismay, a cold sweat seeped through my cotton nightshirt beneath my housecoat, as if I'd run miles instead of having walked a small stretch. A wheeze punctuated my once steady breaths. My pace slowed.

I pushed forward, taking one, two, three steps.

My head swam. The world tilted on its axis. Seeking stability, my shoulder leaned against the copper-toned wallpaper. A weakness seized me, and the cane clattered from my clutches. The soft carpet muffled the thump as it landed. My brow furrowed. The crutch laid just beyond my reach, but I didn't have time to focus on the walking stick as a fit overtook me. A choking sensation akin to a vise gripped my windpipe.

I gasped. This mortal coil relented against my sheer stubbornness. Frantically, I rummaged through my robe pocket for the remedy that would ease my symptoms and open my airways. My hand laced around the glass vial. The pale green elixir sloshed in the container. My fingers trembled as I tried to yank the stopper out, to no avail. A wheeze wrenched through me. Spots speckled my vision. Hastily, I lodged the cork between my teeth. The spongy texture ripped free. Yet I swayed off-kilter from the force. My wobbly legs buckled. Similar to a foal, I stumbled, and the medicine jostled from my grip.

The vial tumbled onto the sage-hued rug, its contents spilling onto the plush fabric. My eyes widened in shock at the wet spot where my tonic pooled and caused the light-colored carpet to darken. The muscles in my ribcage squeezed, wringing the life from me.

I gasped. No air came. My waning strength faltered. Gravity tugged against me. My nails dug into the wallpaper, shredding the delicate lining into strips. I tumbled.

Thud.

Pain shot through my head, rattling my brain as my skull connected with the wood floor inches shy of the soft runner.

Stars filled my vision. I strained for the empty vial, hoping to consume at least a few drops. As a last effort, my hand snaked over the soaking rug for the container. The coolness of the glass seeped into my palm. I brought the vial closer and placed it on my lips. None remained.

The tightening in my lungs intensified. Terrified, I used my final dregs of strength to roll to my side. My fingers dug into my throat, as if I could rip my neck open and allow oxygen to enter me. Pain seared where my nails scratched against my flesh. But nothing could help me as blood and phlegm coated my lungs.

Arianna! I cried out for her through our bond, in this last-ditch effort to save myself, but only silence echoed through the connection. The once strong cord had weakened as I inched closer to my end. Now only a fraying thread held us together.

A tear ran down my cheek. Why was fate so cruel, giving me Arianna, then separating us once our souls had finally found each other? I couldn't abandon her, not while the threat of the Aralians loomed and her relationships lay in shambles after the horrors that occurred at Terrell Estate.

I clung to our connection, yet it blinked in and out of existence like a candle flickering in the wind. Regardless of my hope to remain by her side, I would perish without oxygen.

Arianna. I beckoned her again, as if she were my lifeline.

Tears rolled down my cheeks. A silent prayer to whatever deity of life or death churned in my soul. That they would wait until she was next to me before they took me. The edges of my world grew hazy. Time seemed irrelevant as I floundered like a fish out of water. Seconds stretched as if they'd become hours as I teetered toward my impending doom. I wanted to live, but my body wouldn't acquiesce to my desires.

"Silas." Arianna's scream rang through the hallway. The thundering of boots drew closer, like a storm approached.

She slid to her knees and shifted my head into her lap. "No. No. No! Don't you dare go, Silas. I won't let you." She rummaged in her pocket and pulled out another tonic.

Warmth enveloped me. My beloved, my bride. My only regret was the autumn wasted not accepting what was between us. At least I'd relished these stolen days this winter. My reward for the future I forfeited for hers.

She pried my lips open and poured the bitter remedy onto my tongue. Trickles of the tonic dribbled out. She clamped my mouth shut, and the liquid slid down my throat. Heartbeats passed, but my breathing didn't regulate.

"Don't you dare leave me, Silas! Not you too. You can't." She sobbed.

Her trembling hands stroked through my hair. The sensation soothed the tightly coiled tension a fraction. I had her here: my beloved, my lifeblood. We anchored each other to these mortal coils.

The scent of ash filled the space, and a surge of energy crackled from her fingertips. It washed over my scalp, as if it could keep my soul tethered to this broken form. Her eyes flickered wholly black, then returned to blue. She whimpered, pressing her forehead against mine.

"I love you. Please don't leave me alone." Her hot, salty tears streamed, dripping onto my forehead. My heart shattered for her. I never meant to cause her pain.

A wheeze rattled out of me. No sound came from me, despite my desire to declare my love for her and my wish for her to live on. But I was too weak. My limbs were going numb, and my sight faltered. Only darkness prevailed. With the last of my strength, I sent a promise to her.

I will always come back to you, Arianna. Always...

CHAPTER 2

Arianna

EACH DAY, A PIECE of my soul withered away, as if I were vanishing. This long existence without my love haunted me in a way akin to a specter wandering this copper-colored corridor where death had come to claim him. My curse churned, an internal warning that the spot I'd loathed walking across loomed nearby, causing a shudder to course down my spine. My boots slipped off the scorched padded rug and onto the marred wood where my blight had unfurled from me like an inky darkness, charring this segment of hallway where he'd lain, dying within my arms.

As I traversed the path Silas had two days ago, I chastised myself for not sensing his intentions. However, the tether that lived between us, feeding us one another's emotions, had dwindled with each day since he'd awoken from his coma after the blast at Terrell Estate. The fact that I'd heard his cries through our bond as he lay dying, despite the connection having been threadbare, had been miraculous. As the thought rushed forward, a knot pressed against my windpipe. I hastened my pace, weaving around the dreaded spot and past the portraits of the previous overseers of Presspin. My steps echoed as I headed for the study where Beatrix waited to finalize the transfer of power. Today, she'd officially become the Lady of Belmont Manor.

I halted at the threshold, having no desire to enter nor acknowledge the bleak future that unfurled before me. However, if I lingered here, Mrs. Potter would likely pounce upon me with trays of delicacies that I'd be forced to choke down. My fist rapped against the door.

"Come in," Beatrix's somber voice called out.

As I entered, a wave of sorrow crashed against me, nearly breaking my heart. It had been months since Silas had sat at his desk, his hair askew, with ink staining his fingers and a cold cup of tea by his side. He hadn't occupied this space over the past few months, despite his intentions. This winter, many things had changed, including the study. A vase of lilies perched on the small table by the sofa, and a soft yellow blanket lay on the couch. Even the scent of coffee wafted through the air, replacing the aroma of chamomile. The once luxurious tang made my gut twist in discomfort.

"Have a seat. I just need to finish this request for Vincent before he returns from morning training with the army." She turned her attention from the thick ledger to me and gestured to the couch.

I huffed a sigh. The Belmont siblings struggled to disengage when in the depths of managing the village, so I moved to the sofa and took a seat amongst the cushions. Numb, I spun the onyx ring Brielle had crafted to replace the one lost at Terrell Estates. The black stone glimmered in the soft winter glow washing through the massive windows. Sitting in this space without my love caused a fog to coat my perception as the clock on the mantel ticked, as if none of this were truly real.

"Coffee?" Beatrix's question pierced through my dissociation.

I blinked. Her face remained neutral, and her eyes held a glint of coolness where warmth had once lived. She'd hardened under the weight of the abuses she'd endured from her dastardly husband, Duncan Archer. She never spoke of her ordeal—when Duncan held her captive in her own home—yet the perpetual frown that pulled on her once joyous face was impossible to ignore.

"No, thank you." I waved away the tray. Since the escapades at Terrell Estate, food had lost its splendor and my appetite had diminished.

She pursed her lips in thought as she took in my frail frame. The robust health I'd gained during the fall had declined. Uncomfortable, I shifted on the cushions, the skirts drowning me and rustling from the motion. A beat of silence passed as her brilliant mind whirled.

"Very well. I'll have to let Mrs. Potter know you refused refreshments. I'm certain she'll be joining you for lunch and spoon-feeding you soup." She lifted the silver craft and poured a cup.

I pulled on my gaping sleeve, unable to hide the stone I'd lost over the past few months. Despite my lack of appetite, I heaved a sigh and nodded.

A hint of a smile tugged at the corner of her lips in a rare reappearance of her jovial demeanor. It clashed with her tight chignon and navy day dress, as if the carefree girl she once was warred against the overseer she'd soon be.

The clicking of the silver spoon against the cup punctuated our awkward quiet. Though we were friends, we were both coping with unpredictable futures that coated our relationship in a sober gloom. Seconds later, she handed me the steaming brew. The porcelain warmed my icy palms, but even this comfort couldn't thaw the chill within me.

Begrudgingly, I sipped the beverage, sensing her watchful stare as she settled on the other end of the couch.

She lowered her beverage to the table with a clink. Her skirt rustled as she pivoted, pointing her knees toward me. Concern etched across her brow. "You don't have to do this. You should become the overseer of Presspin. As Silas's wife, it is your right."

I chewed the inside of my cheek. Silas had bristled against my desire to step down from the position and place the town's well-being in Beatrix's capable hands. But I was a farmer's daughter with minimal education. For months, I'd been far more concerned with Silas's failing health and my fruitless attempts to find a cure for his ailment. Beatrix, with Vincent's assistance, had stepped into the role and was managing the village with the same efficiency her brother once had.

"You're better suited to rule this territory." My brow pinched.

"If I can't get you to change your mind, then perhaps you'll listen to Silas." She rummaged in her pocket, tugged out a letter, and handed it to me.

Silas. The cup shook on the saucer, unsteady in my grip. I lowered my beverage to the side table and reached for the message. My heart hammered. The Belmont crest gleamed against the faint candlelight. My fingers trembled as they pressed into the crisp paper with Silas's scroll upon it.

"What is this?" My voice warbled.

"He updated his testament. I suspect it's why he was out of bed." She rubbed her forehead.

My thumb trailed over his handwriting, and a pang of sorrow washed over me. I'd wondered endlessly why he'd ventured out of our suites and to the study. Now I'd have an answer. My index finger slipped between the seam, dislodging the stiff wax. The letter tumbled open, and with bated breath, I read.

Beloved,

If you are reading this, then I assume that I've passed onto the Great Beyond and Vincent found my updated wishes. Weeks ago, when we crafted my original testament, you were hesitant in expressing your plans for the future, so certain that you'd save me from the wasting sickness. I understand that unyielding desire, for it was the same one I'd possessed when my uncle became ill with this ailment. Now that I am gone, this foolish search for nonexistent answers can be laid to rest along with me.

I hope you'll reconsider your position at Belmont Manor. Though you've expressed sentiments of inadequacy regarding governing Presspin, I do not agree with your tainted self-image. Over the fall, you blossomed from the shy farm girl you once were. You took on the mantle of Lady Belmont with poise and grace. Your compassion, consideration, and natural inclination to guard the less fortunate shall serve you well when you take on the mantle that belongs to you as my wife. Beatrix and Vincent will serve as your guides as you learn the daily rhythm of managing the town. I believe in you. More importantly, the title of overseer of Presspin will function as your shield. Any acts of aggression made against you will revoke the Presspin/Hallowhaven treaty of 1712 and be considered an act of war. If Delphine or the Aralians ever come for you, our militia are committed to protecting their sovereign. Please trust in our people to provide for you, as you shall provide for them.

I love you, Arianna, forever and always.

Silas

Tears brimmed as I read through the legal jargon that high-lighted his wishes.

"What is it?" Beatrix plucked the pages and withdrew them from my grasp. Silence stretched as she scanned the contents. Then she spoke. "He's not wrong. This is the most logical course of action. I was never meant to govern this town, and it would provide you with protection."

My gut twisted. The Aralians were searching for me, and my bounty had marked me. Though the winter had been quiet, my blight twitched, as if sensing their looming malicious intentions. I shook my head with untethered frustration. "We made a plan weeks ago. You were to become Lady Belmont if this happened, and I would…"

My words trailed off, because my plans and those highlight-ed with the original decree were vastly different. I'd requested to be bequeathed the gardener's cottage at the eastern border of Belmont Manor, and I'd asked that Naomi receive a monthly allowance. Alternatively, I'd created a secret plan to enact if Silas died, because I had no intention of staying here. No, I'd leave for Hallowhaven alone and turn myself in. This would leave Presspin out of the Aralians' clutches. Naomi's safety would be secured, and then I'd meet Silas in the Great Beyond. Unwilling to divulge my true intentions, I stood and strode to the window.

The white-capped mountains surrounded my people like sentinels, keeping them safe from the harm lurking just be-yond the range. Yet glimmers of green peeked from the once snow-covered evergreens, denoting that spring drew near. Once the pass cleared, the Aralians would likely be knocking on our doorstep to seek their revenge. For Silas and I had killed their sistren, and they would stop at nothing to exact their punishment.

"Arianna." Beatrix's boots clicked along the wood floors as she approached. "His judgment is sound. If the Aralians come, we'll protect you. Our militia—"

"Militia," I scoffed. "Do you believe three dozen hastily trained volunteers are strong enough to defeat the Aralians?"

A pained silence hung over us, and I sensed her internal battle. For it had been her husband, Silas's adviser, who'd suggested the once hearty army be disbanded. It had been a time of peace, and the soldiers were draining the village's coffers. Sadly, many of the unemployed soldiers left. Worse yet, some may have joined Hallowhaven's ranks.

"Peter's certain they are a strong lot and growing in numbers. We can double the yearly income and draw in more recruits. You do not have to fight this war alone." She squared her shoulders with determination.

"It doesn't matter. They would all die in minutes. Silas and I...we couldn't. I couldn't."

Summoned by the conversation, flashbacks of that horrible day at Terrell Estate overwhelmed me. The tinge of blood coated my senses. My sister's wails echoed through my mind, and my mother's unseeing eye stared at me as if I was reliving the events. The sip of coffee churned in my stomach. Bile crawled up my throat. I pressed my eyes closed and grasped the window seal, but darkness seeped through my skin and sizzled the wood. The tang of charring filled the air, locking me into the horrific memories instead of pulling me out. Sweat beaded my brow. The nightmare wouldn't relent.

"Arianna." Beatrix touched my shoulder, jolting me.

I flinched away from her, terrified of harming her by accident. My grip on the charred ledge loosened. I blinked and focused on the mountain range, counting the peaks: *one...two...three...four...five.* I repeated the ritual Peter had taught me until my control returned. A long puff of air pressed through my lips. Steady again, I turned to her.

Her olive complexion blanched to a ghostly white. However, she remained unmoved, as if terror had rooted her to the spot. I had likely transformed before her, my curse unleashing and showing her the monster that lurked beneath. My lips trembled; it was the same horrific stare Naomi had worn after the incident in the conservatory. I reeled back, giving her some distance.

To my relief, the door opened, breaking this fraught moment, and Vincent stepped in. "Beatrix, I..."

His gaze flicked from his papers, and the stack he carried nearly toppled from his clutches. His relaxed demeanor tightened to that of a professional. "My apologies, ladies. I can return later. I was just checking to see if Lady Beatrix needed my services this morning." A flush crossed the steward's cheeks, crawling up the shells of his ears.

"No, that is unnecessary." I squared my shoulders, forcing some level of authority into my voice as Silas used to do. "I'll sign the paperwork this afternoon to solidify that you shall be the rightful overseer of Presspin."

Beatrix huffed an exasperated sigh, then strode to the desk and sat in the large chair that Silas had once occupied.

Vincent gave a half-hearted bow as I brushed past him.

The door closed, ending a chapter of my life I'd once hoped for. Silas and I discussing business before delving into an afternoon of companionship. My lip trembled from the swelling sensation threatening to drown me. With haste, I marched down the hallway, my gaze locked straight ahead to avoid the space where my love had once been.

Minutes later, I arrived at the master suites that had once belonged to Uncle Oliver. Throughout the winter, my husband had insisted on convalescing here because he didn't want to mar my quarters. I was grateful for this consideration as the stench of sickness melding with eucalyptus assailed me. A soft light crested through the floor-to-ceiling windows overlooking the town. The room remained the same, with its outdated copper and crimson motif.

Rough, raspy breathing punctuated the silent suite, causing my stomach to sink. An ashen Silas lay tucked within the thick quilts, his slow respiration barely keeping him alive. A soft sniffling melded with his ragged breaths as Mrs. Potter softly cried at his bedside. Like a guard dog, she'd settled beside him at the foot of the bed, as if her ferocity would battle death herself to protect the boy she'd helped raise.

The door clicked behind me, drawing the matron's attention to me.

She blotted a handkerchief over her damp eyes. "My apologies, my lady. I excused Hannah to be near Silas. I didn't mean for you to see me like a watering pot."

"It's all right." I tiptoed toward the bed. Nothing would rouse him at this point, aside from a miracle, but I wouldn't stop searching until his dying breath.

Fresh tears streamed down her face, coating her cheeks, and she stifled a sob. "I'm sorry. I shouldn't be blubbering like this in front of you. I'll collect myself and fetch you breakfast. Perhaps you'd eat some honey buns Agnes sent this morning?"

The tray would grow cold, but I nodded, needing to be alone with him after reading over the letter that led us here.

Mrs. Potter gave a watery smile, and a whisper of hope softened her gaze. She bobbed a curtsy and scurried off.

Exhausted, I settled on the edge of the mattress. It dipped under my weight. Silas's chest rose and fell with quick, pained breaths, and a sheen of sweat beaded his forehead. His once olive skin had grayed to a sickly pallor.

"You foolish dunderhead," I whispered.

Sadly, there was no reaching him in this near-death state. I sucked in a sharp inhale and blew it out, expelling all the pent-up emotions I carried. "You know me far too well, don't you? That I'd leave this safe haven the second you perished as a final resort." My heart cracked open like an egg as I leaned closer, my lips pressed against the shell of his ear in a revertant promise. "Hear this: I won't relent, not until you draw your last breath. I'll save you, even if it kills me."

CHAPTER 3

ARIANNA

SUNLIGHT GLIMMERED OVER THE sidewalk, causing the melting patches of snow to sparkle akin to diamonds. Children giggled as they splashed through the puddles where precipitation pooled. The usually gray clouds that had cast over Presspin cleared, revealing a perfect crystal blue sky. Bright yellow birds flew through the air, denoting that warmer days would soon be here. If Silas were not dying, I'd have enjoyed a glorious day like this when winter began its transition to spring.

Yet my focus remained on my task—procure the medical tome Jamie had found hidden in his annex. With Silas's ailment worsening since his collapse, I'd requested that Jamie scour the dusty storage area in case we'd missed any tomes. To my luck, he stumbled across a book last night and sent word for me to stop by the bookstore in the morning.

Though I hated leaving Silas's side, I couldn't sit beside him sobbing instead of searching for a cure. Fortunately, Mrs. Potter and Agnes had spent many hours watching over him while I scoured Presspin for answers or trained with Peter to keep my deadly blight at bay.

Determined that this book would finally hold the needed answers, I weaved through the townspeople. Each person nodded in acknowledgment as they passed on the narrow lane. To my relief, no one asked about Silas's well-being. Most likely because of the widespread rumor that Silas was suffering from long-term complications from pneumonia, which they believed had taken my mother's life.

Minutes later, I turned the corner toward the row of tidy basalt buildings that housed the bookstore. The yeasty aroma of fresh bread from the bakery assaulted my senses. The once pleasant smell sank into me like a heavy stone. My empty stomach grumbled as a wave of weakness seized me. My brain chided me. I should have choked down the coffee and mush Mrs. Potter had begged me to eat. Feeling faint, my legs wobbled.

"My lady." A firm grip caught my elbow, steadying me.

I blinked, registering Mateo Reed. Sunlight washed over the man, highlighting his angelic features. For a moment, a sense of ease washed over me. He had that effect on people. His easy charm had been why Brielle had become so besotted with him. Moreso, he'd become a welcome sight in my home. Over the weeks, he'd often accompanied Brielle to Belmont Manor while she'd tended to Silas or checked on Naomi. His presence often lifted the sourest of moods. He'd also done the unthinkable—he'd won Brielle's heart.

As if sensing my thoughts, the furrowed lines in his brow smoothed, and a grin tugged on his lips. "You know, I seem to have this swoony effect on women, but I thought you'd at least be immune, my lady."

I huffed a sigh and straightened. "As we've discussed before, please call me Arianna. You are Brielle's paramour and Naomi's friend. There is no need for formality."

"As you wish." He flourished a mocking bow. "But you are obviously unwell. May I escort you to Brielle's? I wanted to check on her before I headed out for my rounds with the militia. She snuck out of bed without breakfast again." He lifted the wicker basket and smiled.

I flicked my glance away, as if caught also having forgone my meal. He studied me, then huffed an exasperated sigh. "My gods, you and Brielle are the same. That's why you're so wobbly. Well, luckily for you, I packed enough to feed an army. Come now."

He grabbed the crook of my arm and guided me past the bakery and bookstore, leading me straight to the herbalist shop.

As we entered, the bell chimed, announcing our presence. I breathed in the battling herbal aromas, which left a tinny tinge in my nostrils. Sweat beaded on my forehead from the overheated space that blazed to keep the various vegetation alive in the icy months. Vines crawled along the brick walls, and potted plants hung overhead.

"Brielle. You have a punishment waiting for you tonight. I've warned you—you mustn't sneak out of the house without eating," Mateo bellowed.

A flush crept up my cheeks at his blatant banter. However, in the past few weeks, the pair hadn't been shy about their ardor. They went as far as to cavort loudly in the closet at Belmont Manor shortly after they announced their newly fledged relationship.

I followed in tow, certain that Brielle was concocting remedies in the back room. A pang of panic twisted in my stomach. What if Naomi was minding the storefront today?

The rear door flung open, and a bedraggled Brielle stepped out. Heavy bags lay under her green eyes and a speckling of bright colors dotted her once crisp white apron, but despite the fatigue, a sultry smirk tugged on her lips. "Why would I wait for tonight when you can punish me right—"

Her mouth snapped closed as her gaze shifted from Mateo, who stood next to the counter where patrons paid for their items, to me. She smoothed her palms over her smock.

"Why didn't you mention we had company, dear?"

"Oh, that is my fault." He shrugged and lowered the basket to the surface beside the register. "She nearly fainted because she, too, refuses to take care of herself. No wonder you are friends. You both enjoy working yourselves to death and then refusing to meet the most basic of needs."

"That is not true at all. I have a basic need you are constantly taking care of." She leaned over the counter that separated her from Mateo, her eyes gleaming with mischief.

I cleared my throat, reminding the amorous pair that I was still here. They both turned to me.

"Well, I best be off. I'll have to pick up an extra patrol shift if I'm late for militia training." He pivoted to Brielle, placed a quick kiss on her cheek, and scurried off.

A smile softened her weary expression as she watched Mateo leave, like a lovesick fool. But the door never clicked closed. Instead, soft footsteps clipped on the tile floor behind me.

Brielle's eyes widened in a wordless plea to whoever had entered. I knew in the depths of my soul that it was my sister.

"What are you doing here? I made it abundantly clear that you should never set foot in this shop. I don't want to hear your apologies, nor do I want to see you," Naomi sneered.

I pivoted to her. Sunlight streamed from the windows, highlighting her rosy cheeks and golden hair. But fury pinched her features. I stepped closer, having missed her so desperately since she'd left Belmont Manor to come and live here.

She balled her gloved hands into fists and looked past me to Brielle. "I don't want her here."

"And yet you forget you are my apprentice and living in my home. Arianna is not only my friend, but Lady Belmont. If you don't want to be near her, then you may leave." Brielle crossed her arms over her chest and cocked an eyebrow.

Naomi shuddered with rage, clamped her mouth shut, and stormed off. The door smacked closed behind her, rattling the plants in the rafters. Pain radiated through my ribs. A desperate need to chase after my sister tingled down my legs. However, she wanted nothing to do with me. Between the death of our mother, her captivity in Terrell Estate, and being forced to live here, I didn't fault her for blaming me. I'd hoped we could reconcile until the incident in the conservatory a month ago, which caused our once tenuous relationship to shatter and Naomi to seek refuge here. Luckily, Brielle had somehow broken through her dense walls by offering her a purpose—an apprenticeship.

I remained stone-still, unsure of what to do. Should I chase after Naomi or head to the bookstore?

Brielle blew out a long breath. "No more sulking. Besides, I have something for you upstairs." She strode toward the exit.

Had Brielle perfected a stronger remedy, or had Naomi's experiments yielded an elixir to help with Silas's wasting sickness?

I hastened after her, leaving the shop. We climbed the icy steps and stepped into her apartment above. As we walked the hallway, we entered the familiar sitting room with the leather chair Silas had once occupied and the floral settee by the window. Brielle dropped the basket on the small side table and plucked out a crumble-topped muffin.

"Lemon blueberry. Mateo must have gone to the manor to request the fruit from the reserves. He's the sweetest." She plopped onto the sofa and took a hearty bite of the pastry. "I swear to the gods, I've been famished lately. It's probably because of all those rigorous hours entangled with Mateo. Have I told you about his cock? It's glorious."

My palm scrubbed over my face. "Is that why you dragged me up here, to talk about your escapades? Spare me the details of your activities. I have errands to run."

"Ah, yes. Your endless task to find a cure." She reached over the edge of the couch and lifted a heavy burlap bag. "I ran into Jamie this morning on my way home from Mateo's. He mentioned the medical journal." She shook the sack in triumph. "I saved you at least fifteen minutes of Jamie pestering you about no longer working at Layla's."

My fingers laced around the entwined handle. Hope blossomed in my belly. Perhaps this tome would hold the answers to Silas's ailment. I'd spent months combing through every book throughout Presspin, only to find outdated methods for helping those with respiratory illnesses.

From my research, the wasting sickness hadn't been recorded in texts because the Aralians had rewritten history, wrongfully casting the cursed as villains. They'd blotted the truth from memory. Few knew Aralia was the Goddess of Darkness and not the Goddess of Light. There was no mention of the disciples draining the life force from the blighted through the enchanted rooms and masks. Only after seeing it firsthand in battle had I deduced that they collected our power to create weapons. Only as Silas slipped away, much like his uncle before him, did I realize the true cost of these wards—the wasting sickness. According to Brielle, the ailment likely took root when Silas expended enough energy to destroy a battalion of Aralians and Terrell Estate. He shouldn't have lived to tell the tale. He should have died that day.

With a cleansing exhale, I pulled out the thick tome. My thumb traced over the engraved words *Medical Journal of 1762*. Rage blazed within. I'd already read this pointless edition about the healing practice of bloodletting. My ears rang, as if warning bells chimed. My vision heightened, allowing me to see the tug of every faint line on Brielle's face. Fury sparked through my fingers, igniting the book. In a second, only ash remained.

"Gods above." Brielle chucked the half-eaten muffin to the floor and approached with her palms showing. Despite my likely monstrous state, fear didn't cross her expression. "Breathe."

My shoulders tensed. Smoke roiled through my fingers. I had to leash my darkness before it took root and burned down my friend's apartment. My focus skittered about the sitting area, searching for something to anchor me. To my shock, Brielle stepped forward and cupped my cheeks in her hands.

"Focus on me. In...out...in...out," she chanted, and my respiration followed with the beat she set.

Minutes slipped by, and eventually, my blight settled, tethered by my friend's steady cadence. My curse had untethered from my control, threatening to harm another person I cared about. My chin wobbled, and the anguish I'd held at bay spilled from me. She wrapped me in her embrace.

"That edition was in the library. I thought...this was the answer. There has to be an answer. Someone. Anything." I sobbed against her shoulder, and she tensed tight as a bowstring. A sensation pinged in my gut at the sudden shift in her energy.

"What's wrong?" I stumbled back, fearing my darkness had leaked from me without my permission.

"No. It's not you..." Her emboldened countenance tightened. She shifted from one foot to the other, her gaze flicking beyond me. Whatever she was hiding seemed to eat at her usually bold demeanor.

I reached for her hand, and my fingers squeezed a pulse of reassurance. "You've kept Silas alive and helped my sister. You have been my sole confidante throughout the winter. Whatever burden you're carrying, you can share it with me."

She pulled away and fidgeted with the frayed edge of her braid. Her face fell. She shook her head as if she could dislodge whatever bothered her. As if overcoming some internal battle, she took a deep breath, then spoke. "I've been having nightmares about Wren since Silas collapsed."

Despite my shock, I schooled my features. Brielle rarely discussed her lost mate. To remain composed, I folded my hands in front of me, anchoring my emotions.

Her focus shifted from me to a painting over the mantel that depicted women dancing, as if she were not here but somewhere else. "Every night, Wren's bound to a cell. I'm scouring a dungeon for a way to free her. Then I hear you in the distance. I run to you, and there you are with the key. But you refuse to assist me, even when I fall to my knees and beg. You let her rot there."

She shuddered, but I remained unmoving, holding space for her in this fraught moment.

"My heart breaks all over again as the door between Wren and me remains bolted shut. In my anguish, I wake up screaming her name." A tense beat of silence clung to the air as her lower lip trembled a fraction.

My shoulders softened at this shared horror of watching our soulmates drift away while we are unable to save them. "I promise you, if I'd known Wren and you all those years ago, I could have rescued her."

"I know. The dream is not an accurate depiction of you," she leaned forward and whispered, "but a reflection of me."

That pang of danger sizzled down my spine, ready to strike. I breathed through the unease, anchoring myself to the moment, waiting for her to continue.

A deep crease cut across her brow. "I've been lying to you. At first, I used Silas's threats of throwing me in the brig as an excuse. Honestly, I've feared what would happen to my life if the Aralians ever came to Presspin. Would they strip another love from my clutches and leave me a hollowed shell?" She shook her head. "No, I couldn't allow it."

A knot formed in my throat. "I don't understand."

"I never wrote to Martha like you asked. I lied, saying I'd sent word, and she never responded."

The admittance hit me akin to a ton of bricks, nearly bowling me over. I blinked, aghast.

"It was too great a risk. Of course Martha had provided me with assistance when I escaped the Aralians, but with a bounty as large as yours, can anyone truly be trusted? To further sway me, Silas threatened to imprison me if I sent word when his symptoms flared. Unwilling to put everything I love in jeopardy, I agreed." Her glance darted to the carpet.

My hands balled into fists. Silas had again superseded my wishes, going behind my back to protect me. It was the foundation our relationship had been built upon. Me being the frail girl, and him being my savior. But what he hadn't realized was that our roles had reversed, and I was no longer the damsel in distress.

"Why tell me this now?" I hissed through clenched teeth.

"Hopefully, speaking this truth aloud will stop Wren from haunting my dreams. I want her to be at peace. Perhaps that is self-centered, but I'd do anything for my mate, even for her ghost. If admitting my wrongdoing finally allows her memory to rest, then I shall bear whatever consequence you'll unleash on me."

Rage boiled through my blood, heating my body. My curse lapped against my skin, ready to leach out. "There could be a remedy. Silas could be well already. Both of you have been shortsighted."

She squared her shoulders, as if she truly could battle me. "Shortsighted? Aren't you the one so obsessed with finding a cure that you've ignored everything around you?"

I sucked in a sharp inhale. Yes, my relationships outside of Silas had dwindled. Yet what was I supposed to do? Watch him perish?

Her lip flickered into that knowing smirk. "You're finally listening. Then let me tell you a harsher truth. I studied under the temple herbalist, and I know of no remedies. There was only death."

A low cackle curled through me. A whisper of the blight slipped forward, as if the words on my tongue belonged to it instead of me. "You'll send that letter right now. If Silas dies because of this, then I'll banish you. Presspin will be nothing but a distant memory. Where would you run then? All the way out to Seaside? Would you make it to the territory before they found you? No more tricks. I'll watch over you until the task is complete."

CHAPTER 4

ARIANNA

THE WARM RAYS OF dawn seeped into my training leathers. The tang of perspiration tickled my nostrils, and my lungs burned from an hour of exertion. Peter eyed me warily, shifting his weight slightly as he held the sword with ease, waiting for my next attack. The wind rustled between us, echoing our panting breaths through the still meadow east of the manor. Patches of scorched earth dotted the space where my darkness had sizzled from me, creating divots in the ground. Sensing my opening, I darted forward, but my boots sloshed over the snow that had turned to slush as the temperatures slowly warmed. My heel slid, causing my attention to slip from him to the soggy patch beneath me for a millisecond.

Whoosh.

The fine hairs on my neck prickled. My once dormant power snapped under my control, fueling my motions. I spun. The blade's tip grazed my upper arm, slashing through my sleeve.

"Sloppy." Peter's lips tugged into a tight line.

Fury roared in my skull. My blight boiled, heating my body. Inky tendrils laced along my palms. He charged. Despite being in his seventies, he possessed the agility of a cat. His sword arced at me again with the full force of the war-hardened general.

Whoosh—Clank.

My bare hand encompassed the steel, and shadows blossomed from my palm, looping over it. The gleaming metal disintegrated under my touch. An acrid metallic tang wafted through the air. The wind whipped the fragmented ash, leaving nothing but the hilt in his tight grip.

"That's the second sword this week." He chucked the handle to the ground, then scrubbed his gloved hand over his face, drawing attention to the many lines that denoted his years of life.

"Sorry." I leashed the blight, locking it within the deepest recesses of my soul.

It hissed at me, delighting in the destruction I'd just caused.

Quiet, I mentally retorted with the same ferocity. It had been nearly two weeks since Silas collapsed, and my curse had grown more unruly with each passing day. The blight simmered, wanting to burn the world for a cure for our beloved.

Unaware of my internal struggle, Peter meandered toward a log on the border of the meadow and settled upon it. His brow furrowed, and for a heartbeat, exhaustion washed over his features. As it smoothed, he yanked the waterskin from the satchel he'd discarded at the beginning of our session and took a long swig. Then he raised the receptacle to me.

Reluctantly, I approached, my boots trudging through the melting ice. Resigned, I settled upon the log. The frigid bark nipped at my thighs through the leathers, but the sensation wasn't unpleasant. Instead, it cooled my heated blood, anchoring me to the present. My fingers laced around the smooth skin and tipped the brass knob against my lips. A gush of cold water spilled into my mouth, calming me.

"That's my girl." He patted my shoulder, and warmth washed over me.

Peter had become a father figure of sorts over the winter, showing me an unconditional compassion while he guided me. It had taken time to become accustomed to Peter's presence in this almost parental role. I'd never been close to my father. He'd either been working on the farm, arguing with my mother, or squandering our meager funds at the tavern. He'd never visited my rooms after my curse had ignited, likely pretending that I'd died the day I became a monster. My gut twisted at the mere thought of my family. But my blight panged within me, delighting in the heavy emotions like fuel for the fire.

"Any more power surges?" he asked, dragging me from my ruminations as if he could sense the inner turmoil that churned.

I twisted the metal cap onto the canteen. "Not for over a week, not since Brielle's."

My impatient blight burned beneath my flesh, itching to get out, which was why I continued these daily training sessions despite Silas's ever worsening condition. If I stayed confined to the manor, waiting for answers that would likely never come, my curse would set my home ablaze. Now a hopeless future laid before me as my comatose husband slipped closer to death. Sorrow pulled at my heart as he teetered toward the Great Beyond. I closed my eyes and searched for the faint cord between us, reassuring myself that my love was still living. It pulsed in tune with my heartbeat. A sigh escaped me, and a fraction of the tension I carried loosened.

"And Silas?" His grip tightened on my knee, and he stared straight ahead, taking in the mountain range. The early dawn painted orange hues against the dwindling snow caps. He asked this question each morning after our sessions, even though he visited Silas every evening.

"He's getting weaker. I can feel it. His breathing is so shallow, and it's a struggle to get him to keep down any of his remedies or water. Brielle doesn't know how long he'll last. It could be days or a fortnight. We're unsure." I gritted my teeth, angered that no word had come from Martha; that no cure existed, only death.

"I'm so sorry, my dear." Concern furrowed his brow. A haunting twinge of sadness colored his expression—the same one that Silas's other loved ones often wore.

A knot formed in my throat. The thought that plagued me as Silas crept closer to his demise swirled through my mind. *Silas was dying because of me.* My blight bristled against this truth, hissing. My palms heated, and smoke curled at my fingertips. I gulped down the guilt, jolted to standing, and thrust my hands behind my back, hiding the creeping darkness from Peter.

"Is everything all right?" His lips drooped into a frown. He stood, yet caution tightened his shoulders.

My stomach tensed at the protective posture. It was as if he was preparing to flee if my dark power unraveled from me.

"My curse feels a bit unruly. Maybe my blight senses that I'm not ready for Mrs. Potter's pestering." I forced a watery smile.

He heaved a sigh of relief. "Perhaps a run would help expel whatever lingering energy you have, but I wouldn't keep Mrs. Potter waiting. You know how she frets."

I gave a curt nod, agreeing with this course of action. Peter's scuffling steps echoed as he headed back to town. I went in the opposite direction, to the line of dense pine trees. The second my boots crossed onto the shadowy trail, I ran.

The tightly coiled inky tendrils unraveled, wrapping about me like a cyclone. The giant trunks groaned as my shadows whipped across them, searing scorch marks into their bark. I breathed in the ashen scent of wood, but pushed myself further, as if I could outrun my fate. A rotten log sprawled before me, blocking my trail. A snarl escaped me. Darkness leaked, disintegrating the tree bases and melting the snow beneath.

An hour later, I'd scorched a path from the meadow south of the manor toward the northern edge of the property. Thankfully, my blight finally stabilized. The copper tang of a hard sprint blazed in my lungs, and perspiration caused my clothing to cling to me. My muscles burned from the exertion.

Disoriented by my mindless run—running in my blighted state was thrice as fast as walking—I spun around, taking in the unfamiliar terrain. Silas and I had never traversed this far. The property sprawled for hundreds of acres, with the manor house settled within the center. My brows knitted in frustration. As the clouds crested over the morning sun, I realized that I did not want to linger here in case a sudden storm swept in. Agitated with myself, I turned to the route where soot and ash lay, akin to a beacon home. My nose wrinkled at the long walk back to the manor.

Snap.

I whirled, facing the cracking of a branch in a bush behind me. The hairs on my nape rose. A sense of danger swirled within me. My curse snapped over me like a second skin. Darkness danced on my fingertips. I aimed. A squirrel burst from the bushes, unaware it had almost been fricasseed.

My blight slipped away, and I shook my head at the gray animal munching on a seed. "Lucky for you, little one, I expelled enough energy to control myself. If not, you'd have been—"

Snap.

Whoosh.

I pivoted seconds before the arrow could pierce my shoulder.

Smack.

The white shaft and onyx feathers protruded from the trunk behind me less than a foot away. It reverberated in the thick bark.

Had a hunter stumbled into this area? My fingers grazed the raven fletching. No, the townsfolk preferred pine, not aspen shafts. I remembered Silas and Beatrix discussing the need to harvest a grove of trees weeks ago to bolster the weapons reserve. These arrows were not from Presspin.

Whoosh.

A tingling sensation ran down my spine, and raw dark energy cocooned me. I twisted out of an arrow's path a millisecond before the spearhead lodged in the trunk.

Furious, I leapt for a wide tree, using it as a shield.

This was no mere hunter. The villagers didn't venture this far, nor would they have shot twice. My eyes closed as my heightened hearing scanned my surroundings for the thumping of a heartbeat. The sounds of the forest faded, and a faint pulse pinged through the space.

Thump...thump...thump...thump...

My focus shifted to the thicket of trees to the southeast of me, some twenty paces away. Their ragged breathing punctuated the air. A rush coursed through my body. The bloodlust my curse craved rang in my ears, like a beast hunting its prey. The click of an arrow being removed from its sheath reverberated through my skull.

Fueled by the blight's destructive delights, I bolted from my cover, sprinting at an inhuman speed. My body leapt into the person's hiding spot. Simultaneously, the young man's face blanched with terror. He shot his arrow. The onyx head pierced through the protective shield surrounding me and grazed my cheek. My fingers wrapped around his wrist, sending wisps of smoke to curl over his arms, melting his simple wool coat. His thin lips wobbled under his mustache, but a steely resolve entered his eyes despite the agony he endured.

"Hateful bitch. Kill me," he spat.

"Who are you?" I hissed, my voice coated with an otherworldly tone. "You're not one of my people. How did you get here?"

He cackled a maddening laugh. "The boss's informant was right. You were hiding here all along, and what a pretty price he'll get for you."

"Who's your boss?" Power surged through my hands.

His jaw quivered. The stench of burning flesh filled the air. He cried out in pain. His ragged breaths came in quick, clipped pants. "Someone with a vendetta against your husband. It's a shame I'll die before bringing you in myself. I was looking forward to a cut of the bounty. But the boys will find you, or they'll burn your town down trying."

He cackled. The sound boiled my blood. My people. The tight leash on my control slipped. Energy surged along my fingertips, crushing him into ash.

Whispers of his remains floated on the wind. I blinked, and the curse curled back within me, like a cat settling in for a long nap.

Shock seized me. My body trembled. Bile crawled up my throat. A watery vomit spewed from my mouth, coating the spot where the man had once stood. My heart pounded. The world tilted on its axis. I wanted to shrivel into myself, unable to cope with the life I'd taken.

I clenched my jaw, fighting back my warring feelings. I couldn't linger here. Not while my people were in danger.

CHAPTER 5

ARIANNA

SWEAT TRAILED ALONG EVERY inch of my skin, the unseasonable warmth adding to my discomfort. The damp leather chafed my flesh after the hours' run from the northern boundary, where I'd been attacked, to the south of Presspin, where the militia trained in the flat farmlands. My lungs burned, and a tinny flavor lingered on my tongue as the familiar flat terrain came into view. Discomfort blazed through every muscle, but I didn't slow my pace, not when I needed to inform Peter of what had occurred. The sun arched high overhead, washing over the space where only footprints remained from the hand-to-hand combat drills. My teeth gritted. I should have run to the manor to request a horse. However, my panic-addled mind had feared the time it would have taken. Yet, as my feet slowed, a tense ball curled in my belly. I scanned the fields surrounded by the dotting of farmhouses. The reserves were not here.

A muttered whisper floated through the air, tugging my focus toward a large elm tree. A swell of relief unfurled in my tight muscles as I took in Peter, who was settled on a thick root. His brow pinched as he scribbled notes in his pad. I rushed for him, my breathing rasping with each step, punctuating my exhaustion. Sensing me, his gaze shifted up from his journal. His eyes widened at my likely bedraggled state, then his features smoothed to those of the general.

"Arianna, what are you doing here?" He tucked the log into his coat pocket and rushed toward me.

I gasped, bracing my hands on my knees. "I was attacked."

"Are you harmed?" He placed a warm hand on my shoulder as I sucked in a harsh inhale to steady my respiration.

"No, just a scrap." I lifted my head and tilted my chin, showing the faint scratch that stung on my cheek.

His gloved fingers cupped my elbow. "Tell me what happened."

I rushed through the details of the attack, recalling the unfamiliar arrows and the man's desire to deliver me to his group for a bigger cut of the bounty, then finishing with the unidentified leader who had a vendetta against Silas and the unknown informant.

"Duncan." He shook his head. "It has to be that bastard." His fingers grazed over the hilt of his dagger sheathed at his side, as if he'd happily use it to slice the man's jugular. His hatred of Duncan Archer was bone deep. Beatrix's husband had forced Peter into early retirement when the army was disbanded. Then he'd betrayed the Belmont siblings, whom Peter viewed as his kin. But whatever personal grudge he felt smoothed along with his expression.

"We'll focus on the leader later. We must alert the militia at once." He brushed past me with long strides, cutting through the soggy trail to the heart of the square.

Fifteen minutes later, we crossed through the farmlands and pressed onto the cobblestone path. Unaware of the looming threat, the townspeople milled about their morning. My stomach dropped. Would everything I held dear be destroyed? My existence had been a beacon of danger. This internal belief had been why I'd created distance from those I loved after the incident at the Terrell Estate, fearing my blight would soil this lovely place. I was still a harbinger of doom. This knowledge fueled my decision to sign away my rights as Lady Belmont, train with Peter daily, and remove myself from frequenting the village.

A raven flew overhead, cawing. A shudder crawled over my skin, as if the shriek warned that the life I loved teetered toward destruction. My gaze skittered from the sidewalk and to the sky, where looming gray clouds blotted out the sun, casting my home in shadows. A shiver slithered down my spine. My teeth chattered, and a wave of fatigue coursed through me. Despite bottling my darkness before heading down the mountain, I'd still pushed my body and blight too hard. A trickle of liquid washed over my lip. My fingertips grazed along my nostril. Sticky black blood coated my pale skin.

Ring...ring...ring...ring...

The bell Peter had installed in the center of the square rang out through the bustling village, dragging me from my ruminations. The once unaware villagers slowed and peered at the elderly man who rang the bell with full force as if he'd grown a second head.

"Another drill. Old man's trying to relive his glory days," Mr. Collins, the disgraced banker, snorted as he passed me, uncaring as the alarm tolled.

Yet, to my relief, clomping of boots sounded from the surrounding lanes. The newly established militia weaved through the people. Despite having trained for only two months, they all shared the same rhythmic march, as if the chiming had snapped them from civilians to soldiers. Moments later, thirty-four individuals stood in front of Peter, forming almost perfect lines of six, standing at attention. Men and women both, ranging from those in their early twenties to those likely into their late fifties. Regardless of their inexperience, they'd formed a formidable group who would protect Presspin or die trying.

"Today we are to begin our first military game." Peter braced his hands behind his back. The onlookers continued on their way, assuming this was just a drill. "Team A will investigate the southern border for signs of a breach. Be on guard. Team B is to form a perimeter around the town, making sure no one enters the inner sanctum. Team C will secure supplies and weapons from Belmont Manor and create a command post, which shall be run by Lieutenant Gallager."

"Permission to speak, sir," a voice shouted from the rear.

"Granted, Private Collins." Peter nodded to Rosalind. I wouldn't have expected her to sign up for the reserve, but from her tense brow and rigid posture, it seemed to somehow be a perfect fit for the tightly wound lady.

"Lieutenant Gallager and Private Reed are not here. They were on patrol this morning and never returned for debriefing, sir." Her blue eyes blazed with ire, as if she was the rule keeper.

Peter's brow furrowed. "Thank you, Private Collins. I'll have a word with them. They are likely at the manor house on Lady Beatrix's command."

"Yes, sir." Rosalind nodded, placated that they would be reprimanded for breaking protocol.

"That is all. To your stations," Peter commanded.

Without another word, the soldiers dispersed to their tasks. I sidled beside Peter, who stared past the town and to the mountains near Belmont Manor, his lips dipped into a heavy frown.

"What is it?" I asked, fearing the truth.

"Mateo and Vincent were patrolling the northern area. Let's hope they became distracted and headed to Belmont Manor, as I said."

"How likely do you think that is?" I wrung my hands, knowing that Vincent was a stickler for the rules.

Silence stretched between us, and the implication burned in my soul. It was unlikely that the pair had shirked their responsibilities.

"Come. Let's take my carriage up to the manor. Hopefully, Vincent will be there when we inform Beatrix of this issue." Peter strode forward, heading for the Owl's Nest, where his residence and conveyance waited, without a glance back.

CHAPTER 6

Arianna

Dusk crept along the master suite's windowpanes, casting Presspin in shadowed purple hues. Heat blossomed behind me from the blazing hearth, causing condensation to bead on the glass. My thumb traced over the moisture as if the motion could show me where Mateo and Vincent had disappeared to. Yet I was no soothsayer, and the swirling design didn't denote some mystical pattern to guide me to the missing men, no matter how desperately I wished it would. My finger crossed an X over the village Peter and I had spent hours scouring, to no avail. Even our search north, where I'd been attacked, and south to the border, had been fruitless. My friends had vanished.

"Arianna," Mrs. Potter clucked from the cozy sitting space. "Come, before your dinner grows cold."

I pivoted to her. Determination lived in her brown eyes, halting my desire to argue. An hour ago, Peter had deposited me into her care with strict orders that I eat and rest after expelling immense amounts of energy throughout the day. However, my focus couldn't remain on this motherly maid. My gaze shifted to an ever-weakening Silas, who struggled for breath in bed. For a heartbeat, guilt ate away at me. He'd been creeping closer to death while I gallivanted through the woods.

She chimed in, as if sensing my thoughts. "If he were awake, he would have spent the afternoon searching with you. He may love you most, but he cares deeply for his people."

Despite Mrs. Potter's reassurance, I struggled to grapple with the heavy responsibilities that seemed to duplicate with each passing day.

I made a beeline for Silas. Sweat beaded along his forehead, and a perpetual crease knitted his brow. His knuckles blanched against the quilt he clutched as he strained through each painful respiration cycle.

"I'm so sorry I haven't been by your side today." I reached out and placed a hand over his, wishing I could revive him from this unconscious state.

She approached. Her firm grip cupped my elbow. "Come now. You must eat. You're practically skin and bones."

Like a doting mother, she pulled me away from Silas and toward the warm fireplace. I lowered myself into the crimson chair, and my body melted into the oversized cushions. The warmth from the fire lapped against me, heating my cheeks. An exhale expelled from me, loosening my tightly wound muscles a fraction. In this more relaxed state, the exhaustion I'd carried since this morning coated me in a way akin to a heavy blanket threatening to pull me under. Yet I couldn't drown under the fatigue, not when my friends were missing. Reluctantly, I'd choke down a few bites of this meal. Then I'd find Beatrix and concoct a plan.

Seconds later, Mrs. Potter lowered a silver tray onto my lap. Heat seeped from the metal and through my wool pants. Her fingers wrapped around the scalloped handle and revealed a heaping dinner plate. Steam curled from the roasted lamb and root vegetables. My stomach twisted in discomfort, for the usually luscious scent fell flat, as if I were only breathing in the remnants of food.

She picked up a slice of bread and pressed it against my mouth. "Bite."

Half an hour later, she'd forced me to eat every bit of the bland dinner.

Satisfied that I'd capitulated to her will, she removed the tray from my lap and placed it onto the small side table with a clink. "Now to get Silas to swallow some broth and his evening dose of tonics."

I blinked at her, processing her words, and a horrific realization emerged.

"Brielle. I didn't tell her about Mateo. When I went to the shop this morning, it was closed. I need to—"

"Do nothing of the sort. There's no reason to alarm her or anyone else in Presspin. I told her that Mateo was assigned the night shift in the military exercise when she was doing her afternoon rounds here, checking on Silas."

I pursed my lips, and the lie soured on my tongue. We had continued with the training game ruse and hadn't mentioned Vincent's or Mateo's disappearance to the militia again, fearing it would cause widespread panic. Many assumed they were at Belmont Manor. Though I was comfortable keeping the truth from the town, I was unsure about hiding this from Brielle.

She wiped her hands across her apron. "We don't want her so out of sorts that she stops tending to Silas, do we?"

I opened my mouth to argue but clamped it shut. If Brielle found out, would she withhold care? I doubted it, but love made people do crazy things. I hated lying to her, but maybe Mrs. Potter was right. Besides, if she discovered the truth, she'd likely stomp off to the woods and get herself hurt.

Resigned, I unfurled from my comfortable seat. My aching muscles protested, but my mind pushed forward. *I needed to find Mateo and Vincent.* Instead of heading for the door, my feet moved toward my love.

"I'm sorry to leave you again," I whispered.

She settled onto the rear corner of the mattress and gazed at the fading Lord Belmont. "Go be the leader he wanted you to become. Besides, you're giving me more time to tell him stories from his childhood. It makes me feel useful, being here for him." She blinked, fighting tears.

"I'll return soon." I pressed a kiss against his perspiration-laden forehead. With my husband securely in Mrs. Potter's care, I strode out of the master suite.

Minutes later, I approached the study, but before I could knock, the door swung open.

"Beatrix." I gawked, confused. "What are you—"

"Not out here." Her fingers looped around my arm, and she tugged me in.

I stumbled over the threshold. Before I could get my bearings, she hastened back to the mahogany desk, where large, wrinkled canvases sprawled over the top. She stared at the pages, with no additional information as to her abrupt behavior.

However, discovering that Vincent and Mateo were missing had left her fretful. Hours prior, I'd departed with the promise of finding our friends, but I'd returned empty-handed. This evening, her fine hairs popped out from her usually sleek chignon, and her gray dress bore thick wrinkles. Even the skin on the thumb she often nervously nibbled had cracked open. Her face remained smooth like granite, a trait so unlike her and so similar to her brother.

My slippered feet clicked over the hardwood then slipped onto the plush rug. As I reached the desk, my mind registered the scrolling lines and depictions of the Presspin territory and the scribbled letter sprawled atop of the maps.

"What is this?" My fingers grazed the unfamiliar distressed paper, and a pang of horror twisted in my gut at the words.

We have your men.

She slid the note closer to me, but her gaze remained on the charts she studied.

With trembling hands, I picked up the missive and read.

Lady Beatrix,
We have kidnapped two of your patrolmen. For now, they are both alive. I would be happy to return them to you unharmed in exchange for the traitor, Arianna Park, whom we know you are harboring within your town. You're to bring Arianna Park, masked, to the old miner's settlement at the edge of the Presspin forest by sunrise. If you protect her, we'll murder our captives, then burn the village down to find her.
The Huntsman

Bile crawled up my throat, and I regretted allowing Mrs. Potter to force-feed me the meal. The page slipped from my grasp and floated onto the maps Beatrix studied intently. My knees buckled, and I swayed. Vincent and Mateo had been kidnapped because of me. I gulped down the burning sensation in my chest and breathed through this discomfort.

"I have to—"

"Sit," she commanded with an authority so reminiscent of her brother's that I shifted to the chair on the opposite side of the desk and sat without thinking.

"Where did this come from?" Unease settled in my bones.

She rummaged through the canvases. "Grey delivered the letter fifteen minutes ago. He found it pinned to the back kitchen door. No one saw who left it. I assume it's someone within the huntsman's party who wanted to go undetected. Sadly, Grey was preoccupied with the well-being of his barn cat, Mr. Pickles, to notice anyone on the estate. No servants have noticed anyone on the property, either. I have had them on high alert since this morning. The note could have easily been posted hours prior, given his timeline."

She settled her thumb on the last leaf and tugged it free. The crinkling of paper punctuated the tense silence lingering between us. My blight pulsed through me, ready to fuel my body into battle. Yet Beatrix worked methodically, smoothing out the canvas atop the stack. My fingers thrummed over the wooden armrest, setting a beat to my impatience.

"I only wish Peter had been here when the note arrived. He's headed toward the southern border. He's certain that a breach must have occurred because of the diminishing snow, despite reports from the militia that it is secure. But given this letter, I suspect there's an abandoned route through these condemned mines. Here." Her nail pressed into the top right corner of the paper; blood oozed from the skin, marking the spot where an old settlement lay on the edge of the mountains.

I rose from my seat, taking in the atlas dated 1607. It had been created nearly two hundred years ago. The village in the center of Presspin appeared minuscule in comparison to the sprawling town it had become.

"Then what are we waiting for? This is roughly twenty miles, correct? We can reach the northern area in a few hours on horseback. We can rescue our friends and dispatch the huntsmen before risking the lives of the militia." My curse churned within me, humming for the fight.

"What if there is an entire army? Do you believe yourself capable of battling a hundred enemies on your own? The logical choice would be to alert Peter, send scouts north to the settlement, and prepare the territory for the attack. We must protect our people, no matter the cost." She brushed her palms over her skirts, ironing out the wrinkles. Though her tone held no sign of doubt, heartbreak blazed in her eyes.

"Very logical, sacrificing the few for the greater well-being. Then let me pay the price. I'm the reason these huntsmen are here. I'll go on my own, either to dispatch the men or die trying. If I'm killed, at least it will be in service of this place. Silas isn't long for this world. Perhaps facing our enemies shall seal my fate, and I can wait for my love in the Great Beyond." I spun on my heel, ready to depart, but she rested a hand on my shoulder, stopping me.

"Wait. If we are attacked, you are our strongest fighter. We'll need your power to protect the town. Regardless of whether you sign over your rights to oversee Presspin, you are also the wife of Lord Belmont, making this an act of war against you and our territory by extension."

I spun to her, my blight fueling my boldness. Logic ruled the Belmont siblings unless they were pushed to guard the ones they cared about most. "And what of Vincent, then? You'd let him die because I'm a stronger fighter than him and have a higher title? I've heard the gossip and am well aware of your tryst. Shall you sacrifice your happiness again for mine? I'd rather perish than allow that to happen."

She sucked in a sharp inhale, and the act of Lady Belmont she'd played melted away. She crossed her arms over her chest, but that smooth countenance diminished. A whisper of the cunning woman I met in Krella stepped forward; my words had landed. "Fine. Since you're determined to traipse into the woods without the cavalry, then let's at least devise a strategy where the four of us can return home...alive."

"The four of us?" Disbelief coated my tone.

"Do you really believe I'd let you head into an enemy camp alone? I might present like a blathering lady, but never forget that Peter is also like a grandfather to me. Do you think you are the only one he's trained? No, while Silas was busy studying with Uncle Oliver to contain his curse, Peter taught me how to wield a sword. Though I may be out of practice, I can provide some support. Sit down, and let's devise a strategy to save Mateo and Vincent." She gestured to the chair.

Despite my inclination to run headlong into danger, she was right. We needed a plan.

CHAPTER 7

ARIANNA

MOONLIGHT GLIMMERED OVER THE painted porcelain mask that had once suffocated me. It smiled blithely, mocking me for the turmoil it had caused. In answer, my curse churned, silently protesting against the spelled container in my grasp. My nails dug against the wards carved along its hollows. I itched to chuck the horrific contraption, leaving it buried in the ankle-deep snow. However, nothing could erase the memory of having my power and vitality siphoned from me for nearly twenty years. This thing played a role in my torment, yet now it served as a key piece of the plan to rescue Mateo and Vincent.

"Are you ready?" Beatrix whispered from the forest's perimeter, where she'd hidden the black mares.

The wind whipped along the forest floor, causing the overgrown pines to sway and creak in ominous warning. The fine hairs on my nape rose.

"Of course not." Despite my uncertainty, I held my bare wrists out to her.

She approached, clad in training leathers and a hood that obscured her features. Her fingers worked the cord, tying my hands together to solidify this prisoner ploy. Yet with each passing second, the curse rattled through me, whispering Silas. His name didn't unfurl from the blight as if it were searching for him. Instead, it coiled in my gut in warning. My throat burned, and I fought the panicked protest on my tongue.

A tug yanked against my wrist, chafing where the fibrous strains scratched against my delicate flesh, bringing me back to the present. Sensing my unease, Beatrix grabbed the mask and placed it on my face. The smooth porcelain caressed my cheek, akin to a long-lost lover. A shudder slithered down my spine. My curse bellowed through my skull, as if it could rip the offending object from me. I slipped the onyx ring off my finger and clutched it in my fist. A burning sensation, similar to being scalded from boiling water, coursed through me as the porcelain sealed against my skin, locking my power away.

I swayed from the heaviness of the wards, as if a brick wall had erected itself between me and the curse I'd become accustomed to. A small thread inched through—the blight could no longer be fully contained. It wafted through the air, invisible to the eye, and beat in rhythm to my heart, connecting me to Silas. I'd always assumed our curse-bond was stronger than the spells, and that had allowed me to blast through them at Terrell Estate. Sensing Silas in the distance, this theory must be correct.

Despite this temporary relief, the pressure of the containment spell pressed against my shoulders, subduing me. My legs swayed. For a heartbeat, I feared I'd faint from the intensity. How had I lived under this heaviness?

"Are you all right?" Beatrix whispered. "We can stop, return to the manor, and inform Peter of what has transpired. The militia will fight for you. We don't have to do this."

I shook my head, yet the weight bobbed, as if my skull were made of bricks.

"No...we stick to the plan," I panted through heavy breaths, understanding that this bone-weary fatigue was due to the wards draining the power and life force from me. "But we need to hurry."

To my relief, Beatrix didn't argue. She grasped the end of the rope and tugged me through the thick forest. I blinked, waiting for my vision to improve, but it never came. I trudged through the woods wholly human, without access to the powers that had plagued and protected me. My legs burned from this unaccustomed exertion as we headed for the encampment.

As we approached, a flicker of light cut through the shadows where a bonfire blazed. A gust blew through the trees, carrying smoke and the echoing laughter of men at ease.

"Look over there." Beatrix pointed to the north.

Twenty feet ahead lay the dilapidated settlement camp. Rotting wood buildings sat on raised platforms that would protect the dwellings from the snow in the onslaught of winter. The rickety pier posts peeked through the pockets of ice. At least a dozen were scattered throughout the area surrounding the mountain where the cave lay.

A fire roared at the edge of the forest nearest to us. Three men chuckled as they sat around the flames, enjoying an evening despite being in enemy territory. The moon stretched over the clearing, washing over a speckling of guards standing in rough tanned jackets made of animal hide. They focused on the thick evergreen grove where we hid amongst the overgrown thicket of trees.

"There they are." Beatrix gestured to two bound prisoners where they knelt on the ground many paces from the bonfire.

"Just as we planned. You get Mateo and Vincent out of danger. I'll handle the rest." My fist squeezed, pressing the onyx ring against my palm. Once I slid it on, the mask would fall and the ropes would disintegrate, unleashing my wrath.

"All right." Beatrix yanked me forward from the shadowy hiding spot and into the enemy's camp.

The guards directed their attention and their swords toward us, prepared to deliver the killing blow.

Beatrix tugged off her hood, revealing her face. "Is this how you treat the Lady of Belmont Manor and overseer of Presspin? With swords drawn? Your leader has requested a prisoner exchange. Arianna Park for the captives. Lower your weapons." Command laced through her tone.

The guards glared at Beatrix, who tilted her jaw in defiance. As our presence had been sensed inside, the door of a dilapidated shanty home swung open and a cloaked figure emerged. The stranger clapped their hands, and a deep tone echoed from under the figure's hood. "Beatrix Belmont. You've grown from a flimsy flower into such a bold leader."

Uneasy, I tightened my grip, creating the ring's indentation in my palm. An exhale pressed through my nostrils, and despite my desire to rip the mask from my face, I stayed silent at Beatrix's side, portraying a prisoner.

"What poor manners you and your comrades have! You know of my name, but I do not know of yours." She tilted her chin in that haughty Belmont way.

"Who knew you'd have such a feisty spirit under that flighty façade?" The stranger yanked his hood off.

Puffy pink scars ran along his face like rough patchwork where the skin had been seared together, as if he had been plunged into a blazing fire. His bald head bore equally painful marks, causing hair to grow in chunks if it were not shaved clean. The shiny hue of his uneven flesh glinted in the firelight. A shudder racked through me, his gruesome appearance discomforting. Yet Beatrix remained unmoved.

"Don't you recognize me?" His laugh twisted into one of deep malice. "No one does. Not after the damage your brother did to me years ago. Let me reintroduce myself. Kaine Darkmont of Presspin, but you can call us the huntsmen." He gestured to his allies, who lay in wait behind us, and those sitting at the campfire.

Unease washed over me as I studied the disfigured stranger. My mind harkened to Silas's story about the three miscreants who'd beaten him when he was in his adolescence.

I grew angrier, and my curse fed upon it. I was young and rash, lacking control. When the darkness seeped out of me, the two who held me were consumed by my blight, but their ringleader survived. The darkness had burned his body and scrambled his brain. He fled.

Though the man's appearance bore the signs of Silas's power, his once jumbled wits had healed. Panic twisted in my stomach. Beatrix was unaware of the history between the men, and I feared we'd miscalculated. This transaction wasn't simply about my bounty. From the malice in his soulless stare, it was about revenge.

Beatrix, ever the tactician, smoothed her composure. "Whatever ill will exists between you and my brother has nothing to do with me. You've requested Arianna Park in exchange for my people. Now let's get to it."

He clapped again, as if amused. "Goddess, you are a spirited one, aren't you? I have a better idea. I'll take this monstrous bitch for her ransom, slaughter these boys, and then have you for my pleasure. It would destroy your brother, knowing I'm putting that saucy mouth of yours to good use."

"Damn you, you bastard! I swear if you lay a finger on her, I'll gut you," Vincent screamed from the corner, drawing Kaine's attention.

Vincent's shoulders rose and fell in heaving breaths. Bruises bloomed over his jaw and nose, eroding any trace of his usual good-natured aura. His arms were tied behind him, and the bindings were connected to his ankles, causing him to remain on his knees. Mateo squirmed at Vincent's side, in a similar kneeling position. He bore facial bruises, but determination flared in his hazel eyes as they locked with mine.

"Bring them here. Let's kill them first," Kaine ordered.

The three huntsmen watching by the bonfire strode to their prisoners.

Mateo squirmed, as if in a last-ditch effort to untie himself. As the henchmen lingered mere steps away, he burst free from his binding and pounced on the guard nearest to him.

"Stupid boy. You can't—Agh!"

Mateo jutted a knife through the huntsman's eye. The inertia caused the pair to collapse into the snowpack. He retrieved the weapon, then stumbled to standing, a bit off-kilter but alive. Simultaneously, Vincent scrambled onto unbalanced feet and knocked the distracted enemy onto the icy terrain with the force of his weight.

Time slowed as the third huntsman outside of Mateo's periphery ran for my friend with a dagger aimed at his back.

"Watch out!" Beatrix shouted beside me as she sprinted.

The blight skimmed the wall separating us, sparking like a match in the dark because of the looming danger. It needed to be set free. I had to save Mateo.

I slipped on my ring; the mask clattered to the frost-bitten ground. Darkness disintegrated the ropes that bound my hands together. I flicked my wrist and sent a bolt of energy surging toward the attacker. It sizzled through the ether.

Thump

The huntsman flopped with a thud to the ground. Simultaneously, crimson splattered from Mateo's mouth, marring the white snow below. He took a step, slowed, then shifted, showing the blade lodged in his back.

"No!" My scream echoed through the chaos. I was too late. I was always too late.

Hearing my cries, Mateo locked eyes with me. His knees hit the ice as he fought to stay upright. A watery smile brushed his bloody lips, as if he were trying to convey to me that everything would be all right. Even as death approached, he tried to provide a sense of peace to the monster who had caused it. His eyes fluttered closed. He collapsed with a thud.

My pulse climbed, the horrific seconds ticking by with it. The screaming huntsman behind me roared. Beatrix's boots sloshed against the sleet in a frantic rhythm, rushing for Vincent. The steward struggled with a guard, who lunged for him with rage in his twisted features.

Help them, something deep within me bellowed. I remained rooted to the spot, unmoving. Horrified memories overwhelmed me, delaying my reaction time, trapping me in the past. Mateo's warm smile as we danced at the Kesere festival. His subtle jesting tone in conversation. The loving way he looked at Brielle. My fingers dug into my scalp, tugged at it as if I could rid myself of the truth.

He died because of me.

My mind shattered as if a mirror had broken as I witnessed the death of another loved one. Shards scraped holes in my resolve, cutting it to the core.

Destroy them. Destroy them all. That otherworldly internal voice rose above the chaos, coating my jagged emotions, deepening the rage and shifting it externally.

Energy churned internally, overheating like a pot boiling over. Overwhelmed by grief, I tipped my head back, taking in the night sky. The stars sparkled, lulling my consciousness into a half sleep. The tight leash I clutched against my curse slipped, letting the beast free.

Boom.

A dense fog surged from me, as if my pain unraveled from every nerve ending in my spine, engulfing the guards at my rear. Their curdling screams ripped through the battlefield, then faded into nothing in the blink of an eye. The char of burning flesh filled the air. The wind curled the remnants of my attackers into the space between Kaine and me.

Kaine's jaw ticked as the ashen remnants of his underlings wafted between us. A beat passed as we maintained this tense stare-off.

"Dodge this, you bitch." He charged with an onyx dagger held high, ready to make the striking blow.

I leapt for him with animalistic agility. The sheer force of my motion caused him to stumble. He fell backward with me atop of him. His skull smacked against the ice. He aimed his weapon at my chest. Dark tendrils curled from my fingers through his shoulder and laced his arm, halting his movements. Fear flashed across his hard features.

"Ah, you remember this pain, don't you?" My voice twinged with a haunting timbre.

A pulse of power washed through me. His grip on the dagger loosened. The weapon crashed to the sleet beside him. A whimper escaped the man.

"There shall be no mercy for you. You've killed my friend and threatened my town. Now die." Heat seared through my palms and into him, boiling him alive.

His terrorized cries reverberated through the space, serving as a beacon to his allies that remained. Shouts emanated from the rear shanty homes, and half a dozen foes rushed into the clearing. Energy surged through me, turning Kaine into dust. I pounced to my feet, then turned to the next threat, coated in the leader's soot.

"Get the monster!" A grizzly, bearded bloke charged from the settlement, pointing at me.

Four enemies veered from the pack, running for me, while a pair rushed for Beatrix and Vincent. Concerned for my sister-in-law, my attention shifted to her as she sliced through the ropes binding Vincent's wrists. Blood pooled under their boots, and a huntsman lay unmoving to their rear. Beatrix, hearing the battle cry, arced her sword, standing between the approaching foe and the beaten steward, preparing herself for the fight with the two incoming attackers.

Whoosh.

The subtle shift in the air forced my focus to my opponents. A dart flew, possibly filled with some sort of paralytic to knock me unconscious. My body spun on instinct, and the projectile missed me by an inch. Before completing my full pivot, whips of crackling energy flung from my palms like webbing from a spider, grasping my four attackers' torsos and extremities while they were still many meters away. They shrieked as the inky tendrils encompassed them, holding them in place. With the flick of my wrist, the sizzling energy cleaved through them.

Thump...thump...thump...thump.

Human remains collapsed to the marred, steaming soil, leaving a macabre jigsaw puzzle.

I spun on my heel, facing Vincent and Beatrix. To my surprise, my fierce sister-in-law yanked her sword from a man's stomach. The man stumbled. He clasped his throat. He tumbled to the floor, dead.

Whoosh.

A sixth sense hummed an internal warning, drawing my attention to an arrow in the moonlight careening for an unaware Beatrix.

"Beatrix," I shouted.

Her gaze shifted to me. Yet Vincent's stare locked on to the incoming projectile, only seconds from lodging into her chest. He bolted from her side and threw himself in front of her, knocking Beatrix out of the way.

Thump.

Vincent stumbled. Blood oozed through his dirty jacket. He blinked, staring at the aspen shaft lodged precariously between his heart and shoulder. His face blanched.

"No! Why would you do that?" Beatrix wrapped her arms around him, catching him before he landed in the slush where death lay.

"You know why," he wheezed before falling unconscious in her embrace.

Clink.

My heightened senses followed the sound of the arrow being removed from its quiver. My vision strained and caught on the flutter of a tan coat peeking from the shadows of one of the old buildings nearest the pair. He lodged the reed into the bow, but before he could make his second attempt, inky energy shot from my fingertips and pierced through his heart.

Smack.

The man crashed against the decaying wooden wall he'd used for cover, then he sank into the decaying pier.

My pulse surged and my blight thrummed, searching for the next opponent. *More...*

Inky tendrils oozed from me, whipping around me akin to a cyclone. "Please, please stop."

More! it roared.

My shoulders tensed like a puppet on a string. Thick, tarry smoke unfurled from me, inching over the steaming soil. The darkness expanded from me. Steam emitted through the slush as the frozen earth thawed. My fingernails cut into my palms, but the pain didn't anchor me to the present. Exhausted, my knees buckled, and I landed on the heated forest floor. Screams burst from me.

More, more, more! it shrieked. My skin thinned as if the blight would explode from me. Black blood oozed from my nostrils. The world became hazy, as if I were underwater.

"Arianna! I can't move him fast enough. If you don't calm down, you will kill us," Beatrix cried out.

Her sob racked through the piercing shriek in my mind. I anchored to it, forcing my consciousness to take over. The blight balked as I forced it back into its container, sealed in my depths.

As my awareness returned, bile crawled up my throat. Black ash encircled me, stretched until it stopped only inches from where Beatrix cradled an unconscious Vincent. Blood coated her hands, and tears lived in her usually gentle gaze.

"I...I..."

She hovered over Vincent, as if shielding him from me. She wept against him, trembling in fear. My body shook. I'd been seconds away from killing them. I couldn't stay here, not until I could be certain my power was under my control. Without a word, I ran for the shanty homes.

CHAPTER 8

ARIANNA

VOMIT BURNED UP MY throat and spewed from me, coating the pristine snow with chunks of mushed roasted lamb and a putrid mix of bile. The wind whipped, melding the acrid tang of blood and my regurgitation with the crisp pine scent. After long, agonizing minutes, my gagging ceased. To my relief, no sounds echoed through the forest. My back pressed against a trunk, and thick bushes hid my trembling form fifty paces from the closest cabin on the settlement's northwestern edge. I'd run far enough from Beatrix for her to be out of earshot. Yet, given her horrified expression, she wouldn't search for me. I'd nearly crossed the line with her, just as I had with Naomi all those weeks ago. After today, she too would abandon me because of the monster I had become, and once Silas died, I'd be alone.

Overwhelm seized me. My nerves sizzled. The buzzing of bees swam in my ears. A cold sweat washed over my skin. My equilibrium shifted. Off-kilter, I swayed on my feet. My fingers dug into the trunk of an evergreen, holding me steady. I had to center myself, making certain the curse wouldn't hook into my sorrow and free itself. I gulped down the growing knot pressing against my windpipe and searched the silent miner's encampment for anything to anchor me. My focus settled upon the decomposing shacks, and I began counting.

One, two, three, Mama...

Visions of my mother leapt forward. Her blue eyes stared lifelessly into the sky, and an arrow pierced through her heart. An ache tightened my chest. No, I couldn't focus on Mama now. Not ever. I locked the memory of her death away in the pit where all my dense emotions lived. My attention shifted to the pines, to my right, to try again.

One, two, three, Mateo...

Flashes of his dying smile invaded my mind, entwining with the joyous expression he'd worn when we'd danced at the Kesere festival. A heaviness pushed against my chest. Overwhelmed by the pressure, I heaved. Watery bile expelled from me.

Once my stomach emptied, I collapsed and sat amongst the roots. What had I done? I'd ventured into these woods to save Mateo and Vincent. Instead, my hands bore the blood of more souls. A guttural moan bubbled, and I curled into myself, stifling the noise into my knees. My tears pooled in my leathers as I wept over my dead friend.

A crow cawed overhead, the sound melding with my soft sobs, drawing my attention from my many minutes of mourning back to the present. It circled a miner's cottage, then landed on the roof. The wind howled. A creaking rolled through the once still camp. Was that the breeze blowing through the wobbly shacks or were those footsteps? A twinge of unease curled in my empty belly.

My brow knitted. Despite my anguish, I couldn't linger here. Currently, Vincent lay wounded, and Beatrix had been out of sorts. And my ability to control my blight remained uncertain. My jaw trembled as logic fought to overrule the flood of emotion. My gaze shifted toward the shadowy shanty settlement. Had we dispatched all the huntsmen, or did others remain hidden to devise a plan? I needed to make certain.

Unwilling to watch more friends perish, I forced myself to my feet and wiped the sleet off my cloak. Fortunately, the darkness remained tethered but still edgy.

With determination fueling me, I entered the encampment. Footprints marred the snow-covered ground, likely from the chaos that had ensued. To begin my search for hidden enemies, I veered for the closest shack. My boot slipped from the icy mush onto the wobbly steps. The weathered boards sank under my heels as if they were seconds from giving out. The rickety door sat askew on rusted hinges, barely holding on. I held my breath, pushed the bloated wood open, and crossed the threshold.

Drip...drip...drip...

Water trickled from gaping holes overhead, where the dense snow had eaten away at the roof's wooden shingles. A flicker of light from the stone fireplace illuminated the tiny room, no larger than a linen closet in Belmont Manor. A pair of makeshift beds made of moldy straw were nestled beside the hearth, and a man slept upon each. My fingers itched to send power surging through them, serving them with a killing blow. However, my now steady head prevailed, urging me to capture the intruders to gain more information.

With the men within arm's reach, my body reflexively took a fighting stance, ready to take down the huntsmen without the use of my power. I inched forward until I loomed over them like a harbinger of doom. A shudder racked through me as their lifeless eyes stared at me. My brain hitched. They were already dead. Confused, I squatted, searching for any sign of wounds, yet there were none. Both wore the huntsmen's uniform and tan hide coats, with packs beside them. I rummaged through them, pocketing the tranquilizer darts I found. A jug of gin sat between them. I picked up the foggy glass and drew the liquor closer. A pungent scent wafted from the container.

"I wouldn't drink that," a rich male voice called out from behind me. "Poison. Not as fast-acting as I'd hoped, but I was supposed to have until sunrise. It really is a shame that you barged in and ruined my plans."

Confused, I stood and spun toward the intruder, who leaned against the doorframe akin to a rogue pirate. Unlike the huntsmen, who wore tan hide jackets, he wore a gray coat of a simple cut but made of fine wool thread, as if he were playacting a vagabond. From his sleek raven hair and his unweathered complexion, he didn't seem to be a huntsman by trade.

Uncertain if he was friend or foe, a flutter of darkness inched along my fingertips on instinct, ready to dispatch the stranger. "You killed them?"

Sensing my shift in demeanor, he straightened and showed his palms. However, he smirked, as if wholly amused by the interaction. "Is this how you repay an ally? By dredging up your blight to strike them down? For shame. And to think Martha sent me all this way to help you. But if you're able to use your power, then you are not who Brielle wrote about. If you're not ill, then…" He drew in a sharp breath, and his grin dropped. "Silas. Silas is dying." He lowered his hands and balled them into fists at his side.

I stepped back, as if slapped. So few were aware of Silas's curse. We'd only provided the information to Mrs. Potter, Peter, and Agnes after our return from Daviel. To the best of my knowledge, before then, only his Aunt Ophelia, Uncle Oliver, and Beatrix knew of his blight.

My shoulders tensed. "Who are you?"

"It doesn't matter who I am. Right now, I'm the only chance he has of survival. You must listen to me and do exactly as I say." He slipped a hand into his pocket and plucked out a vial containing a shimmering golden liquid.

I didn't approach the man, still uncertain about his intentions. Despite stating that he'd come at Martha's behest, he'd broken into Presspin with the huntsmen who'd wanted me for my bounty.

Sensing my hesitation, he eased closer. His movements were similar to a cat on the prowl. The shining tonic he held between us illuminated his face, highlighting sharp cheekbones, deep green eyes, and full lips. Had we passed each other walking along the street before meeting Silas, I may have swooned at the strange mix of masculine aura while possessing such delicate features. As I studied him, something tugged within me. Had I seen him before? The ease of familiarity caused me to drop my guard.

"What is this?" I asked.

"A temporary remedy, made from a special flower grown from the blood of a dear friend of mine. An oracle blessed by Cassius with immortality. It will temporarily return Silas's vigor. If he has a week to live, his life force shall dwindle it down to days. However, during that time, he'll burn hot like the sun before fading away."

My nose crinkled. "Martha sent you to give me a handful of moments? I don't want a few days; I want a lifetime."

His features twisted with annoyance, then smoothed. He blew out a long breath. My fingernails dug deeper into my palms. A whisper of frustration coiled in my belly, whirling near my darkness. For a second, I feared it would fully awaken.

"Yes, days," he hissed, then cocked his head, assessing me. "There is an antidote. To obtain it, Silas needs to be strong enough for the journey."

A pang of warning slithered along my spine. "A cure? Why not bring it here?"

His lips pulled into a straight line. "Because the elixir of life loses its potency the farther it travels from the source. From Hallowhaven, it would be as helpful as water by the time it reached here."

"Hallowhaven." My body snapped tight like a bowstring, on high alert. "I'm certain this is a trap. Why else enter my territory with my enemies, then spout tales of an immortal oracle, magic remedies, and an elixir of life? Do you think me a fool? You've come here to capture us both and return us to the Aralians."

The air pressurized. My curse reignited, pulsing through me. The barely contained blight leached forward, curling around me like a second skin. The floorboards buckled. He didn't recoil. His jaw ticked, then set in a hard line.

"You stupid girl. You have no idea of the risk I am taking. But go ahead. Kill me and destroy Silas's only chance to live. You are such an impetuous child. Barging in here without a plan and leaving death in your wake, then threatening your only ally. What did Silas see in you? I heard he'd become a levelheaded man, but..." He paused, as if grappling with some new information. "Gods above. He is just as brash as you are, isn't he? The explosion in Daviel. That was him, wasn't it? That is why he's dying." He scrubbed his free hand over his face. "I'd hoped Oliver would have taught him better, but I guess he is his mother's son."

I paused. Did he know Silas? The way he spoke of him seemed personal. Who was this stranger? My dark aura dissipated, and the air settled.

He lifted the vial. "Give him this, and by morning's light, he'll rise again. Then we will leave to Hallowhaven to secure him a drink from the elixir of life, which heals any ailment."

I stepped closer, my gaze flicking between the medicine and the stranger. He bore minimal wrinkles, and his shoulder-length hair was a shining raven color with a few strands of silver scattered throughout. Even his delicate features bore few signs of aging. He talked of Silas's long-gone relatives as if they'd been acquainted.

"You speak of Silas's uncle and his mother as if you knew them. They both died many years ago, but you can't be much older than my husband. Did you know them as a child?"

He let out a dry chuckle. "Dear girl, you are mistaken on both counts. Yes, I knew Oliver and Juliette, the original Belmont siblings. You can say we were very well acquainted. For I'm not your husband's age, but nearly sixty years old." He gestured toward himself. "As you can see, the elixir of life works. I've partaken of it for decades. Take the tonic. Come morning's light, you'll see that I mean you no harm. I only want to help."

My mind reeled, and I asked again, "Who are you?"

"Sadly, that is not a question I can answer until Silas is revived. Once he is well, my identity shall be revealed. Hopefully, he will be less stubborn than you. But knowing him, I highly doubt it. Take it." He dangled the vial before me.

Though I didn't trust the man, I'd run out of options. If I continued to do nothing, Silas would die, and if I gave him this medicine, perhaps he would live. Or it could be a horrific trap to lure us both to the Aralians, leading to our demise. The weight of the world pressed against my shoulders. I closed the distance between us. My fingers wrapped around the container. It warmed my skin, as if energy exuded through the glass.

My hand slipped into my pocket and dropped the remedy. My thumb grazed the tranquilizer I'd pilfered, and an idea took root.

"Good. I'm so glad you've come to your—"

I thrust the dart into the man's neck.

His eyes widened, and he stumbled forward, then collapsed to the ground with a thud.

CHAPTER 9

Arianna

Click.

My hand tucked the brass key to the liquor storeroom into my pocket, locking away the stranger until I could decide what to do with him. A draft pulled through the old rock walls that lay beneath Belmont Manor, causing my teeth to chatter. I paused, worried that the rogue might freeze, but it was unlikely, given his coat, the discarded blanket I'd tossed into the room, and the shelves of alcohol. Knowing my luck, the tranquilizer would have worn off and he'd be well within his cups when I came to check in a few hours.

"My lady, is there anything else you need?" Roger, the burly footman, loomed behind me, drawing my attention from the antechamber of the expansive cellar.

I whirled to him. The light from the gas lamp he clutched illuminated his brunette locks and fatigued, honied eyes. Despite the earliness of the hour, he donned his black livery bearing the Belmont crest. Unsurprisingly, I hadn't been the first to request his services this morning.

"No, that is all. Please remember that this captive's presence must be kept a secret. It is of the utmost importance not only to the town, but to Lord Belmont's safety." I placed my finger against my lips, gesturing for him to remain silent.

"Who is this man? Does he have anything to do with Mr. Gallager's injury or Mr. Reed's disappearance? An hour ago, Lady Beatrix had me hauling Mr. Gallager upstairs. Shortly thereafter, another footman fetched Ms. Brielle to tend to his wounds," Roger said.

My stomach dropped at the mention of Mateo and Brielle. I blinked, and Mateo's bloody smile enveloped my mind. I shook my head, dislodging the memory before it could pull me under.

"I'm sorry. I can't speak of this any further." I strode away from the door, passing him.

Without pressing further, he followed, casting soft light over the dank cellar. Our boots clicked over the hard stone floors. We weaved through the floor-to-ceiling shelves that stored preserves of every color, then toward the stack of sacks of dried goods, and finally around the wooden barrels of pickled vegetables. Without another word between us, we traversed the steps, then entered the servants' hallway.

"Mrs. Potter is with my lord, in case you need someone to speak with," Roger whispered before turning in the direction of his quarters.

My muscles groaned as I dragged my body up the servants' stairs. They deposited me on the second floor between the east wing, where Silas lay, and the west wing, where Brielle likely tended to Vincent. For a heartbeat, I lingered in indecision, tugged between which crisis I should handle first, but the pull to my mate after this horrible night was too strong. My feet moved of their own accord through the hallway, past the portraits of the previous overseers, leading me to the master suites.

Minutes later, my fingers wrapped around the cool metal knob of the door that led to my quarters. Inside, I breathed in the familiar tang of medicinal herbs melded with the faint scent of sickly sweat. Despite being unpleasant, the aroma soothed me. However, the fleeting sensation evaporated as I locked eyes with a frazzled Mrs. Potter.

"Where have you been?" Mrs. Potter pounced from the chair beside the bed, where Silas slumbered.

Her slippered feet padded over the carpet, and her thick robe rustled from the motion. As she reached me, her arms opened wide, and she yanked me into her embrace. "I was so worried about you. When Beatrix returned, but you didn't, I feared something horrible had happened to you."

She pulled back, then cupped my cheeks in her hands. "Don't you ever scare me like that again. Between you and Silas last night." She huffed a sigh. "You're going to put me into an early grave."

"What about Silas?" My gaze shifted from the haggard maid to my husband, who appeared stable. Yet as a shallow inhale echoed through the quiet room, a warning tugged at my gut. Something wasn't right.

She rubbed her fingers along her forehead, drawing attention to her sunken brown eyes and the loose braid she wore. "I swear. His heart stopped beating for at least a minute or two. He was breathing, then it went shallow, then nothing. I prayed to the gods to spare him. As if Cassius himself answered me, Silas gasped."

"His heart stopped?" I rushed to his side, then pressed my ear against his chest.

Thump...thump...thump...

I breathed out a sigh of relief at the steady beat in rhythm with my own. Satisfied, I stood and pivoted toward Mrs. Potter.

Her ashen complexion and the distress in her countenance spoke volumes—his symptoms were worsening. Either I had the possibility of a cure in my possession or poison. My mind scrambled, weighing the options. I could ask Brielle to test the remedy for harmful substances, but if we waited, would his heart give out again? Moreso, would she help us after hearing of her paramour's death? Tears threatened. How had I let her love die?

Sensing my unease, Mrs. Potter's hands grasped my shoulders. "Dear girl, you are as white as a ghost. What happened in those woods?"

My lower lip trembled. So much had occurred, yet only one truth tumbled from me. "Mateo...he's...he's dead."

She gasped at the revelation. Sorrow filled her gaze. A soft rasp entered her voice. "Oh my gods. That sweet boy."

The confession uncorked fraught emotions. As if summoned, his last moments rattled in my skull, a scene that would haunt me for a lifetime. My knees buckled. The fatigue of the past day pushed upon my shoulders akin to a knoll stone. I swayed.

She wrapped an arm around my waist. "Blasts. You need to sit before you, too, fall unconscious. Then what? I'll be a blathering mess with my lord and lady abed. Come."

She guided me toward the chair by the fireplace and deposited me. I heaved a sigh as my weary body eased into the soft cushions. The warmth from the hearth washed over my ash-covered skin. Last night seemed like a nightmare. Maybe I'd fallen asleep after Mrs. Potter force-fed me dinner, and what occurred thereafter wasn't real.

"Arianna." Her voice chimed softly through my illusion. "It's all right, dear. You're safe. Tell me everything."

I blinked, drawn back to reality. With a shaky breath, I summarized the events. I began with the note delivered to Beatrix, to the showdown in the woods, then finally settled upon the stranger.

A whisper of heat swirled in my pocket, beckoning me to speak of it. I slowed, detailing every aspect of the man and our conversation. She leaned forward with each detail. As my recounting ended, I plucked the vial from its hiding spot and held it out to her. "This is the temporary remedy."

She stretched out a finger and touched the glass. "It's warm."

Silas heaved a watery cough. A fraught tension filled the air. I needed to make a choice: trust the rogue or watch my mate slip away.

My shoulders tensed. "I don't know what to do. Perhaps this is a concoction meant to kill Silas and capture me." My lips tipped into a frown. "Though he'll have a difficult time doing so locked in our cellar."

She nearly teetered out of the chair. Shock washed over her expression. "You captured him?"

"I did. I tranquilized him. But I think he may be an ally. Afterward, I checked the shacks. He'd poisoned two dozen huntsmen in total. Had he not killed them, our battle would have been far more difficult."

"Exactly, you foolish girl." She rose and swatted me on the shoulder. "This stranger saved your hide and gave you this magical remedy, and you threw him in the liquor storeroom? I'd be laying out a king's feast for him."

"Yet he has a propensity for poisons. It could be a trick." My brow furrowed. My fingers popped the cork free. A sweet scent akin to spring flowers wafted through the air.

"What if he's telling the truth? If he says Martha sent him and killed those men, then perhaps you should have faith in him. Besides, Silas is dying. It might be tonight, tomorrow, or in a week. This remedy is a miracle. It gives him the one thing he doesn't have now—choice."

"Then what if this works? What if he won't search for the cure? Must I hope, only to lose it again, or worse, sentence him to death?" My nostrils burned, but I refused to cry.

"We can only worry about the problems before us." She stood and placed her hand on my shoulder. "I know what I would do, but he's your husband, and you must decide."

I nodded, the pressure of making the incorrect move bearing down upon me. My gaze shifted to the hearth, where the fading embers crackled. Only a faint whisper of heat exuded from them.

"I'll go prepare a bath for you." Mrs. Potter's palm gave a final squeeze, then she left, leaving only Silas's rasping respiration as company.

Each horrific wheeze curled through the air, fortifying this impossible decision. My brow knitted together, and I hoped to whatever gods that listened that I was correct. Reluctantly, I closed the distance between myself and Silas. He had withered over these winter months, from his thinning frame to his hollowed skin and sunken eyes. However, I had to believe that a fighter's spirit blazed inside him, one that would give life a chance, no matter how slim.

My jaw trembled, and something in my soul soothed for a half second, like a compass point to true north.

"Please stay with me. Please." My thumb pressed against his chin, jarring his mouth open, and I poured the elixir down his throat.

With a gut-wrenching sob, I pushed his lips closed, hoping that I hadn't doomed him to death.

CHAPTER 10

SILAS

HEAT SEARED THROUGH MY veins, as if sunlight infused my blood. Warmth sprawled through me, unfurling every aching muscle. A pins-and-needles sensation tingled in my extremities. My lungs expanded, allowing my first full breath in months to flow through me. Each cycle of respiration came with ease. The fatigue that clung to me akin to a second skin dissipated.

Had I lost my battle and died? I gulped down the knot in my throat, fearing that if I opened my eyes, I'd see my uncle's and mother's faces. Yet if I had finally succumbed to this moment, perhaps I could find peace, having given everything to protect my wife.

I blinked. Sunlight streamed through the floor-to-ceiling windows of the master suites in Belmont Manor, washing the gaudy room in a hazy glow. The pungent scent of sweat and medicinal herbs stung my nostrils. Was this an illusion like the stretching meadow I'd been trapped within?

I studied the swirling pattern in the plaster, afraid the horrific pains of dying would rush back to me. A familiar presence curled on the mattress beside me swayed, entangled with the quilt. Arianna. Understanding washed over me, for I must have died, and this was paradise. I reached for this beautiful illusion. My fingers laced around my wife's. Heat radiated into my skin, soft and warm, giving me pause. In the meadow, I'd felt nothing, only bland oblivion, as if trapped in an oil painting. The gentle rasp of her respiration filled the air. My brow furrowed as my thumb traced her wrist. She was no wraith, but flesh and blood. My brain faltered. How in the gods was this possible?

"Silas," Arianna whispered, as if she spoke a reverent prayer. "Please tell me I'm not dreaming and that you are awake."

"This isn't a dream?" My voice rasped from disuse. My head lolled toward her, and I took in my wife. In that shared heartbeat, I understood that somehow, my vitality had been restored.

Her jaw quivered. "Oh my gods. I thought I'd poisoned you." A sob racked through her, and her dense sorrow poured down our bond like inky tar.

I blinked, the words heavy as bricks, shifting my wonder to unease. Poison? What blasted concoction had Brielle, or worse, Naomi, tinkered with to revive me to this state? Presently, I didn't care. Not as my beloved wept. Desperate to comfort her, I rolled to my side, facing her. To my surprise, my motions were swift, as if my original vigor had returned to me.

I reached for a stray lock cascading over her face and tucked it behind her ear. Then my thumb caressed her cheek. She leaned into the touch. Her blue eyes sparkled with an intensity I hadn't seen since the events that occurred at Terrell Estate. Her worn features had softened, as if the ravages of these months had reversed. Yet from the furrow in her brow and the downward slope of her perfect lips, whatever had occurred wore on her mind.

"I seem well, yet something is vexing you."

Her lower lip wobbled, and tears streamed down her cheeks. "I did something...bad. You were dying. Brielle told me the truth about Martha and..." She croaked a sob. "I forced her to write to Martha. In doing so, I've unleashed chaos."

My shoulders tightened. She wrote to Martha. The knotting anguish coiling in our connection caused my gut to twist. Was it the outcome I'd feared, hence my threats to Brielle to keep the ex-Aralian out of our business? My jaw ticked. There would be no reveling in my revival. Given Arianna's distress, it seemed my awakening had come at a steep price.

Despite my trepidation, I schooled my features. "Tell me everything."

Her brow pinched, and she nodded. Then, as if a dam burst, she recounted the events since I had fallen unconscious. Over an hour span, she divulged details of a huntsman who tried to kill her on her run, Vincent and Mateo's disappearance, the ransom note, her and Beatrix's rash rescue attempt, Mateo's demise, the stranger who'd provided the elixir, and the journey we would have to take if I wanted to stay alive.

With each revelation, my jaw tightened until I feared I'd break a tooth. Vexation overtook any whispers of awe that had crept in since I'd awoken. How could I be unconscious for roughly a fortnight and everything fall to shambles? I'd assumed those left in charge of Presspin, my people, and my wife's well-being, would act accordingly. Worst of all, Arianna, with her lack of self-preservation, had nearly gotten herself killed. I'd hoped that with my end looming, she would have ceased this foolishness and taken on the role of Lady Belmont. Apparently, I'd been mistaken.

Too focused on her own frantic feelings from the events to notice my swelling frustration, she continued on.

"After I locked him in the cellar, I came upstairs and gave you the tonic. Then Mrs. Potter forced me to bathe and change into my nightclothes, though it was past dawn when I crawled into bed. I tried to stay awake, but I fell asleep." She wiped her palm over her tearstained cheeks. "The good news is you're awake."

Silence stretched, with only the clock on the mantel ticking harsh seconds by. My lips remained closed, halting a sharp retort. I should be grateful that I was alive, but my mind harkened onto the looming target on Arianna and her foolish decisions.

"Please say something." She reached for me.

I pulled my hand away and ran it through my hair, then cupped my nape. Did she believe I'd run off to Hallowhaven with some stranger for a whisper of a chance? Was that her wish, for me to venture straight into the lion's den where enemies lay in wait? Gods, it would have been easier had I died in the hallway. My muscles tensed. Overwhelm pierced through my stony façade. "What a disastrous mess."

She blinked, taken aback by my comment. Perhaps I should have softened, given the circumstances she'd endured to get me here. However, my usually stable emotions flared like a spark in the night.

I sucked my teeth. "This isn't what I wanted...for you to place yourself in danger for my sake."

Unable to remain here a second longer, I scooted to the edge and swung my legs off the bed with ease. My feet landed on the rug, and I stayed rooted to the spot. To my relief, my knees didn't buckle, nor did my body sway. However, given the circumstance, there wouldn't be pause for celebration.

"What was I supposed to do? Watch you die?" The mattress creaked, and the pattering of Arianna's feet on the carpet sounded.

Without a retort, I strode past the plush armchairs, then toward the rear corner of the suite. I veered behind the gold leaf dressing screen and to the mahogany armoire.

Her footsteps stormed as she approached. "That's exactly what you wanted. For me to sit here protected in Presspin while everyone I care about dies for me. Have you considered what I wanted?"

I remained unmoved as she continued this one-sided argument. "Of course not. If you did, then you would have to stop making decisions for my well-being. Do you know how livid I was when I found out you threatened Brielle with imprisonment if she wrote that letter, and then left our suites to update your will after I implicitly told you my wishes?"

My attention stayed on my task. Reaching the dresser, I grasped the brass knob, tugged the drawer open, and plucked out a crisp tunic. Frustrated, she yanked the shirt out of my grasp, then skidded backward, creating space.

"What are you planning to do? Torture the man for information, blow up the mines, and then die?" She balled the white linen garment. Her accusations rippled through the air, weighing heavily.

My fingers curled into fists, my bottled frustration spilling. A dry chuckle pressed through my chest. "I should torture the rogue. He entered our territory with those who wanted to capture you. Or did you expect me to go to the cellar and thank him? If he were truly a friend, then why not come directly to Belmont Manor?"

Her nostrils flared. "I don't know. Maybe he couldn't. He did dispatch of nearly two dozen huntsmen, give you a temporary remedy that revived you, and offer you a future. Besides, there's something about him..."

My jaw ticked. I cocked an eyebrow. Had another dared to pique her interest? Did this rogue believe he could seduce her to his side? A pang of jealousy curled inside me, taking root. My inner darkness devoured the spiraling emotions I'd carried over the last hour, fueling me. The gears in my mind shifted from interrogating the man to staking my claim.

A swell of possessiveness surged through our connection, an entanglement of lust and frustration.

She shivered, then shook her head in a feeble attempt to disengage from the bond's thrall. "We don't have time—"

I closed the distance between us and kissed her hungrily, sealing her protest. My tongue traced the seam of her lips, tasting of her. My overwhelming feelings coalesced into this one—a need to unite with her. Her tense muscles loosened. The tunic she clutched slipped from her grasp and onto the plush carpet.

I trailed soft peaks from her cheek to her earlobe. "I'm tired of not having enough time for what I want." The longing I'd buried unfurled from me in a low rumble.

She placed her palms against my chest and stepped back. "Then let's depart for Hallowhaven and secure the elixir of life. We can have decades of this."

My nostrils flared. In the dense silence, she retreated farther, creating space. Her eyes pleaded with me to acquiesce to her wishes. Yet this torrent of emotions overwhelmed my logic, and a frenzy entered my blood. There was only the now. I needed her like breath itself.

I lunged for her. She leapt out of my reach, having become far faster due to her morning trainings with Peter. My lips tugged into a feral smirk. Our bubbling battle of wills caused my blight to pulse in my blood, driving me forward like an animal on the prowl. For a sizzling heartbeat, we stared at each other.

She sprinted for the oversized chairs, using them as a shield. But my stamina had returned. I bolted for her, eating up the distance in seconds. I pounced. My fingers grazed the hem of her silver silk nightgown. She darted out of reach. Her eyes widened, but no protest bubbled from her. Instead, a flush colored her cheeks. Her passion ballooned through the bond, for she couldn't resist its pull.

"You can run, but I'll catch you, my troublesome wife," I growled.

Yet woven through the strands of lust lay a cord of bone-deep longing. This chase served as a whisper of what could have been if I'd capitulated to my love sooner, had Duncan not kidnapped her, had I not nearly died.

As if sensing this beating sensation in the depths of my soul, her tight countenance softened. To my relief, she smiled slyly in silent acknowledgment that we both required this release.

A willing participant, she ran to the opposite end of the room, toward the shelves of books.

My blood buzzed with anticipation and my blight pushed me after her.

Arianna...Arianna...Arianna. It sang to her through our bond, as if her name were the sweetest caress.

As if under my thrall, her feet faltered inches from the desk. Sensing my opening, I pounced upon her, pinning her lithe form between my hard body and the thick wooden frame. I bent her over the top, pressing her face against the cool wood. Her shoulders rose and fell with quick breaths.

"Tell me to stop." My thumb grazed her nape, causing her to inhale sharply.

"Never." She whimpered, fueling my frenzy further.

Unable to wait, I yanked my bed shirt off and stepped out of my drawers. Nude, I settled my throbbing erection along the crease of her covered rear, ready to burst. The weeks since I'd possessed the strength for this intimacy drowned logic further.

Aching for release, I slid my fingers up the silky fabric of her nightgown, trailed her inner thigh, and parted her drenched folds. My thumb swirled over the sensitive nub. She arched into my touch, mewling in pleasure.

"You enjoyed this chase as much as I did, but you can't outrun me. I'll always catch you." A growl emanated from me.

Her knees buckled, and she clenched the desk's curved ledge. "Please don't make me wait any longer."

Lust overwhelmed me. My other hand skimmed through her scalp and tangled into her hair. She moaned. I removed my digits from her dripping core, grasped along the scalloped edge of the flimsy garment, and lifted it to reveal her bare lower half. I squeezed the sharp curve of her hip and tilted her pelvis until her slick entrance aligned with my throbbing cock. With a harsh thrust, I filled her to the hilt. As she cried out in a mix of pleasure and pain, I paused.

"Don't stop." She laid her forehead against the desktop.

My hold on her hair tightened, tugging on her scalp. She gasped. Fueled by the blight and this restored vigor, I drove into her, causing the wooden legs bearing her weight to creak in rhythm with my onslaught. Arianna jostled against the swaying desk, taking every inch of me with shuddering whimpers. With each passing minute, her fingernails dug deeper into the mahogany ledge, indenting the patina. With each rough slap of flesh upon flesh, the sweet scent of musk replaced the stale medicinal tang, marking this room as our own. Pleasure surged down my spine, teetering toward release.

Unwilling to find completion first, I circled her sensitive nub with my thumb, swirling patterns with each swift buck of my hips. Her keening mewls heightened. With a final pluck of the bundle of nerves, her core spasmed. A moan reverberated from her, punctuating her release. Her inner walls squeezed my cock, forcing out a climax as my seed spilled into her. Heat coursed through me, subduing my fraught feelings from earlier.

Spent, I laid my forehead between her shoulder blades, sucking in a breath. My mind spun with euphoria. The once pulsing energy fueling my actions fizzled away as my blight retreated, allowing logic to reign again.

Arianna trembled beneath me, and a soft cry emitted from her.

Horror replaced my ease. I stumbled back from her, terrified that I'd pushed her too far. "Did I hurt you?"

"Yes." She slipped off the desk and onto the floor, curling into herself.

My stomach dropped. I was a mindless, stupid brute. The curse's predilections had driven me forward, using my lack of practice controlling its full depth as its foot hold. Needing to rectify this issue, I retrieved my cotton undergarments and slipped them on before sitting next to her.

Her blond locks washed over her, hiding her features from me.

"I'm so sorry. I shouldn't have been so rough with you. I'll never—" I clamped my mouth shut, because that romp would likely be our last. An uncomfortable knot pressed against my windpipe.

"No, not that." She flicked her wrist but kept her face buried within her knees. "You've hurt me in all the other choices you've made. This can't be our ending. I want so much more—to see the prescar flowers bloom with you, to have summer picnics in the meadows, to sip hot beverages in the fall by the fire and spend winter nights wrapped within your warmth. But when you realized you had the wasting sickness, you gave up. You didn't try. Now we have a chance at happiness, and I'm terrified you'll refuse and wither away, leaving me alone."

My heart plummeted into my stomach. For weeks, I'd resigned myself to my end, thinking that this fleeting winter with Arianna had been a gift. Death should have claimed me that day when my wrath unleashed against the Aralians. However, somehow, I'd survived. In spite of death's looming grasp,

I kept dodging her. Could I outmaneuver her again with this stranger's help?

I blew out a long exhale. I still struggled to convey my sentiments, but I no longer possessed the luxury of time to fumble through my feelings. My arm wrapped around her shoulder, and I tugged her against me, as if I could protect her with my strength from all the horrible things that awaited us the second we crossed the threshold of this suite.

We settled into this tender moment, no longer driven by lust or my impending doom, just truth. She leaned her head against my chest. For the first time in months, I considered this past winter through Arianna's perspective. Perhaps I had fallen into my old ways, desperate to protect her no matter the cost.

My shoulders slumped. "I'm sorry, beloved. I've been a brash ass."

Despite my plans to safeguard her, the die had been cast. I'd be a fool to squander a chance to live, even one presented by a stranger I hesitated in trusting. I'd believed my plight had been hopeless; yet somehow, she'd rescued me from the brink of death, not once, but twice.

I rose and offered her my hand. "I can't promise that I'll go to Hallowhaven, but at least I can speak with this man."

She shifted, tilting her face to me. The morning light washed through the windows, casting away the shadows of doubt that lingered. She grasped my palm and stood. My lips pressed against her forehead. In our master suites, a spark of hope took root.

CHAPTER II

ARIANNA

CANDLELIGHT FLICKERED IN THE gold sconces along the corridor, washing away the shadows of the past few months. However, a heaviness clung to my shoulders, caused by the weight of the lives I'd destroyed. Sensing my heavy emotions, Silas squeezed my hand, flooding our once fraying bond with reassurance. The warmth of his palm seeped into mine, anchoring me, as we walked hand-in-hand toward a future I'd give my last breath to preserve.

Crash

Eggs, sausage, and toast splattered the carpet runner at the other end of the hallway near the servant's stairwell. Uncaring about the mess she'd made, a shaken Mrs. Potter leapt over the discarded meal and ran to us.

"Silas." Tears of joy streamed down her face.

"I see you're as overwrought with emotions as ever." Warmth rang through his tone, and a smile tugged on his lips.

We quickened our pace, meeting the housekeeper in the middle of the long hallway.

Her palms pressed into his cheeks, and she squeezed them as if he were a lad. "My gods! The remedy worked. You are a hearty young man again."

Since he'd awoken, the dark bags under his eyes had dissipated, and his amber irises now radiated life. Candlelight from the sconces overhead glimmered through his raven hair. The whispers of silver that once streaked his temples had disappeared.

Seconds skittered by. Under Mrs. Potter's hopeful gaze, the stoic persona of Lord Belmont fizzled away, and he laid his fingers upon the tops of her hands. My heart warmed at the tender reconnection with the woman who'd raised him and acted as his nurse over these grueling months. However, we couldn't dawdle here. He cleared his throat.

A flush crawled over her cheeks and straight nose. Embarrassed by her outburst, she smoothed her hands over her apron. She cocked an eyebrow at me. "And you. Why didn't you ring for me the moment he arose?"

A blush heated my skin. My mind harkened back to our intense interlude. At the memory, a heady sensation pulsed through our connection.

Sensing my flustered feelings, he rolled his shoulders, causing his gray jacket to strain against him. His once gentle features hardened to that of Lord Belmont. "There is much for me to navigate, and quickly. Send a summons to Peter and inform Beatrix of my revival. I expect both of them in my study within the half hour." He fidgeted with the button on his cuff, tugging at the tight fabric. "And have someone fetch me a larger coat and breaches. I'll not be wandering the manor like this."

My lips pursed at the clothing. From the nearly popping buttons and bulging seams, he seemed to have gained a stone since partaking of the tonic, which restored some of his body composition.

"Of course. I'll have Roger fetch your old wardrobe, and Peter is already here. Beatrix requested his presence to discuss the events of last night."

"Is Vincent awake and well?" A heaviness pressed on my shoulders.

"Praise be to Cassius, that the arrow missed his heart. He's weak, but shall remain at the manor to convalesce. Brielle has provided tonics to help with the healing process."

A choking sensation twisted around my throat like a noose. "Where is Brielle? Has anyone told her about Mateo?"

Mrs. Potter shuffled from foot to foot. "I lied to her. She believes her paramour is at her shop awaiting her return."

I opened my mouth to argue, but she held out a hand, stopping me. "Please understand. I needed her to focus on Vincent's injury. After she finished tending to his wounds, I sent her and Ms. Naomi to the sitting room with an expensive bottle of whiskey as a distraction. Fortunately, her curiosity about the remedy Silas partook of helped my cause. I deposited them there half an hour ago. Beatrix and Peter are currently discussing how to divulge the truth to her."

My mouth dried, and no words formed.

"I'll deliver the news." Despite Silas's level tone, a flicker of frustration panged through our bond. Mrs. Potter often placed those under her wing at the forefront of care, doing anything to protect them. Her long-term distaste for the herbalist juxtaposed with her concern for the steward had escalated into an already difficult predicament.

Sensing Silas's irritation, the matron gave a hasty curtsy, spun on her heel, and walked in the opposite direction.

Despite the urgency of the situation, my feet refused to move. My stomach churned. Once Brielle discovered the truth of Mateo's fate, our friendship would be struck down. She would hate me. My mere existence had brought nothing but suffering to those I cared about. Brielle had lost Mateo, Naomi had lost Mama, and Silas had been teetering toward death for months.

"You don't need to be present when I speak with her. Let me handle this." His thumb traced along the top of my hand, soothing me.

"No. I won't hide. I'm not a coward," I said.

He pushed warmth through our connection. The sensation reassured me and uprooted my feet from the spot. Silently, we made our way to where the herbalist waited, unaware of the horrific news we carried.

As we reached the sitting room, my pulse skittered, as if I were readying myself to face a firing squad. He paused, a silent offer to allow me this final opportunity to escape. Unwilling to relent, I squared my shoulders and unfurled my sweat-slicked fingers from his grasp.

My hand wrapped around the cool metal knob and opened the door. To my dismay, an eerie quiet settled over the space. Naomi sat stiffly in the corner of the beige sofa, staring into her crystal snifter while Brielle stood beside the gilded drink cart, pouring herself a glass of whiskey. For a fleeting second, neither looked up, and I wished I could keep this moment forever, where they believed Mateo had lived. Reluctantly, my boots crossed the threshold.

A sullen Naomi shifted her stare from her libation to me. Her lip curled in disgust as our eyes locked. As Silas stepped in behind me, her mouth hung agape like a fish.

"Oh my gods." Brielle's voice pierced through the air.

The herbalist kicked her drink back, swallowing it in one gulp. She lowered the glass to the cart, then closed the distance between us, studying Silas as if he were a medical marvel to decode. She circled him akin to a hawk. "Mrs. Potter mentioned an ally who'd brought a remedy, but this is miraculous. Is there another dose of the tonic so I can study its properties?"

He cleared his throat. "There was only a single vial. But my revival isn't what is important currently. We have much to discuss, and it's best you sit down."

She gestured toward her blood-splattered apron. "As you can see, I'm in desperate need of a bath. I only waited to see whether this tonic worked. Since it has, I can examine you later. We can chat about whatever occurred then. I must tell Mateo about Vincent's injuries. I'm certain he's worried sick about his friend." Brielle stepped forward, but Silas remained a blockade between her and the exit.

I fiddled with my ring. Had we lied to Brielle so thoroughly that she hadn't realized Mateo had been in danger? My gaze trailed to the floor. A tense silence stretched over us.

Brielle tried to veer past my husband. "Get out of my—"

Smack.

All eyes shifted to my sister, whose fingers laced around the now empty glass on the side table. Her jaw squared. It was the same look she bore when she'd completed a puzzle. My stomach dropped.

"Something isn't adding up. I'm guessing the training games were a ruse. From Vincent's injuries, he was attacked, meaning someone must have breached your snow-packed fortress. But you didn't want to scare the town. Right?" Her thumb trailed along the edge of the snifter.

Neither Silas nor I answered. Brielle's brow furrowed, as if the realization had begun to unfurl in her mind as well.

Naomi rose. "Then Mrs. Potter, the crone, who's never shown us an ounce of gratitude, decided to turn a new leaf and ply us with expensive liquor as gratitude for helping Vincent? I think not." Her eyes bore into mine. "And then there is Arianna's guilt-ridden expression. No, they are hiding something."

Brielle straightened, her body tight as a bowstring. She sucked in a sharp inhale as realization dawned on her. "Mateo was on patrol with Vincent yesterday morning. I haven't seen him since before then." Her voice warbled. "Please tell me he is at home."

"I wish you'd sit down." Silas gestured again to the couch.

"Where is he?" She remained rooted to the spot.

"He's gone," I whispered, unable to withhold the truth a moment longer. "He was captured with Vincent, and the huntsmen killed him. I'm so sorry."

Brielle's hands balled into fists. "No. He's not. You're lying. Mrs. Potter said he was safe." She shook her head. "He wouldn't. He knew how hard it was to lose Wren. No, this is a mistake. He wouldn't do this to me. We...we were building a life together."

Naomi tiptoed forward but lingered many feet away. She kept her gaze trained on Brielle, as if she'd rush to her side. For a heartbeat, hurt twisted in my gut. Naomi had once looked upon me with that same concern, ready to hold the broken pieces of my heart. But this wasn't the time to focus on my grief.

I swallowed my emotions down. "I'm so sorry. I tried to save him, but I couldn't—"

Slap.

Pain radiated through my cheek. Brielle's nostrils flared with fury. Before I could speak, Silas stepped between us, shielding me from the herbalist's wrath. "Don't ever touch my wife again, or it will be the last thing you do."

A maddening laugh left Brielle, causing a shiver to crawl along my spine. "Mateo's dead because of your wife! That is why these huntsmen were here, right? For the bounty on your pretty little bride's head. And you." She pushed her finger into Silas's chest. "Mateo is dead, and you are revived."

She swiveled around Silas and pointed at me. "How did they know you were here? It was that letter, wasn't it? I knew in the marrow of my bones that sending it would be my undoing, but you forced my hand, and now my love is dead! And Martha? Oh, that two-timing bitch betrayed me. She's a damned madam! Of course the bounty would sway her loyalties. This little potion you were provided must be a trap. I hope you fall for it and suffer."

Silas slid in front of me, blocking me from Brielle's view. His shoulders rose and fell in quick, clipped breaths. Unbridled fury pulsed through the bond, and his untamed blight fed upon it.

"You'll not treat Arianna this way. She's devastated over what happened. Now get out before I truly lose my temper."

Brielle snarled, "You're such a coward, hiding behind your husband. Grow a gods' damned backbone, you pathetic—"

"Enough. If you continue this, he'll kill you. It doesn't matter that you kept him alive through the winter. His curse will sizzle you down to the bones." Naomi's voice rose above the chaos. "We don't need either of them. Not anymore." She approached, and her hand gripped Brielle's shoulder. "Who needs a friend or a sister who is destruction incarnate anyway?"

My chest ached, but how could I argue with them when everything they said was true? Instead, I studied the muted paisley pattern of the carpet. To my relief, the door clicked closed, leaving Silas and me alone. Yet a heaviness remained in my soul, coating me with guilt.

"I should lock them in the brig for how they treated you." He spun to me and blew out a long breath. His tense features softened as he took me in. Sensing my devastation, he cupped my cheek. "No matter what Brielle says, you didn't cause his death."

"I may have not provided the killing blow, but he died because of my presence here." I withdrew and hardened my resolve. Mateo's demise wouldn't be for naught. "We don't have time to dwell on my broken relationships. Not while that remedy within you is fading with each passing second. We must focus on what we can do—saving you. Please, no more delays."

He huffed a sigh. "Listen to me. Though I'm not amused with Brielle, she may be right. This could be a ruse to lure us out of

Presspin's protection. I want to live, but I don't trust this man. I make you no promises other than to meet with him."

My jaw ticked. Why was he being so stubborn? Yet, at least we were moving forward. Perhaps this stranger could provide him with the certainty he needed to go on this journey.

Solemnly, we exited the room, leaving the ghosts of my now destroyed relationships behind.

CHAPTER 12

SILAS

SILENCE SETTLED BETWEEN ARIANNA and me as we veered down the steep stairs leading to the cellar. With a lantern in hand, I walked ahead of her, illuminating the dank basement. With each step downward, a coolness overtook the warmth that lived within Belmont Manor, melding with Arianna's unsettled feelings curling through our connection. Despite my desire to whisk her back to the safety of our quarters, I'd promised to speak with the stranger. Yet Brielle's rant rang through me like a bell. This indeed could be a ruse. If it was, I'd extract information from the prisoner and use my stolen time to protect my beloved.

We weaved around the wooden barrels of pickled vegetables, past the sacks of dried goods, and toward the tall shelves of preserves. As we reached the annex, Arianna stepped in front of me and unlocked the door.

Squeak.

The rusty hinges announced our arrival. Yet the stranger didn't stir. As I crossed the threshold, my fingers latched the lantern on to the metal hook on the doorframe. A soft whisper of light illuminated the space, highlighting the rows of liquor along the stone wall, but only reached to the soles of the boots of the man who seemed slumped in shadows.

Arianna lingered at the entrance. She squinted. "Is he unconscious?"

"Not asleep, just drinking in the moment." He stood but remained cloaked in darkness, where only his outline could be seen.

The hairs on my nape rose at the familiar voice. I shook off the impossibility.

"I'm glad your wife isn't as stubborn as I feared. She gave you the remedy." He let out a wry chuckle. "Though I didn't expect her to tranquilize me and hold me captive in a storeroom. You've found yourself quite the fearsome match, my boy."

At the endearment, my body snapped tight as a bowstring. My pulse climbed, for there was only one person who'd ever referred to me that way. This must be some trick, because he'd never provide me aid.

"Show yourself." My voice rang with authority.

A chuckle curled through the ether, making my blood run cold. Arianna's eyes trailed from the shadows and settled on me, concern evident in her gaze.

Click...click...click...

He strode into the soft light. My shoulders slumped in on me as I took in his face. Why was he here? How was this possible? He hadn't aged a day since I had last seen him over two decades ago. His features were smooth, without any denotations of age, his hair still black, and his green eyes as bright as ever.

"Surprised by my appearance? Didn't your wife mention the effects of the elixir of life?" He gestured to Arianna. "It slows the aging process, son."

She gasped. "Son? You're his father?"

She flicked her glance between Xavier and me. Though my features resembled my mother's side of the family, I possessed his raven hair and angular jaw. Even our statures were different. I stood a head taller than him, and he had a lithe frame. More-so, our mannerisms were the opposite. While I favored Uncle Oliver's reserved countenance, he bore charm like a weapon.

"I haven't been his son for years." My attention shifted from her and settled on Xavier. "What was it you called me the last time we spoke? Oh yes, a monster." My boots clicked on the slate floor, but halted, keeping distance between us.

He smoothed his long raven locks, so similar to mine. His fingers wrapped his shoulder-length hair into a knot, then tied his tangled mane with a string. He possessed the same non-chalance he had during my childhood. Even being locked in this tiny storage room with two cursed beings before him, he was unaffected by the looming danger we posed. This smooth countenance made him a valuable piece in Delphine's game. She'd likely sent him here to lure Arianna and me right into her clutches.

At the realization, my nostrils flared. Any whisper of hope extinguished. He couldn't be trusted. I needed to reconvene with Peter and Beatrix to form a strategy before I succumbed to the wasting sickness.

Without another word, I walked to the door, but Arianna remained rooted to the spot, blocking the threshold. Her eyes locked with mine in silent determination.

"Move." Command laced my voice.

"You're the same sullen child, too emotional to face your problems. That's fine. Leave me here while you sulk, wasting precious time." Xavier clucked his tongue.

Ignoring him, I glared at my mate, who remained rooted to the spot.

He continued, "But what will happen to your beautiful bride after you perish? Delphine believes she killed her sistren and will stop at nothing to capture her. So go ahead, slip away and die. Leave your wife unguarded."

My back stiffened at the threat. I spun on my heel and sucked my teeth. "I'll kill you if you or your whore Delphine dare lay a hand on her head."

"And how do you plan on shielding her when you're dead? I had hoped Oliver would have broken this emotional streak you have. Apparently not." He tutted, as if I were a lad.

"I'm not emotional." My mouth clamped shut, yet pressure built within me akin to a lightning storm ready to blaze through the sky. The thin atmosphere densified, causing the wine bottles nestled on the wooden shelves to shake. The gray stone cracked underfoot.

"Once you calm yourself down from this tantrum, we'll speak like civilized men." He cocked a haughty eyebrow, as if he still held authority over me.

My hands curled into fists. I glared at him. Flickers of the past harkened forward. For a heartbeat, I wasn't in the annex, but in the soot, weeping in the ashes of our destroyed home, with him looming over me. The blight swelled, feeding off my wrought feelings. Energy akin to a gust of wind surged from me. A cork popped from a bottle, and sparkling wine arced through the air.

"Breathe." Arianna clasped my bicep.

But I couldn't focus on my beloved, not as he stared at me disapprovingly. In that moment, I no longer felt like a man but a child. The memory of that horrible day overtook me, and his last conversation looped through my mind.

You're nothing but a monster, boy, a monster no one will ever love.

My body shook with rage. I'd used the moniker he'd given me as a badge, to keep everyone at a distance, before Arianna came into my life. Under his scrutiny, the horrific ache in my chest amplified. I'd hated myself for two decades because of this man. It was time he paid for his transgressions.

My blood boiled, churning with a fury. He'd never loved me, nor was he our ally now. Xavier Veronin was a snake serving as a prominent member of the high council and bedfellow to High Disciple Delphine. He believed I was a monster. Today, I'd show him the true beast I'd become because of him. My curse delighted in my anguish, feeding upon it. It anchored into my body, using my lack of practice as a foothold for its predilections. A single thought rooted inside me—*protect Arianna*. The only way I could keep her safe was to kill him.

My sight heightened. The blight blazed through my veins. Darkness swirled about me akin to a storm in a bottle.

"Don't do this. He's the only one who can help you." Arianna's words came out a muffled cry, drowned out by my curse's murderous intent.

A maddening laugh left my throat. He hadn't come to save either of us. He would destroy us. My power pulsed like a gust of wind rattling through the small space. The bottles clinked. Her nails dug into my arm, as if the pain could anchor me, but my mind was too far gone. Instead, I held Xavier's glare. The man remained unmoved, as if I were a lad fussing over a broken toy.

Crash...Pop...Crash...Pop...Pop...Pop.

Jagged bottle shards speckled the ground. Sparkling wine sprayed throughout the room, no longer able to withstand the force. He shielded his face with his arms as liquid, glass, and splintered wood flew. He hissed. Crimson oozed from under his coat sleeve.

"Stop this instant." She tugged at my arm, but I couldn't trust him. He needed to be exterminated.

Shadows unfurled from my body, curling along the floor. The slate tiles fractured. The oak cabinets sizzled to ash. Darkness crawled, skating closer to him. Yet no fear radiated in his countenance. Instead, he straightened and rolled his shoulders, uncaring that death would befall him in seconds.

Gasp.

A searing pain lanced through my ribcage. The world tilted. The once pulsing pressure radiating off me vanished. The inky darkness mere inches from his feet dissipated into the ether. My body swayed. Arianna's arms wrapped around me, slowing my descent as I stumbled backward. A respiration attack? Sweat beaded my brow, and my once easy breath stifled.

Cough.

Black blood oozed from my lips and sputtered onto the crushed stone before me.

"Silas, what's wrong?" She shook her head in denial. "Oh my gods, it was poison. This was a—"

"It's not poison." His boots crunched over the glass pieces as he approached.

"This tonic isn't a cure-all. It will burn through your vitality more quickly but provide a boost in stamina. Accessing the curse power likely spends an immense amount of energy. Despite appearing healthy, Silas still possesses the wasting sickness. The symptoms will probably return more quickly the more he accesses his blight. So stop being so damned petulant and let me help you."

"I'm rightfully enraged to see your face." Unwilling to be held up by Arianna, I unraveled from her embrace and rested my back against the ash-coated wall.

Free from my weight, she approached Xavier and pressed her finger into his chest. "Why didn't you tell me you were his father in the woods?"

He brushed her hand away and chuckled. "After the warm welcome I received, I'm glad I kept my identity a secret. You would have either chucked the elixir into the river or Silas would have dumped it into a chamber pot." His gaze flicked beyond Arianna to me. "Now shall we continue on to Hallowhaven? Or shall you just sit here and die?"

"We are not going anywhere with you. I don't trust you." I wheezed, attempting to catch my breath.

Arianna turned toward me, her features soft and her eyes pleading. "You promised you'd listen. Please."

My jaw ticked, but in my current state, I likely couldn't haul myself up the stairs for at least a few minutes. To appease my bride, I waved to Xavier. "Fine, speak your flowery words, but don't think I'll be so easily swayed by your antics as the high council."

He paused, then tugged on his coat sleeves and smoothed his hair. He straightened as if he were giving a speech on governance instead of as a prisoner in a dank storeroom.

"There's an ancient wisdom that the enemy of my enemy is my friend. I originally came to assist Arianna. When Martha received the letter, I was in Daviel tending to a..." His lips pursed for a half second, then smoothed. "A personal matter. Martha is a confidant of mine. Because of the vagueness of the correspondence, I assumed Arianna had contracted the wasting sickness. All of Hallowhaven and its surrounding territories believe she murdered the Aralians and Terrells. But since she was well when I discovered her, it meant that you were dying."

"Why not capture her and leave me to die?" My nose wrinkled.

"You are still my son, and no parent wants their child to perish. Despite what you think, I sent you away for a reason. You were such a gentle boy. When your curse awoke, I knew that a life bound to the wards would destroy you. That is why I never returned. I faked your deaths and made certain you hated me enough to never search for me."

My mind reeled, trying to piece together his words and my lived experience. However, he wove lies for a living.

My brow furrowed. "What a martyr you've been. Dumping your offspring in Presspin, lying about our existence, and then slipping into bed with Delphine, the high disciple. Do all men fuck their enemies?"

For the first time, a flicker of rage hardened Xavier's expression. "When they want to keep their children safe, they do. Do you know the lengths I've gone to in order to hide your identities? Do you not wonder why no one ever connected House Veronin to Presspin after your mother died? Or why no one came searching Presspin for Arianna? Why in the blasts didn't you change her name? Even if you had called her Anna or Aria, it would have helped your cause. I've been working behind the scenes to protect you."

I pinched the bridge of my nose. Not giving her an alias had been my greatest mistake. A beat passed between us, heightening the injunction we faced.

"Are you bleeding?" Arianna's question broke the silence. She stepped closer to Xavier. Her fingers curled along his wrist, lifting his hand toward the light. Crimson dripped down his palm and onto the floor.

"I believe I am." He studied the stained fabric. "Well, that's a shame. This is the only coat I brought on the journey."

"Why are you showing him such tender care, beloved? Do you not remember what I've told you?" I crossed my arms over my chest.

She blew out a long, pained breath and spun to me with his bloody wrist cupped in her grasp. "I'm not amused with either of you. Don't mistake my compassion for acceptance. But we can't just linger in this destroyed room while your father bleeds out and while you seem intent on killing him. He may be lying, but he might be telling the truth."

"He's not leaving this cellar," I spat out.

She tilted her jaw and held my stare. Her determination surged through our bond. "I'll take him to our rooms to tend to his wounds while you go update Peter and Beatrix. Perhaps your sister can sway you to see reason. Besides, he's bleeding. You are unsettled, and this space is in shambles."

The light swayed, casting its glow upon the destruction I'd left in my wake. Only the rear corner where Xavier once stood remained unmarred.

Without awaiting my response, she tugged him out the door. Alone, I dragged my hand down my face. Had Xavier been a double agent all along, hiding me from Delphine, or was he still the villain of my story?

CHAPTER 13

ARIANNA

"A DAUGHTER-IN-LAW WHO CAN tend to a wound, destroy a group of bounty hunters, and deescalate a situation. My suspicions were correct. You'll make an excellent ally." Xavier examined his wrapped forearm. The clean bandage gleamed in the firelight from the hearth in the master suite, the white a stark contrast against his dirty olive skin. He sat perched on the edge of the oversized chair.

As I withdrew, he settled into the cushions. The faint scent of ash, filth, and wine wafted off him, causing my nose to wrinkle. I should guide him to the bathing chambers and provide a change of clothing and perhaps some food. Yet as he fiddled with the dressing, I'd little desire to show any additional kindness to this enigma of a man. An hour ago, Xavier had pushed against Silas's long-harbored emotional scars, revealing that this slick courtier, despite having potential access to a cure-all, the elixir of life, could be an enemy in disguise.

"Are you pouting as well? Still upset about my fib regarding my identity? You, of all people, should understand the importance of secrecy." A few black locks fell from their tie, framing his face, as he gave a rakish smirk. He was deceptively beautiful. It added to his air of unpredictability, from lecturing Silas in the cellar to lounging in relaxed nonchalance here.

My palms itched with barely tethered energy, ready to smite him for the pain he'd caused my husband. Unwilling to take the bait, I grabbed the water basin and retreated to the dressing area in the rear corner. The murky liquid sloshed in my grip due to my quick, clipped pace, but my footsteps didn't slow. With the dressing screen acting as a shield between me and the man, I placed the dish on the dresser and breathed through the tension coiled in my shoulders.

As I inhaled, the tinny tang of blood filled my nostrils, triggering flashbacks from last night. *Mateo's dying smile, Beatrix's terror, and the dispatched men* popped into my mind like sparking embers. My hands trembled, and my gaze locked on my blood-drenched fingertips. A knot formed in my throat. My steady respiration escalated as the weight of my sins crushed my chest, attempting to extinguish the final flickers of light in my soul. My lower lip trembled. Tears welled, but I couldn't relent to these emotions. Not now. I plucked a clean towel from the armoire and scrubbed my fingertips until the rough fabric chafed my skin. Nothing could quell the memories.

"Enough." Xavier grabbed the towel and tugged it from my grasp, pulling me to the present. I blinked, reorienting to the suite, no longer trapped in the ruminations. My gaze dragged from the floor to his face, and concern softened his green eyes. His lips pulled into a thin line, and he chucked the towel onto the dresser top.

He cupped my elbow and guided me to the chair beside the hearth. Wordlessly, I sat. The numb sensations coating my perspective melted, as if every moment leading to this one blazed through me akin to a raw nerve.

He strode for the bellpull and yanked it, signaling for a servant, as if he'd done so a hundred times before. His boots slid over the carpet, and no sound emanated from him as he rejoined me. Had I been within my wits, I would have likely lectured him for his impertinence. He was a prisoner, not a guest. Yet, I was completely drained at this silent moment.

"You're a formidable force but not battle hardened. Don't worry. I'm certain Maggie will come swooping in with a tray of honey buns and a pot of chamomile tea. At least I assume she still works here. She rarely left Oliver's side." He cocked his head.

"Maggie?" My mind reeled. I'd learned the entire staff, but the name didn't register.

"Yes, the young widow, Maggie Potter. She always followed Oliver about the manor. I dare say she carried a torch for him, but she understood the unbreakable bond between Ophelia and Oliver."

"Mrs. Potter had feelings for Uncle Oliver?" I asked in shock.

His eyes lit with delight, as if the story had transported him to happier days. "Once at the Kesere festival..."

He wove a tale from years past. My heart warmed as he described an elated Silas playing with toy soldiers and a chipper Beatrix dancing about the town square as if she were the queen of the event. With each passing minute, as I was drawn in by his anecdotes, pieces of my defenses against the charmer faded. He spoke of this memory as if he'd replayed it for years, detailing the smallest interactions.

I leaned forward over the armrest, in rapt attention as the recollection shifted to Mrs. Potter's longing glances as Uncle Oliver and Ophelia danced a country jig.

"And then when the song ended—"

"What are you doing?" Silas's voice boomed through the space, drawing me out of the story.

A flicker of frustration curled through our connection. I stumbled to my feet, taking in Silas's rumpled hair, darkened eyes, and tense jaw. Pain surged through our bond, as if these calm moments listening to his story were akin to betrayal. My gaze shifted beyond my brooding husband and onto Beatrix, who waited hesitantly behind him.

Xavier stood, smoothed his hands over his dirt-covered pants, and turned toward Silas. "I was just telling your bride a story about our last Kesere festival."

A beat of silence stretched over us as Xavier registered Beatrix hidden behind a seething Silas.

"Oh, my sweet girl." Xavier's voice warbled. "You look just like your mother. So beautiful." He beelined for the daughter he'd abandoned.

"Papa." She veered around Silas.

The swish of her black skirts punctuated the quiet space as she rushed forward and tugged him into her embrace. "You came. I knew you'd return some day, especially after I found your letter. Is it true you're here to save Silas? You won't let him die?"

"Yes, I'm here to help him. Now let me look at you. Tell me about your life in the brief moments we have here." He took her hands in his and led her toward the chair I'd once occupied.

"Arianna," Silas bellowed, sending a shiver of delight and a twinge of fear coursing down my spine. "Come, we have much to discuss."

He gestured to the door. Not wanting to interrupt the reunited pair, I weaved past them and approached Silas. His glare burned into me, and the bitter tang of betrayal lay on my tongue. I followed him out of the suite and down the corridor. We stopped in front of an unoccupied guest room.

"Let's speak in here." He opened the door.

As we crossed the threshold, a stale musk wafted through the air. Heavy cloths covered the furniture, leaving it devoid of personality. Faint whispers of sunlight washed through the windows, peeking through the gray storm clouds that churned within the afternoon sky. They cast over him, further hardening his unsettled menace.

"I leave you with him for less than two hours, and he already has you under his thrall." His jealousy pulsed. "He's a notorious rake. After my mother died, he slept with every gods damn person who'd jump into his bed. At least those were the rumors my uncle shared when I was old enough." He closed the distance between us. His nostrils flared. He tugged me closer, melding my body against his. "He's trying to seduce you to his side."

My heart pounded, matching Silas's beat for beat. His desire to claim me again beckoned me. Arousal pooled in my belly. Despite the desire to capitulate to his curse's carnal nature, I forced logic to rule. He couldn't sway me with lust again, hoping I'd acquiesce to his foolish desire to die.

My palm sprawled over his hard pectoral, and I pushed him back so he stood an arm's breadth away. "He's your forbearer, and I was captivated because he spoke of your childhood. Nothing more. But that is not what is important. We've already wasted enough time. Have you made your decision?"

His arms unfurled from my waist. His gaze drifted to the window, where storm clouds roiled. He dug into his coat pocket and retrieved a letter. My brow wrinkled as he handed it to me.

My fingers pressed against the paper, yellowed with age, then brushed over the wax seal bearing an oak tree. "What is this?"

He sucked his teeth. "It's from Xavier to Oliver. Beatrix found it. Apparently, it had been lodged in a hiding spot beneath the desk and..." He shuddered. "Somehow, she and Vincent shook it from its hiding spot. I didn't ask for details."

I blinked at his obvious discomfort. Realization of the likely carnal act on the desk in the study dawned on me. Had the circumstances been different, I may have teased him about the Belmont siblings' desktop proclivities. As the tension loomed between us, I nodded in understanding, plucked the seal on the missive, and read.

Oliver,

This shall be my last correspondence from this point forward. The children's names have been changed in the archives in Hallowhaven. Silas and Beatrix Veronin are no more. I mourn Stephan and Bella Veronin. Any person who's known of their true identities is no longer living to tell the tale. Many fatal accidents have befallen them. I only thank the gods that your sister had no taste for courtly life and primarily remained to herself, at home with the children. I've also made certain to change their lineage to you in the records. Beatrix and Silas Belmont are your kin from a cousin twice removed, a poor relation from Hallowhaven who died of influenza. It is best that they never return to Hallowhaven or the surrounding territories for their safety. The treaty should prevent anyone from entering your town unannounced. Despite this safeguard, it's best to keep Silas hidden, separate from the town as much as possible.

I'm sure you're aware the runner bearing this missive can't live. My apologies that you must use your blight to smite an innocent.

Xavier.

"This proves he cares for you and that we can trust him." I held the page up.

His lips twisted into a frown as he walked toward the covered chair and plopped into it. His fingers drummed against the armrest. "But he's still entangling with Delphine, a member of the high council. This shows that he'll stop at nothing to achieve his plans. The question is, what does he want? Is it to protect me or to gain more power?"

I stowed the correspondence in my pocket and walked to the seat beside him. My body remained tense on the stiff cushions. I huffed a sigh. "You're hesitant in trusting him, and rightfully so, but if we stay here, all that awaits you is death. Why not try to live, for me, for Beatrix, for Mrs. Potter?"

He leaned back, and his gaze settled on the fireplace. "You sound just like Beatrix and Peter. After reading the letter, they both believed that my leaving with him was the best course of action." His gaze shifted to me, and his hand reached for mine. "Is that how you want me to spend my dying days? On a wild goose chase with my estranged forbearer instead of here, tangled in the sheets with you?" His thumb caressed my skin.

My jaw ticked but smoothed again quickly. That whisper of vulnerability lingered in his gentle touch, the one that secretly asked me to push against his stubborn nature. "Yes, and we must leave at once. We've wasted precious hours in mulling over this decision. Please, my love. I want you to live." I lifted his fingers to my lips and placed a gentle kiss on his knuckles. "Please."

A heavy silence lingered as he warred between distrust and hope. My blight curled around the flicker of optimism, tugging on the raw emotions.

His features gentled, and the seed rooted in him, unfurling against the heaviness that pressed against us both. A soft pang crested from him, a sweet emotion that tasted of sunshine. "Then I'll depart with Xavier."

My chest cracked open like an egg. "Thank you for trying, for trusting."

He nodded, but the moment darkened akin to dusk turning to night. With his decision made, the calculating mind of Lord Belmont overtook my sweet husband. He withdrew from my grasp, stood, and pulled his hand through his hair. "Then we shall enact the tentative plan I devised with Beatrix. Peter is to expand the militia's patrols to include the mines starting tomorrow morning. If I don't return to Presspin through the tunnels in a week, then you're to collapse the entrance, to protect yourself and the town."

I gaped, then snapped my mouth shut. Whatever warmth lingered between us fizzled into the air. Frustration pulsed through my blood, and I leapt from my seat. "You're going with him alone? Are you mad? You can't access your power, and the journey may be perilous."

"Exactly. He acted on my behalf as a child, but there is no certainty that he'll safeguard you. You're a wanted criminal with a bounty on your head. I won't be able to protect you. You are to remain here."

"You're doing it again. Deciding without me. You and Beatrix planned out everything, right?" I pressed a finger into his chest. "You must be daft if you think I'll allow you to run into danger headlong without a plan. What are you going to do? Tranquilize me? Lock me away?" A pang of terror cut through me. Had he lured me to his uncle's old rooms? My glance darted to the doorframe and, to my relief, no wards laid in the wood.

A sinking sensation of his disbelief prickled and settled into my belly.

"Do you really think me that heartless?" He scrubbed a hand over his face. "For once I wish you'd use logic and ignore your need to save everyone at your detriment. Venturing into Hallowhaven is suicide."

"And it's not for you? Gods above. Do you not understand what will happen if you leave without me? I'll blast the mountain down in order to find you. This is my life, and I'll not be parted from you." Heat seared through my palms, as if my blight would burn the world to find him—to save him.

He shuddered. "Arianna, I—"

The door flung open, and Xavier strode in, uncaring as he walked in on our discussion. His once smooth features tightened. He opened his mouth to speak, but Silas interrupted him.

"Do you have no decorum? Can you not see we are having a discussion? And where is Beatrix?"

"Apparently, the steward who was injured has awakened. Maggie...Mrs. Potter is awaiting your instructions in your suites." Xavier ran his thumb over his jaw, drawing my attention to the red splotch. "I forgot Maggie is not to be trifled with. Between Silas's outburst and Mrs. Potter's right hook, I fear I won't make it through this journey alive. But in all seriousness, we are running out of time on your elixir. However, there's a more serious matter lurking that must be addressed with haste."

Silas's jaw ticked, and I blinked, taken aback. Silence stretched for a heartbeat.

Unfazed by our shock, he continued. "The huntsmen's reserve remains at the inn. An ally infiltrated the group with me. However, they are more spy than fighter. She's a crafty girl, but these damned bulky brutes took far more poison to kill than I expected." He studied his dirty nails. "We'll have to head to the inn they overtook and dispatch them before they try to enter Presspin." He let out a low whistle. "If they find their leaders have been killed, they'll slaughter your town. So we really should be off."

My fists curled into balls, my nails digging into my flesh. "Why did you tell me about the Kesere festival instead of this information? Or after we dispatched the huntsmen at the encampment?"

"First, you tranquilized me before I could say more. Second, when the cellar door finally opened, Silas nearly killed me. Finally..." His features softened a fraction. "When we entered your suites, I feared it wasn't news you could handle. Not when you were clearly spiraling out of control. There is no knowing how your curse would have fed upon more dreadful news. So I wove a happy tale. It calmed you down, didn't it?"

I gritted my teeth and surged past my husband and toward his father, ready to throttle the man.

Silas grasped my shoulder, anchoring me to the spot. Menace laced his tone. "And how many are there?"

Xavier counted on his fingers, as if trying to remember. "I'd say two dozen. But with Arianna's powers—"

"No. She won't be coming—"

I unraveled from my husband's grasp. Months ago, Silas may have been more powerful, but the tables had turned. Now, my love was the damsel in distress, and I was his valiant knight. "And you shall not venture into danger without me. You are not well. You have no ability to access your blight. And from what

Xavier said in the cellar, your symptoms will return. You expect me to let you gallivant off into danger with our enemies at the base of the mountain? I'm coming, and you cannot stop me."

CHAPTER 14

SILAS

AN EERIE SILENCE STRETCHED over the ash-covered miner's camp. The typically swaying pines remained still, sentinels encasing the destruction. The wind whipped the smoky residue, stinging my nostrils. My boots sloshed through the mud as I followed Arianna, silently bearing witness to last night's battlefield. As if unaffected by the carnage, she strode in quick steps through the epicenter of the soot circle. Yet as she crested the outskirts, her posture tightened. Her fists curled into balls. A sinking sensation exuded from her and crashed over me like a wave, threatening to drown us both.

As we prepared for the journey, I'd hoped for this moment. One where her steely determination wavered long enough for me to persuade her to stay. For hours, despite my efforts, she'd been unflinching, even when we'd said our goodbyes to Beatrix and Mrs. Potter. Now, as we waited for Xavier to find his messenger bird bearing the news of our fates, she faltered, providing me my opening.

Gently, I approached and placed a hand on her shoulder. Before I could speak, a crow cawed, flying south. I held my breath, hoping that Xavier's ally had sent word that she'd dispatched the enemies at the inn and no threat loomed, providing me with a stronger argument to convince Arianna to remain hidden here.

"The reserves are heading our way at dawn. Kaine's men were given detailed instructions that allowed them to navigate the caves," Xavier called out, shaking the note from the closest shanty home where he had a pack stowed. "My associate Robin has poison for half a dozen men. She'll take out the most brutal of them. So that leaves the rest to us. Best be off to reach the inn before daybreak." The porch creaked as he walked off the rickety wood and strode north to the mines.

My heart sank. With the threat looming, she wouldn't send me into danger unguarded. Neither Arianna nor I moved. My hesitation lay in the journey ahead, yet her gaze focused on an ash-covered skeleton. The bitter sting of death remained on my tongue. Her sorrow settled between us, heavy as a knoll stone. My brow furrowed, and understanding took root. This had once been Mateo Reed. Her blight had scorched his corpse the night before, and this consumed her. Though it was unkind, I'd finally found my foothold to sway her.

"If you continue on, you'll be forced to kill again. You don't have to do this. You can stay here," I whispered in an unaccustomed plea.

Her spine straightened. She spun to face me. "I'm well aware of what I must do. As you were at Terrell Estate. Do you not think my love for you carries the same weight? That I too am willing to sacrifice everything for you, including my soul?"

I blinked. I'd known of the depth of her affection but believed she simply had no sense of self-preservation. It wasn't the weight of her words that captivated me, but the affection that blazed from her akin to a bonfire. She was the fire that warmed me. I gulped down the realization, battling between my awe of her and my desperate desire to protect her.

Without awaiting my answer, she strode past me.

I didn't follow. Instead, my gaze landed on the mountain range and the town in the distance. For the briefest of seconds, my heart ached. Before I left, I'd made peace with my final farewells, but the journey ahead caused a choking sensation to wrap around my neck like a noose. Would this journey lead me to my salvation or my demise? A shudder crawled over my skin. Whatever these bubbling feelings were, I couldn't linger on them. Not as she edged closer to the mines. Not as we followed Xavier, who had yet to earn my trust.

Stay close to her, my blight whispered in warning.

The hairs on my nape rose. As if my body moved of its own accord, I hastened to the caves, leaving my home behind.

⬧◆⬧

In the sunless space, time shifted. Hours and minutes collapsed onto each other, as if the caverns were endless. Downward we spiraled, through the narrow passageways, with the rough rock walls closing in. We walked in stilted silence, with nary a word spoken between us. This quiet often served as my solitude, but after many miles of stretching darkness with only Xavier's lantern softly casting away the shadows, a looming dread sank into my soul.

The whispers of uncertainty I'd had before entering the mines intensified as I drew closer to my impending doom. For this space mirrored that of the pitch-black world in which I'd been trapped. As reality and nightmares converged, my once steady respiration escalated, heightening to a fever pitch after a long stretch of weaving corridors. My body tensed as if I were still running through the macabre abyss Arianna had extracted me from. The memories hooked on to me like specters, tugging me into a descent of madness.

Despite the chill in the caves, a prickle of sweat beaded on my forehead. I ran my sleeve over my damp skin. My footsteps faltered. I blinked, my vision swimming. My breathing acceler-ated. My tongue thickened, choking me. In this nothingness, a truth I'd spent months ignoring overtook me. Without a cure, I would die with no future before me. The realization sank, halting me.

Unaware of my panic, Arianna and Xavier pressed on, taking the whisper of light with them. It glinted over the limestone shimmering along the path, leading deeper into the unknown. They walked onward in a narrow line. I tried to force my feet to move, to chase after them before I was cast into the shadows, but my body didn't acquiesce. When did I become so weak? Self-doubt clawed at my mind, drowning me.

"Xavier, stop." Arianna's voice echoed through the caverns.

Her quick steps clicked on the rocky ground as she returned for me. The lantern flickered behind her, casting her in a soft glow, the harbinger of my salvation coming to drag me from the darkness. Warmth seeped along our connection, easing the coiled tension through my chest.

She closed the distance between us. "What's wrong?" Her fingers laced with mine. "Is the remedy fading? Is your strength weakening?" Concern edged into her voice.

"No. I'm fine. It's just..." I shuddered, not wanting to speak the issue aloud.

Her eyebrows lifted as the realization dawned on her. "The darkness." Her thumb ran along the top of my hand. "Like your nightmares."

"Yes." A twinge of embarrassment coated my tone. I was her husband. Shouldn't I be resolutely strong and unfazed by these bothersome emotions?

"Yet I found you. I will always find you." She squeezed my hand.

A pang of relief washed over me, and I could breathe again. I shouldn't allow her to support me in this way, to promise to be my salvation. Yet hadn't she blazed a determined path to follow me into Hallowhaven, rescued me from the abyss, then illuminated my life that was once nothing but shadows? Perhaps I needed her as much as she needed me.

"We will overcome this together." She tugged me forward, and I finally moved with her by my side.

A few paces ahead, Xavier shifted impatiently on his feet. I waited for some sort of admonishment. Instead, he cocked his head. "Please stay close. I don't want anyone to get lost. Though I did mark the way."

He smirked and leaned against the stone wall. The flickers of light illuminated an X marked in crimson on the jagged gray rock.

"X for Xavier. How clever." Sarcasm dripped from Arianna, causing a flicker of a grin to tease the corners of my lips.

Was she using this bravado for my sake? It was likely. I could still feel the anguish that had roiled within her for months, but she'd learned to craft a new mask. She no longer presented as my meek bride, though both fear and fierceness battled inside her.

"Thank you. I had to mark the cave with my blood." Without awaiting our response, he turned and walked onward.

Time ticked by with the beat of my steadying heart. The endless nothingness continued as we weaved through the tunnels. However, the pangs of unease continued to tug at my mind. Still unsettled, my apprehension bled into our connection. For once, I despised silence.

Arianna shivered as my feelings settled into her being. Her pace slowed, and her gaze softened. An unspoken understanding lived between us.

"How did you infiltrate the huntsmen? Was that how you planned to gain access to Presspin?" Arianna asked Xavier, freeing me from the heavy quiet.

I blew out a breath. It was a question I'd wondered and a conversation that wouldn't spark unneeded tension. She refrained from delving into the uncertainty of his character and his loyalty. Perhaps we'd find a sliver of his true intentions.

"No. It was a fortunate twist of fate." The light he held forward highlighted the downward slope of his shoulders, pulling against the ill-fitting coat Mrs. Potter had provided him before our departure.

"My spies had been tracking Kaine's group throughout the winter. We'd heard rumors he possessed a map that could lead an army into Presspin, even during the snow-laden months. My intention was to steal the atlas and burn it before the Aralians discovered this intel."

I scoffed, but he continued on, ignoring me. "But, you see, it wasn't on paper but in Kaine's mind and in the details shared with his men. I'd been set to execute them when Brielle's letter arrived. So my plans changed, though I assumed that the aid was for your wife."

My jaw ticked. "My curse hadn't rattled Kaine's brain. Given the circumstances, I'm unsure if I'm grateful for that fact or not."

He huffed a wry chuckle. "Oh, it rattled him. It filled him with unbridled rage. He'd borne a grudge against you for some time, but the hefty price on Arianna's head, along with some intel that she may be in Presspin, apparently, and a desire to cause you pain, drove the man to action."

"Who informed him of my whereabouts?" She squeezed my hand, anchoring herself.

He shrugged. "I'm unsure." His free hand scratched his neck, then settled on the nape. "Kaine was a private man, untrusting even of his crew. Lucky for me, his second-in-command, Declan, had a taste for raven-haired men."

I cleared my throat, and he peered over his shoulder. "Uncomfortable that my tastes vary?"

My nose wrinkled. "I have no issue with your choice in partner. My issue is that no child wants to hear of their parent's proclivities."

He let out a barked laugh. "Ah, so I'm your father when I'm speaking of my interludes, but only then. Noted." He paused as we entered a fork in the corridor. The lantern highlighted the crimson X shown to the right. He veered, and we followed.

"But how did Kaine navigate these corridors? It's a maze down here." Arianna gestured toward the ever-cramping space around us.

My brow pinched. A memory harkened forward. "Kaine would often explore the tunnels when he lived in Presspin. I recall many conversations my uncle had with his father. He'd say that if Kaine perished within them, it would be the young man's own fault for ignoring his warnings. I just never expected he'd return. Honestly, I assumed he'd died some time ago from the injuries he sustained from my curse."

He nodded. "I gleaned as much from Declan. It sounded as though he'd spent a lifetime in these caverns and wandering through them was second nature, even decades later."

My gaze shifted to the wall, to another crimson X on the rock. The symbol was unnoticeable to a passerby but obvious enough for the trained eye.

Her body tightened beside me, then a ripple of frustration sizzled, cutting off my bubbling quandary.

"And when you arrived, why didn't you just come to Belmont Manor? Or help Mateo and Vincent escape? Why not slaughter them all upon arriving?" she asked.

He halted. He pivoted, and the light flickered along his tight features. "Because Kaine didn't trust me, and rightfully so. Luckily, I'd been allowed to trail the group, which is how I left the marks unnoticed. However, I had a guard on me the second we entered Presspin, despite Declan's protest. I did what I could, using stealth instead of an outright attack. When Declan fetched me for a private interlude, I poisoned him. A true shame, but one that couldn't be helped. Then I snuck toward the captives and provided that boy with the pocketknife. I'd told him I'd release them but to keep the weapon in case of an emergency. They waited as I began lacing the drinks, and well, we know what happened after that."

She stilled, and that mask of strength dropped. Her jaw trembled. My fingers clasped around hers.

"You could have freed them, then gone to poisoning the men." I squared my shoulders, voicing the sentiments that could have saved my wife from this pain.

"Don't be so naïve. Saving them would have drawn attention back to me. I had greater plans, securing an ally in Arianna and, more so, one in you. The boy acted out of instinct instead of logic. Because of that, he died. I carry no guilt for the lives I've taken. Had I not, we wouldn't be heading south to secure the cure for you, son. Perhaps no more questions for a while. Besides..."

He turned back toward the corridor where heavy rocks lay, so narrow that I feared I wouldn't be able to get through.

He glanced over his shoulder and smirked. "It's going to be a tight squeeze for a while. Best save your breath until we get through."

CHAPTER 15

SILAS

THE SWEET PINE AROMA wafted through the wind, overtaking the sulfuric scent that had permeated my senses for hours. The coiled tension in my shoulders loosened with each inhale of fresh air that pressed through my lungs. For a heartbeat, I allowed myself this moment of relief as the stars twinkled overhead and the moon highlighted the valley floor.

"Are you going to help me with this boulder?" Xavier pushed his shoulder against the large stone that we'd rolled moments earlier to free us from the endless mines.

My jaw ticked. The cave mouth shouldn't stay open, not when danger lurked about, threatening my people. I slogged through the ankle-deep snow, closing the distance between us. As I reached him, my hands gripped the cold stone. With all my might, I pushed against the boulder until it scuffed across the mountain face, causing a scraping sound to punctuate the night. It slid into place, blocking the entrance to Presspin.

"We should blast the damned cave closed." He straightened and wiped his gloved fingers along his pants.

My shoulders tensed as my glare burned into him. To my relief, the tight corridors had been too confining for any further lengthy chats as we slithered through the cramped crevices. However, here, there were no such impediments. Though my broad form had been nearly stuck between the sharp rocks in that damn cave, now the claustrophobic space was far more palatable than speaking with Xavier.

"No. A blast would draw attention, giving up the element of surprise." The half-truth hid my genuine sentiment to leave a failsafe for Arianna to escape Hallowhaven and reenter Presspin if everything went awry and I perished.

"Silas is right. Besides, the mountain range will be unpassable for at least another few weeks. It's our only way to return after Silas is well. We can't stay in Hallowhaven, where danger is lurking at every corner," Arianna chimed in from the perimeter of the woods where she lingered.

She pressed the waterskin against her lips, yet her gaze remained on us. Xavier adjusted his too-tight coat, shifting under her scrutiny.

His lips twisted, as if withholding a retort. His green eyes narrowed. He secured his sack and strode forward. "Suit yourselves. I'm not the Lord or Lady of Presspin. Best believe, just because the Aralians haven't infiltrated Presspin yet doesn't mean that they never will."

His gaze locked with Arianna's as he brushed past her. My jaw ticked.

As if sensing my irritation, he paused at the forest's entrance, where the gibbous moon poked through the thick canopy of evergreens, casting him half in shadows. "Now, shall we thwart the enemy, or should we linger here, wasting precious minutes chatting?"

Without waiting for a response, he stepped onto the path flanked by trees, walking until he was no longer in sight.

"The man is insufferable." I hissed through gritted teeth.

She placed her water skin in her pack. Her boots sloshed through the snow as she approached.

"That he is, but..." her words drifted off as she scanned the forest. "He's kept his word. For now, we'll tolerate him. After we secure your cure, you may deal with him as you see fit. But Beatrix would likely be bereft if you killed him."

A knot formed in my throat at the mere mention of my sister. We'd embraced as if it would be our last time seeing one another before I'd left. She believed we'd return. I couldn't shake the pessimism that still clung to me from our half day in complete darkness.

"He's right. We need to dispatch the huntsmen." Despite the sentiment, she remained rooted to the spot. Conflict churned within her. Her blight nearly sizzled between us, ready to strike a killing blow, but the soft-hearted woman who'd revived me recoiled at the task at hand.

"Let Xavier and me handle this. Though I haven't practiced with daggers in an age, my uncle required that I possess combat skills outside of using my curse." My hand brushed the dusty debris from her braid. As I assisted her, my gaze slipped past her to the ground. My brow furrowed at the unusual footprints sunk into the snowpack.

"What is it?" She spun around, taking in the snow-covered earth and woods behind her.

"Footprints, a pair." I pointed to two small sets of boot prints leading from the mines toward the forest.

"It could have been from the huntsmen." She shrugged.

My thumb rubbed at my temple. Scouts could have trekked to the cave mouth, but the size and shape of the imprints gave me pause. Unaffected by my curiosity, she stepped into the pine grove. However, I lingered, as if something tugged at my mind.

Silas, her curse called through the bond, unraveling me from my ruminations.

Like a dog on a lead, I followed behind her, ignoring the pang of uncertainty that blossomed through my chest.

An hour later, a flicker of light pierced through the woods as Agnes and Peter's inn came into view. Smoke curled from the chimney. A wash of lamplight glowed through the lower windows, illuminating the stone home. Fortunately, the dense evergreens and bushes hid our lurking forms as we lingered fifty feet away. We assessed the huntsman who guarded their stronghold, though the intense darkness within the thick forest made it difficult to see.

I blinked, searching the thick tree line for Xavier, who'd been minutes ahead of us. A sinking sensation pulled in my stomach. Had he scampered off to warn the huntsmen? Had this been a trap to lure Arianna and me into captivity? My fingers yanked Arianna's bare wrist, and I readied myself to retreat through the woods and the maze of caves to keep her safe.

"*Trust us*," her blight whispered against mine, soothing the desperate need to intervene on her behalf.

"Good, you finally made it. There are three to the south, two to the east, and two to the west," Xavier whispered some distance to my right.

My shoulders tensed, then smoothed. My eyes strained to see him. Unable to access my curse, my vision remained human, taking in only his outline in the shadows.

"And there are three more here. That makes ten outside. And inside?" Arianna asked.

"Hopefully Robin took out a few. If not, then over twenty men total." He stepped out of the darkness and back toward us. A whisper of moonlight was cast over his face. To my surprise, worry tugged at his features.

He strode closer to Arianna, wholly ignoring me. "I'll dispatch the groups to the south and east. That will allow me access through the kitchen. You'll focus on the three huntsmen here. After that, clear the western perimeter leading to the main entrance. Try to kill them before they sound the alarm. If we are fortunate, we can slit the necks of those sleeping within the inn."

"I'll handle them. Silas, you can provide me cover. It is best if he doesn't enter the fight." She peeled off her gloves and tucked them into her pack, then lowered the satchel, leaving it hidden in the thickets.

"The blast I will." My gloved fingers laced around the daggers in my sack, and I slid them into the holders attached to my belt.

"She's right. Have you used a dagger recently?" He placed a hand on my shoulder.

My fingers flipped the knife, catching it in a swift motion. As it returned to my grasp, I arched toward Xavier, placing the blade against his jugular. "I'm good enough to slice your throat."

"I'd love to see you try," he goaded.

"We don't have time for this." She spun to face me. "Silas, do you trust me?"

My chest tightened at the layered question. She'd felt I made unilateral decisions for us, but my motivations were always to protect her. Despite her growth, I still yearned to protect her. She'd dispatched the huntsmen without my help already, and she had guided me through the mines like a beacon. Xavier's murky motives gave me pause, but he was the only ally we had at present.

"I do." My hand slid the last dagger into my holster.

"Then believe I can do this." Warmth coursed through our bond, but I could still sense the bitter tang of fear.

I let the words settle on me but couldn't answer her. Instead, I lowered my pack and tucked it behind a bush. When I stood, both she and Xavier were gone. An expletive bubbled within me as the faint moonlight whispered over my beloved, where she stalked mere steps away from the safety of the dense pines' shadows and toward the huntsmen who laid in wait.

CHAPTER 16

ARIANNA

ICY WIND WHIPPED ALONG my face as I sprinted through the forest for the inn. After tonight, this scenic retreat would no longer house the memories of my hasty wedding. Instead, the lives I would take would forever tarnish this place. Despite my soul recoiling at the task ahead, my blight fueled me, its carnal savagery coating my tongue with a lusty flavor. Overwhelmed by the incongruent sensations, my mind disconnected from my body, allowing it to act as the weapon it must be to keep Silas safe. With my consciousness quieted, my form moved like a predator searching for its prey.

Arianna, Silas bellowed through our bond, an order that I wouldn't capitulate to.

The curse heated my blood, warming me from the inside out. Snow sizzled under my boots, causing steam to coat my presence in a thick fog. As I entered the edge of the woods, my senses heightened. The two hazy figures guarding the east end became clear as day, cast in moonlight. Hidden in the mist, I padded forward, preparing myself to strike the killing blow.

"What in the goddess above is that?" A red-haired huntsman adorned in tan leathers straightened from his once relaxed position, where he'd leaned against the stone wall. He stepped forward, blinking at the fog that hid my form.

My focus shifted to the blond man he spoke to, the man closer to me. He scratched his short beard and squinted at the steam.

Inky lightning shot from my fingertips, buzzing toward the baffled fair-haired bloke.

"Aye. Must be—"

Oof.

A hole burrowed through his chest. He slumped against the stone building, then slid onto the icy ground underfoot. The distracted redhead ran for his comrade. Power surged through my hand, piercing through the atmosphere, targeting the unaware guard kneeling beside his departed companion.

"What happ—"

Energy punctured his skull. He crashed atop his friend, joining him in death.

Arianna.

Silas drew closer. Fury rattled between us. For the duration of our time in the caves, I could sense his uncertainty about my presence on this journey. Yet I was the key to his survival. Without waiting for him, I rushed forward, not wanting him in this skirmish.

My boots sloshed through the snow, but as I surged for the entrance of the inn, the lantern light permeated my smokescreen. Two guards lounged against the knoll posts with nonchalant ease. As their gazes locked on mine, they fumbled to straighten. They reached for their hilts, but they were too slow.

Inky tendrils sizzled through the ether, piercing both of them through the heart. They crumpled like puppets whose strings had been cut.

The tang of seared flesh stung my nostrils, reconnecting my mind with my body. My once steady pulse climbed. Sweat slicked my palms. My stomach churned. Their lifeless eyes stared at me. My jaw quivered as I took in their youthful faces, so similar to Mateo's. A knot pressed against my windpipe.

"Arianna." A shout jolted me from my panicked pause.

I spun on my heel. A huntsman lunged with a sword arched high. Fury curled along the man's lip. Caught off guard, my movements were sloppy. My arm rose to block the weapon from barreling into my chest.

Oof.

His footsteps faltered. Shock replaced his anger. The blade fell from his fingertips inches from making contact with my forearm and slipped into the snow. Crimson spurted from his mouth. His strength waned, and he collapsed before me. A ruffled Silas stood a few meters behind me, and a dagger protruded through the back of my attacker's neck.

No relief crossed Silas's expression. Instead, he panted through quick, clipped breaths. His nostrils flared, and chastisement likely waited on this tongue. Before he could speak, his attention skittered to the entrance.

"After," I whispered.

He sucked his teeth. "After."

Tension coiled in my belly, but I pushed the sensation away and forced myself to move swiftly over the path. Silas loomed a half step behind me. My fingers laced upon the knob. Slowly, the door opened. My feet crossed the threshold, and the breath I'd been holding expelled from me at the silent entryway. Perhaps Xavier had been right. Were the remaining huntsmen asleep, unaware that we'd slaughtered their brethren?

Creak.

My attention flicked to the staircase to my left, where the sound had emanated from. A man leapt over the banister, pouncing toward me. He arched the black blade in his grasp toward my heart. I pivoted and lifted my hand to shoot power through him, but I was too late. The dagger pierced the spot between my shoulder and my breast. Searing pain lanced through my being, as if a piece of my soul were being untethered.

Thud.

The horrific sound rang through my skull as someone behind me collapsed to the ground. Was there another enemy lying in wait who had also harmed Silas? Panic coursed through me, radiating through my being. To my horror, the connection between Silas and me flickered out. Silence reverberated through me. But I didn't have time to react as I stumbled backward.

Whack.

My back careened against the hardwood floor. My skull ricocheted off the surface. Stars splattered my vision. The heavy weight of the beady-eyed huntsman landed atop me, forcing the air out of my lungs. His whiskey-ladened breath wafted over me. My palm flattened against his belly. I willed energy to pierce through him, but nothing came.

He snarled and twisted the hilt. A shriek bellowed from me. Agony coursed through my extremities. Frantic for relief, I recalled my combat training with Peter. *Remain calm and free yourself.*

With all my might, I kicked my knee upward, connecting with my attacker's testicles. He howled in anguish. I squirmed beneath him, but with each slide, the dagger dug deeper, causing blood to pour from my wound. To my dismay, my window for escape had closed. The man's grimy hand wrapped around my neck.

"You'll pay for—"

Thump.

His mouth slacked. He collapsed on top of me. His weight pushed the knife into me. A sob escaped me. A tinny tang accosted my senses. Haziness skittered over my vision. My teeth gritted as a sharp ache radiated through my shoulder and down my arm. A hand grasped the corpse's arm and rolled it off me.

I blinked, taking in a gore-covered Xavier. He grabbed my uninjured wrist and pulled me to standing. I swayed, lightheaded. Xavier's glance passed over me to the entranceway. My blood ran cold as I followed his gaze. Silas lay face down on the porch, unmoving. Yet there was no enemy near him. Confusion took root.

But we didn't have a moment's respite. Footsteps thumped from the second floor overhead. My knees buckled, and Xavier grasped my elbow, steadying me. None of us were in any shape to continue the fight, yet our doom barreled toward us from the upstairs landing.

"Gods damn it." His thumb trailed over the hilt of the dagger embedded in me. "It's a warded onyx blade. As long as it remains, you're powerless."

Sweat coated my brow. My stomach roiled from the anguish. The heavy footfalls thundered, drawing closer. I blinked, my mind swimming between consciousness and the bliss of nothingness. I shook my head, trying to keep myself rooted to the present. With Silas unconscious and Xavier worse for wear, there was no way we could defeat our enemy if the circumstances didn't change, and quickly. A bone-deep realization took root. If my curse possessed me, I could dispatch the remaining enemy, but I might accidentally kill Xavier. However, if we waited, we were all as good as dead.

Clomp, clomp, clomp, clomp...

"Take it out. Now," I screamed.

His features screwed into an argument, but as his gaze shifted toward the approaching enemies, his demeanor smoothed.

"I'm sorry." He grasped the knife and yanked it free.

A scream reverberated from me. Blood oozed from the wound. The world went hazy. My legs swayed, and only one option remained. My fingers tugged off the onyx ring keeping my deadly blight at bay. Hastily, I thrust the jewelry into my pocket. Simultaneously, tarry blackness coated my awareness. The curse took over my body, making me its conduit, slipping over me like a second skin. My soul retreated, and the darkness surged forward as a separate entity. It secured me within the cage, and I watched my being act as if it were not my own.

An inhuman shriek left me. Despite my injuries, my legs sprinted up the stairs for a group of men barreling toward me. The fastest, a lithe, pale huntsman, lifted his sword, but I was faster. My unrestrained power hummed through my limbs, giving me unnatural speed. My hand wrapped around his throat.

His jaw quaked. He gasped for air. I hated the image. The curse delighted in his terror. Darkness surged through him from my palms until he popped akin to an overheated amber. Ash filled the cramped area, and though I wanted to gag, I couldn't. Instead, my tongue darted over my lips. The blight fluttered, delighting in the taste. I recoiled. It laughed in the shared space of my being as if we were two people trapped in one form.

Let me handle this. Look away if you can't stomach what must be done, the curse hissed.

I gulped down the discomfort and forced myself to remain present, unwilling to fully slip under its control. It would overtake me if I relented. I didn't know if I'd regain command of my being if it ever did. The curse cackled, delighted, as a dozen men barreled down the stairs in a row.

My jaw unhinged, and dense tar spewed from me. Their expressions twisted in horror, and they staggered backward. They were cramped in the narrow stairwell. They crashed upon one another, similar to dominoes falling. The inky darkness sprayed over them. The sizzling of flesh melded with their horrific cries. Yet the vomitus spittle continued to leave my gullet until nothing was left but a thick, sticky goo mixed with random bones poking through the mess. My mouth closed. My throat worked, swallowing the bilious flavor. A smirk curled my lips as my feet tiptoed past the unrecognizable men. A clatter sounded overhead. My head whipped, tracking the unseen person.

No mercy, the blight rattled in my brain.

I leaped over the last remnants. My boots settled on the landing with catlike ease. Despite the surging power, my skin overheated. Would I burn through my vitality like a firework bursting in the night sky? Before I could assess the situation, a clang drew my attention. My feet rushed down the hallway to the room where a subtle scuffling punctuated the now silent corridor. Energy whipped around me, blasting the door off its hinges.

A white quilt with violet irises lay askew on the four-poster bed. The soft scent of lemon and lye wafted through the air. An almost inaudible whimper emitted near the pine dressing table.

The chattering of teeth echoed through the space. It came from an adolescent girl curled in the corner. Her knees were pulled against her chest, tucked beneath her flannel night-gown. She clung to a kitchen knife, causing her sepia knuckles to blanch.

"Get up. Face your end." The blight's inhuman reverberation caused my soul to shudder.

The wisp of a young woman stood no taller than me. Her violet eyes shone with tears, and her full lower lip wobbled. "I-I-I-I'm a friend. Please don't kill me."

A bellow bubbled from my throat, but I forced my mouth shut, stifling the horrific sound. I may have become a monster, but even I couldn't kill a child.

My palm splayed of its own accord at the young girl. She trembled and held the weapon between us.

"Stop," I ordered in my voice.

Stop? The blight curled, trying to force me deeper into the prison I'd created for it.

"Stop," I whispered and shut my eyes. I scoured my being for the darkness that raged through me, hunting it within my mind as if it were an entity of its own, separate from me. It snarled in the recesses of my memories, desiring the death of this girl. I wrestled against the bitter emotions, the bloodshed that tinged my hands. It screamed against my brain. My nails dug into my skull. The pain seared through my shoulder. I anchored myself to the agony burning through my flesh. My sentience rose, as if I slid into my skin. With great internal force, I shoved the curse into the mental prison.

I fell to my knees, panting. Tears streamed down my cheeks, and my heart ached for the death coating me. A sob racked through me. My hand pressed into my pocket and slipped the ring onto my finger. The coursing energy faltered like a river being blocked off by a dam. Despite the fight, the warmth of unconsciousness tugged against me, and I faded into the abyss.

CHAPTER 17

SILAS

Sunlight pierced through my closed eyelids. Wasn't it too early to be dawn? My mind scrambled for recollection, settling upon my very last memory—Arianna crossing the threshold and a huntsman stabbing her in the chest.

"Arianna!" I jolted to sitting. A bright blue sky glimmered overhead, as if azure paint had been spilled across the atmosphere. Sunlight sparkled through a puffy white cloud, but no warmth permeated my being. A knot formed in my throat, and my fingers moved along my neck to loosen my cape. Yet no string lay against my windpipe. Instead, a gauzy cream tunic and matching breeches had replaced my clothing. My nostrils flared at the meadow I'd been trapped in after I nearly perished in the hallway. How had I ended up here again?

I shot to standing. The rolling meadows sprawled for miles in an endless sea of grass.

"Arianna!" My gut twisted. Internally, I scoured for our connection, but something dampened my senses, as if many glasses of whiskey muted them.

A guttural growl emanated from me. She was injured and in danger. Desperate to find her, I stomped through the ankle-deep grasses.

As I searched, time flattened. The sun illuminated the space but remained fixed. Yet I strode on through the endless emerald meadows. This was no darkness realm, but no peace lay within this eerily picturesque world.

"Arianna!" I continued to call out her name.

Only silence answered my pleas.

After trudging for an eternity, my patience frayed at the edges. I must free myself from this prison. Agitated, I kicked a small rock nestled in the soft grass. It sailed through the air, then veered slightly to the left. As it landed, there was only silence. My glare flowed away from the stone, but as I focused upon the horizon, a shadowy shape loomed in the distance.

Relieved to see something other than these damned rolling hills, I surged forward. As I drew closer, the hazy silhouette sharpened to a leafy elm, larger than any I'd ever seen before. My vision strained until a woman came into view.

Arianna? I ran for the person, but my steps slowed as she came into focus. She smoothed her palms over her frock and stepped toward the edge of the tree. The whispers of sunlight filtered through the canopy of leaves washing over her olive complexion, her raven hair, and her amber eyes.

"Silas." She stretched her hands out, gesturing for me to join her.

Impossible. She shouldn't be here. Perhaps this was a dream? Uncaring of how she came to be, I sprinted to her like a lad coming home from lessons. "Mother."

Her fingers reached for me, and I leaned my cheek into her gentle embrace. "My sweet boy. I've waited so long to see you." A tear rolled down her face. "There's so much I want to ask you, but..."

However, a cold gust blew across the field, dampening our reunion. A chill slithered over me. The once fluffy clouds darkened and cast over the sun, casting us in shadows.

"You are too young to be here, but it seems your soul isn't freed from your body yet. Thank Cassius that something still tethers you to your mortal coil, keeping me from ushering you to the Great Beyond." Her gaze softened as she studied me.

Darkness overtook the sky as night befell us. The temperatures plummeted. My teeth chattered.

The warmth within her expression hardened to that of determination. "But you cannot linger here, in the realm between realms. It is her prison, and I fear what will happen to your soul if you remain. You must return to the mortal world, to Arianna and your father. Trust him."

Thunder rumbled through the sky. Mother's face blanched. My gaze drifted past her, to a shadowy figure lurking on the other side of the thick elm. A flicker of white hair flowed from behind the dark trunk. My mouth dried. Something about this place was horribly wrong.

Mother's spine went rigid. She pushed from beneath the tree's shade and into the meadow. "Go home. Now!"

Smoke bubbled from the shade of the leaves. The all-consuming fog crawled toward us. The haze consumed the green grass. My pulse skittered. Goose bumps rose. I reached for Mother's hand to rescue her from the darkness, but she stayed rooted to the spot.

"Arise, Silas. You must live, or all will be lost." She shook out of my hold.

My chest ached, but a flash of light absorbed her before the smoke could devour her form. The creeping mist surged.

Fear prickled along my spine. Panic fueled my limbs. I sprinted in the opposite direction. The miasma nipped at my heels. My feet tripped over that damned rock I'd thrown minutes ago. My body smacked into the ground. I turned onto my back and stared at the fog only seconds from overtaking me. I closed my eyes and—

"Son, wake up. Son." A fist pounded against my sternum.

I sucked in a sharp breath and coughed. Pain pulsed through my ribcage, anchoring me. The gibbous moon reflected off Xavier's inky locks. His hair tumbled out of its tie and over his furrowed brow. The snow whipped through the porch and curled along the eaves of the inn's entrance. Somehow, my soul had been yanked from the realm between realms.

"My gods, your heart stopped. There's no injury. You just collapsed." Xavier choked out a sob, and a tear streaked down his nose.

With a hiss, I shifted to a seated position. A haze covered my perception as my mind tried to reorient to this place. Had that meadow simply been a dream? Before I could ponder what had happened, reality crashed upon me. Arianna. Concern for my love lanced through my mental fog like a hot knife cutting through butter.

I inhaled sharply, tasting the tang of blood and ash on my tongue. "Where is she?"

I moved to stand, but Xavier placed a palm on my chest, halting me. "She's upstairs, clearing out the last of the riffraff. I'll help her, but you—"

I smacked his hand away and scrambled to my feet, but reality tilted. Off-kilter, I crashed shoulder-first against the doorframe. Sweat beaded my forehead. What in the blasts had happened? Minutes ago, I'd been well; now fatigue coated me. Seconds before I toppled, I'd felt as if something had severed my strength, somehow causing me to drift into that otherworldly space. Despite my waning strength, a single-minded desire fueled me: protect Arianna.

"Silas." He wrapped an arm around my waist. "Please sit—"

"Help," an unfamiliar female voice screamed from the top of the stairwell to my left.

"Robin?" He cocked his head toward the bottom floor to our right.

"Yes. I'm fine. Hurry! Arianna's injured. She's losing a lot of blood. I need you to boil water and grab a sewing kit," the female voice ordered.

Xavier looked between me and the stairs, hesitating for a fraction of a second.

"Go." I tugged myself free from his grasp and leaned against the wall.

Xavier leapt over the corpse of the man who'd accosted Arianna before I'd lost consciousness, then rushed for the kitchen. My focus shifted to the landing. I scoured my soul for my connection to my beloved. The thread between us blinked in and out. Terror consumed me. She was slipping through my fingertips. I had to get to her.

My feet dragged along the wooden floor, skittering past the dead huntsmen. Then I rounded the corner to the stairwell. The putrid tang of ash and tar washed over me. A petrified onyx goo covered the path upstairs, akin to molten lava that had cooled. Bile rose, but I swallowed it down. Without focusing on the substance, I trudged up the steps. My fingernails dug into the banister as I hauled my body forward. Brittle bones poking through the plaque crunched underfoot. What dark power had Arianna accessed in order to cause this level of destruction? I couldn't focus on the carnage, not when my energy waned. Finally, my boots landed on the carpet runner in the hallway.

"Where is she?" I growled through panted breaths. The corridor was empty, but I sensed her sluggish pulse beating through me.

"Over here. Hurry," the voice shouted from three doors down.

My palm pushed into the wallpaper along the hall as I lugged my weary body to the room. Perspiration dotted my brow. Finally, my legs crossed the threshold. Yet the scene before me caused panic to bubble. Charred footsteps were seared into the wood that led into the quarters and ended where Arianna lay lifeless like a rag doll on the soft yellow rug. An adolescent girl leaned over my bride with her hands pressed against her chest. Blood coated the cloth in the girl's hands. Her violet irises blazed with anxiety, but her countenance remained level, as if she'd dealt with death before.

"Arianna." I rushed to my wife's side and knelt beside her limp form.

"Xavier, is he getting the supplies?" the girl asked.

Crimson stained the once-white rag in her grasp. The ruby shade on my beloved's lips and the rosy pink of her cheeks had vanished. If she continued bleeding out, she'd die.

Long ago, I remembered Brielle having to act quickly on a footman who'd severely injured himself by cauterizing the laceration. Warm coals simmered in the fireplace, casting a faint glow over the space. However, the dying embers would not create enough heat for what I must do. My jaw clamped as my gaze scanned over my love. In a second, I'd made an important decision—we'd return to Presspin together, or neither of us would.

"Do you have anything metallic and flat? A spoon? Anything will do." My hand nudged the girl's, taking over the compression, as my palms placed pressure against my wife's contusion. "And any type of alcohol?"

The girl's nose wrinkled, but she didn't ask questions. Instead, she rushed about the room, rummaging through drawers. The shuffling of clothing punctuated the silence, mixing with Arianna's ragged breaths. Blood oozed through the rag with each passing heartbeat as the girl searched. My stomach sank as crimson leached onto my fingertips. The world grew hazy, as if I'd also been mortally injured. Finally, the girl approached with a metal hair comb and a bottle of spirits. She held out the items.

"Pour the whiskey on the laceration." I tugged off Arianna's cape and the gore-stained tunic that covered her injury.

A wide gash pierced the juncture above the soft top of her breast and under her shoulder. Fortunately, the blade had been mere inches from piercing her heart. The girl poured the amber liquid. It sloshed over the deep abrasion. My beloved winced, and her face paled. Would she perish? I swallowed a swell of pain; was this the agony she'd lived with for months? No wonder she had been determined to save me, no matter the cost.

"Go find herbs that help with infection. Quickly."

Thankfully, the girl didn't argue. She dashed out of the room. I poured whiskey on the long end of the steel comb, then slathered my hands with the alcohol. Arianna's breaths slowed, and her skin blanched further. I gulped down my distress, and as if tied to hers, my own respirations hitched. The edges of my vision blackened, as if I would also succumb to unconsciousness.

"Just hold on." I gripped the handle, curling my fist around it.

I pulled against the fizzling curse. The power surged, and I directed the energy into my palms, heating the metal. Sweat beaded down my forehead. I inhaled through a tightening in my ribcage. A warning tolled in my mind. If I continued, I'd burn through more of my life force. Uncaring of the consequences, I continued until the alloy blazed a molten red, as if it had been plunged into a fire.

"I'm so sorry, beloved," I whispered and pushed the scalding steel against the laceration.

Arianna screamed as her flesh seared together. Her eyes flew open, then rolled into the back of her head as she slipped deeper into unconsciousness. Sweat dotted her clammy skin.

As I extracted the molten tool, an angry puffy mark with a rose indentation remained where the gash had once been. Needing to fully stop the bleeding, I rotated her to her side. Crimson dribbled through a hole pierced her tunic. I ripped the clothes from her back, exposing the oozing exit wound. With no time to spare, I gripped the bottle and splashed whiskey on the abrasion.

A barking cough rasped from me. Ringing entered my ears. A cold sensation coursed down my spine. Despite the internal warning, I reheated the comb with my power. Fatigue coated me, but I held steady. Moments later, I removed the metal from my palm and placed it against the lesion. The acrid scent of burning flesh hit my nostrils. She whimpered beneath me, but to my relief, she didn't stir.

With her injury sealed, the handle fell from my grasp and tumbled to the carpet. A cough rattled from me. Black liquid dripped from my nose.

"What in the blast?" Xavier ran through the doorway, clutching a bucket of water. His brow furrowed as he peered down at Arianna and her heat-fused tissue. He whipped his head toward me. "What have you done?"

Exhausted, I collapsed beside Arianna. My hand stretched for hers, and I wrapped her fingers in my embrace. I blinked one last time, taking her in, before I slipped into the abyss.

CHAPTER 18

Arianna

Snowflakes pelted the floor-to-ceiling windows of the conservatory in Belmont Manor, causing the light to distort through the foggy glass. Despite the persistent storms churning through Presspin, the restored orangery had become an oasis. Heat blazed from the furnace along the brick wall, providing a balmy warmth to the budding plants. Weeks ago, brokenness had filled this desolate place; now it brimmed with life. My boots clicked over the polished tile. My fingers skimmed over the old metal table that housed a line of medicinal herbs, scribbled papers, a pestle, and a mortar.

Somehow, Naomi had found a purpose in Presspin, serving as Brielle's herbalist apprentice and tending to the sick. Yet a pang radiated in my chest, denoting the distance that had grown between us. I ignored the sensation, focusing on the relief that she was no longer lingering in her suite, unkempt and silent. Given her recent renewal in spirit, I didn't push for connection, hoping that one day we could be sisters again. Instead, I snuck into her safe haven when she was busy, hoping to glean some comfort from the whispers of her presence.

Settling into the space, I surveyed the rear wall, where canvas speckled the once blank gray brick. Unlike when I'd last lurked here to view her progress, there was a new sketch of our mother lying between our old farmhouse and the meadows of Krella.

A knot formed in my windpipe as Clara Park stared back at me, immortalized in charcoal. I swallowed the lump. Despite the blaring internal warning to flee, my feet moved of their own accord, as if drawn to her portrait. My heart plummeted into my stomach at the softness in her gaze, the gentle smile on her lips, and the warmth in her countenance, for it was an expression I'd never experienced.

The pressure against my throat tightened, choking me. To my dismay, the past leapt forward, and the last words Mama had uttered to me rattled through my skull. "I'm sorry." It wasn't lost on me that she couldn't muster the words "I love you," like she'd whispered to my sister. Instead, her apology haunted me most nights. Had her remorse been because of the mistreatment I'd endured or a bitter acknowledgment of her displeasure of my existence? I'd shouldered her abuse for a lifetime and still was unsure whether it had been because of her failing or mine.

My fingers curled into a fist. My nails dug into my palms, trying to anchor me against the swelling anguish. But I couldn't look away from her portrait. Memories toppled upon me one by one: Mama's icy stare, her distance, her sharp words, her allowance of the Aralians to subdue me, then, finally, her selling me to the Terrells for her comfort.

Overwhelmed by the flooding ruminations, my skin heated. Wisps of crackling power curled from my fingers. I inhaled sharply, filling my lungs. A desperate desire to remain in control rooted in my gut. But the question that had plagued me unfurled from the recesses of my mind. Was it the curse that made me unlovable, or simply me?

"What are you doing in here? This is my sanctuary. You have the whole damn manor," Naomi shouted behind me.

When had she entered the room? I blinked, being yanked into the present.

"Get out!" she commanded.

My shoulders tensed at her order. The blight boiled in my blood, clawing against my mental boundaries. I spun on my heels to face her. Her lips puckered and her nose wrinkled, as if I'd marred her haven with my mere presence.

Fueled by the churning darkness, my bitter tongue spewed vitriol. "Yet this is my home. Mine. I've spent all winter honoring your wishes. Skulking about these halls, hoping not to upset you. How much more must I apologize? I'm sorry your mother died."

As soon as the harsh truth rushed from me, the curse took hold of the horrific honesty I'd never acknowledged. Mrs. Clara Park had never truly been my parent, but my warden, begrudgingly keeping me because of obligation.

A sharp cackle left her. She crossed her arms over her chest, bunching the pristine white apron she often wore when experimenting with herbs. "What are you expecting from me, a thank you? All right. Thank you, Arianna, for running off with Silas, leading to Mama and me being captured and shoved into that dank cellar at Terrell Estate for a fortnight. Thank you for taking your dear sweet time to get to us, and then..."

Her cheeks reddened. Tears welled in the corners of her eyes.

"Not being able to save Mama."

My heart ached as if I'd been stabbed with a knife. In the core of my soul, I knew she blamed me, yet hearing it spoken aloud stung like poison. The emotions I'd kept buried rose to the surface, untethered.

"You told me to go with him. I would have stayed; I would have married Theo, and I would have…" I swallowed down the harsh truth, that the wards would have slowly drained my vitality until I became ill with the wasting sickness and died.

I shook my head and forced out what she wanted to hear. "You're right. I am the villain in your story. The horrific monster you've been saddled with. I should have wed that wretch so you could be happy."

"You should have," she sneered.

I sucked in a sharp breath, as if she'd slapped me. Anguish burrowed into my gut. The curse clung to this pain. My mind fought against the darkness, yet it tempted me with relief. I was so tired of fighting. In an instant, the light within me snuffed out, as if I were consumed by a thick haze.

Flooded by my misery, a shriek left my mouth. The high-pitched squeal reverberated. The windows pulsated, and the pots on the metal desk shook.

Pop…pop…pop…pop.

The jars of herbs exploded. Colorful powders splattered the sheets of crisp paper.

Crash.

The windowpanes shattered. She screamed. Shards of glass flew about, whirling through the thick, unyielding wind. Inky tendrils crawled out of me, cracking the tiles underfoot. The legs of the metal table wobbled, melting as my power licked upon it.

Time sped from a trot to a gallop, for it could have been mere seconds or long minutes as the dense energy sizzled along the conservatory, turning all it touched to ash.

"Arianna," Silas boomed. My consciousness scrambled, as if the curse were trying to drown me and my husband was my buoy.

Heavy footsteps surged toward me, and concern laced his countenance as he bore witness to my activated form. He clasped my shoulders, tugging more of me forward. "Breathe. You're safe. I am here, and you are safe. Please stay with me."

His hands cupped my chin. "Beloved, come back to me."

Oxygen rushed through my lungs, and I anchored myself to the sensation. With a heavy exhale, I blinked, pressing the blight into the cage where it belonged. As my awareness returned, horror replaced my anguish.

Destruction had unfurled from me, and ruin encompassed the once pristine orangery. Naomi wept, curled in a corner, having been trapped by my power's predilections. Cuts gashed across her arms, which shielded her face. Blood oozed from the wound, dripping over her apron. A frozen wind sent snow whipping through the broken windows. Frost covered the once beautiful blooms, the fractured pots, and the lopsided table. The sketches had burned to ash. Nothing remained of the life she'd rebuilt.

My stomach dropped. Wholly myself, I left the comfort of Silas's embrace. My boots crunched over the pottery shards as I approached Naomi. I reached for her to examine her injuries.

She scrambled backward. "No, don't touch me. You...you...monster." Fear lived in her haunted expression.

I raised my hands, showing my palms, and withdrew.

Silas's steps clipped against the tile floor as he neared. "Naomi. Don't say that. She's—"

"No." I spun to him, pressing my fingers against his pectoral. "She's right."

"I hate you," she hissed between sobs. "I wish you had never been born."

A shiver slipped down my spine and pooled at its base. "If it helps, I wish I'd never been born as well."

Unable to remain a moment longer, I strode through the destruction and exited.

"Come back," Silas bellowed through our connection.

Jolted awake, I studied an unfamiliar ceiling overhead. My palms pushed the comforter covering me, causing a stinging sensation to lance from my breast and radiate down my arm. I winced. My fingers trailed the vee of a fresh gray tunic, then skated over the bandaged wound where the blade had once been. I sucked in a sharp breath as recollections flooded me—the inn, Silas on the ground, the knife being pulled from my shoulder, and then the blight using me like a puppet. A cold sweat washed over me. I'd killed again, and with each death, I slipped closer to being the monster Naomi claimed me to be. However, my guilt would have to wait. I needed to find him. Internally, I searched for our bond. To my relief, it beat in rhythm with my heart, but the once strong thread before we'd entered this place had weakened. What had happened while I was asleep?

Impatient, I hoisted myself into a sitting position. A hiss of pain whooshed from me.

"You're awake. Xavier will be relieved," a voice called from the shadowed corner.

I blinked, trying to make out the hazy figure perched on a stool. Moonlight streamed through the gossamer curtain, casting a faint glow over the space. The embers in the hearth blazed, keeping the room warm without it being sweltering. A dressing table sat in the corner, hiding the stranger. They unfurled from their seat and moved to the dresser.

Flickers of firelight washed over her violet irises, wide nose, and springy black curls. She donned a plain gray dress, making her look more like a servant than a huntsman. Her lips pulled into a thin line. She plucked a pouch from a drawer, poured a glass of water, and closed the distance between us.

"Here. Chinchona bark powder to help with the pain." She emptied the contents of the envelope into the liquid, then swirled the snifter about, turning it a rust hue. She shoved the concoction forward, urging me to take it.

My fingers pressed into the cool crystal, but I didn't imbibe. Instead, I stared at the remedy, then at the girl, whom I'd almost dispatched before I'd lost consciousness. "Why would you help me? I nearly killed you."

"You stopped yourself from harming me, which I'm sure was quite the internal battle. Besides, any friend of Xavier's is a friend of mine." She shrugged.

Realization dawned on me—the ally that he'd mentioned. I'd expected an adult, but she was a girl not even at her majority. Why was a child assisting him? Despite my confusion, only one person mattered—Silas.

"Have you seen my husband?" I ignored the medicine and squirmed to free myself from the tangled sheets. A heaviness burned in my muscles, making it difficult for me to escape.

"Drink this first, and then I'll take you to them." She pushed the brew to me. A determination blazed in the stubborn tilt of her jaw. Blindly, I accepted the tonic and chugged the bitter contents. "Now, where is he?"

She lowered the cup to the floor, walked around the four-poster bed, and held out a hand. With great effort, I dangled my feet over the edge of the plush mattress. My fingers laced with the girl's, and she helped me to stand. My legs wobbled, but I forced myself to steady.

"Ready?" She tugged my uninjured arm over her shoulder, then took a tentative step.

I nodded, and together we exited the room. The scent of ash accosted my senses the second we stepped into the hallway. My stomach churned, and bile rose up my throat. Not wanting to vomit all over her, I leaned into my curiosity to distract myself from the destruction I'd caused.

"What's your name?" The question tumbled from me as I focused on the singed runner with my boot prints scorched into the fibers.

"Robin." She smiled. A bouncy determination entered her tone as she continued unbidden. "I'm part of the Opposition and one of Xavier's best spies. No one thinks that a flighty girl of fourteen posing as a kitchen servant would be sent to infiltrate groups, but I was."

I cocked my head toward her, confused. "You're just a child. Aren't you afraid?"

Her nose wrinkled as we stopped at the door. "Of course, but you see, I need to help Xavier. My sister was captured by the Aralians. It's my life's mission to rescue her or take the disciples down."

My eyes widened at the girl's words. Before I could press for more information, we crossed the threshold.

Xavier sat on the edge of the mattress, near a slumbering Silas, who was tucked beneath the quilts. My husband's rasping breaths punctuated the silence, causing a chill to prickle my skin. It was the same horrific sound that had haunted me for weeks; that gurgling respiration denoting his decline.

"Xavier," Robin called out, tugging his attention from his son and onto us.

A whisper of relief cut across his tense features as he took us in. "Thank Cassius, you're awake." He stood and rushed forward. "Did you give her the medicinal powder? Has she eaten?"

She huffed a sigh. "Yes. I gave her the remedy and water. Shall I fetch some deer jerky and a biscuit for our guests?" A twinge of sarcasm laced her tone, the sound so similar to Naomi that it made my heart ache.

"Please do. She needs to rebuild her strength." He flicked his wrist then offered his hand to me. "We have much to discuss."

Hesitantly, I accepted Xavier's assistance while Robin simultaneously unfurled from me. Without a goodbye, she left the room.

Still weak, my knees buckled. He anchored me, placing my arm against his as if we were promenading in a park.

Before I could ask about Silas's well-being, he began speaking. "You've both caused me quite a lot of frustration. We are a full day behind schedule, but it's not safe to travel with two slumbering passengers who could likely be hauled off by bandits, huntsmen, or worse—disciples. At least you've risen."

My brow knitted. Had a day passed? But my concern remained with my husband and what had triggered his collapse.

He guided me to the bed, then released me where a sleeping Silas lay. My palm pressed against the smooth pine post of the frame for balance. My love breathed shallowly. The heavy bags that had dissipated after sipping the tonic Xavier provided had returned. A gray pallor tinged his olive skin, and his cheeks had hollowed slightly.

"Where is he injured?" I asked, hoping that the wound hadn't been life-threatening.

"That's the odd thing. His heart stopped beating. Then, moments later, he inhaled, and his eyes flew open, as if nothing had happened. He was shaky but seemed fine." Xavier patted Silas's foot tucked under the cream-colored quilt. "With him awake and you injured, I ran to the kitchen to fetch supplies. He somehow made it up the stairs and used his power to cauterize your wound. When I arrived, it was already too late. He's been unconscious ever since. And don't worry; Robin applied the bandage and changed your shirt."

I grazed my fingers through Silas's locks to reassure myself that he was here. He'd been foolish; however, I didn't know if I would have survived without his assistance.

As if sensing my thoughts, Xavier said, "He's always been sensitive, willing to sacrifice himself for the good of others. He gets that from his mother." He shook his head, then strode to the desk near the window.

I drank in Silas's feeble form. Panic churned in my belly. What did using his curse mean regarding his dwindling vitality? Would we have time to cure him? Or had that stunt weakened him further? Would he wake up again?

"Stay with me." I leaned over Silas and placed a kiss on his clammy cheek. Then I pressed my forehead against his and said a prayer to whatever god was listening, asking that they revive him for the rest of our journey.

A few moments later, Xavier whispered from behind me. "I have something to ease your nerves."

As I pivoted, Xavier thrust a snifter of whiskey toward me. "Here."

My fingers curved around the etched crystal. The oaky aroma wafted forward. My mouth watered. Exhausted, I drank a sip but lowered the rest of the beverage to the nightstand, unwilling to risk losing control and giving my blight a foothold.

He downed the spirits and then settled the cup beside mine. He shifted to his son. His features softened, reminding me so much of that sketch Naomi had drawn of Mama, of a parent looking upon their child with love.

A hard knot formed in my throat, but I locked the memories of my nightmare away. With Xavier lost in his own thoughts, my mind focused on the mystery of my husband's unpredictable health. Though Xavier had glazed over his heart stopping, something in my soul caused me to focus on it. I played through the events, beginning in the woods and then settling on the moment he collapsed, which coincided with the dagger being plunged into my chest. My blight stirred. The same prickling sensation arose, so similar to when I'd discovered our curse-bond.

"Where is the warded blade?" I asked.

Xavier's hand settled on Silas's foot as if he could will him to rise.

"Right here." His fingers grazed the tan huntsman jacket he'd likely pilfered and plucked the weapon from a hidden pocket. Soft candlelight glimmered over the familiar etchings, similar to those on the eaves of my childhood bedroom door.

My fingers traced the grooved markings. My blight hissed in my mind.

"I wouldn't touch this if I were you. If it lodges in your body, you won't be able to access your power. Not as long as it's embedded within you." He pointed at my bandage.

I studied the symbols on the dagger. Silas had risen after this was removed from my flesh. Were these incidents connected, or was it a coincidence?

Xavier's fist curled around the hilt. His knuckles blanched from the pressure. "After studying this damned thing for a day, I still have no idea where it came from."

He walked to the window, and the bored expression he often bore shattered as frustration etched into the soft lines of his face. The quandary over this weapon apparently unsettled both of us. A beat passed as he stared into the night sky as if it held all the answers. A tension settled over the space.

"Damn it. I shouldn't have been distracted at Daviel. But I didn't have a choice, did I?" Xavier sheathed the dagger. "I thought that hiding him in a brothel would keep him well entertained. No, he had to cause a ruckus. First the gambling, then his wicked tongue getting him into trouble with Martha, and finally offending the toughest courtesan in the bunch, Jasmine. I knew he was a rakehell, a true scoundrel. Just like his father." He snorted then softened his tone. "Just like his father." He scrubbed a hand over his face.

"I can't blame Wolf, can I?" He turned to me.

My brow furrowed. He spoke of this person as if I knew of them, or perhaps the incidents over the past few days had finally rattled the unshakable man.

Not waiting for my answer, he pressed the empty snifter to his forehead. "Forget about Wolf. Focus. Who gave the dagger to the huntsman? Think, Xavier. You are not in Delphine's bed persuading her anymore, leaving the spot open for someone new. Who's entangling with her to gain access to this weapon? Wobbleton wants her. No, she has no interest in that bloated buffoon. Perhaps Malrik? No, he prefers men. Damn it. There are too many players." He chucked the crystal cup across the room. It crashed against the wall and shattered into pieces.

In the past, an outburst may have frightened me, but not anymore. Hadn't he witnessed me kill a dozen men in the blink of an eye? The man remained unruffled by my darkness, sharing a drink with me without flinching in fear. He and Silas had both borne witness to my darkness and remained by my side.

Tentatively, I grasped his shoulder. "We have a long journey tomorrow. We can figure out who our enemies may be then. Have you slept?"

"A bit in the chair. I couldn't leave him." His gaze remained fixed ahead, but a gentleness entered his tone. "Even if I had a good reason to part from him as a child, he's still my boy."

A tug of warmth swirled in my heart. Oddly, I believed him. Perhaps I'd wished my mother had reached this same conclusion, or maybe I simply wanted Silas to feel the love of a father once again.

"I'll stay by his side. You should get some sleep, so you'll be rested for our journey."

"All right." He spun toward me. His green gaze held mine and, for a heartbeat, that strange familiarity tugged within the recesses of my mind. Where had I seen him before? Why were his eyes and the tilt of his smirk so eerily familiar? I forced a watery smile.

"You're a walking contradiction, you know that? Forceful enough to kill, but gentle enough to soothe my old soul." With one final glance at his son, he turned and exited.

Alone with Silas, I crawled onto the mattress beside him and hoped that he'd awaken with the dawn.

CHAPTER 19

Arianna

A DAMPNESS CLUNG TO the air, penetrating my cloak and seeping into my bones. My gloved fingers tugged the black wool fabric, yanking it tighter around me. However, I found no relief from this chill, not as dark storm clouds rolled overhead, casting us in shadows. Despite our delay, at least we'd avoided the precipitation that had swept through the territory last night, leaving the road waterlogged. However, the deep puddles dotting the dirt path leading to Daviel caused the cart to bob and dip. I swayed, nearly knocking into a sleeping Robin, who was curled in the corner near Silas's feet. Yet somehow Xavier remained unfazed, his back straight and his stare intent upon the route as he clutched the reins.

A cough barked from my husband, who lay unconscious by my side. Fortunately, the wagon was long enough to contain Silas. His head touched the pine-board of one end, and his boots pressed against the rear. Robin and I sat cramped along the edge, with little room to sit comfortably as Silas's slumbering form took up most of the space.

As I drank in my love, I wondered when he would emerge from this comatose state. To my dismay, he hadn't risen with the dawn. With his health deteriorating, we'd loaded him into a wheelbarrow to transport him out of the inn, then we'd secured him into the cart. As the morning slipped into afternoon, he'd stayed trapped in his slumber. His teeth chattered. Concerned, I tugged off my glove, then grazed my fingers over his forehead. Blistering heat seeped into my skin. Despite the brisk air, the fever he'd suffered from for months had taken hold of him again.

Needing to help him, I dug into my sack and retrieved the willow bark powder and respiratory blend Mrs. Potter had packed before we departed. However, there'd only been a single dose of each left, and with Brielle's rightful hatred of me, I hadn't requested more. My brow pinched as I studied the concoctions.

"Are we stopping in Daviel? You'd sent a missive to Martha saying we'd be passing through, correct? Does she have access to medicines to replenish our supplies?" I called out over the horse's sloshing hooves to Xavier, who'd been lost in thought, likely trying to deduce who'd provided the warded dagger to the huntsman. A while ago, he'd mumbled some unfamiliar names. I'd assumed they were council members, but soon after, he'd grown silent.

"Yes, we'll collect supplies, medicines, and fresh clothing. Then we'll venture to Hallowhaven, where I have a safe house. We can use it as our hideout after we acquire the elixir of life." His eyes remained fixed on the landscape ahead.

Satisfied that we'd be able to procure additional tonics, I grasped a tin cup I'd pilfered from the inn and dumped the powder into it. My free hand retrieved my canteen and poured the cold water. I swirled the contents until the medicine disintegrated into the liquid. Gingerly, I pried Silas's mouth open and tipped the remedy down his throat.

He swallowed the bitter herbs with a groan. Another blustery gust of wind blew. I slipped my glove on and then tucked the quilt covering Silas tighter around him, fearful that his condition would worsen in these elements. As my fingers moved over the soft down fabric. A realization panged, I'd been so preoccupied with getting to the inn and dispatching the huntsmen, then Silas's unconsciousness, that I hadn't pushed further about the cure's location. This morning, Xavier had been vague, continuously saying it was in Hallowhaven, but that could be anywhere.

My brow furrowed, and a sense of foreboding pooled in my gut. "After we rest in your safe house, how will we access the elixir of life?"

Minutes passed with only Silas's rasping breaths and the sloshing hoofbeats to punctuate the silence.

"What are you not telling me?"

He rolled his neck; his raven locks swayed over the huntsman's jacket he bore. "Let's just get to Martha's. We can discuss the matter then."

My jaw ticked. He'd been evading providing details during each portion of our trek, insisting that we concentrate on the next leg of our journey. Perhaps it was the fatigue clinging to my being, Silas's deteriorating health, or my heart breaking the closer we drew to Daviel, where my nightmares lived, but I'd grown tired of these antics. "No. Tell me now."

"Or what, you'll kill me?" he chided, taking on that lazy tone he'd used previously.

"Of course not," I snapped, agitated that he'd even joke about me dispatching him. "I take no pleasure in harming others. Besides, you're Silas's father."

"Maybe he'd prefer if you rid me of this world." He shrugged, and a hint of the man I'd seen the day prior peered through his nonchalant façade.

"If you start being honest, perhaps you can rebuild a relationship with him. Telling me where the elixir of life is would be a step toward developing a much-needed trust between us all."

A long beat stretched. He adjusted in his seat, then grumbled to himself. Finally, a heavy sigh left him, and the words came out in a muddled whisper, as if he'd hoped they'd be lost in the ether. "The Aralian temple."

I sucked in a sharp breath. "My gods, are you mad? How in the blast are we to enter the Aralian temple?" My hands balled into fists; my leather gloves squeaked from the tension. Entering the disciples' stronghold, with a bounty on my head, could easily lead to my capture and death. I believed Xavier's intentions were not malicious, but Silas would feel otherwise.

As if sensing my thoughts, he continued, "I have a plan. Tomorrow night is the full moon celebration, where the disciples entertain the high council and its dignitaries for the evening. As the predawn crests, we'll sneak in. The residents of the temple should be asleep, drunk, or occupied. I've attended these parties; after hours of unbridled debauchery, no one will be coherent enough to catch us. It is our best chance to snatch the elixir." His back remained ramrod straight, unflinching.

My stomach plummeted and settled in my boots. I was going to be sick. How could I enter the temple as a wanted criminal?

Silas hacked a watery cough. A groan pressed through his pale lips. My gaze dragged from my feet to my love's anguished face. Reality hit me like a ton of bricks. Without this elixir, he would die, so I'd confront whatever I must in order to save him. My mind spun over the possibilities of how to penetrate the stronghold.

As I shuffled through my ruminations, the cart jostled over another pothole. This time my elbow crashed into Robin's side. I winced as pain radiated through my arm and toward my injured shoulder. To my dismay, tenderness still pulled from the sealed wound.

Her violet eyes flew open. "Ow. Can you try not to hit every divot? Some of us are trying to sleep." She pouted, but levity softened her features. A whisper of light peeked through the clouds, shimmering against her sepia skin.

"Pardon me. I'll focus on the path," he said.

Unaware of the tense talk between Xavier and me moments prior, Robin bubbled with youthful excitement. "Gods above. I can't wait to be back home. I need a bath, a hot meal, and some fun. Perhaps a game of poker with Jasmine, or I'll convince Wolf to play a song for me."

My awareness hooked on to the name Xavier had mentioned the night before. This mysterious person who'd frustrated him. Curious, I leaned forward and whispered. "Who's Wolf?"

She grinned mischievously. "He's a resident at the Scarlet Rose, Martha's brothel. He's cursed like you and wears a wolf mask. But the ladies who've bedded him say he's handsome as sin, with dangerous scars across his face."

It was strange to hear of someone like me talked about so openly and without fear. Though I'd always known that others existed outside of Silas and myself.

Unaware of my wandering thoughts, she placed her palm against her forehead and pretended to swoon. "He's an accomplished violinist. When he's bored, he often plays, and I love to sit by his door and listen in the evening. When he is not entertaining the ladies, of course." She gave a wink.

"How did he end up in the brothel?" I leaned in and cupped my chin in my hand, trying to appear nonchalant as I gleaned information from her.

She tilted her head toward Xavier, then lowered her voice. "He's Xavier's ward. Wolf was badly injured when his curse awoke. Fortunately for Wolf, a spy notified Xavier of a blighted young man in need of help. Xavier paid for his care and had him settled in Martha's brothel, hidden. The Aralians have been imprisoning the cursed in their homes, so he's confined to the Scarlet Rose or the Gilded Serpent next door. Though he disappears sometimes. It drives Xavier mad, but Wolf is too sly to be captured."

A pang of sympathy tugged at me for this man, trapped within the confines of the spelled rooms. It was a fate I'd endured for nearly two decades, and one I wouldn't wish on my greatest enemy.

"It's not safe for the blighted. Officials have taken and imprisoned anyone walking the streets. They've locked them in the temple..." Her shoulders fell.

Though she didn't say it, I picked up on the implication. The Aralians had enforced more restrictions since the incident in Daviel, when Silas and I had fought against their oppression. Whomever the disciples had captured were probably dead. They wouldn't risk curse-bond mates finding each other as Silas and I had. A pit formed in my belly. Hadn't she mentioned her sister being detained? I forced down the knowledge that her sibling was likely long gone and focused on keeping my expression steady.

"But we'll save them all. The Opposition will rise and thwart those dreadful disciples." She lifted her fist to the sky. "We have you now. We have Silas when he's well. And Wolf." She lowered her hand and scrubbed her chin. "Though Wolf needs to learn to control his temper. It's why he's bound to the mask. The last time he and Martha trained was a disaster." She wrinkled her nose.

I forced a watery smile as the lie tumbled from my lips. "Let's focus on getting Silas well. We can see what the future holds after that."

Her eyes widened, and that same naiveté and hope shone through her, reminding me so much of Naomi before I'd destroyed her world.

No longer wanting to dwell on the Aralians, I switched the conversation to find out more about the girl. Elated for my questions about her life, she chattered on about living on the top floors of the Scarlet Rose after her sister was abducted, how she had infiltrated the huntsmen by posing as a cook-maid, and more tales of the elusive Wolf, whom she was quite smitten with. To my relief, the grown man seemed to pay her no mind outside of general politeness.

Despite the heaviness of the day, being near Robin lightened a piece of my soul. For a heartbeat, I felt as if I were speaking with a young Naomi. Despite the looming chaos, I allowed myself to soak in this fleeting warmth with a girl who reminded me of my sister.

After hours of companionable chatting, Robin grew bored, shifting her attention to a book in her pack. Lost in her own world, she pulled her knees into her chest and read. As the tall evergreens of the northern forest gave way to the rolling green hills of Daviel, my focus slipped, spiraling into suppressed memories of that horrible day at Terrell Estate.

As we drew closer to the place where I'd become a monster, the hairs on my nape prickled, as if danger loomed. My palms itched, ready to shoot darkness, eager to protect me from a threat that was no longer here. Unwilling to be overtaken by the blight, I watched the black sheep dotting the terrain like tiny dark markings throughout the lush grasses.

The once gloomy clouds overhead darkened with a brewing storm. The icy breeze blew, pressing the tang of dung and hay into my nostrils, gagging me. A chill ran along my spine and settled at my base as the familiar path nearing Terrell Estate drew closer. My heart raced. My skin dampened beneath my gloves. The heaviness I tried to ignore for all these months choked me like a noose. My lips twisted as I held in the silent scream rattling through my being. A shriek melding all that I and the curse had become.

As if summoned by my torment, the skies opened and heavy drops fell upon us, cold and wet. The sudden storm seeped through my cape and straight to my bones. Yet I relished the icy wind as it soothed the brewing tension within, dampening the anguish.

"Gods damn it," Xavier growled from the perch. "Just another blasted thing I didn't calculate."

CHAPTER 20

SILAS

ARISE, SILAS.

My eyes flew open. Yet I wasn't staring at a plaster ceiling; instead, dark storm clouds opened overhead. Rain pelted my fevered flesh and soaked into the thick quilt covering me. The sharp tang of dung and hay clawed at my nostrils. Sneezing, I jostled. My entire body winced as the pain I'd forgotten but grown accustomed to sizzled through my nerves, reminding me that I was a dying man. I blinked; my hazy mind grappled to register my surroundings.

Two-story buildings with red clay tile roofs loomed on either side of the cart I lay within. Daviel. I remembered this city center from my trip to the northern territory. How long had I been asleep? When had we left the inn? A sense of foreboding overwhelmed my confusion as the last memory I held pressed forward—Arianna bleeding out. I licked my dry lips and rolled my head toward the figure curled beside me. Blue irises shone through the shadow of the thick black cloak hiding her face. She reached for my hand, intertwining her fingers with mine. With a quick squeeze, she sent emotions through our connection—relief at my revival, anguish at our proximity to Terrell Estate, and fear due to my recent comatose state. I wanted to comfort her, but our conversation required privacy.

We veered to the right, and my attention shifted from my love to the changing architecture. The once pristine ash-wood storefronts gave way to old, dilapidated shops with broken brown stucco roofs. The cart jostled roughly along divots. My muscles tensed with every bump for the minutes we traveled.

The wagon turned left, and the once fractured path smoothed, and older, well-kept buildings came into view. Despite the blustery weather, raucous music and laughter echoed. My brow furrowed. I'd heard of the pleasure district in Daviel. It was brimming with buxom beauties, bountiful bottles of booze, and endless rounds of poker to entertain the wealthy businessmen who lived too far north to have mistresses in Hallowhaven. The horse slowed as the red brick structure stood like a beacon against the gray sky. *The Scarlet Rose* was etched upon a sign secured above the doorway. Thick black curtains fluttered over the windows, blocking onlookers from the intimate acts that occurred. Hoots and cheers roared from the neighboring tavern, causing Arianna's grip to tighten. My jaw ticked as we rolled into a shadowed alley between the brothel and the boisterous bar.

"Whoa," Xavier's voice echoed.

The horses halted near a side door between the two brick buildings.

"Let's go before we catch our death from this damned rain," he said.

Then the cart swayed, and boots splashed through puddles. My gaze flicked to Xavier's familiar form. He donned a tan huntsman's jacket as he bounded the steps to the door and knocked. The cart dipped toward my feet.

"I'm soaked to the bone," an unfamiliar female voice muttered.

As I strained to see, my mind registered the girl from the inn. In my desperate focus to help Arianna, I hadn't questioned how this girl had known Xavier. Now, as she barreled behind him, ready to push her way into the bawdy house, I wondered who she was. Yet my temples pulsed from the blistering fever, making it difficult to focus.

The dark wood swung open. A tall woman with umber skin and a shaved head stood before Xavier. A quick whispered exchange passed between the pair, then he gestured to us. The lady nodded. Without a second glance, the young girl who traveled with us ran into the dwelling. Did she live here?

Suddenly, Arianna released her hold, and the cart bobbed as she scrambled over the high-backed wood siding. Her boots hit the ground with a splash. "Do you need help?"

My gaze held hers for a heartbeat. I rolled my ankles, but the motion was sluggish. My legs felt fused to the wooden bottom of the wagon. Perhaps it was from the hours of sleep, or from the bone-deep fatigue that had settled in my marrow, but I wouldn't be able to exit unassisted. I shook my head.

"I'll—"

"I'll bring him in." Xavier's voice cut over Arianna's whisper as he loomed near, taking in my feeble form.

Arianna opened her mouth to argue, but his tone tightened. "Go inside. You can't linger here."

Her brow furrowed, but hesitantly, she nodded, then glided up the steps, disappearing into the building.

I clenched my jaw. "I swear if this is a trap—"

"It's not. I promise on your mother's grave, your wife will be safe here. Now let's hurry." He strode for the rear and unlatched the wood by my booted feet. He hoisted himself into the tight space.

I expected him to haul me roughly and tug me out of the conveyance. Instead, his thumb brushed over the locks clinging to my forehead from the precipitation. "You're burning up."

His eyes brimmed with concern, but his features remained neutral, confusing me.

"You're going to be uncomfortable, but we'll get to your suite and get you cleaned up and tucked in with a bowl of beet soup like your mother made when you were sick."

My brow knitted. However, discomfort replaced the bubbling reminiscences as he yanked the soggy quilt off me. The icy deluge pelted against my tunic, causing my teeth to chatter. His hands wrapped under my armpits, hefting me to a sitting position. My muscles protested and my lips restrained a groan from escaping me.

"It's all right, son. You'll likely feel better in the morning. You've been asleep for a day and a half."

A day and a half? My mind latched on to the fact.

With great effort, he twisted my form so my back was facing the opening, then tugged me until my ass nearly toppled over the ledge. "Can you dangle your legs over the end?"

With some effort, I pivoted, forcing my feet to hang over the edge. "I'll walk."

"All right, son. Use me to brace yourself." He straightened and offered his body as a cane.

Though I wanted to argue with the affectionate title, I could not simultaneously banter and unfurl from this conveyance. I pushed my weight forward. My boots thumped onto the gravel road. My knees buckled, but my fingers dug into his shoulder. His hand snaked along my waist, steadying me.

Sweat beaded my forehead, and the world swayed, but I refused to collapse here in this alley. I forced my limbs to move slowly around the brimming puddles, then up the three steps leading to the doorway where the woman lay in wait. Her dark eyes widened as they locked on mine.

"We don't have time to dawdle. The evening rush will start in an hour." She clicked the lock behind us, shutting us inside the brothel.

I blinked in the dimly lit corridor, searching for my beloved. "Where is…" A cough burst from me, and I pressed my mouth against my arm, catching the spittle.

"Robin's showing your wife to your quarters. It's a private wing, reserved only for my highest priority guests, as requested, Mr. Smith. I hope your journey from Seaside was a pleasant one, but from the look of you, it seems it was more arduous than expected." Her glance flicked from me to Xavier. Then she spun on her heel. Her crimson skirts fluttered from the motion. "Come, we must get you to your rooms before my girls take their calls."

We followed her down the hall lined with golden-hued wallpaper. We passed doors with carved flowers and nameplates denoting the courtesans who likely occupied the quarters. Lily, Rose, Violet, Iris, Marigold, and Jasmine. Were all the women named after flora here?

Before I could voice my question, violin music wafted from the floor overhead. The painted ceiling depicted beautiful ladies as angelic figures dancing amongst the clouds. Despite the opulence of the space, the music lacked the same ambiance. Quick, intense chords flew through the air. Franticness moved through the melody, matching my escalated heartbeat.

Xavier peered above, as if he were entranced by the song, and an indistinguishable look crossed over his expression as he stared at the ceiling. The violin crescendoed, and the agony that lived within the notes amplified. A knot formed in my throat as I connected with this unseen figure who played on.

"He's in a mood," she clucked under her tongue. "You need to speak with that boy about disappearing. He missed his curfew again."

"Of course he didn't listen to my last warning." Xavier heaved a sigh, then his gaze shifted to me.

I held his stare, confused about who this musician could be. Was it a lover? Or perhaps another spy?

"He was probably playing cards all night." Xavier fluttered a wrist, dismissing her. "I can only take care of one problem at a time."

She smoothed her palms over the sides of the crimson silk gown that was far more appropriate for an evening event than an afternoon. "Of course. I'll just continue babysitting this little wolf cub. I'm sure Lily or Marigold would be happy to entertain him. Neither have partners tonight, and he seems to match their tastes. They were quite elated with his rough handling of—"

"Please don't share his proclivities with me." He shuddered.

I cocked my head, studying Xavier. Hadn't he been open about his dalliance with the huntsmen's second-in-command? Whoever this man was, Xavier seemed repulsed by whatever escapades he took part in. My nose wrinkled; the musician wasn't a lover, then.

The woman slowed at a tee in the hallway. A stairwell sat to the left. To the right, there was an alcove housing guest rooms. Xavier paused and flicked his attention to the stairs and then to me.

"Help your guests. I'll deal with Wolf. At the very least, he should pick a chipper tune." Without waiting for an answer, she turned to the steps, leaving us.

"Come on. Martha has you in the regent suites." He guided me to the private alcove, where a single entrance lay before us. As we reached the suite, he lifted his fist and knocked thrice. "It's Xavier."

The door opened, and he heaved me over the threshold. A moderate-size room sprawled ahead of me. Gold-vined paper crawled over the walls. The leaves shimmered in the soft candlelight, creating an optical illusion, as if they were aspens dancing in the wind. Surprisingly, there were no windows. Velvet curtains framed a painted fresco. A fire roared, a pink sofa settled near it. To the right sat a bed large enough to sleep five.

"Hurry, take him to the settee." Arianna gestured to the couch, then rushed to a white oak dresser nestled against the wall.

I couldn't focus on her sporadic movements as Xavier guided me in the opposite direction to the divan. "Sit."

He lowered me to the edge of the soft cushions, then knelt before me. His fingers unraveled the laces of my boots and then pulled them off one by one. A sigh escaped me as the soaking footwear fell to the floor with a clunk. I stretched my exposed heels toward the fire, allowing the heat to soak into me.

"We have to get him undressed and into a bath." He stood, then walked to the back of the suite, where another door lay. Then a trickle of a stream emitted from the bathing chamber.

"What is that?" Arianna placed a pair of clean night garments atop the crab apple-hued comforter.

"Running water." He popped out of the antechamber. "It's a luxury here. Though it's becoming far more common in Hallowhaven, at least for the elite."

My lips pursed into a line at the comment about the governing swine, but my features softened as Arianna walked toward me. Her blue eyes focused on mine, but heavy bags hung beneath them, as if she hadn't slept in days. The hollows in her cheeks had reappeared virtually overnight, and a sallowness washed over her complexion.

"I'm quite cross with you." She offered a hand. "But I'll lecture you once we get you out of these damp clothes. I'm certain this rainstorm will not break by nightfall. We may be stuck here until the morning." She hoisted me to a standing position and wrapped my arm around her shoulder. She hissed as my palm pressed against the wound I'd cauterized.

"Sorry." My thumb trailed down the waterlogged tunic clinging to her skin.

As we approached the bathing chamber, Xavier stepped out. "All right, the tub is filled and towels are in the cupboard. I'll have some food and fresh travel clothing gathered for you."

"And medication for Silas," she chimed in.

"Yes, and a salve for you. I'm sure that wound burns like the dickens." He pointed at Arianna's shoulder.

Her expression flattened, but she didn't deny the pain that likely pulsed through where the blade had pierced her.

He nodded, then strode for the exit. As he reached the threshold, he turned around. "Don't answer the door for anyone but me or Martha. We'll knock with three short raps. Don't venture out of here. If anyone sees you, all will be lost."

Without awaiting our acknowledgment, he slipped out of the room.

"Come on." She tugged me into the antechamber.

My bare feet transitioned from the lush carpet to the cold tile floor. Pine shelves lined the walls, brimming with glass vials of bath oils and rose-shaped soaps. I breathed in the familiar tang of eucalyptus and mint, which loosened the tightening in my chest. Settled in the center was a tub large enough to house three people. Metal piping ran along the wall, then attached to a spigot curved over the tub's edge. Steam curled, filling the space, as we inched closer.

"Amazing." Arianna unfurled her grip from me.

My balance wavered, and my fingers clutched the smooth porcelain rim. Her brow pinched. She slowly unbuttoned my shirt and peeled it off my damp flesh. A pang twisted my heart. How many weeks had she spent acting as my nursemaid instead of my wife? This wasn't the fate I wanted for her when we fled her betrothal months ago. But with my waning abilities, I worked with her, moving my limbs until I stood before her naked.

I tugged my heavy legs forward and slid into the tub. The heat soaked into my skin, providing instant relief to my cramped muscles. The slap of wet clothing hit the tile. Seconds later, the water sloshed, and her leg grazed against mine as she joined me in the bath. Yet her tight features didn't smooth. Grief and concern churned through our bond. She fiddled with the onyx ring on her finger and blew out a long sigh. My spine tensed.

"We need to talk."

CHAPTER 21

SILAS

My hands clenched around the rim of the bathtub as Arianna divulged the events of the last two days, starting with the dagger that had cut off her access to her power, her waking from unconsciousness, the girl, Robin, who had ties to the Opposition, Xavier's worries about a spy who'd provided the blade, and finally ending with the location of the elixir of life hidden in the Aralian temple.

She spun her onyx ring and studied the bottles behind me, unable to hold eye contact as she spent the hour outlining the endless details.

With each new revelation, my fingers dug into the smooth porcelain so tightly that had I been at my full strength, it may have cracked under the pressure. Tension ballooned in my ribcage. I was unsure if it was from the anger that loomed or if it was caused by the wasting sickness retaking hold of me.

"Xavier has a plan. Tomorrow night is the full moon celebration. After the festivities, we'll sneak into the temple and retrieve the elixir." She held my gaze. Fear sizzled in our bond, a melding of her anguish at the thought of losing me and the uncertainty of entering into the disciples' territory. However, an overwhelming sense of determination pressed forward.

She wanted me to capitulate, to allow her to run blindly into battle with no allies. She wanted to save me, but the threat was too great. I'd no desire to thrust her into danger for my well-being, yet if we continued on this path, Arianna would be right within the epicenter.

"This is madness. I don't want to die, but I can't risk your life for mine. You are to stay here at the Scarlet Rose. I'll leave with Xavier. Alone." I ran my hand through my hair and settled it on my nape.

She sucked her teeth. Her nose wrinkled. Rivulets dripped off her skin. Her wet hair lay over her shoulders, covering the wound she'd sustained from battle already.

"You can barely walk, and your stamina will probably falter." She tilted her chin skyward, and impetuousness glimmered in her eyes. "What if you're accosted by highwaymen or huntsmen? Or worse, a group of disciples? There's no way for you to fight in your condition. Though Xavier seems skilled, if you worsen, can he keep you safe? Leaving without me is suicide."

"Coming with us is just as dangerous for you." My jaw ticked.

A beat of silence lingered between us. She opened her mouth to disagree, but three sharp knocks punctuated the tension. She slipped out of the tub, tugged a large drying cloth out of the cupboard, and wrapped it around herself. Her footsteps padded over the tile, then the carpet. A few moments later, a familiar male voice cut through the air.

"Glad I'm not interrupting anything," Xavier said. "Do you need help getting him into bed?"

Booted footsteps approached. The door swung open, and Xavier loomed in the doorway. In the past hour, he had bathed and dressed in fresh clothing. He wore a white tunic unbuttoned at the collar; a navy jacket with gold threading lay atop, and he donned matching trousers. I shifted, sinking deeper into the murky water.

"Nothing I haven't seen before, son. No need to be embarrassed. We don't want you to slip, fall, and injure yourself further. With Arianna's shoulder, I dare say it might be a challenge for her to hoist you from the bath." He stripped off his navy coat and placed it on a hook on the wall.

"I don't require your help. Turn around," I grumbled.

He huffed a sigh, closed the door, and stared at the etched wood.

Agitated, I clutched the porcelain ledge and pushed myself with all my might to stand. My legs wobbled akin to those of a newborn foal. The world swam. To my horror, my feet slipped from the slick surface, and my body slid back into the tub.

Splash.

Water sloshed over the edge, covering the tile floor. I stared up at the crisp white ceiling, flustered by my weakness.

He tutted. "Come now, Silas. Just let me help you, and then you'll have your medicine and a meal, and hopefully, you'll be able to move easily in the morning. Stop being so damned stubborn."

My lips pursed, trapping an expletive between them. I wouldn't allow him to see me rattled. I refused to sulk but had no inclination to ask for assistance. However, the heated bath had cooled. The comfort I'd found previously in the warm temperatures had dissipated, leaving me freezing.

"Fine," I hissed through my clenched teeth.

Without a word, he fetched a towel from the cupboard. He draped it over his shoulder, then turned to me and outstretched his palms. Begrudgingly, I slipped my hands into his as he hoisted me up. His eyes remained locked on mine. My weight shifted forward, but his grip tightened, allowing me the extra stability to wade out. With my feet on solid ground, my fingers tugged at the drying cloth and covered my lower half.

"All right. Nice and slow." He guided me out of the bathing chamber and into the rose-shaded room.

To my relief, Arianna had dressed in the time it took him to assist me out of the bath. Her damp hair hung loose over a gray day dress more suitable for a servant than the lady of Belmont Manor. Martha had likely provided the bland outfit to disguise her as a maid instead of the wanted Arianna Park. She clutched a black robe and rushed for me.

"Here." She held out the garment, making it easier for me to slip into.

My brow pinched. In less than a day, I'd transitioned from a vigorous man to an invalid. Resigned, I pulled out of Xavier's grasp, allowing her to clothe me. She wrapped the sash, and the towel dropped to the floor.

They watched me with bated breath.

I waved my hand away. "I'm able to walk the ten paces to the bed."

Stubbornly, I straightened, despite the world tilting slightly, and forced my sluggish steps forward. The pair followed behind me like baby chicks on the tail of a mother duck. Had I really grown so weak that they feared I'd tumble? But sweat beaded my brow as I took the last three strides. My body protested as my knee arched toward the mattress. Fortunately, my leg swung through the motion, and my form collapsed onto the plush cushions.

An audible sigh of relief escaped her. "Help him get settled, and I'll grab the medicine."

My glance flicked from Arianna as she moved to the table beside the hearth and then to Xavier, who approached. I expected a sarcastic retort to brim from him. Instead, he pulled the comforter over my legs. A soft hum rumbled through me. For a heartbeat, I didn't feel like a dying man, but an ill child being tended to. My nostrils burned. A cracking sensation reverberated through my chest as if it were softening. Hadn't my mother told me to trust him in that dream world? But was it truly her speaking to me or simply a figment of my imagination? Regardless, a flicker of hope took root in me. I wanted to believe he had my best interests at heart, but he'd led us here aware that the elixir of life was in the temple.

"Here." Arianna handed a cup to me, drawing me out of my rumination and into the present.

My fingers laced through the delicate curled handle, then tilted the rim against my lips. The bitter flavor washed over my mouth and down my throat. My nose wrinkled, and I thrust the drink her way.

"Still don't care for medicine, I see. Want a spoonful of honey? It helped when you were a boy." Xavier stepped back but lingered within the suites.

My brow knitted as I studied his features, and a mix of emotions curled through me. Frustration at his lies and pain at his abandonment, but a whisper of something else pushed through the grief—a desire to be loved by the man I'd once called father. I shuddered at the realization. Drawing on my earlier vexation, I buried the brimming feelings.

Arianna's eyes widened, and sensing the storm brewing between Xavier and me, she scurried away, busying herself with the tea set on the table by the fireplace.

"Why did you hide the elixir's location? When were you going to divulge this critical information?" I tilted my jaw skyward, attempting to draw on my mantle as Lord Belmont, despite having been aided by him mere seconds ago.

He ran his tongue over his teeth and shoved his hands into his pockets. "I was hoping to wait until we reached my safe house in Hallowhaven, but I see your wife is a chatty one." His glare flicked to Arianna, who held his withering stare.

"You expected her to lie to me? We are united in more ways than you realize, but I've decided. Arianna is to remain here with Martha while we continue on."

He chuckled, but his features smoothed as he took in my stoic countenance. Whatever gentleness lived in his gaze dissipated.

The clink of a spoon against porcelain in the background behind him punctuated the tense silence.

He scrubbed a hand over his face. "You can't be serious."

"Oh, but he is." She approached with a teacup and thrust it at me.

My palms cupped the steaming brew, allowing the warmth to soak into my skin. She didn't settle on the edge of the bed, but remained standing, with her arms crossed over her chest.

"He's being a stubborn fool. I'm assuming it's a trait he gets from you." She arched an eyebrow.

A flicker of a smile tugged at my lips, a fleeting delight, as my wife directed her fire at my forbearer.

"Don't you smirk." She pointed a finger at me. "I'm tired and my shoulder hurts. And I would prefer to spend this evening resting, not listening to you two argue."

She rubbed her temples and closed her eyes, as if trying to think. He gaped at her, and despite my frustration with her desire to throw caution to the wind, she was a sight to behold—brilliance personified.

"We'll be leaving just after dawn, the three of us. Xavier, I swear to the gods if you are hiding anything else, I'll kill you. Best lay out the truth." She placed her hands on her hips.

He blew out a long breath and studied his nails. "That's all. We make it to the safe house, we wait until the morning after the full moon celebration, and we grab the elixir. Then Silas is as good as new. We can decide on our next steps from there."

Her features pinched. "No. Once Silas is well, we'll be returning home. Thank you for your assistance, but I'd like to speak with my husband alone now. We'll see you at first light." She gestured to the exit.

He smirked and cocked an eyebrow at me. "Good luck, son." Then the door closed behind him.

She stared, and I took a long sip of the tea, trying to postpone the quarrel I knew I would lose. However, she didn't take my stalling tactics well. Her fingers curled around the teacup, and she gently removed it from my hand and lowered it to the side table. Her palms cupped my face.

I expected an argument, but a question tumbled from her. "How did you feel watching me bleed out?"

I tried to avoid her gaze, but her grasp melded against my cheeks, keeping my eyes on hers. My nostrils stung as the horrific sinking sensation burrowed into my chest. "My world crumbled."

"How do you think I've felt all winter? Sitting by while you slowly die? Like my heart is being ripped out, and at the end, I don't know if I'll survive. Please believe in me. I've grown stronger. I can battle the Aralians. It's time you trusted me with your life." Her thumb grazed along my cheekbone.

A knot formed in my throat. The agony I'd felt at the inn had nearly consumed me, and I would have happily died to save her. Had my beloved experienced this same ache for months—this horrific torture? I swallowed hard. I wanted to argue, but I couldn't accomplish this task alone.

"Stop fighting me. I'll need the strength to fight our enemies so we may live another day." She leaned her forehead against mine. "Please let me be your savior; let my love be enough. Let me be enough."

Remorse washed over me, coating me akin to a heavy blanket. Desperation in our connection rolled off her. Did she truly believe that she'd fallen short?

"You've always been enough, beloved," I whispered.

She shook her head slightly, her brow rubbing against mine. Her body tightened like a bowstring.

My tight expression softened. She'd struggled with what had happened for months, but the cascade of choices had been far out of her control. If she didn't save me, would this self-doubt consume her? Not wanting to continue inflicting pain, I pressed my palms against her hands, then slid her fingertips over my lips. I peppered kisses over her knuckles. A soft sigh eased from her. My thumb traced along her jaw, tilting her mouth and capturing her in a sweet kiss. She melted, this tightly coiled woman who carried the weight of the past upon her. A tear rolled down her face and caught on my skin.

She inched back. "I can't lose you. I can't lose everything. I won't survive. We return to Presspin together, or not at all."

My heart ached at her words. From her perspective, she'd lost her family and her friends, and now I teetered toward death. She dreaded the loneliness looming for her. This driving force pushed her toward either our mutual destruction or to salvation. Hadn't I been ready to die for the same reason? Without her, life wasn't worth living. How could I doom her to the same fate?

"All right. We'll leave for Hallowhaven united. We'll return to Presspin together, or not at all." I sealed our fates with a kiss, hoping that we'd faced the last of the obstacles in the way of our mutual salvation. But I worried only destruction awaited us.

CHAPTER 22

ARIANNA

I BLINKED, TAKING IN the parlor of the old farmhouse that had served as my prison. The familiar aroma of must and lemon polish wafted through the air, and the faded sofas sat upon the worn wood floors. Despite the frigid temperatures, the hearth remained unlit, but somehow a soft glow emitted from the space.

"You're a monster." Mama's voice dripped with vitriol.

A chill slithered down my spine and pooled at its base, but I didn't turn to her. Instead, my eyes shifted to the staircase that led to the path to my once-sanctuary.

"Arianna, did you hear me, you worthless child? You're to blame for this," Mama shrieked. As soon as her words left her, the once sepia-toned dreamworld darkened, consumed by shadows.

A knot formed in my throat. I gulped. Part of me screamed to run to my room, but nowhere was safe in this house. Not the closet-size warded chamber that drained me of my life force, nor the open space in my home where I wasn't allowed to dwell.

"Look at me," Mama snapped.

I shook my head, not wanting to see her. Hadn't that been the crux of these months? These heavy emotions regarding our relationship that I struggled to address? I'd promised Silas I was strong enough to continue on to Hallowhaven, but grappling with my feelings regarding my mother's death caused my stomach to sink. Yet I wasn't Arianna Park anymore; that girl had died along with her mother that day on the hill of Terrell Estate. When I'd risen from bed, burdened with the consequences of my sins, Arianna Belmont had fully taken hold. Hadn't she? Using every ounce of my title as Lady Belmont, I tilted my jaw skyward, then spun on my heel to confront her.

As I took her in, bile crawled up my throat. My gut twisted, and I feared I'd spew all over the vintage couch. My feet stumbled backward, and whatever bluster I'd possessed faltered, revealing the weak girl I'd always been.

"Can't look at me?" She gestured to her remaining blue eye. The other was nothing but a black pit. Blood oozed from her chest where the arrow had pierced through her. Crimson and grim stained her fine gown. Something about this wraith felt off. Perhaps it was the death consuming her that made her seem more akin to a puppet than a person.

Overwhelmed by her gruesome appearance, I studied the rough patches on my worn boots. She was dead because of me. The heaviness of my transgressions weighed upon my shoulders, causing them to slump.

"Ah, there she is. My weak, worthless daughter. You know why I apologized to you the day you died? Because I was sorry that you lived after your curse enacted." She closed the distance between us, and her fingers trailed my chin, forcing my focus off my worn footwear and onto her decaying face. Her breath fanned over my skin. The putrid scent of decomposition wafted off her, deepening my horror.

Her dry lips cracked into a smile. "The world would be better off without you. You've brought nothing but misery to everyone who's ever had the misfortune of crossing paths with you."

Tears streamed down my cheeks. It was a harsh truth I'd battled with internally. One I attempted to hide from but no longer could. Not as the ghost of my past stood before me. I was the catalyst for the pain that plagued those I loved.

"I'm sorry, Mama. I didn't mean for this to happen. I should have just married Theo. If I had, Silas wouldn't be doomed, Naomi would be happy, you would be alive, and even Brielle wouldn't have lost her love." My shoulders shook as sobs racked through me.

"You are a burden. But you might have some use left within you. When the time comes, I hope you make the right choice." Her nails cut into my flesh, drawing blood. She pulled a vial out of her pocket, catching the droplets into the container. She smirked and placed the glass against her mouth, devouring my life force. I blinked, my world growing hazy. If I fell under this wraith's spell, all would be lost.

"Arianna," Silas's curse shouted through my skull.

Gasping for air, I jolted awake. My cotton nightgown clung to my sweat-laden frame. Heat seared through my blood, as if my blight blazed internally, prepared to thwart a looming danger. On alert, my head swiveled around the dim, unfamiliar quarters as I tried to regain my grasp on reality. A shaky exhale rushed through my lungs as my body and mind aligned, registering the suite in the Scarlet Rose.

I inhaled, and a twinge of ash tickled my nostrils. My spine went rigid as I blinked down at the singed cotton below my fingertips. My brows knitted. I pushed the marred fabric away.

In my dream state, the darkness must have leached from my hands, permanently altering the lovely crab apple comforter.

A raspy snore emitted from a slumbering Silas, anchoring me to the present. His lips twisted into a frown. Was he also wrestling with nightmares? His breathing remained steady, but perspiration dotted his brow, denoting the fever had retaken hold. I huffed a bone-weary sigh. Despite his earlier prideful speech about venturing to Hallowhaven with Xavier alone, he'd continued to weaken.

Imagine how much better everyone would be without you. My mother's words pressed through my memory as I drank in my love.

I gulped against my dry mouth. I wanted to deny her, but Silas was dying because he had saved me. My curse, feeding on my unsettled emotions, itched under my skin. My nails scraped down my bare arms, trying to soothe the sensation. However, my flesh still burned, and my blight hissed to escape the jail in my mind.

Agitated, I rose. Pushed on by the adrenaline of the nightmare, I paced the suite. Despite being far larger than my cramped quarters in my childhood home, the windowless room rattled me. As if I were a trapped animal, instinct overtook logic. I needed to be free from this prison.

Hastily, my feet padded over the plush carpet to the bureau. I grabbed the gray servant uniform Martha had provided from the drawer. The damp nightgown fell to the floor, and I slipped into the fresh clothing. I skirted toward the roaring fire and plucked my dried hood from the hook on the mantel and my boots from beside the hearth. As I tugged on my footwear, a realization took root. These nightmares had haunted me because of the destruction I'd caused at Terrell Estate. If I confronted the past, perhaps I'd find peace.

With my decision made, I slipped out the door. The scent of sweet wine melded with amber hit my senses. My nose wrinkled, and my hand tugged the cloak lower. Tittering laughter floated down the corridor, and a harp played a lovely tune in the distance. If I hurried, I could slip through the side entrance, journey to the demolished Terrell Estate, and return by daybreak.

As I reached the tee where the back stairwell lay, the click of heels echoed on the steps, heading in my direction. My pulse skittered. Panicked by the approaching person, I searched for a hiding spot and noticed the small storage closet under the stairs. My fingers grabbed the pulley and yanked the wood open. My body squeezed into the cubby. However, I was too large and could not close the door fully behind me, leaving a crack for me to peer through.

Seconds later, a young woman with brunette hair in a sleek braid and sharp features entered the alcove. Her black cape fluttered as she strode purposefully toward the hall where the courtesans' chambers lay, but she froze as footsteps approached from the opposite end of the corridor. Her brown eyes widened, then slammed into slits. She rolled her shoulders back and smoothed her expression.

"Couldn't secure a bedfellow again tonight, Jasmine?" A man's voice cut through the shadows of the hallway ahead.

Her jaw ticked. Her glare burned as the figure approached.

The man stepped into the light. My hands laced over my mouth, withholding a gasp, fearing they'd hear me. The candlelight from the gilded sconces caught upon the maw of a wolf crafted in painted porcelain. Where my mask had denoted a placid smiling façade, his caused a shudder to course through me. The arched teeth along the lips, the protruding snout, and thick eyebrows conveyed menace.

"Come to beg me for a romp? No coin could convince me to find interest in a monster like you. I'm sure Lily or Marigold would give your short cock a quick ride. I'd estimate sixty seconds at best." She smirked.

She shifted to veer around him, but he moved in tandem with her, blocking her exit. "I have no desire to bed you. You're not my taste." He flicked his wrist in dismissal. "Besides, you have a pretty redhead waiting for you at the Lace Dove down the street, right?"

Her body stiffened, and an ease entered the man's posture. He tutted. "Martha thinks you're her golden girl. So obedient. Won't she be displeased to hear that you're cavorting with an unvetted outsider? I saw you swoop her away from the Scarlet Rose yesterday afternoon when Martha was running errands."

"Oh, that's sweet. You've finally come to accept your place here as Martha's little cub. Do you plan on babbling to her about my new paramour? I'm sure she'll praise you and give you a treat, like the dog you are." She crossed her arms over her chest and tilted her chin skyward.

"I don't care about this prison Xavier trapped me within. I've come to make a deal with you. I know you saw me in the alley last night." He cocked his head, the move causing him to look akin to a predator ready to pounce on its prey.

She tittered a vicious laugh. "Ah, yes, the blonde. Pretty little thing you carried off the streets. I'm guessing you whisked her away to your shanty in the woods. Is she your new plaything? Fine, I'll keep your pet a secret as long as you keep quiet about my affairs. Now that we agree, I have business to attend."

With a flourish, he stepped out of the way, allowing Jasmine to pass. My heart thundered in my chest as I studied the man who lingered. He pulled the hood he wore off, revealing raven hair that curled around his ears. The cloak lay over his sleek form, mostly covering his simple black tunic and trousers. For some reason, he remained, as if in some sort of internal battle. His fingers scratched at the seam between his jaw and the mask.

The soft tap of heels overhead signaled yet another person entering the first floor of the brothel. I'd expected the man to run. Instead, he held his ground and glared up the steps. His chin tilted upward, causing his wolfish façade to point toward the stairwell.

"Where in the blast have you been? I told you to stay in your room for just one night. Are you not entertained here? I hope you weren't so stupid as to venture to the Gilded Serpent," Xavier hissed.

My spine stiffened. If Xavier caught me here, I'd endure a tongue-lashing from both him and Silas. I drew my knees closer to my chest.

"Of course I could only be drinking, gambling, or fucking, right? A chip off the old block." The masked man turned to depart.

"Wolf," Xavier called out and then approached his ward.

Wolf's gaze remained on the hallway, and his fists curled.

"You can't continue gallivanting about anymore. The Aralians have been pushing farther north, and huntsmen were at the Gilded Serpent. It's not safe for you to roam Daviel when bound to the mask. They are collecting the cursed. If you are caught, I won't be able to help you."

Xavier stepped closer, and his tone softened. "If you would begin your training again with Martha, you could wield a ring and walk the world unencumbered. But you must learn to control your temper first."

"Control my temper?" Wolf spun on his heel. His cape fluttered in the wind as he faced Xavier. "How am I supposed to do that? By finding peace?" A raw laugh escaped Wolf. "There will be no solace for me. I'm a blackguard, which means I'll be trapped in these damned spelled rooms until I die."

My heart sank. Hadn't I fled the suites here for the same reason? The enchantments had imprisoned me for nearly twenty years, keeping me a prisoner behind porcelain. Despite the man's intensity, a sense of kinship rooted within me.

"I'm trying to help you. We can figure out a way to keep your blight at bay. It will take some time and practice." Xavier's tone softened, and he reached out to place a hand on Wolf's shoulder.

Wolf swatted it away. "Stop speaking to me as if you are my father. I'm heading to the hunting lodge for the night. I'll stay hidden like you want."

Xavier scrubbed a palm down his face. Before he could retort, Wolf stalked down the hall for the exit. I expected Xavier to chase after him, but he didn't. Instead, he leaned against the wall and blew out a long breath. A weariness coated his features. It was an expression I saw in the mirror daily. One of a person trying desperately to hold a crumbling life together. He pinched the bridge of his nose.

The rustling of skirts punctuated the air. Xavier straightened, and whatever emotion he'd held vanished. He donned an air of nonchalance and smoothed his fingers over his navy trousers.

"Perhaps arguing with Wolf in the hallway isn't the best for business, nor for keeping our secrets from listening ears," Martha crooned as she emerged from the shadowy hall and into the tee beside the stairs where Xavier stood.

Her dark eyes sparkled, and a copper gown lay against her skin, shimmering akin to melted metal. "You're losing your touch. Let Wolf wander into the woods. It's better he's not here while your guests are, anyway. Besides, he's bound to that mask. It leaves him with little ability to venture beyond the hunting lodge or the pleasure district. Now, go get some rest. It's already well past midnight, and you're departing at daybreak, correct?"

Xavier ran his hand through his long locks and nodded.

"Will you stop to see Yulia? She summoned me yesterday afternoon, demanding a visit before you leave for Hallowhaven. She has a message for them," Martha said.

"She gives nothing but poetic ramblings. Besides, I don't have time for delays." He tapped his foot in impatience.

"And yet it was her blossoms that revived your son enough to get him here, wasn't it?" She cocked an eyebrow. "And you owe her a price for her favor. She wants to see them."

He grumbled under his breath, then huffed an exasperated sigh. "Fine. Tomorrow we'll visit Yulia, but please keep an eye on Wolf. He thinks he's indestructible since his curse awoke, and it makes him act like a damned fool."

Martha nodded, and he retreated up the stairwell. His boots clicked until the sound dissipated into silence. She didn't leave. Instead, her gaze settled upon the steps for a heartbeat longer, then shifted onto the small cubby. "And what about you? Are you going to remain hidden in that closet, or shall you join me for a chat, Arianna?"

CHAPTER 23

ARIANNA

I FOLLOWED MARTHA INTO her private sitting room. The gibbous moon and stars glimmered through the glass-domed ceiling, casting the space in an ethereal incandescence. Ivy crawled along red cedar rafters, lacing over the skylight. Violet wallpaper with lilac wildflowers and golden leaves shimmered against the soft glow of the hearth to my right. The familiar tang of herbal remedies wafted through the air from a metal workstation in the rear. It was covered with tonics, reminding me of Naomi and Brielle. My nostrils burned, but I ignored the stinging sensation, turning my attention to the wall of leather tomes nestled in bookshelves stretching toward the roof.

"Come." Martha's voice pulled me in the opposite direction of her vast book collection, where she sat beside a small table. Soft candlelight danced along her silken skin, and the metallic colors of her dress glimmered, as if she were a beacon in the darkness.

My boots slipped over the plush purple rug and to the chair across from her. I settled on the ornate cushion seat.

"Do you play?" Her fingers moved swiftly as she laid a chess set before her.

I nodded, then followed suit, securing the onyx pieces in the corresponding squares where they belonged.

With the gameboard prepared, a smile tugged at her full lips. "Guests first."

The pieces clicked against the polished board, cutting through the tense silence as we played.

Ding...Ding...Ding...

The grandfather clock chimed in the shadowed corner, denoting the midnight hour. My brow wrinkled. Twenty minutes had passed since we began, and within that time, Martha had outmatched my skill. With my knights and bishops in her possession, my cavalry had dwindled. A few petty pawns protected the royalty. My fingertips grazed over the king. Did I leave his side to venture into danger? Or stay close to protect him? My eyes trailed the board, and an open spot, out of peril, called out to me.

She clucked her tongue. "I wouldn't do that if I were you. Don't you realize the queen is the most powerful? Without her, the king shall fall." She arched an eyebrow, and in the depths of my soul, I knew this conversation extended past chess.

"But if she stays, you will overtake my rooks, leaving me with nothing." I kept my grasp on the queen, uncertain if I should push on or remain, sacrificing a pawn to create an opening. I sucked my teeth; the board felt as hopeless as our current predicament.

The blight bubbled within me, feeding off my frustration. My hands itched to toss the table to the ground and allow everything to fall. Sensing my agitation, she cocked her head. "Perhaps a change of perspective can help you see things more clearly."

Her long nails glided to the spot I'd been eyeing, the seemingly safe space for the queen to land, to prepare for her next attack. However, her finger trailed toward where the bishop lay in wait, ready to snag the powerful player. "Sometimes it's challenging to see what danger may befall us when we are so focused on anticipating our moves."

My face fell as I reassessed the situation and realized she was close to declaring checkmate. I'd been absorbed in my offensive strategy, allowing her to create a defensive trap. My nose wrinkled.

Her dark eyes softened. "Exactly. Now why did you abandon your king this evening? It would have been far safer to remain in the suites, yet you wandered my halls despite Xavier's warning."

I rubbed at my temples. My foolishness in this situation became clearer—had I ventured from this brothel, I likely would have been caught. A headache took hold, pounding against my skull. Why was I continuously making the wrong choices?

"Ah, a migraine." She stood and walked to a table with jars of herbal poultices strewn across it. My lower lip bobbed, and I swallowed the knot in my throat. The room reminded me so much of Brielle's shop and Naomi's conservatory. My body tensed. They had every right to hate me; my heart broke at the loss of our relationship.

"Here." She pressed a cup into my hands.

"Thank you." I downed the saccharine contents in a single gulp, eager for relief.

As she took the glass, her delicate hand wrapped around mine. "Let's forget about the game."

I stood, and she guided me to a purple sofa beside the hearth. The flames flickered and danced, warming my cold soul. The heady sensation from the migraine tonic relaxed my tense shoulders. A hazy aura coated the room, as if I'd consumed glasses of wine.

She smoothed her hands over her skirt, then settled them upon her lap. Gold rings glimmered on her fingers. She was likely my mother's age, but her complexion remained unblemished by time. As if drawn in by her beauty, and with my tongue loosened by the remedy, the question swirling in my mind tumbled from me. "Have you taken the elixir of life?"

Her soft smile fell, and something heavy lingered in her gaze. "No. I have not. That was reserved for Delphine's thirteen noble elite. There are many levels to the temple: girls in servitude, women in training, fully fledged disciples, the thirteen noble elite, and then Delphine, the high disciple, who is rumored to speak to Aralia herself. I fled far before gaining status to drink of the elixir. Not that I would want to. The only people provided the taste of vitality are the seven seats on the high council, the thirteen noble elite, and Delphine herself. My beauty is from my tinctures."

She gestured to the table.

"A madam must always look her best." Whatever moroseness she'd held shimmered away under her performance as the matron of this house.

She gave a wink, and the unexpected gesture caused a slight quirk to tug at my lips.

"Now, child, stop trying to distract me with compliments and tell me why you ventured out of your suite."

I shifted on the cushions, uncertain of what I should divulge to this stranger. Xavier seemed to trust her implicitly, though the man was still a quandary himself. Something about his demeanor toward Silas had softened me.

Fatigued with carrying this burden upon my shoulders, I spoke. "I had a nightmare about my mother. She died during the battle at Terrell Estate."

My gaze drifted from Martha to the fire, as if the flames could coax the words from me. "In the dream, my mother blamed me for her death." I shook my head. However, a softness curled around the edges of my vision, easing the truth from me. "If I'd chosen differently, she would be alive, and Silas would be well. I thought going to Terrell Estate and facing the destruction I'd caused could lead to some semblance of peace. It's ridiculous."

She leaned forward, and her hand lowered onto mine. Her warmth seeped into my skin, soothing me. "It's not foolish to grieve. Grief is like the ocean; it ebbs and flows. Some days it feels far away, and other times it's all-consuming. It can sneak up like a riptide and pull us under before we realize it. It is unwise to leave the protection of the brothel, but it isn't foolish to want to confront your past so you can find peace." Her eyes softened. "How long have you been drowning, dear girl?"

I stared at her. In the safety of this glimmering cocoon of heady sensation, the truth unleashed from me. "Since the moment I awoke to the carnage I'd created and the lives I'd taken.

If I'd stayed in Daviel and married Theo, everyone would have been safe." My nostrils stung. "I should have suffered, but I chose myself for once, and look what happened."

The perpetual tension that clung to my chest lifted. The crushing reality I lived beneath unfurled from me, eased by the lightness of whatever tonic she'd given me. "Everything is my fault. Every blasted thing that has occurred. My mother's death, my sister's hatred for me, my husband…" I closed my eyes. "My husband's dying because of me."

"And he lives because of you too. He is here because of you," she whispered, but her contradiction couldn't penetrate my guilt.

Pain burned in my chest. I was so damned tired. The tears I'd stifled poured from me. I sobbed, and to my surprise, she pulled me into her embrace.

"I'm a destructive monster." My body shook.

"We are all monsters, dear. Each and every one of us. No one is blameless in this world. Sometimes we are pushed past our kindness, and the darkness emerges. Don't fight it; embrace it. I have a feeling fate has great things in store for you." She rubbed her hand over my back; the caress soothed me. My curse swirled under my skin in agreement, as if it had been trying to tell me something this whole time, to accept this blackness in my heart instead of fighting it.

My body shuddered as the pain ripped through me. Tears flowed down my cheeks, and a guttural wail escaped me. Her arms curled around me, and she tugged me against her. We sat in this position for many minutes while I expelled the sorrow I carried. Her fingers wafted over my braided hair, gently stroking my scalp.

"Shh, child. It will all be all right. If everything goes awry, just know you have a home here, as the Opposition's ally. We created this place for the cursed forced into the outskirts of society. You'll always have a haven here."

I tilted my jaw toward her, and her gaze held mine with such maternal kindness it nearly broke my heart. Despite her gentleness, a question pressed forward. "Why help me? Why help the cursed?"

Her features hardened. "Because I want to end the Aralians' shadow rule over the territories."

I slipped from her grasp and leaned into the sofa, numb to the emotions I carried. Not wanting to dwell on my sins any longer, my curiosity overtook my lingering melancholy. "Why?"

She shifted into the corner of the divan and pivoted to me. "Long ago, the disciples found me on the temple steps. I was a babe. When I grew, they forced me to work grueling hours, and then when I reached my majority, my maidenhead was auctioned. It was not a pleasant experience." Her lips thinned, and her eyes drifted to the bookshelf. "I didn't desire sexual acts, not from men nor from women. Needless to say, the monthly full moon festivals where we fucked until morning light left a bitter tang in my mouth."

My eyebrows shot to my hairline, and confusion churned.

As if sensing my bubbling questions, she continued. "Ah, yes. Why be a madam when I don't enjoy the carnality? This space is for weary souls needing a listening ear and advice. I provide that to them—my mind, my companionship, and my comfort. It's also an excellent way to glean information from chatty businessmen. Secrets have fueled our opposition."

Enthralled by her story, the sting of despair faded, wholly transfixed by her. Was this her calling—an ability to soothe with stories? "How did you end up here, then?"

"Roughly twenty years ago, Xavier chose me as his partner for the full moon festival. Unlike the rest of the high council, who enjoyed fucking in the open, he preferred a private suite. Perhaps that is why he caught Delphine's eye. Her desire to break his sense of propriety."

My brow knitted. From what I knew of Xavier, he was open about his exploits, but twenty years ago, he may have acted more similarly to Silas than he cared to admit.

"When he kissed me, I stood stone still. Unlike the others who'd attempt to coax me into these acts, he withdrew and asked if I enjoyed playing chess. We became fast friends after that. As we grew closer, I divulged my hatred of the Aralians' ways, and he proposed a bargain. He would set up this brothel where I'd serve as his mistress in title alone. Once we established the Scarlet Rose, we used it as a ruse to rescue runaway disciples and the cursed and to build the Opposition to take down the temple. No one bats an eye at lost girls ending up in a bawdy house. It serves as the perfect cover."

"Xavier's the leader?" I cocked an eyebrow, trying to make sense of the idea that the man who served on the high council also led a secret resistance.

"Xavier is the creator; I am its leader." Martha tilted her jaw skyward, donning an air of royalty. "He provided the initial coin, but I've been building this faction for two decades. We have worked together to rescue many disciples left for dead on the streets. Much like your friend Brielle. It was Xavier who rescued her from the brink of death and he who summoned me to care for her. As I do with all the women we save, I offered her a place here, but she refused. Though I've kept her abreast of danger that might affect her or Silas, she is unaware of our cause. Only the residing courtesans, the blighted, and our spies know the truth about the Scarlet Rose. She still served a purpose. Xavier knew Silas might need a skilled ex-disciple by his side. So I trained her how to forge an onyx ring, and we sent her on her way to Presspin."

No wonder Brielle had assumed Martha had aided the huntsmen, betraying her. However, Martha's secrets had tainted Brielle's perspective. Brielle had incorrectly believed that my bounty had swayed the madam to betray us and divulge my location. I pinched the bridge of my nose. The need to hide the resistance from outsiders was logical, but the secrecy had created unforeseen issues that had led us here.

"Is Brielle well?" She cocked her head, and genuine concern flashed across her countenance.

My stomach plummeted. "No. She is not." I gulped hard. "She fell in love recently with a charming young man. Mateo." The acrid flavor of ash danced on my tongue as his name slipped from it. My heart twisted. A flash of his sad smile took root in my memory. The bone-deep guilt that had become my constant companion replaced the lightness I'd felt moments ago. "The huntsmen kidnapped him, and he died trying to escape. I tried to save him, but I was too late. I'm always too late."

A heavy silence stretched between us, and the grief that had dissipated only seconds before ballooned again. In this place where nature melded with construction, it reminded me of Brielle and Naomi. I blinked, certain a fresh stream of tears would well from me. My gaze shifted to the clock. The hour grew late, and I needed to sleep before my rumination fully took hold. Martha had sat with my blubbering long enough.

"Perhaps I should return to bed." I stood and smoothed my hands over the plain dress, as if the action could resettle me.

She rose and gently clasped my shoulders. "Of course. Be sure to stay hidden. We don't want any of the suitors to spot you. That would create havoc."

I nodded, then pulled away. As I walked through the exit and closed the door behind me, I realized I hadn't delved into my looming questions about this mysterious Wolf who lived within the brothel. However, monsters like me were welcomed here, and perhaps one day I'd be steady enough to inquire about those within this place instead of spilling my secrets.

CHAPTER 24

SILAS

Silas. Arianna's curse rattled through our connection, forcing my mind to jolt out of my nightmares and into the searing agony of reality.

I blinked my heavy lids. My body protested, as if thick honey coated my perception. Arianna leaned over me, her hands resting on my shoulders. As she took me in, her tightly pinched expression smoothed a fraction, but something troublesome lay in our bond. This thick unease covered me like a heavy blanket. Panic overtook me, thrusting me fully into the present.

Footsteps padded on the carpet from the corner of the room. Xavier rummaged through the bureau like a madman. "Is he awake?"

"Yes." Arriana's knuckles grazed my forehead.

I sucked in a sharp breath at the relief from her cool touch. I licked my dry lips and opened my mouth to ask what in the blast was wrong, but a cough bellowed from my chest. Liquid dribbled from my lips. I lifted my hand, yet it felt akin to being pulled through quicksand, and wiped my cotton nightshirt over my face. As I withdrew the sleeve, crimson stained the pristine fabric.

"He's coughing up blood again," she said.

"We don't need this right now. Give him another dose of the remedies Martha provided." Xavier approached and lowered a small pile of clothing onto the bed. His tight jaw loosened as he took me in. "Son, can you hear me?"

"Of course I can." I sat up, but my limbs ached with each motion. I forced my expression to remain neutral as pain coursed through me. "What is happening? Is it dawn already?"

"Yes, but we must leave immediately." He extended his palms, offering me assistance. Unlike yesterday, I didn't hesitate to grip his hands.

His eyebrows shot to his hairline in surprise but smoothed. With some effort, I rolled my legs toward the edge of the bed.

But before I could stand, Arianna approached and shoved the medicinal brew into my grasp. "For the fever and cough."

I grabbed the cold glass and placed it against my lips. The bitter concoction slid down my throat, though I hoped it would ease the ache in my muscles.

However, as I lowered the cup onto the side table, my attention caught on her clothing. Unlike yesterday afternoon, when she had been dressed in the gray maid's outfit, this morning, she donned men's garments. A pair of trousers hung loosely from her hips, and she wore a black tunic and matching cap that hid all of her blond hair. The night had not treated her kindly. Purple half-moons sat beneath her eyes, her fair skin had paled, and the sharpness to her features had returned as if she hadn't eaten well in weeks. My brow furrowed; how could she appear so markedly different in a day?

"What's wrong?" I gestured to her attire, and her glance drifted to Xavier. Her expression hardened, and she blew out a long exhale. Her fingers laced with mine.

Xavier cleared his throat. "I'll give you a moment. I need to check with Martha to make certain we are ready to leave." He withdrew, veered for the sofa, plucked our packs off the cushions, and then ventured out the door.

In the stilted quiet, a sense of dread took root. What awaited us outside this suite? I braced myself.

"Xavier's spies came here this morning. They informed him that two platoons of disciples are currently milling around Daviel. We don't know the reason for their appearance, only that they are here."

My nostrils flared. My greatest fear was coming to fruition. I was unable to protect Arianna as danger loomed.

She rested a palm on my cheek, soothing me. "Xavier has a friend just south of here who may be able to offer aid. Yulia, the oracle, apparently, has the power to see glimpses of the future. More importantly, she provided the elixir that helped you. Now she has requested an audience. He hopes she might have something to strengthen you for the rest of our trip, and apparently her property is warded against the Aralians. Once it is safe, we'll depart for Hallowhaven along the back roads."

I wanted to argue, but my muscles burned. With the disciples in Daviel, neither the brothel nor Martha could protect her. Sadly, fleeing was the best course of action.

"Now let's get you dressed so we can leave." She huffed a sigh.

Hesitantly, I nodded.

With my agreement, she peeled the damp nightshirt from my fever-laden flesh. The sickly scent wafted off it, reminding me of the sickroom I'd occupied only days ago while creeping closer to my demise. A sinking sensation pulled in my gut as I realized the remedy Xavier had provided was wearing off far quicker than we'd hoped. I couldn't dwell on my faltering health as the disciples loomed. Quickly, she assisted me in dressing, then led me to the door.

A cane leaned against the wall. I gripped the crook of the stick and leaned lean my weight upon it. We exited the suite that had provided us a brief respite. As we ambled through the halls, an eerie silence settled through the brothel. I'd anticipated music or the sounds of vigorous lovemaking. A quiet tension permeated the space, as if the residents sensed the lurking danger. As we entered the alcove by the staircase, Martha and Xavier spoke in hushed whispers.

"Wolf's probably at the cabin. I'll send Robin to check on him. Don't worry." She patted his shoulder.

From his forlorn look, this *Wolf* meant something to him.

Sensing our presence, his features tightened to feigned confidence, but in his eyes I could see the torment, as if his world was falling apart. "Excellent. You can walk. That's at least a mark in our favor."

"Arianna." Martha opened her arms.

My wife strode to the woman and was engulfed in a hug. I cocked an eyebrow. When had they become close?

Xavier walked to me, leaned in, and whispered, "Arianna snuck out of your suite last night."

My jaw ticked.

"Don't worry. Martha found her, and they had a chat," he said.

As I studied the women, my apprehension eased. My wife had struggled for months with what had occurred at Terrell Estate. Then the incident in the conservatory with Naomi had deepened her grief. Now guilt over Mateo's demise consumed her. The whisper of relief penetrating her darkness felt akin to a cool breeze on a hot summer day.

"Don't forget you are always welcome here. Be safe," Martha said.

Arianna forced a watery smile, then withdrew. "Thank you for everything."

Xavier strode ahead, and Arianna slowed to match my sluggish pace. As we exited through the side entrance, whispers of sunlight turned the sky a brilliant purple, deepened by the dark storm clouds. A gust of wind whipped over me, causing a shiver to run down my spine. Slowly, I traversed the steps with my bride hovering behind.

As we neared the cart, Xavier placed a crate at the rear, giving me something to stand on. Sweat beaded on my forehead. My body protested, but I stepped onto the block and forced myself into the conveyance. Arianna swiftly followed suit, then sat beside me. Sacks of wool encircled us, creating the illusion that we were sheep herders heading to market to sell our wares.

Xavier tugged his cloak over his head. He leapt onto the driver's ledge and grabbed the reins. With a flick of his wrist, the horses lurched forward, taking us down the alley and toward the sleepy streets.

My spine pressed against the hard planking, and I slumped into the corner. Pain pulsed through my ribcage, and each breath pulled as if the air caught in my chest. A wheeze escaped, though I tried not to focus on the discomfort. Instead, I turned to Arianna, where she was nestled beside me. Her gaze settled on her boots. Despite her bluster and the brief solace with Martha, anxiety now permeated our bond. Needing to soothe her, I laced my fingers with hers and squeezed her hand.

We weaved through the well-kept pleasure district, then through the slums of Daviel. Much like Krella, the cramped avenues bore dilapidated buildings with broken roofs, dusty windows, and peeling paint. The putrid tang of dung and mildew wafted through the air, gagging me. My glance skittered over the sidewalks as I searched for the white-robed Aralians who would stick out amongst the dull-garbed townsfolk pushing carts toward the city center. To our fortune, we spotted none.

Half an hour later, sunlight sprawled over the dirt path and dawn overtook the darkness. We traversed the green meadows that led to Krella. With the town out of view, my tightly coiled tension lessened.

"We're safe," I whispered to my wife to reassure her.

"For now," Xavier tutted. "It seems we've lost the disciples at present." He huffed a sigh. "Now to visit the oracle. It seems she wants to see you both, and perhaps she'll have another potion to ease your symptoms, son."

My lips pursed. "Maybe we should push on. Create some distance between ourselves and the Aralians." Though every fiber of my being ached, I feared that nothing aside from this elixir of life would restore me.

"You don't understand. She created the remedy that temporarily healed you from the flowers grown from her immortality. I owe her a debt for the tonic, and bringing you to her is the price I must pay."

"How did she come to possess this power?" Arianna shifted her attention from her feet and onto Xavier, who held the answers.

"Since childhood, Yulia could foretell the future. Cassius, when he still roamed this world, blessed her with immortality so she could provide him with guidance. Wards are placed around her property so that those who are devoted to Aralia may not pass. Though I will warn you, she is ancient and eccentric. She speaks in nothing but rhymes, making understanding her quite the headache." He clicked the reins and focused on the road ahead, ending our conversation.

A stretch of silence passed as we traversed the green hills. Eventually, Arianna scooted closer. "How are you feeling?"

Previously, the willow bark would have already eased some of my symptoms, but an unyielding soreness radiated through me, as if no remedy had been taken. Not wanting to upset her, I lifted her knuckles to my lips and brushed a kiss upon them. "A bit tired, but I'm managing."

She smiled wearily, sensing my lie. Yet she didn't dwell on my failing health. Instead, she recounted the events of the night prior. I held my tongue as she described slipping out of our room and her desire to venture to Terrell Estate. To my relief, Martha had interceded. She detailed their conversation, from the emotional release to the information about the Opposition and the mysterious Wolf. I was glad that she'd finally found some solace.

Half an hour later, the cart veered off the dirt trail and onto a lesser-traveled road with dense woods clustered around it. Despite being in the dregs of winter, buds curled along the bare branches. As we bobbed down the broken path, the oaks continued to thicken, transforming from barren to leafy green trees as if spring had fully emerged. The chill in the air dissipated, and warmth beat from the sun. I breathed in a sweet floral scent. Oddly, the pain coursing through me lessened in this respite. The wagon slowed, and I drank in the somehow blue sky above the small cottage.

A picket fence encompassed a grassy patch, where golden blossoms bloomed. A cobbled drive led to the whitewashed house with a straw roof. The gleaming windows were wide open, and the gossamer curtains flowed in the breeze. My mind puzzled over this weather anomaly.

"Let's make this quick." Xavier dismounted and rounded the conveyance, then unlatched the base.

Arianna scurried out, her fatigued aura softening as she took in the flaxen hues coloring the lovely space.

I scooted to the end, and Xavier offered his hand, which I accepted. With some awkwardness, I fumbled out of the cart.

"Here." He reached for the cane and gave it to me. He studied me as he released me from his grasp. "Are you sure you're all right?"

"Of course," I lied, knowing that the walk to the cottage would likely drain me, causing sleep to take hold. But this Yulia had provided a tonic to aid me days ago. Perhaps she could again.

"Don't touch that!" he shouted.

My attention moved from him to Arianna, who lingered beside the gate with her fingers hovering near the magnificent bloom. She withdrew, and a flush crawled over her skin. "Sorry."

"Those flowers are grown with a drop of Yulia's blood, and only she touches them. She's very particular about that fact after some experiments the Aralians performed on her many years ago. It's why she resides here now, in this warded place." He scrubbed a hand over his face, then settled it at his side. "Come on."

He pushed past Arianna, unlocked the gate, and strode down the cobblestone walkway. Slowly, I used the cane to inch to my love. She linked her arm with mine, providing extra support as we walked the path. As we reached the door, he twisted the golden knob and stepped in.

She arched an eyebrow at me, and I shrugged. Xavier had expressed that the pair were friends. As we crossed the threshold, my muscles loosened further. My lungs expanded, taking in a deep breath. My shoulders relaxed and my steps steadied.

Walls of windows overlooked magnificent gardens, and purple blooms curled through the tall grasses, melding with golden flowers. A soft breeze swayed the willow trees that arched in the distance. Despite the apprehension that had prickled in our bond, ease washed over both of us.

The large foyer made little sense. The grandeur didn't match the exterior, as if this entire space was an optical illusion. To the left sat a wooden staircase. To the right, an archway led to a parlor. Heels clicked along the tile from the sitting room. I wasn't sure what to expect, but my mind reeled as a young woman stood before us. Her skin was milky white, which matched her long locks, and her irises were crystalline blue. Only a hint of pink lay on her lips and cheeks. She smiled. Her face lit when she took us in. She clapped and giggled as if she were a girl waiting for playmates.

"Arianna. The dream to me of which it came, it spoke to me, it sang your name." The words tumbled akin to a childlike profession.

My brow knitted, and my glance flicked to Arianna. Were we truly going to stand here while she spouted off singsong prophecies without even a greeting?

Yulia grabbed my wife's hands. She drank in my beloved, as if she'd been waiting an eternity to make her acquaintance.

"Hello. Thank you for the remedy that helped my husband. We were hoping you could provide us with another tonic to help him."

Yulia's brow pinched, and a seriousness replaced her playful expression. She unfurled her fingers from Arianna, then placed both palms upon my cheeks. She closed her eyes, and a long beat of silence stretched between us. When her eyes opened, her blue irises turned wholly white, and she stared at me as if seeing straight into my soul. Her lips curled into a feral grin.

"Death calls you but won't call me. Death calls you. One, two, three. Next time fate won't abide. Not unless saved by your bride."

Arianna shuddered. My stomach twisted as I peered at my wife. She remained transfixed by the oracle.

"How is Arianna to save me? Can you give us any guidance?" I asked.

"For your blight did bind a love foreseen, just like the once eternal king and queen. But unlike them, your love did remain, for you saved him from being slain."

"I saved him?" Arianna repeated, and I could sense her mental cogs churning.

"Yes," the oracle hissed. "Life that binds and bends and ends. Life that finds a way transcends. One heart can't house two. That is why death comes for you. Two lives, one source of power you share. Fate you defied, but you didn't care."

"Two lives? One heart?" I ran a hand through my hair and settled it at my nape, wholly confused.

Yulia drew a harsh inhale. She cocked her head back, as if staring into the cosmos. A shadow shifted over the sun-kissed gardens. "But the blight. The blight will keep the bind, even when erased the mind."

Tears poured down Yulia's cheeks, and a shriek coursed through her. Xavier barreled out of the archway where he had lingered. The woman's knees buckled, but he closed the distance between them, catching her in his embrace before she tumbled to the ground.

He whispered, "Yulia, are you all right?"

She blinked, and the crystalline blue replaced the milky white. Her fingers stretched toward Xavier, and she stroked his jaw. "The kiss of death, it draws near, but neither of us should cower in fear. When the time comes to cross the gates, we all defy the fates."

He lifted her in his arms, but her gaze remained on me. "No medicine I have to give. You must hold on; you must live."

I nodded, but a sinking dread burrowed in my soul, and a question I'd ignored for months tumbled forward. How had I survived the blast at Terrell Estate?

CHAPTER 25

Arianna

The horses' hooves sloshed through the muck as the cart rolled through the meadows between Daviel and Krella. The sweet fragrance of fresh earth after the rain washed over my senses, but the familiar aroma didn't soothe me, nor did the lush green contrasting against the dull blue sky. After our visit to Yulia's, Xavier remained achingly tense. He sat ramrod straight as he white-knuckled the reins. Eventually, he murmured to himself, more names, more theories he didn't divulge with us. However, we had our own mysteries to solve. An hour had passed since Xavier had deposited the soothsayer on her sofa and we'd made our hasty goodbyes and continued the journey south with the Aralians at our backs. Fortunately, the roads had been quiet, with nary another traveler.

I closed my eyes, and whispers of sunlight peeked through the clouds and warmed my skin. Air expanded in my lungs, but a weariness clung to my bones. Perhaps it was because of the lack of sleep, the long journey, or the sting in my shoulder from my wound. However, this malaise ached within me, as it had for weeks before we'd left Presspin. I hadn't noticed the contrast before, my mind so focused on saving Silas that I'd ignored my well-being. Fatigued, I curled my legs toward my chest, rested my chin atop my knees, and shifted my focus from my fatigue and onto Yulia's curious statement.

For your blight did bind a love foreseen, just like the once eternal king and queen. But unlike them, your love did remain, for you saved him from being slain. Life that binds and bends and ends. Life that finds a way transcends. Yet one heart can't house two. That is why death comes for you. Two lives, one source of power you share. Fate you defied, but you didn't care.

Silas mumbled under his breath and shifted beside me. His confusion and concern filled our connection, denoting that he was consumed by the quandary of the oracle's words, as well.

Exhausted, I leaned against the hard wood backing and tipped my head to the sky. If Naomi were here, she would have used her sharp intellect to solve the puzzle by now. I had only my wits to rely on. With great intention, I replayed the prophecy until my brain caught upon one particular line. *Two lives, one source of power you share. Fate you defied, but you didn't care.* Had Silas been meant to die all those months ago? Had we somehow defied fate itself?

"Arianna." Silas's hand reached for mine. His thumb caressed my skin, soothing me.

I turned my focus to my love, who'd withered substantially since last night. The hollows of his cheeks had fully returned, dark bags clung to his eyes, and that grayish hue dampened his shimmering olive complexion. Even his breaths came out as a rasp, caused by a combination of blood and phlegm lodged within his chest. Curiosity blazed in his gaze, driving him.

"Tell me again what you did after I dispatched the Aralians in that explosion."

My lips pursed. We'd gone over the events at least a dozen times over the past few months, detailing every facet that I could remember. Under the curse's control, Silas's memory had fragmented. Though I didn't want to recall that horrific day, something within his gaze pushed me forward. His fingers laced through mine.

"You told me to run. I grabbed Naomi. We sprinted away. Your darkness…" A shudder crawled through me at the remembrance of the menace that flowed down our bond. "It burst. But Naomi wasn't fast enough. She fell, and I needed to protect her, so I pulled off my ring and forced our energy to make a shield around her." I worried my lip, trying to unfurl this knotted riddle tugging in the recesses of my brain.

He scrubbed his free hand over his face, then settled it in the crook of his chin. His eyes flicked back and forth as if he was thinking through the events.

My memory skittered, breaking each moment down into seconds. I'd run, Naomi had fallen, and I had pulled against *our* shared power and protected my sister. I'd used his curse as if it had been my own. But since we awoke, there seemed to be no vast well between us, only a thin cord of connection. That had been the only day that our energy ebbed and flowed; now, it felt as if Silas's portion had shriveled similarly to his body.

I pinched the bridge of my nose, recalling facts Brielle had told me about the wasting sickness and the cursed. The warded masks and rooms drained our vitality. To the best of our knowledge and our experience at Terrell Estate, it fueled the Aralians' weapons. Those who dwelled under the siphoning spells often contracted the wasting sickness. For the curse and its vessel were a symbiotic pair, the life force tied to the darkness. He had expelled vast amounts of energy to dispatch the disciples, but he'd lived when he should have died. The wasting sickness took hold; his curse continued fading, and his life force dwindled along with it.

Minutes passed as we rolled through the marshy meadows. I spoke the soothsayer's rhyme aloud. "*Yet one heart can't house two,*" pressed through my lips. Realizations crested through, connecting her words with recent situations that seemed un-explainable. Silas's heart had stopped twice, once when I bore the mask that stifled my blight and then again when the dagger pierced through my flesh, severing our bond.

Yes, the curse hissed in my skull as I inched closer to the truth.

My nostrils burned as my mind skittered back to when he collapsed in the hallway at Belmont Manor. Darkness had surged from me and into him, an anchor to this realm. I'd been so panicked that I hadn't cared as I marred the carpet. Had his heart stopped then too? My palms itched as if the same unruly energy would burst out of me and surge into Silas.

Sensing my train of thought, he turned toward me and in-terjected the factors that he'd experienced. "The dream, with my mother. She said something binds me to this mortal coil. She couldn't take me to the Great Beyond because I lingered between life and death."

He leaned his head against mine. His breath whooshed over me, filled with the sour tang of sick and medicinal herbs. His grip on my hands tightened, as if I truly was his anchor. "One heart—yours—can't house two—us. I don't recall much of the explosion. However, I remember being dragged back from the darkness, and you were there, Arianna. You were always there. Our curse-bond must have kept me alive. You saved me."

"Impossible." I shook my head. I was so overwhelmed with saving my sister in those moments that I freed my blight from its tether. Could it have not only shielded Naomi but Silas as well? As he had worsened, my curse had become unruly, as if it were leaching from me, out of my control. Reflecting on the winter, other symptoms I'd attributed to grief seemed to correlate with his illness—food tasting bland, the way it had when under the suppression spells; the black blood oozing from my nose when pushing my body too far; losing weight as if I were withering along with him.

As if summoned by my thought, the enigmatic curse pulsed through our bond. "*Yes, save our mate.*"

He held my gaze, and for a heartbeat neither of us could speak. He shook his head in disbelief, as if seeing me in a new light. A knot formed in my throat. I gulped it down. Yet my nostrils still burned. I'd hated myself for months because of the sacrifice he'd made for me that day.

Aware of my swelling emotions, he lifted my fingers to his lips and brushed a soft kiss upon them. "It seems, beloved, that we saved each other."

CHAPTER 26

SILAS

SUNLIGHT BROKE THROUGH THE dark clouds forming overhead and settled upon the deep hollow of Arianna's sunken cheek. My thumb traced along her jaw as she slumbered with her head resting atop my lap. Her soft breaths mixed with the sloshing of hooves as we traversed the mud-laden path. From her lack of sleep and the fatigue of the journey, exhaustion had taken her over shortly after our realization about our connection. Despite my weariness and the pain coursing through my muscles, I feared falling asleep, certain that unconsciousness would claim me.

Instead, I focused on the marshy meadows sprawling along this lesser taken back road north of Krella. My lungs expanded, drawing in the rain-soaked earthen aroma. The air caught in my chest. A cough rattled from me in a gurgling wheeze. Not wanting to mar my beloved, I pressed my sleeve against my mouth. Blood seeped into the white fabric. My lips twisted in a frown. My ribcage squeezed. A haze coated my vision, blurring the edges. If I capitulated to this fatigue, would I awaken again or slip into a comatose state? No, I had to stay by her side. For I needed Arianna as desperately as she needed me. Determined to remain connected to her, I removed her cap. Her shimmering braid unfurled, and my fingers stroked her scalp.

With each pass along her locks, my nostrils burned. The motion didn't provide me comfort but fueled my ruminations. Somehow this fierce woman had saved me yet again, anchoring me to this realm, her curse feeding my own its power. If I died, how would this affect her? Would she contract the wasting sickness? A knot swelled, pressing against my windpipe. In the silence, distress flooded me.

I blinked. A tear rolled down my cheek, landing on her golden hair. My jaw quivered. I'd seen her decline, her frail body, her hollow eyes, and the blight surging out of control. Yet I'd brushed the warning signs away, certain it was the guilt from the lives she'd taken, grief from her mother's death, and overwhelm from my illness that had caused these issues. How could I have been so blind? She'd declined at the same rate that I had.

My body ached, and my shoulders curled in on themselves. Against my will, hot tears slid down my skin, washing over my love, as if I could return the power I'd stolen.

"Silas." Xavier's voice pierced through my swelling emotions.

I shook my head, too overwhelmed to speak. The grief in my heart from her unwitting sacrifice, paired with the looming realization that I drew closer to death, blotted out any sense of propriety.

He didn't push. Instead, his tenor vocals crooned a sweet lullaby he sang to comfort me when I was a boy.

Gods shall rise and gods shall fall

Through the night, we will face it all
When darkness beckons and the light does end
Life survives; it transcends
Noblemen on bended knee
When light comes, all will be free

To my horror, the familiar lullaby wove with the recent revelations, and my impending demise caused a wail to unleash from me. He looped through the chorus, covering the sound of my disquiet with his tune. To my relief, I was so weak that my blight didn't take hold. Instead, it hibernated, conserving energy.

Minutes later, as I sniffled back a final sob, my mind etched this moment into my soul. Xavier's soothing melody, Arianna's closeness, the brief glimpses of warmth upon my skin. Time slowed as I absorbed every minuscule detail, painting what I truly feared might be my last moments.

Her breath whispered against me. The woman who'd saved me in more ways than one. I couldn't allow this uncertainty to drown me. Not when Arianna needed me to remain strong for her. I allowed myself to imagine a perfect world where I was well and we picnicked amongst the prescar flowers or swam in the lakes in the summer. A twinge of hope penetrated my melancholy, and I held on to this flicker of the future. *I must live.*

As a sense of relief washed over me, Xavier sang on, his voice bobbing. My gaze trailed from my beloved to the man. My brow knitted. I'd assumed him to be a heartless rake, yet the sorrow within him oozed. Was he also struggling with what awaited me? As I lingered in this uncertainty, the grudges I'd held against him felt pointless.

I'd wasted months pushing Arianna away before finally declaring a love that I'd harbored since the moment we met, all because of my belief that I was a beast. My hatred of him had poisoned nearly every relationship I had, causing me to keep the world at arm's reach. However, the man who sang this sad tune didn't seem to be a villain. Instead, his countenance reminded me of the parent I'd once known—glib on the surface but compassionate beneath.

My mind drifted past the anger I'd carried and toward the father from my early childhood. The jovial fellow who played hide and seek in the park with us or took me for sweet treats after I'd accompanied him to his high council meetings or his tenderness when I fell ill. The sudden repulsion tied to my curse awakening had been out of character. It was the first time he'd ever acted that way. He had loved us once, and I'd always assumed his abandonment had been because of a deep-seated hatred of what I'd become.

"Father," I said tentatively, feeling like a boy.

His song faltered, as if my use of the title struck him.

"Yes, son." A gentleness I remembered from childhood coated his words.

A question I'd hidden deep within my soul bubbled. "Did you stop caring for me when I became a monster?"

I feared the answer would be yes. That he'd called me a monster because he'd hated me.

He peered over his shoulder. His green eyes softened. "I've always loved you. When your curse awoke, I panicked. Your mother had died, Beatrix was wailing in my arms, and you were so small, covered in ash. I made a rash decision."

His lips tugged into a frown, and he blew out a long, pained breath. "The blighted are in danger under the Aralians' rule. So I said the most vile thing I could and called you a monster. I knew you'd take the insult to heart. And I knew that from that day forward, you would blame me for all your misery. I resigned myself to shouldering that burden for a lifetime, being your villain. Forgive me."

My tongue rolled over my teeth. My brow pinched. The cart inched closer to either my demise or my salvation.

He continued. "I lost myself after your mother died. I was a wastrel, gambling, drinking, and fucking my way through Hallowhaven. Then I met Martha, and she showed me friendship and the ability to turn my pain into purpose. I wanted to build a world where you could roam free without fear."

He scrubbed a hand over his face. "Every cursed person I've helped has been because of you."

Warmth washed over my chest, releasing a fraction of pressure. This must be why he harbored the cursed, like the mysterious Wolf.

Xavier's tone tightened. "But that is not the only reason. I want the temple to fall, not just for you, but for your mother."

"For Mother?" I asked.

"There's much you don't know." His shoulders tensed, and the simple gray coat strained along his back. "As I built my network of spies, I discovered Delphine had poisoned her."

I sucked in a breath, which wheezed through my chest. A barking cough emitted from me. He paused as I righted myself, the air heavy with the revelation.

His gaze shifted from the road to me, and despair coated his expression. "Delphine had been unamused by my lack of desire to attend the full moon festivities because of my devotion to my wife. Years later, after I'd become one of her many lovers, she'd admitted to the deed with a smile. She believes me to be a simple rakehell now that I've lost everything, driven by fucking and fun. I've allowed her to think me the simpleton in order to guide her away from you and the Opposition I've helped Martha build."

A heaviness pressed on my shoulders. "She killed my mother."

"She did. All the council members must be fully aligned with her and her whims or they'll suffer the consequences. Despite the horrid things I said to you that day, knowing I'd kept my children hidden from Delphine has been the driving force for my decisions. Days ago, you asked why I'd come to Presspin to help Arianna. To some degree, she would make a powerful ally. But the truth is, I lost my wife, and I didn't want you to endure the same fate. That's why I came to save her. However, when you saw me in the cellar, with your darkness ready to strike a killing blow, I knew you wouldn't have believed my true intentions." He cleared his throat. "I am sorry, but I promise you every horrible thing I've done has been to protect my children. I love all of you more than life itself."

I closed my eyes, trying to align these words with my past. He had once been a doting parent, and on my most difficult days, I'd allowed the act to erase everything he'd once been. My heart cracked open like an egg. The tiny whisper of hope pressed forward, weaving memories with the present version of my father. But a curiosity also caught on his phrasing. His children—was he including my wife as well?

My fingers trailed over my face and then settled upon my mouth. "Does this devotion extend to Arianna?"

"Of course. She is my daughter-in-law and under my protection until my last breath. Though Duncan Archer, on the other hand, I'd happily strangle to death with my bare hands."

Despite the heaviness of the topic, a whisper of a smirk tugged at the corner of my lips. Somehow, an ease now unfurled between us. "I assumed you or your spies would have killed him."

He gritted his teeth, and his nostrils flared. "He's a bastard. I wish I had poisoned him, but before he wed your sister, his behavior seemed irreprehensible. I suppose it was part of his long con to gain access to your sister and Presspin by extension. I found out about his mistress only after a spy informed me about his brutish acts with Beatrix. He's a slippery bloke, using a slew of false identities. I tried to find him after what occurred in Daviel, but he disappeared. I'm assuming to Seaside. He's likely hiding from the wrath of the Aralians and the broken deal he bartered with them all those months ago. He didn't provide Arianna, and a dozen of their sistren were slaughtered. If I don't kill him, I'm certain Delphine will."

"You'll have to get in line. I owe him a thrashing for kidnapping my wife and harming Beatrix." I sucked my teeth.

He chuckled wryly. "All right. When we find him, we'll dispatch him together."

"Ah yes, our first father and son outing since being reunited—murder." I huffed a sigh.

He let out a laugh, and the sound drifted away. We settled into this quiet ease for many minutes without a word said between us. Something had shifted. My gaze flicked to him, and I wished I hadn't been so stubborn. A swallow flittered through the sky and landed on a branch, chirping a soft song, lulling me. Warmth encompassed my limbs, and fatigue pulled at the edges of my vision. Time slipped by as I drank in the scene and this peace.

With each heartbeat, my back slumped further. As my head bobbed in tune with the horses' hooves, a yawn escaped me. "Father."

"Yes," he whispered, sensing the slumber overtaking me.

"I'll fight to live, but if I succumb to my illness, promise me you'll take my beloved to Presspin. You'll treat her as a daughter, just like Beatrix, and do all within your power to misdirect the disciples until they lose interest in her."

"Of course. I'll protect her as I would all my children, with my life."

CHAPTER 27

ARIANNA

SILAS'S BROW FURROWED AS he sucked in a sharp breath. His head lay upon my lap, and he focused on the sky that peeked through the canopy of branches overhead. The cart bobbed along the lesser-traveled path, bumping over a large tree root. My rear bounced on the hardwood floor. I braced my body, trying to keep Silas, who used my thighs as a pillow, from being jostled. Despite my efforts, I swayed, and my shoulder crashed into a sack of wool cushioning me.

My teeth gritted in frustration at the bumpy road between Krella and Hallowhaven. Though I hadn't traveled to the capital, the central route was likely better maintained than this abandoned way. A while ago, we'd changed horses at a small farm north of my old village. The kindly man had informed Xavier of disciples patrolling the primary pass toward the city. Unwilling to risk our safety, we had veered onto this pothole-laden lane, adding an extra two hours to our journey. We'd avoided the Aralians thus far, though the added time to our trek had created issues of its own.

Silas was worsening.

A coating of sweat beaded on his brow. His eyes had turned glassy. He blinked, studying the barren branches that gnarled above, creating a sinister sensation. Fatigue coated his face. Earlier, he'd dozed for a while; he now refused to capitulate to sleep. To my dismay, the fever blazed through him, so hot that it penetrated through my clothing and into me at every juncture where our bodies touched. Frustratingly, the willow bark and respiratory blends no longer eased his symptoms.

Impatience bubbled, and my gaze drifted to a silent Xavier. His back hunched as he clutched the reins. Though he'd spoken a bit about his late wife and also Silas as a boy, he'd grown achingly quiet the closer we'd drawn to Hallowhaven.

"When will we reach the city?" I asked Xavier, desperate for him to tell me we'd arrive at the outskirts at any minute.

His posture straightened. He pulled his hand through his long raven locks, then settled it upon his nape. "It's hard to say, but I'd guess roughly an hour and a half, maybe two."

My lips pursed, and my agitation built. Had we taken the primary route, we would have already been cresting into the outskirts of Hallowhaven. Instead, we were stuck in these woods as Silas slowly slipped away.

"Arianna." Silas shifted his gaze to mine. His amber eyes held a deep understanding as my fear filled our waning connection, for he too could sense the ever-thinning cord. "If I don't survive, I—"

"Shh. Don't waste your strength speaking of foolish things. You're going to live. We'll make it." My fingers drifted over his sweat-slicked forehead, then to the sharp angle of his jaw.

He sighed at my cooling touch. Regardless of my bluster, we both sensed the fraying connection as it unraveled with each passing minute. I was certain that the elixir Xavier had provided him had all but run out, given the bone-weary fatigue that clung to me despite my earlier nap. My blight remained taut as a bowstring as it anchored him to this world. The sensation was so achingly familiar to how I'd felt over the winter. Now, after speaking with the oracle, I knew that my curse's unwieldy flare-ups were because of its desire to save Silas.

A gurgling cough spewed from him. Blood oozed from the corners of his lips. A groan escaped him as he drew in a pained inhale. My hand dug into my pocket, fetched the soiled handkerchief, and wiped away the spittle. Crimson stained the once pristine fabric. Needing to do something, I reached for my pack and plucked the waterskin out.

"Drink." I pressed the opening against his mouth.

A few drops washed down his throat. I expected him to push and declare his desires for me if he succumbed. To my relief, his gaze settled on the sky. Hues of purple and pink swirled through the ether, though they were quickly blotted out by dark clouds. Soon, the sun would set, plunging us into total darkness. The cart was equipped with lanterns, but I feared that any illumination along this route would draw unwanted attention to us.

Long minutes passed as dusk crawled forward, casting the eerie forest in dense shadows. Each minute dragged, coating time like a thick honey. The curse tingled against my skin, willing to burn these trees to the ground to clear a path for us. My palms itched, and I forced my focus onto the gloomy woods.

The gnarled oaks, muddy road, and darkening sky didn't offer solace. Instead, they denoted the sheer hopelessness of this moment. In this silence, the tight reins on my emotions unfurled, and the buried feelings pressed forward. I'd try to be strong. Yet my resilience had been pointless. The world continued to crash around me no matter how desperately I tried to hold the pieces of my shattered life together. Silas was still dying, my sister hated me, and my mother and Mateo were dead—all because of me. My nostrils stung. I blinked away tears.

Needing comfort, I dragged my fingers through Silas's hair. The fading light caught on the speckles of gray dotting his temples, and purple half-moons hung under his eyes. Time was running out.

Sensing my withering resolve, he peered up at me. His features softened, and his words came out a rasp. "When we return to Presspin, Beatrix will insist on throwing a lavish ball to welcome the Lord and Lady Belmont back to the town. I'll be certain that the hall is brimming with prescar flowers that match the color of your eyes. We'll serve all your favorite foods and play the best music."

The sinking sensation in my soul lightened a fraction. I feared that this fantasy Silas spoke of was nothing more than a delusion. However, we both needed something to anchor ourselves to. Perhaps that's why he'd decided on this fanciful whisper of hope. Despite the uncertainty of the situation, he wasn't gone, and a flicker of the future I desired could lay ahead. I joined in on this tale, weaving in my own ridiculous desires.

"Beatrix shall be the best hostess. She'll create an immaculate space that is welcoming to everyone within the town," I offered, forcing a watery smile. My mind dredged up this beautiful story for me to find respite within. "And Vincent will remain a respectable distance from her, but we'll all notice his longing stares, because Layla will make her wear a scandalous dress."

Xavier peered over his shoulder. "And who is this Vincent?"

"Belmont Manor's steward. He's a good man. Far more suitable for her than that blackguard, Duncan. I've often wondered if he's carried a torch for her over the years. He's soft-spoken but has a kind heart. He was..." My words drifted off.

Vincent was injured because the huntsmen had kidnapped him. I shook my head, trying to escape the flashbacks. I couldn't. The relief I'd acquired began slipping through my fingertips.

"Layla and Jamie would attend too." Silas cut through my rumination, continuing the tale. "And your sister shall pout, but she'll loosen after downing glasses of wine that Brielle provides her. All before Brielle pulls Rosalind Collins into a shaded corner for some scandalous interlude."

My lips pulled into a thin line. Regardless of how much I wanted this fantasy, it would never come to pass. The dark, nightmarish flashes of Mateo dying overwhelmed this dream.

"No, Brielle changed after meeting Mateo. She—she loved him. She wouldn't attend our ball or so easily fall into the arms of Rosalind Collins. After the incident in the conservatory, Naomi would not celebrate my return either." My shoulders fell, and my spine curled in on itself. I carried a modicum of solace from my chat with Martha the day prior, but the guilt from the pain I caused lingered in this internal battle for my soul.

My tongue rolled over my teeth, and my voice warbled. "I am the reason the people they loved the most died. Mama's and Mateo's blood is on my hands."

The lovely imaginary world I painted faded, revealing the darkening forest we traversed. My gaze flicked to my love. My nostrils burned. The hope I clung to diminished. "I should have been better. Done better for them. For you. If you die too, I will never forgive myself."

A hot tear trailed along my cheek. My thumbs brushed over my face, wiping the wetness away.

"Arianna, you are far too hard on yourself. I've told you before; what happened to your mother was not your fault. Mateo's death was a tragic accident. You don't have to—"

"Shh..." Xavier tugged on the reins.

The horses slowed to a snail's pace. The hairs on my nape rose. Panic surged, replacing my heavy emotions. Forced into action, I swiveled around, searching for signs of danger, and landed on a carriage some way ahead blocking the path. I blinked, allowing my darkness to slip over me like a second skin. My eyesight sharpened.

The slick lacquer on the conveyance gleamed against the whispers of light. Though no emblem marked the paint, the mahogany frame denoted a level of wealth unseen by many in Krella. Had someone of means taken this road hoping to avoid highwaymen and gotten stuck in the muck? Given the positioning of the vehicle, it seemed to be free of impediments.

"No insignia. And whoever is in the cart is hidden behind the curtains within," I whispered.

Xavier blew out a long breath, then tugged his hood on, shielding his features. "Arianna, curl into the corner as best as you can and hide among the wool. Both of you remain silent. Let me handle this."

Slowly, I shifted Silas and laid his head on a blanket. Then I scrambled behind the tall sacks of fleece leaning against the backing. This had been our cover since leaving Daviel—that he was a farmer venturing to Hallowhaven to sell his wares. My knees pushed against my chest, and my fingers tugged the closest bushel forward, making certain that my entire body was covered. My heart pounded in rhythm with the horses' increased pace.

Moments later, the cart came to an abrupt halt. A door swung open, and the sloshing of boots on the ground caused tension to coil in my shoulders. Despite my desire to peek, I had to trust Xavier and remain hidden.

"Blessed be Aralia on this beautiful day. How can I be of assistance to the goddess's disciples?" Xavier called out, causing terror to creep down my spine.

CHAPTER 28

ARIANNA

ARALIANS. MY HEART POUNDED. The heavy scent of the wool I hid behind choked me, making it hard to breathe. Yet I slowed my respiration, certain that even a whisper of a sound would draw the disciples' attention. My limbs curled closer into my chest, holding my fear and blight at bay.

"What brings a shepherd on this deserted trail?" an authoritative female voice boomed through the silent forest.

My mouth dried. I stared straight ahead, unable to see anything but the dark brown gunny sack. Not even a sliver of light peeked through the dense fleece covering my head, where I nestled into the corner, only inches from Silas.

To my dismay, he barked a watery cough. The wet sound pierced the tense silence. Boots sloshed through the murky sediment and halted. My curse boiled internally, desperate to thwart these threats.

"Supposedly, highwaymen have been robbing farmers on their way to market. I took the longer route. If I were accosted, I'd lose not only the last of my wool before the spring shear, but I would struggle to guard my ill brother. I'm heading to

Hallowhaven to get coin for treatment for him in the city. As you can see, his consumption symptoms are quite severe," Xavier offered in his unruffled tone.

The woman clucked her teeth. "Hmm...where did you hear these rumors? Do you not believe Aralia nor her disciples to protect you? Ye of little faith."

"You're right." A somber tone coated Xavier's words. "I should trust in our divine goddess; my love for my brother and his worsening condition have blinded me. I'll be certain to tithe a hefty sack of coin to the temple once I sell this wool."

"As you should," she hissed. "May the goddess of light forgive you for your impertinence, but before I release you, the high disciple has tasked me herself to search every passerby. We've received reports of the cursed being smuggled in and out of Hallowhaven. I'm sure a pious man like yourself has nothing to hide."

"Blighted bastards," Xavier spat. "Whoever helps them should be cast out of the Great Beyond."

The cart bobbed at the front. "Let me help you," Xavier offered.

My spine went rigid.

"How many of you are here this fine evening?" Xavier asked.

"Enough small talk." Her boots squelched closer. The conveyance swayed near Silas, as if someone was pulling on the edge. She sucked in a sharp inhale. "And what is this? Why is your ill brother wearing an onyx ring with Aralian symbols?"

My blood ran cold. My curse pressed against my skull, certain the disciple was hovering over my love with a killing intent.

"I won it at a poker game," Silas wheezed through raspy breaths. "I was in the pleasure district in Daviel. A dying man's last wish—a round of cards and an evening with a buxom beauty."

She snarled, disgusted by his smooth lie.

"The man ran out of coin and used this instead. I didn't realize it was anything more valuable than a few coins. Should I exchange this in Hallowhaven to help me procure a doctor?" Silas wheezed again, his words losing air with each passing one.

I remained steady, hoping that she would believe him.

"Of course. If the jewelry is nothing but a token, then you wouldn't mind relinquishing it to me. I'll pay you handsomely, but these artifacts belong to the temple. Or is there a reason you can't part with the warded piece?"

A long beat passed.

"It means nothing to me," he whispered.

My stomach twisted. If he took off his ring in this state, his dwindling blight would leach from him, consuming the very last whisper of vitality keeping him alive. It was too great of a risk.

"*Kill her*," the curse crooned.

Fueled by my earlier unsettled emotions, the darkness ballooned within me.

He'll die, the blight shrieked through my skull.

Unable to wait a moment longer, my leg extended and kicked the sack of fleece. Power pulled at my fingertips. A woman with long brown hair, dressed in white robes, leaned over Silas with her hand wrapped around my love's finger, a millisecond from extracting the spelled jewelry from him.

Her stare shifted from Silas to me, her eyes widening in shock. "You."

Before she could react, an inky tendril shot from my palm and pierced her eye, then exploded through the back of her skull. Brain matter splattered, speckling the mud-soaked earth.

Thump.

She collapsed in a heap. I stood, crouched and ready for the next kill. Assessing the situation, I scanned the space, yet no one remained on the path, just the lacquered carriage. My brow knitted. Where was Xavier? Had he chased another enemy into the woods? Despite the seemingly calm scene, I didn't relax. Something itched under my skin, a sixth sense that denoted danger looming.

Seconds skittered by, and the once still air filled with the echo of boots clomping from the forest encircling us. Terror replaced my brief relief. Time slowed as roughly a dozen women emerged from the shadows of the surrounding trees, clad in dense onyx armor. Blood pounded in my ears. Bile crawled up my throat. In my last battle against a platoon of Aralians, Silas and I had nearly died. My teeth clenched. Where was Xavier? Had he led us here like lambs to the slaughter? Had this been his plan?

The disciples formed a line along the main road, then pointed their bows at the wagon where I crouched. Before I could gather my bearings, arrows arced through the ether toward us.

My eyes flew wide, shifting toward an ashen Silas. He tried to move his sluggish body. Yet he was sluggish in his current state. Needing to save him, I sent energy blasting from my hand. It grazed past my floundering husband and burned through the side of the wagon, creating an opening. I leapt for Silas and landed on him. My fingers clasped his shoulders, and I wrapped my legs around him. With a rough jerking motion, I leaned into the force of my movements to roll us out of the conveyance through the gaping fracture in the panel.

Thud.

My back smacked into the thick muck. Oxygen rushed out of me as he crashed atop my form. I sucked in a sharp breath. Pain radiated through my shoulder, my spine, and my ribs. The whistling of arrows pierced through the air. Unable to focus on the discomfort, I rolled under the cart. The thumping of arrowheads landing in the pine boards above echoed through the tight space.

"Are you all right?" My fingers brushed dirt from his cheeks.

He hacked a cough but nodded.

"That hiding spot won't save you, you cursed monster. It's one against eleven. You can either come with us and live or fight us and he dies," a feminine voice bellowed.

"Run. You can outrun them. Let them take me and Xavier," he pleaded.

Rage boiled in my blood. Ash danced on my tongue. I wouldn't flee, leaving my dying husband to face our enemies alone. Instead, I scooted away from him.

He reached out. His fingers grazed along the seam of my cloak. "Run."

Ignoring his request, I leapt to my feet and raised my hands to the sky, pretending to surrender.

For a heartbeat, I studied my enemy. Unlike the disciple who'd searched the cart, armor that shimmered akin to the night adorned the warriors who stood in a battle formation roughly twenty feet ahead of me. The disciples parted, and a figure stepped forward. I didn't recognize her, but from the gem adorning her helmet, I assumed she was the leader of their troop.

"Arianna Park, how blessed Aralia is to deliver you to us, and on this momentous day of the full moon festival. Blessed be Aralia." She lifted her hands to the sky, the flickers of sunset casting over her.

I searched for an opening in her armor, but there was none. Unlike before, no gap peeked from the neck. The armored Aralians' faces were completely covered except for small holes near their mouths and a strip where their eyes lay. Yet the woman addressing me had lifted her visor, showing her smooth, milky skin.

A huff sounded from behind me, drawing my attention to Silas. He'd somehow crawled from our hiding spot. Grime caked his clothes, and his fingers dug into the wheel as he hauled himself to a standing position. He swayed. His shoulder slumped against the wagon's frame.

A feral smirk tilted the leader's lips. "That is your husband, Lord Silas Belmont, correct? I see he is quite ill. Consumption, that man said? Where is your friend?" She scanned the trail, and her nose wrinkled. "It doesn't matter; he's as good as dead." She snapped her fingers. "Find him, Squad D."

Three women broke off from the rear and ran for the forest, two heading east and the other venturing west.

"Now, Arianna. Why don't you behave for once in your miserable life and surrender? We'll take excellent care of your husband. We have the finest herbalists in the temple, and a blessing from Aralia will strengthen his spirit."

Lies, my blight hissed in my skull.

The wind whipped, making the branches overhead sway. The sun continued its downward descent, causing the gnarled oaks to create long, haunting shadows.

"What will happen to him after he is healed?" I asked, buying time to concoct a plan to get us out of peril.

"Whatever you may wish, if you just surrender. We can return him to Belmont Manor." She opened her arms in an accommodating gesture.

My brow furrowed, and my mind swam with the information. My curse rattled against me, aching to break free. Yet I hesitated. If I relented, would Silas be safe? Would Xavier procure the elixir of life even if they imprisoned me? Or would he forsake his son?

"Never," Silas snarled behind me. Mud streaked over his cheeks, making the fury etched along his sunken features far more menacing. "I will die before you can have her."

She cackled as if amused. "We don't need you, dear Lord Belmont. We need her. But if it is death you wish for, so be it." She lowered her visor over her face, limiting the striking areas.

Let me assist you, the blight crooned. Unleash me.

With the eight fully armored disciples remaining and a weakened Silas at my back, they outnumbered me. Despite the leader's offer, I knew it was a lie. Silas was cursed, and they'd kill him.

"*Yes, no choice. Let me. Let me.*" The curse sang its siren song.

Aware of the danger before us and unwilling to watch my love perish before me, I ripped the ring from my finger.

A cocoon of power enveloped me, and the bone-weary fatigue I'd felt only minutes prior withered away. I pushed the warded piece into my pocket. Energy crackled, encompassing me. The trees swayed under the pressure. The ground cracked under my feet. Destruction laced my tongue, tasting of a sweet delicacy. Though my darkness attempted to suppress me into the subconscious place in my mind. I pressed forward, edging into the joint space.

"No," I hissed through my skull, unwilling to be the blight's puppet yet again. To my surprise, the curse eased, ebbing and flowing with my consciousness.

"Fire!" the leader shouted.

Arrows arched through the sky, their onyx heads glimmering against the whisper of remaining light.

"Duck!" I yelled to Silas.

To my relief, he stumbled toward the rear of the cart, using it as a shield.

My legs moved of their own accord. Blood pulsed through my limbs, and somehow, with the curse working with me, my movements were smoother. An arrow veered toward me, and I spun a millisecond before it made contact. It landed in the muck beyond me. But I didn't relent. I propelled forward at an inhuman speed.

More arrows sailed at me, but I dodged them. My legs picked up speed with each swift motion. As I approached the group, I leapt at the leader. Her arm arched to block me, but she was too late. Black lightning crackled from my fingers, sizzling through her helmet. My power ricocheted, piercing through the mouth guard of the disciple beside her. The pair collapsed as my feet hit the muddy earth in the center of the Aralians' stronghold.

The remaining six enemies encircled me. They dropped their bows to the ground. As they unsheathed their onyx blades, I pounced onto the closest woman to my right, with her fingers laced around a hilt. Before she could fetch her dagger, I'd closed the distance between us. She let out an audible gasp as my palm slammed against her helmet. Inky power surged from my hand through the small slit exposing her eyes.

Pop.

Her head exploded inside the headgear. She tumbled onto the grimy path. Bloody goo coated my skin, but I didn't care. The curse chuckled within me, delighted that I'd finally embraced what Martha had said the night prior. *We are all monsters, dear. Perhaps it was time to fully become the monster I was meant to be.* A savage shriek pressed through my lips, rattling the Aralians as I pivoted to confront them. They paused for half a second, then one lurched at me. She arched a wild swing, but Peter had far more finesse than this enemy. I leapt out of the way, and she stumbled, falling face-first into the sludge-laden earth. My boot stomped upon her hand, causing her to release the blade; before I could finish her, another foe approached.

The hulking woman stood nearly Silas's height; her body seemed dense with muscle. She was a fighter. She clutched an onyx claymore. Despite her size, she sprinted with catlike grace. The other disciples encircled us, as if this were a show instead of a battle. She whipped the sword toward me, and I dodged the blade seconds before it collided with my shoulder.

"We must capture her alive," an onlooker yelled out.

"She'll be missing a limb but alive," the fighter mocked as she took up an offensive stance.

Before I could make a plan, she surged at me again. I pivoted, but my boots slid across the mud, slowing me. The blade skimmed over my tunic, ripping through the fabric. A hiss escaped me as her sword cut along my arm, grazing the skin. Blood oozed from the stinging wound.

She lunged again, hoping to subdue me as I found my bearings. However, I didn't retreat. As she drew close enough that I could see the whites of her eyes, the power unleashed from me in a surge, piercing through the opening in her headgear and into her skull. A horrific cry echoed from her. The claymore sailed through the ether and sliced into the earth at my feet. Its owner fell to her knees and collapsed into the muck.

Time sped up. The frozen disciples pounced into action all at once. Another scrambled toward me, but her movements were sloppy. I leapt over her as if playing a child's game. My heels pressed against her back, and I used the inertia to surge an inky tendril into the disciple behind her. It sizzled akin to lightning finding its mark.

Pop.

Steam curled from her helmet, and the body before me collapsed on the ground.

"Arianna, look out!" Silas shouted from the distance.

I spun as the woman I'd left discarded in the muck before fighting the behemoth thrust a dart into my neck. I grabbed her hand, ripped off her protective glove, and shot power through her arm. She sizzled within the armor and then flopped to the floor. I stood, determined to overcome this paralysis. However, the edges of my vision grew hazy. Two Aralians encircled me. I took a step, then another, but I felt as if I were wading through quicksand. My mouth went dry. The world dimmed until the darkness consumed me.

CHAPTER 29

SILAS

MY MUSCLES TENSED. THE world swayed as my beloved collapsed. I waited with bated breath, certain that I would fall unconscious, yet I remained upright. Was that a tranquilizer similar to the one Duncan had slipped me all those months ago? Perhaps it only affected her body and not our bond. Fortunately, the connection still beat between us, its rhythm the same as my heart's. My knees buckled. But I couldn't relent; I had to save her. Minutes prior, I'd been slowly working toward the mares, hoping to unlatch them from their restraints to provide aid. Urgency fueled my strained movements.

The women's attention drifted from an unconscious Arianna to me. The horses connected to the cart continued to buck, trying to break free from their harnesses. To my luck, they'd dragged the wagon only a few feet forward before the rear wheels lodged into a heavy pothole, anchoring the vehicle.

"Leave him. Let the stragglers in the woods deal with him. We got what we came for." The taller woman flicked her wrist, as if I were no threat at all.

She leaned over and grabbed Arianna's wrists while the other wrapped her grip around my beloved's ankles. Her limp form swung between them, as if she were a rag doll.

"No." My knuckles blanched against the cart's ledge.

The taller woman's gaze flicked to me, and she cackled. "By the time you fumble your way to us, we'll be gone. Besides, judging by the look of you, death is near. Surrender and succumb to the Great Beyond. I'm sure your wife will be there shortly, once Delphine is done with the wretched disciple killer."

I blinked as the last flickers of light dwindled, deepening the purple hue in the sky. The sloshing of the women's boots crept farther from me. The world spun, and a horrific cough rattled through my chest. My pulse skittered. Sweat beaded on my forehead. I dragged my weary legs through the soft sinking earth, trying to get to the horse. I needed to rescue her.

Release me. My blight crackled beneath my flesh, promising destruction on my mate's behalf. I licked my lips, tasting the blood on them. Ignoring the curse, I continued on at a snail's pace as the pair hauled my wife toward the conveyance blocking the route. If I didn't reach them, she'd be lost to me forever.

A raspy wheeze pulled through my lungs. My chest tightened. Only a whisper of air pressed through my lips, but I didn't care. I'd use my dying breath to get to her. I lunged, wrapping my hands around the black mare's hindquarters.

"Steady, girl. Please. Please." My fingers fumbled with the harness.

My glance shifted to the disciples inching closer to the carriage. My jaw clenched.

My curse hissed. *Running out of time. Out of time.*

Even if I unsecured this steed, could I mount it? I rested my forehead against the horse's hindquarters in a feeble attempt to steady myself.

Use me! my blight screamed, uncaring that by unleashing this darkness, I'd likely succumb to the illness. With each passing heartbeat, Arianna was slipping away. My brow furrowed, and in that instant, I disregarded my wilting well-being. I was already a dead man walking, these months stolen from fate herself. Without hesitation, I plucked off the onyx ring, then pocketed it.

Energy surged through my limbs like a fire blazing hot before completely dying out. I sucked in a deep inhale, and the pain I'd felt seconds ago dwindled away. Power coursed through my veins, amplifying my strength. Darkness pushed through my palm and into the harness, vaporizing it. Simultaneously, my body pushed against the steed and mounted it. The frantic horse propelled forward, fueled by its panic. The steed galloped through the muck toward the women who'd captured my love.

"Stop him!" the taller woman commanded.

The stout Aralian released Arianna's ankles, sprinted for her discarded bow on the ground, and lifted it. She yanked an arrow and pointed it at me. It released. I leapt for her, and the projectile sailed past, mere inches from my head. The whites of her eyes flashed as I crashed on top of her. She squelched into the grime. She scrambled beneath me, fighting for freedom, as my hand slammed into her helmet, shooting a shadowy fog through the tiny gaps. A horrible watery scream bellowed from her, filling the ever-darkening night sky. The breeze whipped over us, dragging the scent of ash through the space. The dead disciple lay amongst her counterparts like dispensed toy soldiers in the muck.

As I stood, my limbs buckled. The surging energy faltered. A cough barked from me. Black blood spewed from my mouth.

"Oh my gods. You're...you're cursed too." The last remaining disciple's head swiveled, searching for aid, but she had no allies. She hastened her pace, dragging my beloved as if she were a beast caught in the hunt.

A snarl escaped me, the curse voicing its killing intent.

A scream echoed in the distance to the east. She warbled, "The farmer."

"He is no farmer. He's my father and a killer," the otherworldly tone bellowed from me.

Confirming my statement, a second wail pierced through the night. A smirk tugged on my lips. Perhaps Xavier hadn't abandoned us after all but was simply trying to draw some of the fight away from us. With the two disciples thwarted, he could take Arianna back to safety once I dispatched this final threat.

A gasping wheeze rasped. My legs wobbled, but I forced myself to straighten. Just once more, I whispered to the blight, hoping it could amplify my power for this strike. My chest expanded, pulling in oxygen to fuel my attack. I crouched in a fighting position, ready to deliver the killing blow.

"Don't come any closer." The foe unsheathed her dagger and placed it against the hollow of Arianna's throat. "I'll kill her. I don't care if Delphine wants her alive. Besides, a swift death by my blade is likely far more merciful than whatever torture the high disciple has planned for her."

My nostrils flared. My blight shrieked from me, a scream so haunting that the woman's hands shook. Her gaze slipped from mine and onto her trembling fingers, giving me a millisecond of an opening. Darkness fueled my steps. My muscles spasmed as if the curse would rip me to shreds. I disregarded the internal warning. Energy crackled like dark lightning from my fingertips and coursed through the weak points in her armor. She wailed. The blade toppled out of her grasp, and she plummeted to the murky earth, beside my wife.

With the threat thwarted, my blight fizzled out of me. I swayed. My knees hit the dense mud, and I fell forward. I turned my head just before my face collapsed in the muck. My vision swam. My muscles throbbed. Black blood spurted from my lips and soaked into the grimy ground. A haziness coated the edges of my perception. This was it; death had finally come to call.

Still some feet from Arianna, I dragged myself through the mushy path with aching arms. I had to reach her. If I were to die, it would be by her side. Each second stretched as I wriggled my failing body, trying to close the distance between us.

"What have you done?" a woman shrieked from the west. My throat strung. The Aralian who'd gone searching for Xavier in the opposite direction. How could I have forgotten about her?

Buzzing filled my ears. There was a final disciple. I'd failed. Arianna would be taken. I tried to muster another whisper of my blight to help her, but the faint cords lay limp, having used all the power they had left to give. Needing to safeguard her, I pressed my arms into the mud and squirmed to get to my beloved's side. Despite the pain tightening my chest, only one thing mattered—protecting Arianna.

The squelching of boots in the muck approached me, but I ignored the Aralian. She'd likely kill me, but not before I was by Arianna. I'd shield my beloved with my dead body if I must. My lungs burned. The footsteps grew closer.

"You're still crawling to your wife? How sweet." The voice loomed over me.

I shifted my gaze to face the woman. The rising moon illuminated the onyx dagger she arced overhead, ready to slice down to deliver a killing blow. I closed my eyes, not wanting this helmeted figure to be the last thing I saw.

"But now you d—"

Thud.

I blinked, but the disciple no longer stood over me. Instead, a wild Xavier had crashed atop the woman. Her blade flew toward his skull; he dodged the attack a second before it met its mark. My stomach knotted. He grasped her wrist, hitting it into the ground over and over. The weapon clattered from her clutch and plunged into the grime-coated earth. His fingers dug into her helmet, ripping it off.

Her face twisted in disgust. "Xavier, you traitor."

He reared back, then cocked forward, head-butting her. Her skull landed in the sticky sediment. His hand surged for the blade, retrieved it and then stabbed it through her eye socket, ending her.

Xavier rolled off the vanquished disciple, panting from the exertion. Warmth washed over me, and a sense of bone-deep relief filled my being. I continued my crawl to Arianna. Tears burned as my limp form finally reached her. My dirt-covered fingers pressed against the curve of her cheek. My nostrils stung. Despite my dwindling strength, I inched forward. My forehead pressed against hers. I drank in for the last time her milky skin, her cheekbones, the quirk of her nose. If only I could give her the fantasy we'd painted only moments prior. Of us at Belmont Manor, dancing at a grand ball with our loved ones around us.

As the darkness pulled me closer, I knew I couldn't keep the promise to always come back to her.

CHAPTER 30

ARIANNA

ARIANNA...ARIANNA...ARIANNA, A WOMAN'S VOICE crooned.

My skull throbbed as I forced my eyes open. My back leaned against a hard wall, and my limbs were angled akimbo ahead of me. As my vision focused, a long corridor lay before me instead of the forest south of Hallowhaven. Lanterns flickered along the crimson wallpaper, casting eerie shadows over the cherry wood floor. I rubbed my temples, trying to recall how I'd arrived here. Yet a block seemed to coat my recollections. Only one name rattled through me—Silas.

Desperate to find him, I scrambled to a standing position. My bare feet pressed against the frigid flooring. My hands brushed over my hips, registering the white nightgown that had replaced my traveling garments. Even my hair tumbled around my shoulders as I stood in the desolate hall, akin to a specter in a dream.

Disoriented, I strode down the long corridor, passing door after door. My mind hitched upon the ornamentation adorning the various thresholds. Each had a unique design: one was cedar with metal bolts, another made of copper, yet another with azure prescar flowers etched in a soft aspen. I passed over a dozen more designs that likely led into mysterious rooms. Was Silas behind any of them? Unsure of which to search, I continued forward.

Minutes later, my pace slowed as I reached the end of the hall, where a gold door appeared. It beat as if in time with my pulse. Tears welled as I stared at the blockade. Something lay within there, something sacred. It pulsed like its own beating heart. My fingers trembled as I reached for the metal handle.

"Don't touch that," a familiar voice snapped. "You are too curious for your own good."

My body shook, and a knot formed in my throat. My chin wobbled at the sultry lilt. I spun on my heel, taking in Brielle.

"My gods. What are you doing here? Where are we? What is this place?" The questions tumbled from me as I drank her in.

Something seemed off.

Perhaps it was the overly flirtatious tip of her lips or the smolder in her green eyes. She appeared to be a caricature of the herbalist I'd grown to know rather than the true Brielle.

Concerned, I took a step back. "Who are you?"

"I'm whoever you want me to be. Funny you'd choose a woman your opposite as my embodiment—cunning, alluring, and uncaring of what others think of her. It's so much easier to accept your lack than your worth." She gestured to the green gown clinging to her frame, then huffed a sigh.

"I don't understand." I shook my head.

She placed her hands on her hips. "You've called me many things—power, energy, blight, darkness, curse." She clicked her tongue in annoyance. "However, I prefer a different appearance. Would you like to see?"

My teeth clenched, but I nodded, needing to see the truth.

A dense fog encompassed her. Seconds later, the smokescreen fizzled away, revealing her true form. A mirror image stood before me. Her features were exactly like mine, but an untamed rawness lived in the depths of her blue eyes. Her lips curved into a half-cocked smirk, and her jaw tipped skyward. She smoothed her palms over a sleek black dress that clung to her subtle curves. An onyx choker lay against her throat. Seeing my glance at the necklace, she traced it with her delicate fingers.

"It matches your ring. A collar to keep me in heel." Her nose wrinkled with disdain. "But as you can see, I am you, Arianna. We are two sides of the same coin. I was born of your tragedy, the trauma you endured when you witnessed your mother teeter toward death when you were just a little girl. I flared within you, and here I live, in the recesses of your mind, the ghost that haunts you and the strength that protects you."

My hands balled into fists. "Protect me? You've nearly destroyed me!" My rage blazed, but the curse didn't flicker along my fingertips. Confusion replaced my frustration.

"Oh, sweet child. I'm the power within you. You can't access the well of darkness when you're trapped in my prison. Foolish." She cackled.

"Shall we stay in this hallway, gawking at the portals of memories, or go somewhere a bit more...palatable?" She turned and gestured down the corridor.

My mind spun. Was that what lay behind these doors, recollections from my life? Not wanting to be left behind, I followed. A few moments later, she stopped at a plain wooden door, placing her palm against it. Yellow daisies curled over the hinges, and the pale wood changed to a vibrant green. She turned the metal knob, leading into the vast space.

A warm breeze flowed over my skin, causing my nightgown to flutter. I breathed in the familiar sweet floral fragrance of the meadows near Krella. Wildflowers of every color melded with the long grasses. Puffy white clouds dotted the crisp azure sky. As I drank in the moment, all the tension I felt diminished. An exhale whooshed from between my lips, and my tight shoulders loosened.

"Come." The blight gestured to a blanket amongst the flowers and settled upon it. Despite her dark aura, her presence in this beautiful space seemed right. Hesitantly, I closed the distance between us and sat beside her.

She lay down, her blond hair splayed along the multicolored quilt. She focused on the clouds, and her thumb trailed over the collar. "I'm glad you're here. We can finally have a little chat."

My lips pursed. This organism had tugged within me, pushing me into harming those I cared about. Yet it acted so relaxed, wanting to converse with me as if it hadn't caused me grief. My arms crossed over my chest.

A pout pressed on her lips. "You only desire my help when I'm protecting you or keeping Silas alive. Is that why you repress me? I feed off your indignation, your frustration, and your pain. Yet you deny the complexities of your inner self. Who you are."

My brow knitted, and her words sank to the depths of my heart. Though I knew my unbridled rage fueled her, I didn't have the fortitude to sit with the discomfort.

"How did I get here?" I asked, pivoting the conversation.

"We're in your mind, where I live. You must have fallen into a deep slumber without a barrier between us." She pinched the bridge of her nose.

"A barrier?" I moved to fiddle with my ring. It remained here, a symbol of our symbiotic relationship, but a memory pressed forward. "I removed it."

"Yes. And for once, we fought the enemy together instead of you trying to subdue me or I overcoming you. We were united until that damned bitch injected us with that paralytic. But if we are both here, I assume we're alive." She shifted her gaze to me.

My shoulders fell. "And Silas?"

She held her hand toward the sky, and a thin cord blinked into existence. The gold thread stretched endlessly through the ether. She sucked her teeth. "Alive for now, but I don't know how much longer I can hold on to him. His vitality is waning, and if I continue to feed him our power, it will kill us. We are lucky that, that day at Terrell Estate, when Silas depleted his curse while vanquishing the disciples, you removed your ring to save your sister. It freed me. When Silas's strength waned, I fed him from our life source. But he's used a sizable amount of energy protecting us from the Aralians, and he's slipping through my grasp."

Her once smooth skin wrinkled as if she were an octogenarian rather than in her twenties like me. She snapped her fingers, and both disappeared. My stomach soured. Silas was feeding off my blight, and it was slowly killing us.

"We must secure the elixir before it is too late for both of us," she stated.

I scrubbed a hand over my face. Would I also suffer from the wasting sickness if I continued on like this? Regardless, I needed to focus on how to return to Silas.

"I have to awaken, then." I stood, but she gripped my wrist and yanked me back down.

"You will. For now, we need to rest. Besides, I have a theory I've been wanting to share with you." Her lips curled into a feral smirk. "If we fuse as one, not only will I be freed from this damned prison of memories, but we'll become stronger. When we battled the disciples, we were faster, sharper, better. If you accept me as an intricate part of yourself and not a separate entity, we could be unstoppable."

My brow pinched. "I can't risk your destructive tendencies coming to fruition. You've nearly killed people I care about."

She shot up into a sitting position. Her lower lip curled. "That's because you are constantly hiding from your emotions. If you actually embraced them instead of running from them, I wouldn't be pushed to react as I do. Stop avoiding the truth of who you are—a complex, flawed being who—"

A high-pitched giggle flittered through the space, and the curse's attention shifted to the sound. Her lips pulled into a tight line. "Ah yes, part of the reason you are as insufferable as you are."

She gestured to where the laughter emitted. Some feet away, a little girl no older than six with golden hair ran through the meadow. Her blue irises sparkled, and a wide grin tugged across her cherub features. She dashed around a willow tree, hiding behind the arching leaves, but the tittering kept her from remaining hidden.

My mouth dried, and a heaviness filled my soul as I studied the child version of myself.

"Arianna," my father crooned.

A knot pressed against my windpipe. I'd forgotten how handsome he once was with blond wavy locks, a straight nose, a dashing smile, and his aquamarine eyes. He slunk through the tall grasses and beelined to the willow tree. I blinked as the man embraced the girl, the past me, in a bear hug. "Found you."

A heaviness pushed against my chest. "This, this was our last picnic before..."

"I came to be." The curse nodded.

The high-pitched, elated squeals filled the air. My heart plummeted. Would life have been different had my inner darkness remained dormant? Would everything have stayed the same? As I watched the pair play, a question I'd long contemplated unfurled from me. "I've often wondered why my curse enacted when Naomi was born, but given what happened at Terrell Estate, she has remained unafflicted. And why it was Silas and not Beatrix who was overtaken when their mother died."

She settled her hand upon her chin. "From what I've observed, it's not an exact science. You and Naomi carry the same blighted bloodline, but you are different. You've always been a gentle soul, desperate for connection, while your sister seems to be self-sufficient. I believe that the aspects of your personality, the age of the trauma, and the lack of support systems can affect the reason one's curse is enacted and not the other. You were six when you watched your mother bleeding out. While Naomi was a grown woman when your mother passed. Even how you've grieved her death isn't the same." She shrugged. "I rose from your misery. When I woke, you were overcome with sorrow, though you were far more powerful than you realize. So powerful, in fact, that you kept me at bay when I ignited."

"Arianna, Henry," Mama's voice called through the forest, halting my conversation with the curse.

Sunlight washed over her unblemished skin. Her features still bore the plumpness of youth, and she wore a fine pink day dress that made her complexion rosy. Her hand clutched the handle of a wicker basket, and the other settled upon her rounding belly. Unable to stop myself, I stood and ran toward her, needing so desperately to be reassured that she didn't hate me nor blame me for her death.

"Mama. Mama, please." I rushed forward.

Her gaze remained straight ahead, fixed on the younger me and my father playing around the willow. Tears stung, and my lower lip bobbed.

"She can't see you. This is just a memory." The blight grasped my shoulder. "Watch."

Mama stopped at the edge of the trees and placed her free hand on her hip. "Of course you went gallivanting off to play with her instead of helping me."

My father walked through the string of leaves while the child me hid amongst the branches. I remembered their conversation vaguely, but from this angle, it felt completely different. A shudder ran down my spine at my mother's pinched expression.

"Goddess above, Henry. The least you could have done was take the basket. I had to haul it the two miles through this damned meadow. Why must we have a picnic here? We could have had a lovely meal at home."

My gut twisted. Had mother ever had a happy moment? Father ruffled Mother's quaffed chignon, causing it to unravel. Her nostrils flared.

"Henry, I'm serious." Her lips tugged into a frown.

"*My dear, when are you not serious? Everything must be achingly exact or you'll be displeased.*" *He shrugged, but annoyance replaced his once jovial expression.*

"*And you are always a foolish rogue, wasting our meager funds on ale and poker at the tavern.*" *She lowered the basket to the ground and then crossed her arms over her chest.*

"*My nights out are more enjoyable than having to speak with a shrew like you. Goddess above. Can't we have an afternoon free from your nagging?*" *He lifted his palms into the air and brushed past her.*

"*Where are you going? We were supposed to have a picnic.*" *Mama pivoted to him.*

"*Mama...Papa...*" *Young me emerged from the branches.*

Mama spun to the child, her face screwed into an expression of disdain. "*Go play.*"

My younger self slunk back to her hiding spot. The sun shifted in the sky, casting long shadows as my parents' shouts echoed, marring the beautiful day with their displeasure. All the while, muffled sobs mixed with their screams, but they were too egocentric to notice the weeping girl under the willow tree.

My jaw ticked. Had the child been corporeal, I'd run to her and scoop her into my arms. They'd always ignored my pain and centered their issues over mine. My curse enacting didn't cause their neglect; it provided them with a justification.

Uncaring of the daughter they'd disregarded, Papa eventually strode away, and Mama followed in tow. Minutes later, alone, the small version of me crawled from the tangled branches. Her red-rimmed eyes blinked, searching for her parents, but they were gone. She opened the basket and plucked a strawberry tart, her favorite, from the receptacle and nibbled upon it. There she sat, eating her picnic by herself, until the girl faded as if she'd been a specter in this tableau.

"Did they ever care about me?" I whispered under my breath, shaken by the bone-deep realization that perhaps the blight wasn't wholly to blame.

The curse released her grip. "As much as self-absorbed parents could. Neither of them knew how to love. You were already suffering from neglect before I came. Your mother's near-death experience was the last straw. You'd carried a heavy pain at such a young age. But..."

She stepped in front of me, and the harshness in her features softened. "There were small efforts of affection. Subtle things, like the strawberry tarts. I've watched this memory so many times that I believe your mother sent you to fetch the dessert for your betrothal dinner because when you were a little girl, they were your favorite. She might not have known how to love you, but somewhere in the depths of her heart, she held a sliver for you."

My throat bobbed.

"Though she didn't care for you the way you deserved, she saved Naomi. For that, we can honor her," the blight offered.

My nostrils stung. I'd been so unsure of how to grieve a mother who'd hated me. Yet something within me finally snapped. Tears washed down my face. My knees buckled, and I collapsed onto the soft grass. My body heaved with uncontrollable sobs. "It's not fair. None of this was fair. I didn't want her to die. But I shouldn't have been sold off for her comfort. I couldn't wed Theo. I just wanted to be free."

"It's not." The curse knelt before me. "Life isn't fair, and you deserved better. That's why you are so angry. At the core of who you are, you sense the injustice of it all."

Long moments passed as the gut-wrenching grief unraveled from me a tear at a time. Finally, unable to cry any more, I blinked up at the blight, feeling freer after embracing this darkness.

The flowers withered. The blue sky dimmed, as if the edges of this scene were blackening.

Her brow pinched. "You're awakening. Listen to me. We have little time, and so does Silas. I will continue to aid you, but if you remove your ring once more, I'll assume you've accepted my proposition that we merge, becoming one."

Thunder rumbled through the world. A chill cut through the air.

"Do you understand?" Urgency filled her gaze.

"I do." I nodded. "Thank you for protecting, and for saving our love."

A quirk of her mouth tipped. "Of course. This existence has been far more palatable since I've connected with our mate's blight. Now wake up."

CHAPTER 31

ARIANNA

I GASPED AWAKE, AND my body lurched forward, forcing the blanket to tumble from my chest. My teeth gritted as I took in the nondescript chamber, with plaster cream-hued walls and pine floors. Moments prior, I'd been battling the Aralians. Now a bland room lay before me. Trying to glean any information, I swiveled my head, taking in the fire roaring in a stone hearth to my left and the plain wooden dresser to my right. Even the quilt covering me on this tiny bed lacked any adornment. Nothing about this space denoted any recognizable markers. My pulse raced. Where was I? And where was Silas?

Panicked, I searched my memory, recalling the fight in the forest and the disciple who'd plunged the paralytic into my neck, sending me into the dreamlike world of my subconscious. My blood ran cold. Had they captured me? Did they have my husband, or had he escaped?

My hand pushed against the thick blanket, chucking it off me. I swung my legs to the foot of the bed, stood, and swayed. My nostrils flared at the aftereffects of the paralytic. I pressed a palm into the mattress, steadying myself.

Dizzy, I closed my eyes. Even if I didn't know my location, I could reassure myself of Silas's well-being. My mind pulled the golden cord between us. It blinked to life, but the wear on it gave me pause. The once-bountiful connection now had the density of a hair, hanging on by a mere thread. The curse had been correct. My love wouldn't last much longer.

My jaw clenched. I had to escape and find my husband. Uncaring of my discomfort, I forced my feet to move. They trudged onward, one aching step at a time. Moments later, as I reached the exit, my footing faltered. My shoulder crashed against the wall. Pain radiated through the stinging joint, still healing from my wound. My forehead pressed against the doorframe, but to my surprise, no Aralian symbols lay in the wood. My panic-driven body halted, assessing the situation in a different light.

The onyx ring I'd removed had returned to my finger. A soft cotton nightdress flowed over my form, and the mud-soaked travel garments were nowhere to be seen. My hand wrapped around the knob. It clicked. My brain hitched. Given the details, I doubted I was within the Aralians' clutches. But what was this place?

Cautiously, I stepped over the threshold and into a narrow corridor. The hallway lacked any adornment as well, not a painting nor pretty wallpaper hung upon the walls. Instead, there was plain plaster, with brass sconces holding candles that illuminated the dark spanning space. Confused, I tiptoed along the polished pine floors. Yet I froze when hushed whispers emanated from two doors down. My pulse skittered, sensing Silas's waning presence in the same space. Was he in danger?

Uncertain of the situation, I tugged against my blight. It pressed forward, darkness tingling along my palm to deliver a killing blow.

As if sensing my presence, the door swung open. I lifted my hand, ready to blast whoever had captured Silas and me to the Great Beyond.

A man with short-cropped blond hair and fair skin strode from the door but halted when he saw me. His hazel eyes widened, and he raised his palms to the air. "Xavier," his honeyed voice called out.

My brow pinched. Hadn't Xavier abandoned us on the road? Or was this a continuation of his trap? I didn't lower my guard.

A second later, Xavier rushed from the room and stood between the blond fellow and me. He crossed his arms over his chest and frowned. "Arianna, let's not threaten my friends, shall we?"

My lips thinned into a flat line as I assessed the situation. The men looked between themselves. Xavier no longer bore his farmer costume. Instead, he donned a crisp white shirt with the sleeves rolled, exposing his forearms. Fresh gashes laced his olive skin. He'd seemed freshly bathed, but a bruise grazed along his cheekbone and a slight gash lay above his eyebrow. My mind hitched. What had happened between the forest path and here? And where was I?

The blond gentleman clasped a heavy hand over Xavier's shoulder. "I told you we should have kept them together."

Xavier waved his friend away, wholly ignoring me. "It was best that the doctor didn't see her. I trust him well enough with the cursed, but her fifty-thousand-crown bounty is another story."

I sucked my teeth. My bounty had become a fortune. Why did Delphine want me so desperately? Hadn't the Aralians said I was to be brought back alive? Did she truly desire to relish in killing me herself for the destruction I'd caused? Despite the curiosity, I dragged my mind to the most urgent matter. "Where is Silas? What is this place?"

Xavier gestured to the door. "This is a safe house in Hallowhaven. He is here. Come have a seat, and I'll tell you everything."

I strode past the men and through the doorway of the tiny quarter. The tang of medicinal herbs wafted through the air. Heat blazed from the fireplace to my left. To my right sat a cramped bed, barely large enough to fit Silas's frail form. The space mirrored the one I'd awakened in. Were all the rooms the same nondescript holding places?

A horrific rattling pierced through my thoughts, drawing my attention to Silas, who lay tucked beneath a quilt. Overwhelmed with grief, I hastened to my slumbering husband and perched on the mattress. Fever blazed from him, through the covers and into my thigh that nudged against his side. My fingers grazed along his sweat-laden forehead. A gray hue coated his complexion, and his cheeks had hollowed further. Even the silver strands in his hair had multiplied, making him appear far older. I leaned forward and placed my ear against his chest, listening. To my relief, his heart beat a slow staccato rhythm.

"The doctor says he doesn't have much time." Xavier strode to the bed but settled at its base. Sorrow covered his features as he drank in his son.

My nostrils burned, but I sniffled back the tears, unwilling to cry when my love was alive. Instead, I turned toward Xavier. My brow knitted. I stood and closed the distance between us. My jaw ticked. "Why did you run off? Where are we? Where is the elixir?"

Xavier's expression tightened. He sucked his teeth, and something within the once crisp edges of his aura frayed. He scrubbed a hand over his face. "First, I ran into the forest to draw some of the disciples away from the fight. I had a better chance of defeating them in the woods, where I could use my stealth, than in a battle formation. Second, after I dispatched the two women who'd come searching for me, I rushed to the road. You were unconscious, and Silas..." He shook his head. "All the Aralians were dead except for one, who loomed over my boy. He didn't care about his own well-being. No, he crawled to you. I, however, cared very much. I pounced and killed her."

My tight muscles loosened, and I withdrew. What had my mate done? When I'd fallen under the tranquilizer's hold, there were two more disciples. Had he used his remaining power?

Yes...to save you, the blight hissed in answer. My stomach dropped.

Xavier continued, unaware of my internal dialogue with my curse. "Then I dragged you and Silas into the Aralians' carriage and brought you here to my safe house, near to the city center. You've been asleep for hours, and Silas..." His eyes drifted toward his son.

"He won't make it until morning. We must obtain the elixir at once," I interjected, remembering the curse's warning and sensing the diminishing bond.

Xavier's face fell. "Do you know what you are suggesting? We'll be walking into enemy territory when the entirety of the disciples and high council are partaking of the evening's festivities. It's foolishness. We barely made it out of the woods after facing a single platoon. We must wait. It is the safest option. He's stubborn, so he'll—"

"No, he won't. There are things about our curses that you do not understand. We are connected. I can feel him slipping from me. He'll die by morning light if we do nothing." My shoulders squared.

"She's not wrong. The death rattle has begun; it won't be long before he slips into the Great Beyond," a masculine voice called from the doorway.

My gaze shifted to the man from the hallway. He bore plain clothing, and he stood a head taller than Xavier, though he appeared to be in his late fifties. Perhaps he also served the Opposition?

He took a few steps forward, lingering near Xavier. "We have the garb from the girl you slipped out of the full moon ceremony a few months ago. We can disguise her. The veil should cover her features, and you could move through the temple freely." His hazel eyes shifted between Xavier and me. "I'll watch over your boy while you fetch the elixir. If you wait, he may die. But if we sneak you both into the temple, perhaps there is a chance of at least one of you returning with the remedy."

Xavier shot a glare at his friend. "And what were you just saying—that you are tired of me throwing myself into danger?"

A deep, throaty laugh bellowed from the man. "When have my protests ever stopped you? I hate the idea of you running into danger, but your son is dying, and the medicine the doctor provided didn't help his fever. You'll never forgive yourself if he succumbs to the wasting sickness because you waited too long, like I did with my daughter."

Xavier shuddered. "Lazarus, I..."

Lazarus held up a hand, stopping whatever he had to say, and continued, "I'll fetch the Aralian garb and your finest evening wear." He studied Xavier. "I'll also find a powder to conceal that horrid bruise. We can't have Delphine's favorite courtier appearing anything but pristine." He moved toward the door.

Xavier's gaze followed the gentleman, and something tender lingered in the moment. He watched with bated breath as the blond bloke left the room. A silence clung to the air.

I cleared my throat, breaking the thrall that Lazarus seemed to possess over Xavier. "Who is he?"

Xavier rubbed his nape. A twinge of pink colored the shell of his ears, and a shy expression softened his features. "He's a longtime friend. He had a cursed child. However, his daughter, Christine, passed when she was still young, only five years after being subjected to the wards. We can trust him. He'll keep Silas safe while we secure the elixir. Enough about Lazarus. We must prepare to enter the temple."

CHAPTER 32

ARIANNA

MOONLIGHT PEEKED THROUGH THE crack in the curtains in the carriage. A flicker of light caught on the silver cufflinks Xavier fiddled with. His long fingers twisted the embellished bobble, then smoothed over the forest green coat that caused his meadow irises to sparkle. Unlike the self-assured man I'd grown to know over the past few days, an uneasiness simmered below the surface as he tugged at his expensive evening wear akin to a preening peacock. Despite our earlier scuffle with the armored Aralians, his face appeared unmarred. Lazarus had used a powder to conceal the bruises along his cheek.

As I studied him, his gaze remained plastered to the velvet design on the ceiling rather than the flimsy garment that I bore. The long veil hid my face, similar to a bride on her wedding day, but the density lessened as it reached my shoulders, while only a thin gauzy gossamer covered the shift molded to my body. Though the fabric grazed the tops of my sandaled feet, the material was nearly transparent, leaving the outlines of my breasts, hips, and thighs visible. My arms crossed over my chest in a feeble attempt to hide my exposed form.

He cleared his throat. "I must warn you. The stories of old depicting chaste disciples is a lie. Every full moon, Delphine holds a celebration for the high council and its subordinates. The Aralians believe they are providing a religious act, allowing the council members to partake of their bodies, to rid themselves of their lustful nature and bring them closer to the goddess. Truthfully, these celebrations are one way Delphine controls those who oversee Hallowhaven. In addition, she lines the council members' pockets, using the tithes from those who come on pilgrimage."

My jaw clenched. Though Brielle spoke little of her years living amongst the Aralians, she'd alluded to these festivals on the few occasions she spoke of Wren.

"You are to remain silent and are not to leave my side. We'll slip past the festivities, steal the key to the elixir chamber, and then escape the temple. Hopefully, we will go unnoticed." He smoothed his fingers through his raven locks, which sat unbound, grazing his shoulders.

The carriage slowed, then halted, ending our conversation. My posture straightened, and I feared what lay in wait. A footman opened the door, and Xavier leaped out. Then he paused and held out his palm, assisting me out of the conveyance.

My fingers pressed through the slits in the veil and took his sweat-slicked hand. My glance flicked from the anxious man to the monstrous cathedral behind him. The full moon caused the marble building to sparkle. A hundred steps lay before me, leading toward gigantic statues of beautiful ivory goddesses standing like sentinels guarding the massive white doors with golden handles.

"Always walk a pace behind me and keep your eyes trained on the floor." He released his hold and rolled his shoulders, his tight features smoothing to those of a bored courtier.

His fine boots didn't make a sound as he traversed the stairs. I followed behind him. As we reached the top of the landing, my pulse skittered. The statue of Aralia glared at me as if it were casting judgment upon me, weighing whether my curse would indeed mar the pristine temple. As he pushed the door open, no alarm sounded, nor did I burst into flames as my feet crossed the threshold.

As we entered, an expansive marble hallway lay before us. Ornate golden sconces lined the walls. The lanterns burned brightly, casting away shadows, as if we'd stepped out of the darkness and into the light. From the distance, music and laughter melded with the occasional moan of ecstasy. My belly twisted with uneasiness in response to the rapturous keens.

"Excellent. Even the guards are busy partaking of the celebration." Xavier heaved a sigh of relief.

We continued on, making our way through the abandoned hallway, drawing closer to the ruckus. Yet a high, piercing scream of pleasure echoed through the space, causing me to halt. I didn't want to bear witness to whatever debauchery occurred ahead of us.

Sensing my unease, he slowed. "I intend to avoid the main hall at all costs. You are my guest. Everyone here will believe I've brought you here to partake in. If we run across anyone, I'll inform them that I want to take you to a sequestered suite for privacy."

He strode forward, and hesitantly, I followed behind. Many statues of Aralia lined the ivory walls, each depicting her as light and love instead of the darkness she embodied. My nostrils flared. Though I'd given little thought to the goddess who'd cursed my kind, my bone-deep hatred boiled. It fueled my resolve.

Minutes later, as we neared the main hall, the clomping of heavy boots approaching us filled the air, piercing through the faint music and sensual moans.

My muscles tensed. I curled in on myself, making certain my face was completely hidden. Xavier slowed his pace. A rotund man stomped toward us, his stare trained on Xavier.

"Veronin! Just in time to stick your dick into a sweet, supple virgin. A whole crop came of age this month," the stranger barked.

"Wobbleton, I have a delicacy of my own to devour tonight. We were heading to a private suite." Xavier waved a dismissive gesture.

"Come now, Veronin. Keeping a beauty all for yourself." He stepped closer to Xavier, blocking the way.

My glance shifted from the floor to the gentleman. Though the covering on my face made it difficult to discern his exact features, his bulbous nose and balding head were easy enough to detect. His potbelly protruded through his coat and hung low over his too-tight trousers.

"Trying to make Delphine jealous? Heard she's been fucking some handsome young buck Lexington introduced to her. Is this little treasure to show the high disciple that you're uncaring of her new beau? Or is she a present to share?"

Wobbleton patted Xavier on the shoulder, then pushed past him and stood before me. He leaned forward, trying to see through my veil. His hot, rancid breath rolled over me, and I resisted the urge to gag. "Maybe we can swap. I brought a beautiful, buxom brunette with me. She's dancing right now. I'd happily trade you for your scrawny thing if you help me pass that tax bill you keep blocking."

Kill this idiot, my curse rattled in my skull. My hands curled into fists as I held the murderous intent at bay.

Xavier skirted between us, shielding me from Wobbleton's view. "This isn't the time for politics. It's a night for cavorting. Now excuse me..."

"Perhaps, I should have offered you my footman since your tastes vary as much as your mood." Wobbleton pushed forward, his rotund belly bouncing into Xavier.

My lips pursed. Every fiber of my being screamed to thwart the dimwit for the insult.

However, Xavier cocked his head and tutted. "Oh, Wobbleton. Don't be jealous that men and women come to my bed freely while the disciples who have to service you ply themselves with wine before having to endure your lack of finesse and tiny dick. But at least the romp is a quick one."

Xavier gripped my wrist and tugged me down the hall, away from the bloated buffoon.

"You think you're so superior to the rest of us, just because Delphine fucks you and occasionally listens to your ramblings. Mark my words, your favor with her is coming to an end," Wobbleton boomed down the space.

As we moved farther away from the man, something seemed to cling to Xavier. His posture hunched slightly. Despite my uncertainty about my father-in-law's motives, he had led us to the temple as promised.

"That man is a blathering idiot. After we save Silas, I'll come back and turn him to ash," I whispered. As the sentence left me, I meant the threat. My blight cackled, because the thought of dispatching the vile gentleman hadn't given me pause.

He huffed a sigh. "I don't care about Wobbleton. He's the lowest-ranking council member with no friends, a dwindling fortune, and a dying family line. It's what he said about Delphine. If she has a new bed partner, then someone else is influencing her. She's keeping them a mystery. If it had been an old acquaintance, Wobbleton would have called him out by name. I fear that much has changed in the weeks since—"

The large double doors roughly twenty feet from us swung open. The beating of drums and the musky aroma of debauchery poured through the corridor. Xavier's spine straightened and his grip tightened on my wrist. His head swiveled, searching for an escape route. There was none. Women donning the same sheer veils and sheath dresses danced into the hallways, as if our presence had summoned them. Their arms waved through the air. Their gossamer garb floated around them as if they were ethereal creatures, capturing the light from the flickering lanterns. Three women swayed down the hall while two others headed for us.

"Veronin." A tall, lithe woman approached. Her hips swayed to the rhythmic beat echoing from the chamber ahead. "You made it home. Delphine will be so pleased."

Her movements flowed like the river, her body swaying with the melody, but a tension entered her smooth motions as her attention lingered on me. Xavier stepped between us, blocking me from view.

"Ah, and you brought a guest. Is this why you keep leaving for Daviel? To entertain a pretty little thing? The high disciple has sanctioned your cavorting, but I doubt she'll approve of a mistress. I wouldn't overplay your hand." She leaned forward. A sharp nose poked through the veil and her wine-laden breath washed over us. "Or maybe she'll relish making your whore watch while you fuck Delphine. Come. Let's see how this game unfolds." She intertwined their fingers and tugged him into the fray.

His grip on me tightened as we were yanked off course and into the den of iniquity that he'd promised we'd avoid.

My back tensed as a wave of moans melded with music and accosted my senses. A space twice the size of the ballroom in Belmont Manor stretched before us. Oversized beds with sheer curtains lined the path leading to a dais. On the mattresses, people delved into each other's bodies in a tangle of limbs. My mind registered a glimpse of what unfolded. A woman sucked a bloated man's cock while a gray-haired bloke settled at her rear. She didn't flinch when he barreled into her from behind. My glance shifted away, taking in three women pleasuring an elderly man, writhing over him as if he were a king rather than a wrinkled dolt. The partnering sprawled throughout the ballroom in groups or pairs of every kind.

A dais overlooked the scene. A woman sat upon a golden throne, watching over the fornicators. Her black hair spilled over her shoulders in waves, hiding shapely breasts barely covered by the ornate sheer white gown she bore. She donned an intricate crown of ivory. Though I'd never met her, there was no denying that this regal lady was Delphine, the high disciple.

My hands balled into fists, and my curse coiled in my belly, a serpent ready to strike. She had caused so much despair as the leader of the Aralians. I'd been imprisoned on her orders for most of my life. She'd been the upholder of the lie that Aralia was the goddess of light, when in truth, she was pure darkness. She'd sanctioned my engagement to Theo and had sent her disciples to capture me when I'd escaped my fate. Now she wanted me dead for the murder of her sistren in Daviel.

The music crescendoed as the disciple guided us to the steps leading up to the throne. My eyes settled on the crowned woman. The drumbeat intensified, matching my racing heart. High-pitched keening and the slapping of skin upon skin synced with the clipping of Xavier's heels, as if their climaxes were in unison with this tense moment. The moment when I'd confront the true villain of my story.

As we halted at the base of the steps, Delphine straightened in her seat. Her hand wrapped around the onyx staff that leaned against her side. She lifted it and then slammed it down with such force I thought the marble might crack.

Instantly, silence stretched over the once chaotic room. Soft pants replaced the once rapturous moans. Then the clatter of knees hitting the floor behind me echoed. Xavier yanked me down, and I knelt before this false prophet.

Her onyx irises, dark as the pits of night, drank in Xavier as if he were a morsel. A smirk tilted the corner of her blood-red lips, which highlighted her pale skin. Then her glare settled on me. Her regal nose twitched in disgust. Had she truly believed that he kept running off to Daviel to cavort with a mistress? Had he captivated Delphine so deeply that her jealousy hid the truth of his actions?

"Xavier, you've returned for the full moon celebration." Her metal-tipped fingernails clicked against the gilded armrest, as if she were bored. "I grew so tired of waiting for you, dear pet, that I had to occupy my nights with a new paramour. He's quite the charmer."

Xavier's back tensed and the jacket he wore strained, but his stare stayed fixed on the ground. "If someone else has brought you pleasure, then I should be grateful. Yet knowing another has touched you causes my blood to boil. To think, I ventured all the way to the northern edge of your realm to procure you a gift."

My stomach dropped. My pulse climbed. Had Xavier been lying? Had his plan been to deliver me to the high disciple under the guise of aiding Silas and me? My curse bubbled to the surface, ready to kill this entire temple to escape and save Silas.

"A present?" she crooned.

"Yes, a new servant." He squeezed my wrist in reassurance. "That is why I kept venturing to Daviel. I've been working on collecting a debt. I lent a farmer a large sum of money, and this is his widow. He perished a few months ago, leaving nothing but a few sheep, a worn-down home, and this skilled seamstress. To pay off her family's account, she agreed to a life of servitude. So she is a gift to you, my dearest disciple. What interest would I have in anyone, when divine beauty lies before me?" He released my hand, then pressed his forehead against the marble step.

Her pupils widened, and her smile shifted to a feral smirk. "So that is why you kept leaving Hallowhaven. How foolish of me to have believed you were securing a mistress instead of a present for me."

She leaned back on her throne and spread her legs apart. She licked her lips as her focus settled in our direction. "Prove to me she's not your paramour. Crawl to me."

My gut twisted at the game she was playing. Her gaze didn't leave Xavier. She cocked an eyebrow and trailed her hand over her heavy breasts, toward her flat belly, and then along her thighs, where the fabric split open.

He didn't hesitate as he crawled up the steps, a dog to his master. His eyes locked on Delphine, like a tiger about to pounce upon its prey. As he reached her, his thumb skimmed her ankle. Not wanting to witness the sensual act that would likely unfold before me, I dipped my chin and studied the subtle swirl in the marble floor.

Crack.

My focus shifted to the direction of the sound.

Her knuckles blanched against the stem of the scepter. "If you are not his mistress, then you should have no qualms about watching him devour me. Or did he bring you here to torment me? To force me to watch him fuck you?"

My posture squared, and I tilted my jaw, lining up my sight with the throne.

Her sharp metal nails dug into his scalp, and she pushed his face into her core. "Savor me, pet."

Without hesitation, he shifted the fabric from her thighs. I forced myself not to wince as he devoured her in front of us all. She draped her legs over his shoulders, allowing him better access.

Unable to watch, I screwed my eyes shut. However, I couldn't block out the keening noises emanating from her. My gut soured with each horrific minute that passed. Her breathing heightened, echoing through the tense silence. Finally, after dreadfully long moments, a moan curled through the air, punctuating her release. When I finally took in the stage again, she gazed at him with pupils blown. Her red lips parted. Yet she still had his hair within her grasp, his face now tipped up to hers.

My fists clenched. My jaw ticked. She was testing not only his loyalty but mine. The blight screamed for me to kill her in the vulnerable position, while her mind was hazy with lust. Hadn't she caused so much suffering? She'd been the catalyst for Xavier's abandonment of Silas, the person who'd ordered all the cursed to be locked within their rooms like prisoners. And she'd forced Xavier into these games. My curse hissed to strike, but to my relief, it valued saving our mate over murdering the wretch.

Her once heightened breathing smoothed. She slid her fingers from his hair and to his chin. "I enjoy her watching. Take her to my chambers, have her bathed and prepared for the evening. She'll be our audience. You are fortunate that your mouth is far more skilled than my other bedfellow, or I'd kill the girl on the spot just to prove a point."

A deep, throaty laugh bellowed from him. "Kill her." His tongue flicked out and licked the metal nail. "Kill the entire room, and I'll fuck you on their corpses if it brings you plea-sure."

A flush crawled over her milky skin, and she drank Xavier in as if he were the most magnificent person. "Hmm, that sounds tempting, but who would entertain my guests and who would run Hallowhaven for me?" She cackled. "Very well. Continue the celebration."

As if on cue, the moaning reverberated again, far louder than before. Had the voyeurs become further aroused by the act they'd witnessed moments prior? Before I could further assess the situation, Delphine clapped once, and two disciples in armor stepped out from behind the dais. My stomach sank, but Xavier appeared unfazed, giving me an inkling of hope.

"Escort them to my chambers. Tell Zephira that Xavier's arrived home, and I'll be entertaining him and our guest this evening." The high disciple flicked a wrist, dismissing us.

CHAPTER 33

ARIANNA

OUR STEPS ECHOED THROUGH the long passageway as two escorts flanked us. Fortunately, their scabbards were sheathed at their sides, and they didn't carry shields. However, their onyx armor gleamed in the candlelight flickering from the white halls as if they were dark knights in this ivory palace. Xavier smoothed a hand through his hair, giving off an air of nonchalance, as if the act the high disciple had forced him to partake in was nothing of note.

"Tell me about this new paramour who's occupied Delphine's bed. How long have they been intimate?" he whispered to the guard with short-cropped brunette locks.

A devious smile crested across the escort's hardened countenance. "Jealous? You know Delphine favors those who worship her, and while you were off gallivanting in Daviel, collecting this worthless woman for the high disciple, you left her bed open. Lexington had an excellent candidate lined up. He's younger than you and quite handsome. Plus, he's able to provide her with something you haven't."

"And what is that?" He cocked his head, causing his long locks to shift.

"His undivided attention. Apparently, he is a rake, though he is now fully committed to Delphine. I'm sure she'll introduce you when the time is right. To your fortune, she sent him on a little errand. But you're clever. You'll find a way to regain her favor." She shifted her focus forward, ending the conversation between them.

Moments later, we stood in front of large double doors with a pair of armored sentries flanking the archway. The older, whose gray hair twisted into a bun, snarled. However, the younger smiled, and warmth radiated through her cherub features.

"You're home." The younger lady beamed. The graying woman beside her rolled her eyes.

"Well, we'll leave them in your care. Delphine will arrive shortly." Our chatty escort relayed the information to our new overseers.

The head guard nodded, then unlatched a ring of keys secured to her waist. She slid it into the lock and clicked it open. Without awaiting an invitation, Xavier entered Delphine's quarters, and I followed.

I froze, overwhelmed by the sprawling bedroom three times the size of my suite. Floor-to-ceiling windows opened to a garden where, despite the chill of winter, golden flowers bloomed, like those at Yulia's home. The full moon glowed, highlighting the swirling amber- and cream-patterned marble tile. A bed large enough for six to sleep in lay before me with gossamer curtains hanging around the monstrous mattress. To my right sat a shelf that reached the rafters, brimming with masks, all staring at me as if they were bearing witness to my trespass. A shudder slithered over my skin, and I shifted my attention to the left, where an archway led into a parlor. Along the wall across from the fireplace, bottles of liquor were stored. Just beyond lay doors likely leading to more rooms.

Ignoring me, Xavier beelined for the display of spirits. His fingers skimmed over the labels. He settled on a dark liquor. He plucked it off the shelf, flipped the top off, and took a long swig. He gargled the liquid, then swallowed it with an audible gulp. He clutched the bottle, causing his knuckles to blanch. The smooth persona he'd borne through the ordeal burned away, overtaken by anger.

Slowly, I walked into the sitting area but remained several feet from him. "Are you all right?"

"I'm fine. I..." He took another swig. "This complicates things. I had my sights set on the keys that the old hag Helga holds in the infirmary. She often over imbibes and usually slips into a deep sleep before midnight. We should have gone through the kitchens." He dragged a hand along his face. "But if I had been spotted, it would have drawn too much attention. Why would a high council member enter through there?" He pressed the decanter against his forehead, as if he were playing a game of chess and couldn't quite figure out his next move. "No. We made the right choice. We just need to adapt."

He corked the liquor and then shoved it onto the shelf. "The good news is the chief guard also possesses one of the four keys."

He began pacing down the carpet runner, as if the motion could provide him with the needed plan for escape.

"You're so similar to Silas, milling about while you try to think." My stomach sank at the mention of my love. His faint whisper of life beat between us, a warning that time was limited. "Is there another way out of here?"

"Maybe..." Something flashed in his eyes, as if a plan were taking root.

He strode past me and to the door. His fist rapped on the wood. "Helene, I need your assistance. This damned widow is a pest and refuses to bathe. Now, I wouldn't dare force her, but maybe you could help me. I'll make it worth your while. Besides, I've been dreaming of the taste of your lovely mouth. Please." He scratched against the oak frame, akin to a puppy begging to play.

To my surprise, the latch unlocked. I expected the younger woman who'd blushed to step over the threshold; instead, the older graying lady entered.

"She'll punish me severely for coming into her quarters, but I enjoyed the last time we snuck into her suite." Helene smiled.

Her gaze locked on mine, and her features hardened. She stepped past Xavier, for me. "And you should be grateful that...ouch."

A sudden realization of betrayal flickered across her expression. She swayed. Xavier wrapped his arms around her, catching her before she flopped onto the floor. A tranquilizer dart stuck out of her neck. He plucked it from her flesh and pocketed it. Slowly, he unlatched the keys from her belt, then nodded toward the exit. He crossed the threshold, leaving me waiting in the wings.

"Helene, I swear we are going to get—Xavier, what are you…" The younger sentry's voice trailed off.

A heartbeat later, he returned and strode to the wall of liquor. He plucked a pair of half-filled bottles and rushed out of the suite. "Bring her here."

With a huff, I leaned over, grabbed Helene's legs, and dragged her to the entrance. He propped the women like dolls, creating a scene of two sentinels who had become drunk on spirits and passed out. Then he closed the door.

"Come on, let's go. We've already wasted too much time." He seized my arm and pulled me through the passageway.

Minutes later, perspiration dotted my forehead, causing my veil to stick to my skin. My pulse raced as we rushed through the ornate hallway that gave way to another dimly lit hall. The once-large doors shifted to singular whitewashed wooden ones. My brow wrinkled at the diminishing splendor.

"Past the orphans' barracks, then down the…*Oof*"

My body halted as Xavier stepped back from a red-faced Wobbleton. Unlike before, the man was not alone. His meaty mitt dug into the arm of a girl younger than Naomi. A girl who didn't seem past her majority. Tears poured down her apple cheeks, and her blond hair popped out of her braid.

"What are you gawking at, Veronin? Can't I enjoy a disciple that's not currently on the menu?" Wobbleton possessed the same vicious sneer Mr. Terrell had borne before attempting to rape me.

Fury boiled in my belly.

"Help me, please." The adolescent sobbed.

"Shut up," Wobbleton sneered at her.

Flashes of memories of Mr. Terrell and Theo Terrell's rough handling of me pushed forward. Hadn't I been rescued from those encounters once by Silas, then Naomi, and again when my love's curse flooded our bond, toppling the wards within the room? I knew the fate that lay before her if Xavier and I walked away. My blood boiled with rage. But the blight didn't haze my mind; instead, an understanding crystallized. Martha's words echoed through my soul. *We are all monsters, dear. Each and every one of us. No one is blameless in this world.*

"Pretend you didn't see me, Veronin. I'll pass whatever tax bill you'd like at the next meeting. I promise." Wobbleton tugged the girl's arm.

Her cries intensified. Unable to stand by and watch this injustice unfold, I called upon my darkness. It surged through me, fueling my motions. My body pounced on the rotund man. He gasped. His grip on the girl loosened, and she fell by the wayside. I landed on top of him, with my hands clutched around his throat. His fingers ripped at my veil, tugging it free and revealing my face.

"You." He wheezed as my thumbs constricted his windpipe. "You are..."

"The harbinger of your death," I snarled.

The scent of burning flesh wafted through the air. His features contorted with terror. He attempted to scream, but no sound emitted. Power surged from my fingertips through him until he burst into a plume of ash.

The girl panted. Her eyes widened like saucers as she drank me in. Suddenly, she bolted to standing and sprinted down the corridor toward Delphine's suites. Xavier plucked a dart from his pocket and sent it sailing, but she turned the corner, and the paralytic missed her by a hair.

"Damn it. She's going to report us." He squeezed the bridge of his nose. "I should go after her. Why didn't you let them pass?"

I stood and ripped the tattered veil from my head. To my surprise, not an inkling of guilt flickered. Righteous indignation fueled my resolve. "I couldn't let him rape her. I couldn't allow her to suffer."

Understanding washed over his features. "Fine. Let's hope your heroics won't be the death of us."

CHAPTER 34

ARIANNA

THE LIGHTING IN THIS desolate hallway dimmed, casting shadows over the cold stone corridor. We stood before a metal door with Aralian symbols etched into the frame. My brow knitted as I studied the threshold. Apprehension coiled in my belly, yet this place held the remedy that would save my love.

Danger, the blight hissed, causing my blood to run cold.

Unaware of my looming dread, Xavier strode forward, inserted the key into the lock, and pushed the heavy door open.

"Stay here." He lifted a hand, halting me.

He disappeared into the darkness. I considered his warning, yet the girl I'd assisted minutes prior may have already alerted the guards of our escape. Instead of standing here like a sitting duck, I entered the eerie place.

No lanterns illuminated the dim space. Yet the walls pulsed with a brilliant golden light, like a heartbeat. Within the onyx-lined stonework lay Aralian symbols, where the bright beams shot through. I walked deeper into the chamber, but a sudden weakness seized me, similar to my spelled room at the farmhouse.

I took a tentative step. I swayed, and my shoulder pressed against the wall. Pain radiated through the joint, as if my flesh had melted into the slate. A sharp inhale expanded through my tightening lungs.

"What's happening to me?" Heaviness coated my perception, and sleep beckoned me.

"It will only be a minute. I..." Panic crossed his expression. He rushed for me and ripped me from the onyx-plated stone. "Touch nothing. This place..." He shook his head.

His features tightened, and the heaviness in my skull made it difficult to form coherent thoughts. My legs moved as if pulled through muck. Sweat beaded on my forehead. Blood oozed from my nostrils.

"Xavier?" I cried out. My blight curled internally as if it could hide from this horrific pressure. "What's happening?"

"Gods damn it. Why did you enter? The annex may be draining you. We'd better hurry." He dragged me until we reached a shelf carved into the slate.

"Blasts. There are usually a dozen vials." He snarled as he stared at the nearly empty ledge. A lone vial glowed in the dimly lit space. The crystalline liquid sparkled.

"At least there is one left, but..." His gaze drifted from the remedy to me.

"It's for Silas." I gave a watery smile. Given this horrific ache in my muscles, I feared the wasting sickness was taking hold, and I'd need a dose of the elixir sooner rather than later. Yet, after he'd drugged the guards and I'd killed Wobbleton, the likelihood of being able to set foot into the temple undetected was improbable.

He nodded, but his silence acknowledged the truth. That to save Silas, I'd likely have to die. Luckily, Xavier's love for Silas overrode any desire to protect me. He pocketed the elixir and lugged me to the exit.

As I stepped, my knees weakened. I swayed and pushed against his shoulder. All the strength fizzled out of me. I gasped for air. The beating of the bond between Silas and me slowed. Was he dying? My blight tugged against the connection, holding it in place. He was still alive, but barely.

Securing Silas to this mortal coil caused a cough to rattle through my chest. Blood spurted from my lips, coating the floor. My legs gave out. I toppled forward. Before my skull smacked against the stone, Xavier swooped down, halting my fall. He lifted me in his arms, carrying me through the space that beat in sync with my heart. My blight hissed at the menacing stones surrounding me.

"The wasting sickness has horrific timing," I wheezed.

His brow pinched. "I don't think you've contracted the illness yet. There is something horrible about this place I've kept secret. I feared if I revealed the truth about the elixir of life, Silas wouldn't partake of the remedy."

I blinked; the edges of the world became hazy.

He didn't speak, but the set of his jaw caused my stomach to plummet. What was he hiding? Despite my curiosity, my eyelids grew heavy. I wanted to pry, but it took all my strength to remain conscious. My head swam as we exited the annex and went down the hall. As we crested farther from the room, my energy returned, akin to a wilting flower given water.

But he didn't lower me. Instead, he strode onward, his focus fixed ahead. "There is much you don't understand." He swallowed, and his Adam's apple bobbed. "You see, the wards the blighted live under are a sacred word binding, tied to the Lacrima that lines those walls. Every room, mask, and warded seal is connected to that annex. It is where the stolen energy from the blighted is stored."

My pulse rose. Unaware of my building horror, he continued. "Aralia cursed the bloodlines of those who aided Cassius. But Cassius anointed those like you to control your darkness. A blessing from the god of light is powerful."

A shiver crawled down my spine. A desperate need to run from him sparked internally, but my legs were weak. "I don't understand."

His lips flattened into a tight line. "The cursed are like Yulia; both have received blessings from Cassius. Yulia was granted immortality. However, the potency of the blessing can only be housed in her body. That is why anyone who drinks of her flower tonic will surge with strength but die shortly after. It's why her flowers bloom in the temple gardens from experiments done to her before she went into hiding."

My stomach twisted, and bile crawled up my throat. "But the elixir of life."

He stopped and lowered me to my feet. I leaned against the wall. He placed his hands on my shoulders, as if to keep me from tumbling over. "It's made from the lifeblood of the cursed. The wards weren't just meant to steal the dark power for the Aralians' weapons; the sacred word binding also drained your life force. Filtered through that Lacrima, it is palatable for any to imbibe. It's like drinking divine light, restoring a person as if Cassius himself had blessed them. The blighted's lifeblood is the fountain of youth."

My knees buckled. My mouth watered. I feared I would vomit.

"I'm sorry. I didn't—"

Boots clomped in the distance, drawing near. His head swiveled about.

"Shit, patrols." He grabbed my wrist and tugged me toward an unlocked door a few meters away. He pushed us into the closet. Our backs pressed against a shelf of fresh linens. I blinked in the darkness, and the curse surged forward, fueling my vision. I'd anticipated the same bone-weary sensation to crest through me, but the farther I was from that horrid annex, the better I felt.

I withheld a bubbling scream because of what Xavier had revealed. However, with a patrol on our heels and a remedy in his pocket for Silas, my focus remained on escaping this temple. With my decision made, the blight shifted from strengthening my vision to my hearing. The murmured voices just beyond this small linen closet melding with the clicking of boots became clear as day.

"Helene and Cora would never imbibe while on guard. Now Xavier, the widow, and the keys are missing. What's that wily fox up to?" a woman spat from the hallway near our hiding spot.

"Xavier's days as Delphine's favorite are numbered, especially after this little escapade. First, he promises he'll find Arianna Park, then he sends two platoons to Seaside. They've recently returned and found no trace of her. Delphine's paramour swears she's in Presspin. But I guess we'll have to wait and see who's correct. Besides, I think Xavier is far more handsome than her new beau," another said.

"He is striking, and I partnered with him a year ago at a full moon festival. Goddess above, he is quite skilled. I understand why Delphine turns a blind eye to his antics," the original voice chimed in.

My heart hammered. Their boots stopped at the linen closet. My glance shifted to Xavier, who'd fetched a dagger and was standing at the ready. Perhaps the patrol would slip past us, but I feared they were on the hunt. Apparently, no one had been fooled by the guards Xavier had drugged by Delphine's suites.

My hand lifted, and darkness gathered in my palm. I drew a steadying breath. The knob jiggled, then it yanked open. The pair of disciples gawked in shock, but before they could interject, energy pulsed from me and through their skulls. Xavier lurched, grabbing the patrolwoman closest to him before she clattered to the ground. My body lunged, gripping the other's hands an inch before she fell.

We hauled the women into the closet, and I observed their armor. My brow furrowed, and for a moment I contemplated wearing their garb to sneak away.

Sensing my thoughts, he rested a hand on my shoulder. "No. We can't risk it. You nearly fainted in the onyx chamber. Besides, look at the markings." He pointed at the almost imperceptible symbols etched in the plating. "They are tied to the weapons and the Lacrima with sacred word binding. It's best we leave them here."

I blew out a frustrated breath, wishing for additional cover, but opened the door. To our relief, the passageway was empty. Perhaps the patrols were broken into pairs searching for us.

"Come on, this way." He gestured to the primary hallway.

However, as we peered around the corridor, a half dozen women were lingering in the hall between the orphan dormitory and the annex.

He scanned about, but from the panic dampening his usually aloof countenance, there was no other exit. He took a few steps backward, muttering to himself, as if he could conjure an escape route. I inched forward. The soft pattering of footsteps echoed, approaching the huddled patrol.

My brow pinched as the girl I'd rescued came into view. My nose wrinkled. Xavier was right; she must have reported us.

However, studying the scene, I realized she wasn't with the patrolwomen. Instead, she lingered at the threshold of a barracks room. Her gaze flicked to the gaggle of guards, then stretched toward me. A jolt of panic sizzled along my spine as we locked eyes, and I lurched behind the corner.

"I know where Xavier is. I saw him," a girlish voice said, loud enough for even Xavier to hear. He leaned closer.

My pulse skittered. We should have killed her. I'd made the wrong choice again. Darkness crackled along my fingertips, preparing me for a fight, but before I surged forward, the girl spoke again.

"He went that way, near the main hall." She pointed in the opposite direction.

I gaped. My power fizzled away. Xavier muttered to himself. Shockingly, the primary sentinel nodded, and the patrolwomen left. My racing heart slowed as silence washed over the space.

"You can come out. You're safe." Soft footsteps approached.

She rounded the corner and stood before us. Xavier pushed his hand into his pocket, likely to grab a tranquilizer dart, but I grabbed his wrist, halting him.

"You killed Wobbleton before he could claim me, and I owe you a debt now." Red rings rimmed her brown eyes, and a frown twisted her lips. Her gaze trailed my barely clothed body. "Besides. I know who you are. I want to help you escape this wretched place."

I sucked in a breath at the revelation. Why hadn't she turned me in? She could have been granted a fortune for my capture.

She untied the white cloak from her shoulders and draped it over my nearly nude form, then tugged the hood over my head. She took my hand.

"Don't worry, you can trust me. I hate the temple, and if the rumors are true, you can save us all." Her expression softened. Though she'd been raised by my enemy, something in her brown gaze caused me to believe her.

"We shouldn't trust her. This could be a trap." Xavier worked his jaw.

"What else should we do? They are likely at the main entrance, waiting for us. Besides, she could have turned us in twice already," I said.

"We must hurry. Once they realize you're not in the main hallway, they will come back." The girl tugged my hand.

Resigned, Xavier's shoulders slumped. He nodded. With the decision made, she tugged me back in the direction of the annex.

A wave of panic consumed me. If I had to go through the onyx-laced room, I might die. To my relief, we passed the Lacrima-lined space. At the tee in the corridor, she veered right, down an even more desolate path.

Minutes passed as we weaved through more cramped and abandoned hallways, as if we were in a maze.

"We need to escape, not venture deeper into the temple," Xavier snapped.

"Typical man. You think you know everything, but you don't." She peered over her shoulder. Her glare burned. Had the situation not been dire, I may have found the gesture funny.

Finally, after weaving through what seemed to be an endless labyrinth, we stopped at a dead end. He huffed an exasperated breath. But before he could voice his frustration, she pressed her hands on an odd-shaped rock, and a hidden door slid open, revealing a spiraling staircase.

"Quickly." She grabbed a lantern from the hook and gestured for us to enter.

Without hesitation, we strode forward. Her fingers grazed along the inner wall, and the slate slammed shut.

"Where are we?" I followed her down the narrow stone stairs that seemed to shrink with each step.

She smiled. "An old passage, long forgotten. My best friend and I..." Her face fell. "She's gone, so it's my secret place now. It's the abandoned northern gardens. It's unattended. Not even the herbalists enter. Sometimes trash is heaped in the area, but I've found many discarded treasures with Raya." She gulped.

"Sounds lovely," he drawled.

Her eyes slid to him and flattened to slits. "You are lucky you are with her. If not, I would have happily let the guards find you and I wouldn't have flinched when Delphine beat you half to death. But she saved me like an avenging angel. When she protected me, I knew the rumors were true. That Arianna Park would bring the temple to its knees and free us from Delphine."

My brow knitted. "You don't believe that I'm a murdering monster?"

Her features softened. "Of course. But I won't speak of the gossip with him around." She jutted her chin at Xavier. "He might sell me out, or worse, you, to Delphine."

I paused, my tone gentle. "Xavier is a friend and has assisted me over the past few days." I gestured to him.

She humphed, unimpressed by the man. "He was friends with that cow Wobbleton. Do you know what they do at the full moon celebrations? They sell off our chastity when we reach our majority. But Wobbleton doesn't wait. He slips into the barracks during the festivals and takes what he desires before we are even ripe for the picking. Well, he did." She shuddered. "That's what happened to Raya. He raped her thrice, and when she spoke of it to the headmistress, Delphine beat her to death."

I glanced at Xavier. His face blanched. He'd tried to rescue disciples from this temple, but there was much he wasn't privy to. Perhaps he had overestimated the information he gleaned from his rendezvous with Delphine.

I wanted to broach the topic further, but with the slippery steps, I focused my attention on the path ahead. Many minutes later, we reached the base of the staircase. She pushed a brick on the wall, and it skidded open. A gust of cold air washed over me. Moonlight illuminated through the dark sky and over the barren garden.

"The main road is to the left. But you shouldn't go that way. Head into the old grounds. Roughly a hundred meters from here is a broken panel in the fencing; it leads straight to the carriages." She gestured toward the desolate grove with overgrown weeds and dead trees.

"Thank you for your assistance..." I paused, waiting for her to give a name.

A flicker of a smirk tipped her lips. "Kamy. At your service, harbinger of death."

CHAPTER 35

Arianna

Thump…thump…thump…

The golden thread between Silas and me slowed, as if the rhythmic beats were struggling to remain. The horses' clomping hooves echoed along the abandoned street, cantering back to my withering beloved. Exhausted, I leaned against the carriage's plush cushion. Despite having escaped the temple unharmed, my belly twisted with each passing second. A shudder coursed down my spine, a mix of the panic from nearly being caught and the many blocks we needed to traverse to get to my love with the antidote.

As if sensing my apprehension, a bedraggled Xavier plucked the vial from his pocket and placed the elixir of life into my palm. "Here. Take it."

Overwhelmed by what had occurred this evening and Silas's waning vitality, I'd been too flabbergasted to focus. Yet as the liquid shimmered in my grasp, I couldn't help but wonder how many of my kind had died to provide this remedy. Moreso, how many in Delphine's inner circle had imbibed in this tonic for eternal youth? My jaw clenched. My unruly blight churned internally, feeding off my panic over Silas's well-being and my righteous indignation over the many cursed who'd perished to create this.

"You should have told us about the elixir's origins," I said, cutting through the tense silence.

"Would you have trekked to Hallowhaven for a remedy created from the blighteds' lifeblood?" His gaze dragged from the ceiling to mine, but no guilt lay in its depths, only a steely determination.

"Yet you've taken this for decades? Don't you see how Silas has suffered? How the cursed have suffered?" My nostrils flared. How could he want to protect his blighted son but imbibe of a tonic derived from those like the child he'd hidden? How could he speak of helping an opposition against the Aralians when he sipped the stolen lifeblood?

"I had no desire to drink of the elixir once I discovered its origins. But if I had stopped, my influence over Delphine would have been eliminated. Gods damn it." His fist balled and slammed against the window ledge. "I spent a few weeks in Daviel, and look what has happened. I can't protect my children unless I'm in her inner circle. If she finds them." His head shook, and despair coated his features. "They'll be in danger, and all my sacrifices, my suffering will have been for nothing."

My curse bubbled, wanting to strike a killing blow for the life force stolen from my predecessors. But with the cure in hand and the carriage inching closer to my love, I couldn't let myself be undone by my emotions. Not until Silas was safe. I sucked my teeth. "When he rises, it is your responsibility to inform him of the truth of what has transpired. I won't allow him to perish, but it is you who dragged us to Hallowhaven, and you who shall suffer his wrath."

"I'll happily take on the brunt of his fury. But let's stop pretending you are as morally pure as you portray. Silas would refuse this antidote, and you know it. Yet you'll pour this remedy down his throat even though it's stolen vitality." Xavier's jaw ticked. He leaned forward, his knee knocked mine from across the cramped conveyance. "Besides, you murdered Wobbleton in cold blood without a second glance. You're as Machiavellian as I am."

In the past, the insult would have stung, but it didn't. Now, I teetered between who I once was and who I was always meant to become. Since the woods, the curse had become a partner instead of something I needed to separate from. With each fight, I slipped closer to the monster everyone believed me to be.

"You're right. I would burn this world for Silas and bathe in its ashes if it meant saving him. Perhaps House Veronin's motto should be whatever it takes to save those we love." I crossed my arms over my chest.

"I'll have a new crest created in the morning." He flicked a wrist.

Silence settled over us, in this mutual acceptance that we were cut from the same cloth, willing to sacrifice the greater good for those we cherished.

Thump...thump...thump...

An internal alarm sounded, cutting through the fleeting moment. My focus shifted to the slow pulsing bond unraveling between Silas and myself. My eyes closed, and I focused on the fraying connection, as if my will could make him hold on until I reached his side to give him the antidote.

The beating pulse slowed further, each reverberation taking far longer than the last. My brow furrowed, and my curse surged through me, as if it was grappling to keep him within this mortal coil.

"Arianna."

I blinked, taking in Xavier's concerned countenance.

"Your nose. You're bleeding."

Confused, I brushed my thumb under my nostril, withdrawing black ooze from it. "This isn't good."

My heart pounded, and my stomach plummeted. The cord between us fluttered in and out of existence. A cold sweat washed over me. "He's slipping away."

My throat burned. My shoulders shook. Would we make it?

"We're almost there." Xavier leaned forward and took my hand.

Grief settled over us like a heavy blanket as we focused on our joint love for Silas. The black blood from my fingers trailed over his skin, but he didn't flinch, as if he could keep Silas here with his sheer determination. Excruciatingly long minutes slipped past us as if they were coated in molasses. Finally, as the conveyance halted, Xavier released his grasp on my wrist.

Run! my blight shrieked.

I burst from the carriage, freeing myself before the footman could even dismount. My feet flew up the steps to the townhouse. I pushed through the unlocked door and veered right down the bland hallway.

Thump.

My legs burned, but I sprinted forward. The open doorway to the sick room came into view. I lurched through it.

Lazarus clutched my husband's hand; his attention drifted to me. His tightly knit brow softened. A rattle punctuated the quiet as Silas drew in a raspy wheeze. I ran to Silas, and Lazarus rose. His soft footsteps padded, but he didn't leave. Instead, he lingered near the threshold.

Thump.

Silas drew in a pained inhale. The skin on his neck pressed inward as if the motion could draw in more oxygen. The horrific gurgling noise emitting from him caused goose bumps to rise on my flesh. My hands shook as I withdrew the elixir from my pocket and unscrewed the cap. My fingers tilted his chin back and placed the vial to his chapped lips. The crystalline liquid rushed into his mouth, but droplets spilled from the creases. I clamped his jaw shut and tipped his head.

"Swallow it. Please. Please," I pleaded.

His throat bobbed slightly. When I removed my hands from his face, his lips parted, revealing he'd ingested the remedy.

I lowered my forehead to his. "We did it."

Boots clicked from behind me, drawing my focus to Xavier. As he stared at his son, the sorrow in his expression gave me pause. "Something's wrong. It should have worked instantly. His color should be changing, his skin plumping. I don't understand."

My husband sucked in a bone-rattling inhale. A shuddering exhale left him.

Why wasn't he healing? My eyes flew to him. His olive complexion didn't return, nor did the hollow of his cheeks fill. His once firm body remained withered in the tiny bed, tucked within the cream-colored quilt.

Seconds skittered by, but Silas remained eerily still.

My gut churned.

I trembled. No, this was a mistake. We'd come to Hallowhaven. I'd gone to the temple. I'd procured the elixir. We'd done everything right.

"Wake up." My palm rested on his clammy cheek. A shiver crawled along my spine at his cooling flesh.

Snap.

The fraying cord between us disappeared, like dust in the wind, leaving me with nothing to anchor him to. The blight shrieked through me. Power surged under my skin as the curse searched for the missing thread. A chill pierced through my soul, where a gaping hole now lived instead of Silas's presence.

My sanity shattered.

"No! You can't leave me. Not when we've come this far. Don't you dare." My fists thumped against his chest. He needed to breathe, then the cure would work. I had to get his heart to beat. My fist thumped over his rib cage harder with each thundering smack. "No, No. No! No! No!"

A knot hardened against my windpipe, choking me. Tears welled, blurring my vision. My shoulders burned from the compressions. Moments rushed past me, but I didn't yield. I had to save him. I must save him.

Thick arms wrapped around my waist and yanked me back. "Arianna, stop."

"No!" I pushed Lazarus away. "He's alive. He promised me we would return to Presspin together. He promised he would always come back to me."

"He's gone." Lazarus released me.

A shuddering sob came from Xavier near the foot of the bed. The smack of his knees onto the ground pierced through this horrific moment.

No. It couldn't be.

My shoulders shook as I finally looked at Silas. His rigid body didn't move. No whisper of breath pressed through him. His amber eyes stared at the ceiling, unblinking. His chest remained still. Even his pallor began shifting to that of a corpse. A wordless shriek crawled from my throat.

Silas. Was. Dead.

A watery gasp curled through my lungs, as if grief drowned me. My limbs turned heavy as stone. I crashed onto the floor. A guttural wail so devastating that it would make the coldest man weep unleashed from me. My fingernails dug into the hardwood. Ash marked my descent as I crawled to the bed. The scent of sizzling wood and fabric filled the air as I dragged my body upright to look upon my beloved. A haze coated the world. The echoing of Xavier's cries itched at my consciousness, but I couldn't connect with reality. Not as I drank in the slope of Silas's nose, the curve of his lips, the warm amber of his now lifeless stare. He was my mate. My everything. He was gone.

"I failed you. I'm so sorry." My palm grazed his cheek, but all that remained was an icy chill that settled into the marrow of my bones. I pressed my forehead to his, and tears streamed down my face, coating us both in the inky tar that poured from my tear ducts.

Time twisted. Minutes or hours could have passed as I soaked in these final moments with him. The last seconds worth living.

At some point, boots clicked over the floorboards, returning my attention to reality.

"This, this isn't the elixir." Lazarus's shaking voice pierced through our shared sorrow. "I think it's poison."

"Poison?" I choked out.

I shuddered violently yet rose. My world tipped, as if it had fallen off its axis. I clutched the edge of the bedframe to hold myself upright.

Xavier shook. His broken face lifted and his gaze landed on Lazarus. My mind hitched. Had Xavier poisoned his own son? From the anguish etched on his features, I highly doubted it.

"No, it was in the annex. It was the only one; it looked exactly right...there's no way, unless..." Xavier inhaled sharply. "Delphine knew," he whimpered. "It's why no one patrolled the carriages."

Xavier gripped the edge of the mattress; he rose on shaky feet. His red-rimmed eyes blinked. "It was a trap. She knew. This was all a game to her."

Lazarus closed the distance between himself and Xavier. "They could have followed you here. We must retreat to the other safe house north of the slums."

Xavier's eyes stayed on Silas. He shook his head. Lazarus cupped Xavier's face, drawing his attention back to him. "He's gone, but your other children and the Opposition need you. We must go at once."

They spoke amongst themselves, but whatever plans they made melded into this sepia-hued nightmare. Each piece of the night fragmented. The discarded vial. Xavier's heartbroken expression. Silas's still form. The soft, smoldering fire in the hearth. The sickly scent that wafted through the air.

"Arianna," Lazarus shouted. The tone couldn't break through. It sounded as if he were underwater. "We must leave before it is too late."

"Too late," I whispered to myself.

I turned back, taking in my beloved. I'd failed to rescue him. Now he was gone.

Someone gripped my arm, but I shook them off. "No."

It's time, the blight hissed.

The simple statement from the curse caused the roiling anguish to halt, as if calming the tempest within me. It needn't explain. In the core of my soul, I knew what had to happen now.

I leaned forward and placed a kiss on my husband's icy forehead. "Wait for me. We promised to return to Presspin together or not at all."

I straightened. An eerie resolve coated me, as if the world crystalized. I turned toward the men, my tone oddly still despite the anguish in my heartbroken soul. "It's best you leave now. If any disciples come to this home, where my beloved lies, I'll kill them. Go."

Xavier opened his mouth to argue. A flash of power pulsed from me. The air pressurized, extinguishing the fire in the hearth. Lazarus, heeding my silent warning, tugged a limp Xavier toward the door.

"May Cassius be with you," Lazarus said as he closed the door behind them.

With my decision made, I plucked off my onyx ring and lowered it onto my love's still chest.

Together, the curse hissed.

"I'm ready for us to become one." I closed my eyes.

As if transported, I no longer dwelled in the room with my departed husband. Instead, I stood in the hallway of my inner world. The blight loomed in the black gown. Tar-hued tears covered her pale complexion. She pointed to the bolted door at the end of the corridor. A bone-deep knowing crested through me. Once I crossed the threshold, the curse and I would become something new. Unstoppable. Uncaring of the ramifications to the world that had caused me so much suffering, I padded across the chilly ground, passing by the numerous memories and moments that had formed me into the monster I was. As I reached the ominous entrance, I paused. The blight clasped my shoulder, urging me to unite with her.

"We'll kill them all. The Aralians will suffer for what they did to our mate." Her grasp tightened.

This madness must end. Tonight, I'd finally become the harbinger of destruction everyone assumed me to be. I reached for the handle, and it clicked open. An abyss lay within, so dense that it consumed light. My stomach twisted. I spun toward the curse and grabbed her hands.

She gave a determined smile. "Together."

We fell into the pitch black. For it was the day Arianna Belmont died, and something new arose.

I jolted into my body. Darkness encompassed me, like a beacon of righteous fury blazing in this secret hideaway. The floorboards beneath my sandaled feet splintered. Shards swirled around me, disintegrating in the eye of the storm where I stood. The blight no longer hissed in my skull, pressing for its destructive delights. Only silence remained, along with a surging power far more potent than I'd ever experienced. Oddly, my lips tipped into a smirk as I studied my balled fists. The anguish that had once sparked my curse now sizzled in my soul. Its wrath pulsed in my blood.

My gaze lowered to my beloved's corpse. Toward the man who'd sacrificed everything for me. A sacrifice I would return in kind. Tonight I'd burn the temple to ash for what they'd taken from me, and they would suffer as I had. My fingers grazed through his raven hair one last time. An inky tear rolled down my cheek.

"I'll see you soon, my love." I pressed a final kiss against his cold lips.

The dark aura around me flared. I stepped forward to seek my revenge upon the temple, but a creak along the hallway drew my attention. I cocked my head, catching on a whisper.

"The safe house is empty," a woman's voice said in a hushed tone.

Disciples. Had they been that close on our heels? No, from the icy touch of Silas's skin, a chunk of time had slipped past me. It seemed that the Aralians had arrived to secure this next piece of their trap. Had they hoped I'd be so bereft by my love's death that I'd simply go with them? No, I'd make them pay.

I closed my eyes, counting the beating hearts. One. Two. Three. Four. Five.

They paused at the sickroom's threshold. The knob jiggled. My body crouched into a fighting position. The door swung open.

A woman strode through the doorway, covered in onyx armor, with two soldiers flanking her rear. I surged forward, my speed tripling since my last fight in the woods.

The scene unfolded in an instant.

The leader arched her dagger toward me. She was too slow. I gripped the woman's helmet; a fog sizzled through the openings. Before she fell, I spun to the solider behind her, shooting black lightning through the eye slot. They crashed onto the floor like rag dolls in a heap. I leapt over them, careening toward a third. She swung her onyx blade. I dodged. My fingernails ripped off her shielded glove. Energy crackled across her limb and into her torso, fizzling her to ash. The weapon and empty armor clanked onto the ground.

Heavy footsteps ran in the opposite direction down the hall. I surged toward the fleeing intruder. I pounced on top of her; my hands gripped her helmet and twisted it. A pop sounded as her neck snapped. She toppled before me. One left.

With the carnage in my wake, I rose, then smoothed my palms over my gore-covered shift.

Clapping echoed through the vestibule. I followed the sound until I stood a few feet from a brunette woman in pristine white robes. She wasn't Delphine, but from her fine garb, she looked to be in power. Perhaps one of the Twelve Elite or at least someone who desired to be in that position.

"Arianna, how fortunate—"

Darkness sizzled through my fingers and pierced her skull. She collapsed in a heap on the floor. I'd grown tired of their diatribes.

I tiptoed toward the entrance, cracked the door open, and peeked out onto the street, certain a platoon waited for me. Oddly, a lone servant woman dressed in simple clothing held the reins to an unmarked carriage. Her stare remained straight ahead, studying the horses.

My brow knitted. Perhaps they'd assumed only Xavier was within this place. Yet Delphine's miscalculation was my fortune. I pivoted back to the foyer. I peered down at the dead disciple and her pristine garb. How fortunate that they'd come to seize me but delivered me the perfect disguise to infiltrate their temple again so I may exact my revenge.

CHAPTER 36

ARIANNA

THE CARRIAGE ROLLED TO a stop in front of a slate building a few blocks south of the Aralian temple. My tight knuckles loosened as I lowered the reins. The breeze blew, and the metal sign over the threshold creaked. The flicker of lamplight glowed against the etching. *Francis Key—Undertaker.* My stomach twisted as I dismounted from the landing. My booted feet clipped over the stone, the sound punctuating the night air. As I reached the entrance, my fist thumped against the wood, rapping violently.

Minutes skittered by, and impatience blossomed within me. But before I smote the Aralians for the pain they'd caused me, I had to make certain Xavier wouldn't return to the townhouse and that my love's body would be sent home to Presspin.

The door swung open, and a graying man leaned forward, his lips pulled in a frown. His bushy brows bunched. "Goddess above. It's nearly two in the..." his eyes widened like saucers as he took me in, dressed in Aralian white. His pallor paled, and he dipped his chin in reverence. "My apologies, disciple. How may I assist you?"

My nostrils flared at the instant respect. Had he seen my features beneath this hood, he'd be turning me in for the bounty reward plastered on every wall here instead of assisting me. Not that it mattered, since I'd be entering the temple of my own accord once this last act of care for my love was settled.

"A deceased man's in the carriage. Send for his next of kin, a distant cousin, Xavier Veronin, in the morning." I gestured to the unmarked conveyance behind me.

The undertaker strode past me, his black robe fluttering in the wind. He opened the door, revealing my departed love. The elderly chap didn't blanch at my deceased husband nor at the cold. Instead, a beat passed, then he pivoted to me, taking in my frail form swimming in the garbs.

His heavy forehead bunched, deepening the lines in his brow. "How did you get him in there?"

I clenched my jaw. I was in no mood for this banter, not when my revenge lay only blocks north. However, he was right to be concerned. Even with my increased strength, I'd struggled to tug Silas through the hall, using the quilt to pull his rigid frame down the wooden corridor. To my luck, the servant had been a dullard, fully believing I was the leader of the group when I exited the townhouse. She'd grumbled but had assisted me in getting him into the carriage. She'd reminded me of the undertaker who lived just a few streets away, where the Aralians deposited those they had murdered. I had considered allowing her to drive me here and even leave alive. But as I'd leapt onto the driver's landing, my hood had slipped, revealing my face, so I'd had no choice but to dispose of her.

A bell tolled in the distance, denoting the top of the hour. "I must go. Make certain you notify Xavier Veronin at first light."

The crypt keeper turned to speak, but I crept into the shadows, leaving my love's remains in his care.

With the task settled, my focus shifted to my ultimate goal—kill Delphine.

My pulse climbed as my boots pounded against the cobblestone path. I headed toward my destruction, knowing that I'd soon be joining my beloved in the Great Beyond.

A grand clock near an ancient monument backing the temple ticked in time with my heart. It read a quarter past two. My steps slowed as I approached the place where death waited for me. Moonlight crested over the pristine marble architecture, creating a beacon of white amongst the dark stone buildings surrounding it. Thick clouds loomed, darkening the night further as they blotted out the stars, casting the ivory monstrosity in shadows. My lungs expanded, taking in this final breath, knowing that once I set foot inside the massive doors, I'd never return. For a heartbeat, Naomi entered my thoughts; a gnawing ache pooled in my gut. But I ignored the sensation. Dwelling upon our broken relationship wouldn't stop me, for I had nothing left.

Anger boiled within me. Anger for everything these charlatans had stolen from me. My fingers itched to blast the doors to smithereens, to create a scene. However, causing a ruckus would only draw further attention. My body trembled with rage, but I wouldn't be undone as I'd been in the past. I took a steady breath, drawing in the icy winter air. As eerie calm washed over me, I adjusted the hood, making certain my features were covered, then traversed the steps. As I settled on the landing, the goddess statues stared down at me. A whisper of a smirk tugged on my lips, for this time, my presence would mar the cathedral completely.

My palm pushed against the large door; it creaked open. I crossed the threshold and searched for guards, but none were stationed. Were they fornicating, soaking in depravity and pleasure? My shoulders tensed. Had we stuck to the original plan, it likely would have worked, and Silas would be alive. No, Delphine had made certain that even if we'd procured the cure, whoever imbibed of it would have died from the poison laced within the tonic.

My hands curled into fists, then smoothed. Determination fueled my steps as I walked the long hall. The statues of the goddess served as sentinels, bearing witness to my trespass. Yet after many moments of striding in silence, foreboding settled in my belly. A few hours earlier, this place had been abuzz with revelers and patrols. Had Delphine assumed that paltry platoon would have captured Xavier and me?

Despite my misgivings, I continued on, yet as I skirted the main hall where the festivities once lay, my pace slowed. Music and moans no longer filled the air. Instead, the jangling of metal clicking against metal punctuated the quiet.

"Gods damn it," a voice grumbled, from where the celebration had been held.

My gaze drifted down the corridor where Delphine had cavorted, unaware that I'd entered her safe haven. I paused at this juncture as the rattling and curses intensified behind the cracked double doors. I should have continued on, but a sixth sense caused me to enter the massive hall.

My glance swept over the marble throne room. My brow knitted. The once lavish party had dispersed, and any debauchery within the space from hours prior had disappeared. Now, a lone bed sat in the center. Onyx pillars arched over the bedframe, and a gossamer curtain wafted over the mattress. Chained to the frame was a cloaked figure, their head cast down, keeping their features hidden. They waited on their knees, and their wrists were bound to either side of the stone bedposts with onyx chains. My pulse skittered. Who was this person? My boots clicked over the marble tile, causing them to frantically tug at their restraints.

"I swear to the gods, once I'm free from here, I will kill you, Delphine," the female prisoner shouted.

Her animosity for the high disciple fueled me. My brow furrowed. Whoever this stranger was, she wanted Delphine dead, making her my ally. Without hesitation, I sprinted toward the figure, determined to help her.

Quickly, I closed the distance between us. My hand brushed the gossamer curtain.

She lunged, but the restraints kept her from reaching me. Slowly, my fingers trailed over the dark hood and tugged it away, revealing a beautiful woman. Violet irises shone through thick lashes and highlighted her sepia skin.

Ebony ringlets bobbed as she shook her head. "Who the fuck are you? A desperate disciple trying to gain favor? Is this another of her damned games? She can torment me as much as she wants; I'll never become Aralia's vessel."

My mind reeled. Who was she? What was she talking about? Without time to delve further, darkness curled along my fingertips, then shot energy at the restrains. But they didn't break.

A sharp breath pulled through the woman. "You're her. The blighted they've been whispering about. Listen to me; you must leave before—"

"It's too late, Wren," another voice called from the dais.

Wren. The name pinged through my memory as I took in the sepia-skinned lady before me. Could this be Brielle's mate? I drank her in, registering the resemblance to the love Brielle had described. Realization dawned on me, fueling my resolve to release her further. She was cursed and could assist me in thwarting the disciples.

Frantically, I forced crackling energy into the shackles, but they remained intact.

"Those are warded. Not only do they resist your power, but they absorb it, making the binding even stronger," a voice crooned from behind me.

My spine went rigid as I registered the sultry lilt I'd heard this evening—Delphine.

"Run," Wren whispered.

But I couldn't. I'd come here to face my enemy head-on or die trying. However, as Wren held my stare, my taste for revenge dampened. Perhaps rescuing Wren would free me from one of my sins before I crossed into the Great Beyond. I'd watched one of Brielle's loves die because of my incompetence. My mate was dead, and there was no bringing Silas back. Maybe in freeing Wren, I could provide some solace for Brielle after failing Mateo. My desires pivoted. I would save this woman, then face the wicked Aralians.

"No, I'm going to unchain you. Then we'll slay every damn disciple here or die trying." My shoulders squared. I paced around the bed, searching for a way to free her.

The clicking of heels signaled that Delphine was descending the steps, the sound distracting me from unshackling Wren. My nose wrinkled as the high disciple came into focus. A white dress flowed about her, as if she were the goddess instead of its emissary. A smirk pulled at the corner of her ruby-red lips.

"I love it when a plan works out. Though you strayed a bit," her smooth voice crooned as I continued blasting energy at the shackles, trying to break the bindings so we could face Delphine together. The restraints didn't budge.

"I expected you to rush straight into danger to thwart me after I poisoned your husband, leaving Xavier unguarded, but given your attire, it seems you murdered my recovery team." She tutted. "Where's my little pet now? Hmm? Lying in wait to pounce?"

I remained silent, grateful I'd sent Xavier away and moved Silas's remains to the morgue. Wren tugged against the restraints. Her expression was pleading, urging me to flee. Yet I wouldn't run. Perhaps if I subdued Delphine, I could find a key to unlock Wren. She could escape, then I could bring the temple down. I withdrew from the bed and pivoted to the high disciple, who lingered many paces away. Amusement danced along her features, as if this truly were a game.

Power coursed through me. My senses heightened. I just had to strike a killing blow. My feet pressed against the stone, propelling me forward far faster than ever before. Darkness balled in my palm, then sizzled through the ether, careening for Delphine.

Her expression remained smooth. She held up a hand, splaying her onyx-tipped fingernails. The inky energy split into five pieces, each one absorbed into the jewelry that were weapons. The black rings on her fingers gleamed.

My jaw ticked. Delphine's warded pieces had absorbed the energy. This meant that a long-range attack wouldn't work. I needed to rely on the combat skills Peter had instilled.

"So reactive. You haven't even wondered why we're waiting for you, Arianna. Have you been so blinded by your husband's illness that you didn't consider why I wanted you?" She tutted.

Ignoring her questions, I charged, gathering darkness in my skin to fuel my blows. I lunged at her like a rabid animal. She spun out of my way with ease. Her smooth countenance showed no sign of distress. I pivoted on my heel, using the momentum to strike. Energy coursed along my fist as it arched toward her face. A millisecond before it made contact, she shifted, and my knuckles breezed past her skull. Yet my body continued forward because of the inertia. Her eyes locked with mine. She punched me in the gut. A horrific stinging crackled through my core and expanded through my limbs.

I curled in on myself. Black blood spewed from my mouth and splattered the ivory tiles. Before I could rise, her onyx-clad fingertips latched on to my scalp; she dragged my gaze to hers.

"Do you know what happens after drinking of elixir of life for over two centuries? You gain unspeakable strength and decades of skill to use it." She cocked her head, causing her long, inky locks to tumble over her shoulders.

Enraged by the power she'd stolen, I swung for her stomach, but she was too fast. Her other hand grasped my wrist, and a second wave of crackling bolts surged through me. Blood dripped from my nostrils.

"You are stronger than I expected but still green. From the blood oozing from your nose and mouth, I'd guess the wasting sickness has taken hold. But no matter. I can fix that." She squeezed my wrist harder; another wave of pain racked through my muscles.

My knees buckled.

Her grip tightened. "Guards, bring the restraints. We have a new guest."

"Damn it," Wren called out from the distance. The clank of her cuffs echoed through the quiet space.

Delphine's weaponized fingernails dug deeper into my scalp. My mind grew hazy, as if the shards were splintering my brain. My nostrils stung from the pain. The clipping of boots on the marble floor clattered through my aching skull. I blinked my heavy eyelids, trying to remain conscious. I didn't care about my life, but Wren would provide a sliver of a reason to continue on, at least until she was liberated.

The sharp sting anchored me to the present. Tears welled. I needed to escape her hold. Uncaring of the ache, my fingers within Delphine's grasp extended. If I could shoot a blast through her side. I could...

Snap.

I sucked in a cry as the bone cracked. My mouth watered. My lips pressed together, holding in a scream. A disciple approached and clasped onyx cuffs over my wrists. I gritted my teeth at the pressure of the binding against the throbbing joint.

Delphine released her tight hold on my scalp. Defeat coated me like a heavy cloak. My shoulders slumped and my eyes trailed along the floor. They'd kill me now for the massacre in Daviel. Though it ate within me, at least I'd soon be with my beloved.

"Don't fret, Arianna." Her nail traced along my chin, and she grasped it. "I've faced many foes far better trained than you, but none of them has possessed such a lack of concern for their own well-being. Honestly, it's refreshing. Don't you agree, Wren?"

My gaze moved from the floor to Wren, who'd continued to pull at her restraints. Her expression twisted into a snarl. "Is this why you dragged me out of my damned cell? For another game? I swear I'll make your death nice and slow when—"

"You shouldn't be so combative today of all days, Wren. You see, I finally have the thing in my possession that you want—Brielle."

Brielle? My pulse raced. Why was she here? Was this a trick? Had huntsmen, or worse, Aralians, found a passage through the mines? My jaw clenched. I should have brought the caves down behind us. Instead, I'd left my people and home open to danger.

"Where is she?" Wren screamed. "If you lay a finger on her, I'll—"

"Kill me? Yes, yes, I know." Delphine flicked her wrist, as if unbothered by the woman's hatred.

Two disciples lifted me from the ground, one hauling me on each side. My head lolled toward the bed.

A pair of guards approached Wren. The shorter plucked a key and unlatched the chain from the bedpost. Simultaneously, Wren swung her arm. The metal smacked the escort in the temple. Before she could pivot to the other guard, the disciple shoved a dart into her neck. She blinked and then flopped onto the bed.

Delphine sucked her teeth. "I do hope you'll be more amenable than Wren. I've tired of her unwillingness to submit to Aralia, but I think you shall be far more reasonable. Especially when I tell you what power the goddess can offer you." She leaned forward and a feral smile tugged on her lips. "The ability to raise the dead."

CHAPTER 37

ARIANNA

Soft candlelight washed over a sprawling banquet of plates of smoked meats, fruits, cheeses, and flat bread stacked upon crystal platters. My brain hitched as my escort guided me deeper into the enclosed dining room and to the foot of the table. She pressed a hand to my shoulder, forcing me to settle into the solid oak chair. I wanted to fight, but half a dozen guards flanked the ivory walls, armed to the teeth in onyx. Begrudgingly, I sat. At the head of the feast, Delphine lowered herself into an ornate gold throne. I waited with bated breath for what this villain would do next. Oddly, as if in salute to me, she lifted a goblet of wine, tipped her chin, and took a long sip. Then she nibbled cheese as if I were her guest and not her prisoner.

I studied my surroundings. The space bore no obvious doors, but we'd entered through a hidden corridor between the main hall and here. The marble walls sparkled, portraits of the Goddess Aralia hanging along them. Her white hair flowed about her creamy shoulders, and her ruby eyes settled upon the gardens she lounged within, as if she were the life-bringer instead of destruction. Between each painting stood a sentinel ready to strike me down with their blade. There were six in total, and all kept their attention trained on me as if I could break free from these cuffs. Perhaps if Silas were still alive, I could. I shifted. Pain coursed up my arm from my injured joint as I pushed against the restraints. Even in this heightened state since fusing with the blight, I wasn't strong enough.

"You really should eat something. You're nothing but skin and bones. Aralia won't like that." She gestured to the meal. "Oh, yes. Your hands are bound and your wrist is broken." She smirked and snapped her fingers.

A hidden door behind her opened and a servant stepped over the threshold. She donned a cap, hiding her hair, and her gaze remained cast to the floor. The frumpy frock she wore did little to highlight her age. She could be twelve or twenty.

She bobbed a deep bow. "How can I be of service?"

"It seems our friend cannot eat. Feed her." Delphine pointed at me.

The girl's familiar face came into view. My lips pulled into a thin line, holding in a gasp. Kamy, the youth I'd saved from Wobbleton, the girl who'd led us through the hidden doors to the abandoned gardens, stood before me. Her eyes flashed for a millisecond of recognition as she approached me. My mind raced. Perhaps she could help me once again. Maybe she could free me from these shackles.

"Any preference, Miss?" Kamy motioned to the bountiful plates of food.

"I'm not hungry." I shook my head, uncertain whether poison laced these morsels. Perhaps this was a sick game of roulette.

"Eat, or I'll kill her and every servant who comes after her until you imbibe." Delphine clicked her nails against the armrest.

My nose wrinkled. She held my gaze in a battle of wills, tempting me. Yet it wasn't a bluff. She'd murder Kamy and whoever came next.

"The grapes," I offered, hoping that choosing the unprepared item would be less likely to result in its being laced with something.

Kamy plucked a grape and placed it against my lips. Hesitantly, I chewed the sour fruit, then swallowed.

"That wasn't so hard, was it, Arianna? You were such a well-behaved young lady before this defiant streak occurred a few months ago." Delphine took a bit of a smoked meat, sucked the juice off her fingers, then snapped them. "Arianna's records."

A guard turned and tapped the slate. The hidden door flew open, the patrolwoman scampered away, and the stone slammed closed. I studied the wall, certain that there was some marking that denoted the pulley.

Delphine cocked an eyebrow. To keep up the ruse, I opened my mouth and let the girl feed me another bite. I chewed and swallowed with a gulp.

Minutes passed as the high disciple dined on her dinner and Kamy force-fed me bits of sour grapes, with only our chewing denoting the tense quiet. Finally, the door slid open again, and the guard returned with a leather-bound book. She handed it to Delphine.

Delphine lowered her glass to the table with a click and took the tome. The swishing of pages echoed through the silence as she searched. Her nail trailed along the words, then she began reading.

"Arianna Park, twenty-six. Curse enacted at six because of a complication with her mother's illness. Destruction caused when blight awakened, minimal. Child seems to have a low energy threshold, marked to be drained, not a candidate for the vessel."

The vessel. I glanced at Kamy, but she didn't react to the phrase. Instead, she offered an apple slice. I bit down, wincing as the tart flavor coated my tongue.

Delphine continued. "Engaged to Theo Terrell. Fletcher Terrell, to tithe to the Aralians a yearly sum of thirty-thousand crown, be granted a minority seat on the high council from the vacancy left by the ending of line Kennedy. To gain voting rights, Terrell will establish a trade route to Seaside and provide 10 percent donation every month upon profits made. Your life really would have been much simpler had you married that spoiled shit." She slammed the book shut and flung it across the table.

The guard from before stepped forward, fetched the tome, and then returned to their spot in the row.

"I'm tired of this game. Get to the point," I snarled.

"But you were impetuous, eloping with a backwoods gentry, then, months later, infiltrating Hallowhaven to save him from his consumption. Now that he's dead, you rushed here to claim revenge. Your moves are predictable. But we are running out of time. Guards, leave us. But you, Kamy, stay and attend to our guest." Delphine gestured.

The sentinels turned in unison, then left. My gaze drifted to Kamy. Perhaps this was our moment.

As if sensing my thoughts, Delphine laughed. "Do you think she'll be your salvation again?"

Kamy's features tensed, then smoothed. "My apologies. I don't know what you mean."

"My plan was flawless. The patrols would have flanked Xavier, pushing him to the kitchens, where three platoons lay in wait, ready to capture them both." Delphine picked up her knife and pointed it at the girl. "But you interfered. It is fortunate I created a failsafe, lacing the elixir of life with poison and having a recovery team in the wings in case they slipped away to Xavier's safe house." Her knuckles whitened around the handle. She gritted her teeth. "But you led them through the secret tunnels. We had no idea of the timing of their exit. Now my pet has run off. I'm guessing he's heading straight for his whore, Martha. What is it they call themselves? Oh yes, *the Opposition*. As if anyone could oppose me."

My uninjured hand curled into a ball. My jaw ticked. The details Xavier had gleaned were paltry compared to her intel. She'd been far more knowledgeable than we realized.

The color in Kamy's face drained, making her as white as the apron she wore. "I would never help curse scum—"

"Oh, shut up. I know all about your lofty ideals and your desire to avenge Raya." Delphine rolled her eyes. "Not that you'll be able to." She threw the knife. It whizzed through the air.

Thump.

The blade pierced through Kamy's chest. She blinked in shock. Blood oozed through the fabric of her shirt. She stumbled, then collapsed onto the floor at my feet.

I tugged at my restraints. Pain coursed through me. I had to free myself. But each motion drained more of my energy into the warded cuffs. My stomach sank as I peered down at the adolescent who'd freed us. Crimson soaked the pristine floors and coated my boots. I suppressed a wail, unwilling to give Delphine the satisfaction of witnessing me break.

"Listen to me. Whatever plans you had when you set foot in this space are gone. I'll kill anyone without a second thought to get what I want. I'll drag Brielle in here and make you watch as I drain the life from her. Shall I continue my story?"

My body shook as I took in the blood-drenched girl. Just like Silas, Mateo, and Mama. Death surrounded me. Despite my willingness to die, I had no desire to have the innocent suffer in my stead.

"As I was saying. I spent over twenty years in love with that man, giving him everything—money, power, my body, and the fountain of youth. And how does he repay me? By forming an opposition against me. I was aware of Martha's collection of disposed-of disciples. What could a dozen women do? However, when Xavier started disappearing to Daviel for weeks, I knew something had changed. I admire his analytical mind and his ability to play this little game. But he's gone too far." She reached for a crust of bread and ripped it in half, then lowered the pieces onto the plate.

"How did you find out about Martha?" I asked, wanting to better understand this villain's knowledge.

A beaming smile tugged on her lips. "I sent a spy in months ago. Jasmine."

My eyes widened as the name pinged in my memory. She'd been the one who'd argued with Wolf at the brothel about the red-haired woman she'd had waiting for her. My brow furrowed. Had that been Brielle?

"Ah, you recognize her. You see, I noticed a pattern with Xavier. Whenever I'd punish a girl and leave her in the alley to die, he would disappear. I thought nothing of it because it only happened occasionally, but as he increased his visits to Daviel, I worried he had bigger plans beyond this heroic nonsense of rescuing my discarded disciples. So Jasmine had an affair with a delivery man at my behest to create the perfect backstory for her near-death beating. Like clockwork, he brought her to Daviel and had her patched up by Martha. When she offered her a place in her brothel, she took it. And what amazing information we discovered! It's one thing to tend to my banished girls. It's another to harbor and train a cursed person. That cub, Wolf, shall be his downfall. Then I wondered about his insistence on safeguarding Presspin. My new paramour insisted you were indeed hiding in that backwoods territory. Which meant Xavier was a blighted sympathizer. More so, I suspect he's collecting you, Wolf, and whoever else to thwart me. I can't have that."

My lips pursed closed, and I bit my tongue.

She let out a laugh and then took another swig of her wine. "So I had to secure you for myself. I've been many steps ahead of you this entire time. Jasmine informed me of Xavier joining the huntsmen and his efforts to reach you before I did. So she provided the bounty hunters with the warded weapons. But you were more powerful than them, vanquishing them with ease. We planned to capture you in Daviel, but you fled before the Aralians were able to take hold. Again, when we set up blockades between here and Krella, you defeated my platoons. Don't worry, your skill only further proves your worthiness to house Aralia."

Exhausted by her theatrics, I shifted in my seat. My restraints rubbed against my wrists. "How does Brielle play into this? Did you send Aralians into Presspin? Where is she?"

An amused smile pulled over her lips. "That's the best part. I knew you'd entered my territory and slipped through the huntsmens' fingers. I hadn't concocted an updated plan to capture you yet. Then, in steps Brielle, arriving on the Scarlet Rose's doorstep of her own accord, certain that Martha had betrayed her and sent the huntsmen. In actuality, it was my new paramour who'd hired the men. It was fortunate that Jasmine intercepted her."

"What did you do with her?" I attempted to stand. The world spun, my knees shook, and I collapsed back into the chair.

"Oh, do you want to see her? Make sure she is safe?" She arched an eyebrow. "Send in Brielle."

Moments later, the door swung open, and Brielle pressed through the shadows. Her crimson hair was braided, and she wore a white dress of silk. The usually vivacious woman waited behind the throne with her gaze upon the floor.

"Sit. You're my guest." Delphine gestured to the oak chair to her right, but Brielle stayed stone still.

"Not wanting to join me for a meal? Or is it that you can't look your friend in the face after you betrayed her to save your mate?" Delphine hissed.

My blood ran cold. My stomach plummeted to my sandals. Brielle's shoulders slumped, but her countenance remained stony.

"Our deal is not complete until Arianna agrees to be the new vessel. So if I were you, I'd sit down," she ordered.

Like a dog following its master's commands, Brielle took the seat next to her. She continued to avoid my gaze, instead focusing on the feast before us.

"What have you done?" I asked.

"Come, tell her your tale; it's an excellent one." Delphine lifted her goblet and gestured to her.

A beat passed, stretching in the aching silence.

"Tell her," Delphine said through gritted teeth. "Or shall I let you watch Wren go through the vessel ceremony tonight?"

Brielle's pallor blanched. She poured herself a glass of wine and downed it in a single gulp. Sorrow etched her features but tightened into a familiar determined expression. "Mateo died, and I was livid. All I wanted was revenge against Martha for betraying me, for sending the huntsmen into Presspin." She wrung her hands, then lowered them to her lap. "Naomi divulged a discovery she'd made in the conservatory—a journal with a map of the mines. She was afraid to venture through it without the certainty that it was safe. The huntsmen proved the caverns were passable. We left together shortly after discovering Mateo's death."

"Where is she?" Panic swirled in my gut. Was Naomi here too? Was she also in danger?

"We made it through the tunnel. Then spent the night at a farm many miles north of Daviel. Before dawn, I arose and stole her goods. She had nothing but the map and a note to return to Presspin."

My hand balled into a fist. "You left her there. With strangers."

"Even she's not foolish enough to enter these territories with no money." Brielle shook her head. "She's likely pouting in the manor now."

Rage boiled within me. How could I have believed that she'd ever been my friend?

Brielle shifted in her seat, her glance dragging to Delphine, who tapped her metal nails along the throne in boredom but gestured for her to go on.

Brielle's lips pursed as if the story had a sour flavor, but she continued. "I made it to Daviel and headed for the brothel. When I reached the Scarlet Rose, Martha wasn't home, but Jasmine accepted my summons. It was then that she informed me that Wren was alive and explained the true reason they'd kept my love imprisoned in the temple. They need a vessel to awaken Aralia and had been forcing Wren to participate in the ceremony every full moon. But if they had someone equally powerful," she cocked her head toward me, "another cursed with the ability to defeat a platoon of Aralians and survive, then they could replace Wren."

My mind reeled at her words. She must have told them that Silas had consumption and not the wasting sickness. She'd hidden his blight so Delphine would believe I was strong enough to cause the blast at Terrell Estate and suffer no side effects.

My jaw hardened. "So that was it? You sacrificed us for Wren?"

A dry, unamused laugh pressed through Brielle's lips. "You did the same. You had me message Martha, and now Mateo is dead. Don't be a hypocrite. If you agree, you'll become the vessel and have the power to revive Silas. His consumption would be healed. She'll let Wren and me go." Her hand slipped from the table and rested on her stomach. Her brow pinched. "I've already suffered so much losing Wren for years, then loving Mateo, then losing him too. You can't hate me for trying to save my mate, as you tried to."

My heart broke as my gaze held hers. Her expression pleaded with me to say yes, to sacrifice myself for her and Wren's happiness. Hadn't I been ready to die and take down the temple with me? What if this weren't a lie? What if I could resurrect Silas? Would it be worth it?

"So you see, Arianna, many fates rest on your shoulders. Brielle's and Wren's lives, as well as your husband's." She raised an eyebrow. "If you allow Aralia to use you as her vessel, all will be set to rights, Silas can be revived, Brielle and Wren shall go on their merry way, and your sister..." Her smile curled into something ominous. "Well, she too could live her life in peace in Presspin."

Bile crawled up my throat. I wished I hadn't eaten that horrid fruit. My stomach churned. Heartbeats skittered by, and I worried she might kill Brielle and then me due to my long pause.

What she proposed was utter madness. Yet, what other choice did I have?

"Fine," I hissed. "I'll be your vessel, but you must free Brielle and Wren. Then promise never to seek my sister."

CHAPTER 38

ARIANNA

"Excellent." Delphine rose and clapped. "We have no time to waste."

My mind swam with the implications. What would this mean? Would I now bear Aralia's power? Or would something far more sinister occur? But if I could resurrect Silas and protect those I cared about, then I'd take whatever risk awaited me.

"I'm so glad you are a willing participant. This shall make all the difference. To think I wasted five years hoping Wren would finally concede to Aralia while you were withering away in Krella. You are quite the dark horse, Arianna Park." She lifted her glass.

"Belmont. I am Lady Belmont, and you should address me as such," I hissed.

A cackle bubbled from her. "You have a spark of fighting spirit, don't you? Ester was a fool to believe you were a simple milquetoast maiden. Shall we begin?" She rose, then closed the distance between us.

She offered her metal-nailed hand. My lip curled in disgust, and I pushed myself up to stand. My body swayed from the pressure of the cuffs subduing my energy. I forced myself to straighten, unwilling to require this monster's help. Unfazed, she walked to the wall, pressed the slate, and waited for me at the hidden exit.

"This way." Delphine gestured to the door.

My gaze flicked to Brielle. Her features hardened, but something flashed in her green eyes. Was it regret that her actions had led to Silas's death much like mine had led to Mateo's? Would she be haunted by what she'd done as I'd been? It didn't matter now.

"Don't worry about her." She flicked a wrist at Brielle. "Jasmine will be by to fetch her shortly. She'll get the privilege of watching you accept the goddess, and if you arise untethered to Aralia, I'll kill her. Then I'll hunt down your sister and I'll have her partake in the ceremonies. Is she a virgin? The councilmen have a taste for deflowering, and you'll watch." Despite the harshness of the threat, her words were smooth.

A shiver crawled along my spine as we exited the dining room through the concealed door and stepped into a dark hallway. Torches lined the rough rock walls, illuminating our way through the cramped corridor. My feet trudged over the uneven floor. Was the temple riddled with hidden passageways like Kamy had guided us through?

Minutes later, she stopped. Her fingers splayed along the wall, and another concealed door slid open. The scent of lilies wafted, so sweet it clawed at my nose, gagging me. Unlike the jagged corridor, ivory tile gleamed throughout the antechamber. A pool sat in the middle of the chamber, and two servants dressed in simple frocks similar to Kamy's stood at the edges.

I studied the thin blonde with a heart-shaped face and the plump brunette with her brows furrowed.

"Prepare her. I'll retrieve her in half an hour. Give her a thorough scrubbing. She must be pristine for our goddess." She fished a key from her pocket and undid my binds. They smacked against the marble floor.

My fingers pressed against my broken wrist. For a heartbeat, I considered striking Delphine down, but even before the cuffs and my sustained injuries, she'd subdue me. Instead, my shoulders slumped in defeat.

"That's a good girl." She patted my head as if I were a dog.

I wanted to recoil at the gesture but stayed still.

Satisfied with my humiliation, she backed away and exited.

The door slammed shut behind her. The servants rushed forward. As they reached me, the brunette untied the cape from my neck, and the blonde tugged off the Aralian robes I wore. My gaze remained trained on the steam curling from the pool. Despite the cool tile underfoot, warmth permeated the air.

The frail blonde grabbed my uninjured hand and led me to the edge. "Step in."

Slowly, my toe dipped into the water. My feet lowered into the pool, finding the smooth slate steps. I continued wading into the warmth until my body was submerged up to my neck. The minerals fizzled around my skin, making my limbs feel light as a feather. Even the searing discomfort in my wrist settled to an ache. Despite the tense situation, an audible sigh escaped me.

Moments later, the blonde attendant stepped in fully clothed, clutching a rag. She approached, her expression softened. "I must wash you."

My lips pursed. I nodded, giving my consent for her to begin. Long minutes passed as she worked the cloth over every inch of my body. The clear water darkened as the grime from my battles in the temple washed away. Finally, she rinsed my hair. The brunette handed her a crystal jug. She poured the warm oil over my forehead and through my locks. I stared at the ceiling, denoted with a painting of the constellations overhead. Her fingers massaged my scalp, and a song bubbled from them.

Rise, oh rise, Aralia
Goddess of Light
We call to you
Avenge us, Aralia
Smite the wicked and restore your glory

How deep were the lies? Did they believe Aralia was the goddess of light and not the goddess of darkness? My thoughts dispersed, for at the last verse's end, she submerged me in the water. I gasped as I reemerged, and she began the song again.

She cycled through the melody, then she dunked me into the bath as the stanza concluded. On the first plunge, I contemplated thwarting the pair and fleeing, but I quickly pushed that idea away; facing a platoon in my current state would end in my capture. On the second immersion, I considered fighting Delphine now that my limbs didn't ache and I was free of the cuffs. However, she'd subdue me. By the third time, a cold realization had washed over me. If I wanted my loved ones to be safe, and for Silas to live, this was my only choice—to allow Aralia to claim me.

After the dozenth submersion, she led me out of the pool and retreated to a corner. My arms crossed over my nude form. Water rivulets dripped off me. A chill coursed over my skin, causing goose bumps to form. The brunette approached with a drying cloth and wiped me down vigorously.

Moments later, the blonde returned wearing a new frock. In her hands was a white dress. Now that I was fully dry, they dressed me in the fine garment that covered little. The neckline plunged to my navel and thin straps along my shoulders held the flimsy fabric at bay. One placed soft-soled slippers upon my feet while the other wove my wet hair into a twist, then pinned the chignon. Finally, the blonde crowned me with an ivory tiara. With their task completed, they withdrew and lowered themselves to their knees, casting their gazes downward.

My brow knitted, but before I could react, the door snapped open. Delphine entered.

Delight danced across her face. "You are not as lovely as Wren, but you clean up nicely. Aralia will be pleased." Her gaze flicked to the servants. "You are released. Go join the other disciples in entertaining the dignitaries in their quarters. We must keep them distracted while we perform the ceremony."

The servants nodded but didn't rise. Confused, I looked from the women to Delphine.

"How else do you think this ritual remains a secret from the high council? Men are controlled by their base instincts. If my disciples are riding their cocks, then their focus will remain on their desperate need for pleasure instead of what we do in the shadows. Men truly are simple creatures." Delphine pointed to the warded cuffs.

My gut twisted as the brunette plucked the discarded device and snapped it on my wrists in front of me.

I held back an audible hiss as the metal pressed against the joint, causing my arm to throb.

Delphine turned toward the exit and lingered. "Come, Arianna. We don't have all evening."

Slowly, I exited and reentered the dimly lit hallway. An echo of chants reverberated through the walls in a language unfamiliar to my ears. The mournful sounds pulsed within my blood and ratcheted up my heart rate. With each step forward, the singing intensified.

A high-pitched soprano's voice crooned as we reached the end of the corridor. My stomach plummeted as the rock wall slid open, revealing a domed chamber. Thousands of candles dotted the place. Moonlight illuminated the pristine white robes of the thirteen Aralians. Six cloaked women were to my left, and six stood to my right. In the corner, Jasmine oversaw the chained Brielle and Wren. Wren stared at the altar; my gaze trailed hers, locking on to the onyx slab in the center of the room.

A chill whipped through the slatted ceremonial space from the open-air ceiling. The moon rose overhead, casting a soft glow upon the altar many paces ahead of me. The incantation crescendoed, causing my spine to tingle. A looming dread settled at the base of my back. I halted.

Delphine's sharp claws dug into my upper arm. "Focus on what you are gaining from this, Arianna. Power to resurrect the dead and the ability to thwart any foe."

My glance locked on Wren, who shook her head in warning. She'd gone through this ritual for years, and obvious discomfort tugged along her fine features, causing my muscles to pinch. But there was no turning back.

Hesitantly, my feet moved, walking down the lit path to the altar. As I approached the three steps, I willed myself to move, taking them one at a time. The chanting built, pulsing in my ears like a mournful cry. As I reached the top of the platform, the singing snapped to a wild rhythm, matching my escalating heartbeat. Delphine followed behind me and spun me to face the women. Yet my focus settled on Brielle. Though we hadn't been friends long, I'd trusted her not only with my life, but with Silas's and Naomi's. A knot lodged in my windpipe, and I choked on her betrayal. I tilted my chin and held her stare. How different we were. She'd sacrificed me for her love, and I would be sacrificed to keep her blood from being spilled. She shuddered, averting her gaze to the floor.

The growing cantillation ballooned and then burst in the last overture.

Silence stretched over the disciples who gazed upon me with reverence. Delphine retrieved the key and unlocked my shackles. They clattered to the ground. Wren's eyes locked with mine, as if she willed me to fight. Simultaneously, Jasmine placed a blade against Brielle's throat. Wren's features tightened with defeat.

Delphine's attention slid between the tableau and me. A smirk curled on her lips and then smoothed. She raised her hands. "My thirteen noble elite. Keepers of the truth and knowledge of Aralia's true form. Blessed be this night, when we revive our dark deity, Aralia. The bringer of balance, of death. We've walked too long bound by these performances. May she rise and cleanse the world to start anew. Blessed be this vessel that shall harbor our goddess. The elixir."

The woman holding a golden goblet approached and lowered it into Delphine's hand.

"From the lifeblood of our enemies, those whom Aralia cursed and those whom Cassius placed a blessing upon. The elixir of life. The potion needed to revive Aralia from her prison world." Delphine raised the chalice and handed it to me. "Drink."

The cold metal reverberated through my palm. I brought the rim to my lips. The sweet liquid poured down my throat, warming me akin to sunshine on a summer's day. The heat spread down to my belly, then washed over my skin, stretching through every fiber of my being. I breathed deeply, and a headiness buzzed within my mind, as if I were drunk on a bottle of apple wine.

The empty cup tumbled from my grasp. Instantly, the throbbing in my wrist diminished. I rolled the joint, amazed by the automatic relief, as if it had never been broken. The fuzzy sensation caused me to sway, and Delphine clamped onto my shoulder, anchoring me. I'd expected a dull ache to radiate from the place where Silas seared my flesh together, but no pain came. My jaw ticked. Xavier had been correct. This miraculous remedy acted instantaneously. Had Silas sipped the true cure, he would be alive now. Bile crawled up my throat as my gaze shifted to the villain who'd stripped my husband from me. For that, she'd suffer.

However, my limbs felt disjointed from my body. Delphine grabbed me and laid me on the onyx stone. My stare burned through her, and her lips tipped into a feral smirk. She was wholly aware of the connection I'd made. I tried to move, to wring her neck, but my form fused to the platform, similar to when I'd leaned against the wall in the annex. Though this time it didn't feel as if I were being drained. Instead, it subdued me. My skin buzzed. My head lolled. A shimmering light pulsed through the markings in the wall.

Crash.

Wren collapsed to her knees. Her shoulders curled in. Her breathing came in rasps. Was this place draining her like the annex had drained me?

A brilliant light crawled along etched markings along the path, up the dais, and toward the platform. The altar turned a golden hue. A scream shattered from me as energy coursed through me, as if I were being repeatedly struck by lightning. I gritted my teeth, fearful that my body would explode before the ceremony even began.

"And with the power she provided the curse, we break the seal upon her prison and infuse the vessel to bear her," Delphine said.

My mind scrambled, but my skin pulsed with renewed strength. I gritted my teeth as the realization washed over me. They'd harvest the blighted to fuel their weapons and for the elixir of life. But they also used the dark energy to perform this ceremony to resurrect their deity.

"We sing to you, Aralia, and welcome you to the land of the living. Come, my scribes, mark her flesh to receive our goddess." Delphine traversed the stairs and waited at the base.

Five women bearing needles skittered up the steps. One stood at each limb while the fifth loomed near my heart. The chanting reconvened, swirling through the night air. Pain coursed through my body as they carved markings into my flesh. My mind disengaged, focusing on the brightest star over-head, anchoring me from the painful etchings marked into me. Time bent, and I faded in and out of consciousness, uncertain if I'd endured seconds or hours.

Finally, the endless poking ceased. I opened my eyes and studied my form. Black blood oozed from my skin, coating the Aralian symbols covering my body.

"May Aralia's soul be bound to this vessel with the dark en-ergy of the blighted, the blessing in the lifeblood of the cursed bestowed by Cassius, and the sacred word binding provided by our beloved goddess etched upon this mortal coil," Delphine said.

A soft, mournful melody began, denoting this transition phase in the ceremony. My head tipped to the side, and my glance caught on Brielle. Her features slackened to a look of horror. Her rosy cheeks blanched. A tear rolled down her cheek.

Despite the pain she'd caused me, the betrayal, I wanted to comfort her, as I should have done days ago when Mateo died. I should have held her, apologized. My lips moved, mouthing the words *I'm sorry.*

A wail keened from her. She collapsed beside Wren and pulled her mate into her arms, shielding her face from me.

"The dagger," Delphine called out.

A woman on the far right strode forward, carrying an antique box whose lacquer had worn off centuries ago. She flipped the lid. Delphine withdrew a gleaming onyx dagger with etched symbols. My brow furrowed, but my mind couldn't focus, as if the mix of pain from the ritual and the heady sensation from the elixir drowned my full consciousness.

"My disciples. Tonight, we raise the goddess so she may rule once again and bring true balance to this world. Chant your heart's song to Aralia. May she return to us once and for all."

The incantation began, a rhythmic music that matched my escalating pulse. Delphine walked to the rear of the onyx platform and stood in line with my chest. She faced her congregation. The singing wails filled the space. I blinked. The stars streaked across my vision. Delphine approached. She hovered over me, her wild eyes locked on mine. A high-pitched note pierced at the apex of the melody, drawing my attention for half a second. In that moment, she plunged the dagger into my heart.

CHAPTER 39

ARIANNA

A CRYSTAL BLUE SKY, *as if indigo paint had spilled across the atmosphere, had replaced the twinkling stars from the open-air antechamber. My palms grazed the soft vibrant grass I laid upon. Oddly, despite the blazing sunshine, no warmth permeated my skin. Nor did dew cling to my fingertips. Confused, I pushed against the ground and arched forward to a sitting position. An eerie sensation crawled along my spine and settled at its base. Where was I?*

Only seconds prior, I'd been upon the altar in the temple, and Delphine had loomed over me. Panicked, I traced my thumb down my chest, certain a fatal wound would be there. Instead, my creamy flesh remained unmarred. Had she not stabbed me? Yet flashes of pain burned in my lungs, as if I were drowning. An internal alarm rang. I needed to find Aralia to resuscitate Silas and keep my loved ones safe from Delphine's machinations, but she had not dictated exactly how to connect with the goddess.

I bolted to my feet and traversed the desolate place. To my dismay, the sun overhead did not move, nor did the shadows sway. I couldn't tell how long I searched this space for the goddess. Despite the scenic beauty of the meadow and the azure sky, an unsettling sensation coiled in my belly, growing with each step I took.

Sometime later, a massive tree stood in the distance. With it being the only change to this endless area, I sprinted to it, hoping that answers might lie there. As I approached, the roots unraveled before me. A dense canopy of leaves cast shadows over the grass, and golden apples hung on the vines, ripe for picking.

"I've been expecting you, dear girl." An old woman emerged from behind the trunk.

Her white hair was twisted around her head in a braided crown, drawing attention to her crimson eyes. Wrinkles crackled on her skin, denoting many years of life. Her gnarled fingertips curled along the rough bark, providing her hunched form balance as she walked over a raised root.

"'Tis the full moon ceremony already? Let me look at you." She stretched out her worn hands.

My brow furrowed. Who was she? Was this the goddess of darkness that Delphine worshipped? This fragile crone who could barely stand? How was she to help me?

I stepped back; my heel landed against a root, halting me. "Who are you?"

"Aralia, of course. And you are the new vessel? Not as lovely as Wren, but your appearance is pleasant enough. There is no need to be afraid. I just want to understand you." She outstretched her palms.

Alarm bells chimed internally. However, I ignored the sensation. My safety didn't matter at present. Hesitantly, my feet moved into the cool ground beneath the shade. The shadows washed over the space, casting us both in a filtered light. Slowly, I lowered my hands to hers. Perhaps this was how I allowed her to use me as her vessel?

Her eyes flashed; red coated the whites of her irises. A pang rattled through my skull, as if someone were digging within it. Heaviness covered me, as if the weight of the world pressed against my shoulders. I tried to tug free. Her grasp intensified, causing her knuckles to blanch.

She kicked her head back and stared into the branches as if the tangled vines of my past sprawled before her. Memories flashed before me, and a sinking sensation settled in my gut, warning me to protect Silas's identity. I closed my eyes. I collected the recollection of my curse-bond with Silas, treasures I refused to show her, and hid them within the recesses of my subconscious. If he were to rise, no one could know of his blight. It was the only way to keep him safe.

Finally, her focus shifted to my face. "Arianna. You are shrouded in death, as if it were a perfume coating your skin. Your parents and now your husband. All gone while you are in the summer of your youth. Your husband passed recently. He crossed through here, guided by his mother to the Great Beyond some hours ago. Though his body is cold, I can still save him."

A sour taste laced my tongue at the personal details she'd plucked from me. I swallowed the unpleasant flavor. She released her grasp. Her black cloak swayed as she circled me like a vulture, studying my form as her gaze dragged from my feet to the crown of my head. I crossed my arms over my chest, bunching the fabric of the white gown. A beat passed, but no sound permeated this space, nor breeze shifted through the trees. My muscles tensed at the unnatural stillness.

Her cracked lips tipped into a smirk as she stood before me. "You are an interesting one, Arianna. Barreling into the temple, ready to die, prepared to join your beloved in the Great Beyond, only to be swayed by your tender heart. You even fear for the well-being of the friend who betrayed you. And yet..."

She closed the distance between us. Her icy hand cupped my cheek; the chill settled into my bones. Her eyes bore into mine, peering into the depths of my soul. Whatever bluster I'd had entering the temple fizzled away. My pulse skittered. A cold sweat washed over me. Flashes of the past I hid overwhelmed me, as if she'd summoned my nightmares forward. Each recollection barreled into me, one after another, as if I were reliving them. The sickening crack of Mr. Terrell's skull against the spike of wood. The arrow piercing Mama's flesh. Naomi's terror as the conservatory exploded around her. Mateo dying. Then slowing on the most horrific moment of them all—Silas's death. Pressure built in my ribcage as my beloved's last breaths rattled through me.

"Revenge won't bring him back, but I can," she crooned. "I can finally provide you with what you've been searching for: a way to undo your transgressions. We both know he would have lived had he never met you."

I sucked in a breath. It was a harsh truth I'd battled with internally, now drawn into the light. It took root, curling like a poisonous vine. Since I'd crashed into Silas on the street in Krella all those months ago, his life had been shaken. Silas had only contracted the wasting sickness because he protected me at Terrell Estate. That internal whisper had driven me to search for a cure, to venture to Hallowhaven, and even now to be contemplating allowing this, becoming a vessel, in order to resurrect my dead beloved.

Silas had died because of me.

The façade of a woman strong enough to save her husband and fierce enough to enact revenge crumbled, leaving the shell of a broken girl. A sob escaped me, and the sound echoed through the space. A knot pushed against my throat. My knees buckled, and I fell to the ground. My nails dug into the earth. She lingered, providing no comfort, as my bone-weary weeping curled through me until my cries stifled to subtle sobs.

"Sweet child, you've caused so much hardship. You came here as a harbinger of destruction, to seek revenge against Delphine. Yet the blood of your love coats your hands. Do you really think of yourself as some avenging hero? No, dear girl, you are the villain, and you always have been. But you can undo all this pain."

She crouched down and pressed two fingers to my forehead. An alternative future splayed before me. Naomi on the farm, smiling as she picked apples. Brielle in the herbalist shop with Wren, who chased a toddler with Mateo's coloring. Beatrix and Xavier in the library at Belmont Manor, playing chess. And Silas. Silas lounging in the study with a beaming Mrs. Potter doting over him. Warmth entered my soul.

"You see, if you remove yourself from their lives, their memories, this is the life they could have."

My resolve crumbled. My chest cracked in half as if it were the shell of an egg. I gagged on a fact I'd always known—that had I never been born, everyone I loved would have been happy.

"But you always knew you were worthless. Such a pretty dream you lived for a few months with your love before your curse took hold. Let me fix this for you." She stood and plucked a golden fruit from the tree.

"All you must do is become my vessel. I'll inhabit your body, and it will be like you never existed. All the pain you've caused shall *disappear with the morning light. My shadow shall sprawl across the world, blotting out the memory of your life as I did Cassius's."*

A thought unfurled. Hadn't those in Presspin somehow remembered Cassius? Was there a limit to the goddess's power? It didn't matter; I was no god, beloved by many. No one would remember me. I was nothing.

"You are so tired of fighting. Deep down, you are just a worthless, frail girl. Take a bite, save your beloved, and set everything to rights." She extended the gold-hued fruit in her palm.

The sweet tanginess wafted toward me, reminiscent of the orchards of my childhood home. Unbidden, my mother harkened forward; her last words rattled within my skull. Not her love but an apology. Raw with emotion, fresh tears poured down my cheeks.

"She hated you; both of your parents did. They saw you for who you truly were—a hindrance. Let me set you free." Her fingers wafted through my locks.

A guttural wail coursed through me at the confirmation. My mother had never loved me. I'd always been her burden. My existence had been nothing but a knoll stone for those I cherished to bear. My lips trembled. Every ounce of self-hatred I'd ever felt crashed over me like waves drowning the woman I had become. Perhaps if I'd had more time with Silas, or perhaps Naomi still cared about me, or Brielle hadn't betrayed me, I'd have the will to fight. But I didn't. This darkness coated me, pressing upon any fragments of light within my soul. My transgression weighed me down; I deserved this agony. I deserved to die. Aralia couldn't be fully trusted, yet she was right: I'd caused this.

With my decision made, I straightened and wiped my tears away. First, I'd set everything to rights. "I'll allow you to inhabit my body and erase my existence, but I have provisions."

Her gnarled features twisted in frustration, then smoothed. "Tell me your conditions."

"Silas is to be revived and healed from his ailments. He is to return to Presspin. You are to set Wren and Brielle free, allowing them to leave for Seaside. You'll not harm any of my people." I held her stare.

Her crimson gaze shifted from me to the meadow, as if calculating the weight of my demands. Her features tightened, and for a heart-beat, I feared she would reject my request and overtake me by force.

Her pinched brow smoothed. "A hard bargain, but I will resurrect Silas, fully restored. He is granted safe passage back to his home. Brielle and Wren may leave the temple. Finally, I'll not lay a finger on any of your people within Presspin."

I breathed out a sigh of relief, but uncertainty clung to me as I teetered toward my sacrifice, needing to make certain that my forfeit protected those I loved. "How do I know you are telling me the truth?"

"I'm a deity. My word is the core of sacred word binding, overseen by fate herself. So it is spoken, so it is done."

My mind hitched on the promise, but before I could ask another question, the indigo sky darkened, as if night was full upon us. A chill crept through the atmosphere. I inhaled, but the air wheezed through my lungs. I clutched my throat.

Her features tightened. "Hurry. Take a bite so I can claim your cursed body." With a shaky hand, she pushed the apple to my lips.

I swallowed a wave of nausea. My jaw trembled as it opened. My teeth pressed against the skin.

"That's it, dear. Don't be afraid," she whispered, soothing away any hesitation.

I chomped down on the fruit. A cacophony of flavor danced on my tongue, then morphed into ash. I gasped. My fingers clawed at my neck. The hag's worn face transformed before me into a young woman with sharp, beautiful features, as if she were cut from glass. A smirk tipped her ruby lips as she glared down at me.

The earth beneath me shook, then split. The tree's leaves above me decayed. Mirrored shards rained down upon us as the atmosphere shattered. A dense fog encompassed us.

"Now sleep, child. Don't worry; I will keep my precise words." She cackled.

I collapsed and reached for the goddess as agony coursed through me. Darkness flickered in the corners of my mind, overtaking me. What had I done?

CHAPTER 40

ARALIA

"ARISE, ARALIA, AND CLAIM this cursed creature's body," Delphine commanded.

My nose twitched as the tang of blood wafted with the crisp air. Goose bumps rose on the skin I inhabited. A shiver slithered down my spine at the chilly temperature. Cold, I could feel the cold. A sense of elation coursed through me. I'd been freed from that prison world devoid of sensual pleasures like touch, taste, and smell. My eyes flew open, and the stars sparkled overhead. How long had it been since I'd seen a sky different from that endless sunshine? A sigh of relief caught in my lungs, and pain stung my sternum. My fingers curled around the hilt of that infernal warded dagger that had trapped me in that realm. I ripped it from my chest and flung it to the ground. It clattered along the steps, causing the disciples' chanting to cease. The power fueled by the curse within this form melded with my divinity over death. A tugging sensation crawled through the wound until the flesh sealed shut.

"My goddess, it is you," Delphine cried out.

The echoing of knees clambering across the hard ground reverberated in welcome chorus. I was finally free. Slowly, my hands rested against the ledge. Then I hoisted myself to a sitting position. I took in the stone antechamber, the slate marked with my language. The trace of energy sizzled in the ether, an intoxicating blend of my curse and my once-love's blessing.

The candlelight glowed against the disciples' white cloaks. Their heads remained rightfully downcast before me. I rolled my neck, then smoothed my palms over the delicate dress. Each sensation caused a fresh wave of excitement. Cassius had imprisoned me for too long. A smirk tipped my lips. At least he'd also suffered in my shadow realm, and he must continue to stay there, his consciousness bound to the warded weapon. These next few weeks leading to the new full moon, as my divinity fully claimed this vessel, would be precarious. Besides, I had plans to enact before reviving my once beloved.

"Take the dagger to the catacombs." I pointed to the woman who held the lacquered container. Cassius needed to remain imprisoned until I was ready to revive him, to bear witness to my revenge.

The disciple stood, plucked the warded blade from the step, and laid it in the ancient box. Her heels clicked along the slate floor as she exited the antechamber to do my bidding.

"My goddess. I'm so happy that I've finally secured a vessel. Finding a blighted beauty strong enough to house you while also tame enough to fall under your command was difficult." Delphine rose from her bowed position as if she were my equal and not my usurping underling. My jaw ticked, then smoothed.

"Come here, my child." I held out my palms.

Without hesitation, she closed the distance between us and placed her hands in mine. Her ruby lips stretched into a smile. "I have done what those before me could not. I have resurrected you." Her face lightened, as if she were a schoolgirl waiting for praise from her master.

For a beat, I studied Delphine. She was a far cry from my original disciple, her ancestor, who I'd originally set this plan into motion with. No, she flaunted rings of stolen energy and youth beyond what was natural. She'd played queen long enough, sitting upon a throne that was never meant to be hers.

"You're right. You accomplished something that your predecessors failed to do." My fingers squeezed hers.

A satisfied smirk stretched over her face. Did she truly believe she'd pleased me? My lip twitched, then smoothed. I couldn't act while bound to that prison world. Damned Cassius, my beloved, for trapping me for centuries in the gateway between the living and dead, unable to traverse the Great Beyond nor the mortal world. Now I've been freed.

"My goddess." Delphine dipped a bow.

My nose wrinkled. My connection to her bloodline had allowed me to see glimpses of her selfish ways. She craved power, pleasure, and praise. I remained trapped, unable to feel anything, as she fucked and frolicked. She sickened me. Though Arianna hadn't requested her death, I sensed her desire for vengeance. Perhaps I could provide the girl a small gift for relinquishing herself to me. A decision took root. I grinned, and foolishly, Delphine mirrored my smile.

My grip intensified. Fear replaced her smug certainty. "You broke the covenant. Eighty years to rule, then a daughter of your line was to inherit this throne. That elixir was meant to resurrect me, not provide you with endless youth for over two centuries."

Panic flashed in her expression, as if she were a child caught stealing treats from the kitchens. But I didn't loosen my hold. As if agreeing with my outrage, my congregation remained still.

"I could have been revived far sooner had you not shared this essential ingredient with your paramours. You know you are a bastardization of nature. I am the goddess of darkness, sent to give balance, and your existence has tipped the scales." My stare bore into her.

She tugged away, but shadows pulsed, anchoring her to the spot. Her eyes widened with fear. Forcefully, I yanked her toward me. My lips pressed against hers. My tongue traced along the seam of her mouth, opening her to me. Warmth rushed from her, tasting of long summer days. Panicked, she squirmed, but with each second, the life force she'd stolen crossed into me until she had nothing left. As her movements halted, my hands dropped from hers. Now, a shriveled ancient being gaped at me instead of the once radiant woman.

Her wrinkled fingers clawed at her throat. Her knees buckled. She collapsed atop the steps, dead.

I whipped from the corpse and to the silent disciples who hadn't moved an inch. They remained still, as if they agreed with the punishment I'd inflicted on their leader. Yet my attention landed on the two women in the rear corner, chained and practically snarling at me. My lips tipped upward in amusement. Everything Wren had worked so hard to prevent had finally come to pass. She'd sworn she would never allow me to inhabit her. Now I no longer needed her.

My feet moved along the path, pressing past the reverent Aralians and beelining for the stubborn blighted woman who'd been a thorn in my side. As I stood before her, her violet eyes blazed with fury. She tugged at the onyx restrains. She was powerful, but not enough to defeat me in this form.

"It is a shame. You are more beautiful than Arianna. I mean, look at me. I'm practically skin and bone."

Wren lunged forward, but the restraints were anchored to the slate wall, keeping her at bay.

I clucked my tongue. "But your mental fortitude was stronger than hers. Can you believe you fought my shadows for five years, rejecting the whispers of your past transgressions and anchoring yourself to your beloved?" My gaze settled on the striking red-haired woman. What was her name again? Ah yes, Brielle.

"Is this her?" My thumb traced along Brielle's chin. "She is quite lovely. I can see why you refused to relinquish yourself to me when you had such a pretty mate waiting for you. Perhaps I should kill her."

The moment the threat left my tongue, a bone-deep agony seized my muscles, forcing my arm to drop from her. I'd made a vow to Arianna in regard to the pair. I peered down at my forearm, where the pain radiated. The three golden lines twisted along my wrist, like a shackle created by my oath, enforced by fate themselves. My hand balled into a fist as I reflected on the promise that Brielle and Wren may leave the temple unharmed.

But they needn't know about my restraints, nor their friends' last wishes.

I leaned toward Wren, and a deliciously devious plan formed. Yes, perhaps I'd offer Wren what I'd seen in her dreams, that root of hope she'd clung to, and then destroy it. It would make my revenge that much sweeter.

My finger trailed along Wren's chin and tilted her gaze to me. "I have a better idea. How about we play a little game? I have matters to attend to, a certain someone's husband that is to be resurrected. By mornings light, my shadows will press into your brain, erasing the time you spent here in the temple. You'll believe a beautiful dream that you and your beloved escaped all those years ago. Then, someday, I'll strike when you least expect it, destroying everything you hold dear."

She spat. Hot saliva pooled on my cheek. I raised my hand to slap her, but that horrid sensation burned into my skin, halting my motion, as if I were fate's puppet. Damn it. Once she fled the temple, the vow would be completed, and a line would untangle from my flesh, allowing me to retaliate against her. My thumb swiped the liquid away.

"Release them on the outskirts of Hallowhaven." I flicked my wrist. "Settle them in an apartment Delphine kept for the impoverished pets she was fucking."

The redhead strained in her restraints. "I'll kill you for what you've done to Wren. For what you did to Arianna."

A cackled bubbled from me. "Weren't you the one who sacrificed her? Now you claim to avenge her. Pitiful." I stepped in front of her. Her nostrils flared, and I smiled at her indignation. "What's a little mouse going to do? Besides, once the sun rises, all your memories will be twisted, erasing any knowledge of me being the goddess of darkness. The last five years of your life shall vanish."

Brielle's jaw wobbled. Horror stretched across her face. "Please don't. I can't forget him. I beg of you."

Curious, my hand grazed her cheek. Flashes of a young man flickered, and the warmth of a sweet love unfurled before me. Then a secret revealed itself, one that she'd kept. My eyes locked with hers, and her chin warbled. Perhaps I didn't need to claim revenge immediately. I'd allow Wren to suffer for a bit, because eventually, her mate wouldn't be able to hide this truth.

"Oh, Wren, you've been foolish. While you were battling against me every full moon, your beloved found another. You should be thanking me for blotting her other lover, Mateo, from her mind." I cackled, knowing that doing this would cause more torment to the couple. The confusion that would ensue would create the most horrible division between the mates.

Wren's nostrils flared. Her face hardened, and her glare landed on Brielle, tasting of betrayal. The couple would act as an excellent form of entertainment. Ah yes, what fun it would be to watch Wren suffer. I'd kill her once I'd milked every ounce of amusement from the situation.

My gaze shifted to the redhead. Her lip trembled, and tears poured down her cheeks. I could practically taste the heartbreak that came with knowing that she'd soon completely forget about the man she'd cared for. Moreso, the epic confusion she'd suffer over the next few months.

I wanted to relish their misery. However, sunrise approached, and I had a task to complete before morning light.

With their chaotic future decided, I spun on my heel and exited the antechamber.

An hour later, the wind whipped the scent of decay from the stone building. The sign that read *Francis Key—Undertaker* creaked overhead. The marker blazed in my thoughts as if I'd brought the deceased here and not Arianna, yet as I tried to retrieve her husband's name, I couldn't. My brow furrowed. Had she placed a subconscious block before submitting to me? Internally, a corridor lay before me, filled with locked doors. I sucked my teeth. Her final tricks didn't matter. By the next full moon, my divinity would fully take hold of this vessel, allowing me access even into the deep depths that loomed within her mind.

I breathed in the night sky, relishing the darkness just before the dawn. Time was running out. If he wasn't resurrected before sunrise, his soul would remain in the Great Beyond. Then I wouldn't be able to fulfill my promise. I shuddered at what horrific punishment fate would have for me for breaking that vow. Without delay, I gripped the handle; a shadow unraveled from me, and the lock clicked open.

My feet padded along the floorboards, yet not a soul stirred. The thumping of two hearts in the upstairs bedroom beat a steady tattoo. However, I ignored the pair and followed the pungent aroma of decomposition through the hallway and toward a staircase leading to a cellar.

The cold basement held a table with tools along the wall. A cot stood in the center. Upon the flimsy bed lay a man. From the fluttering of the heart, I knew it was Arianna's husband. I approached and drank in his features. Given his straight nose, high cheekbones, and angular jaw, he'd likely been handsome before the ailment had taken hold. He'd been young, though the illness that had claimed him had ravaged him. Again, I attempted to unfurl more information about him, but none came. My nostrils flared, yet my vow must be kept.

My fingers brushed his salt and pepper locks, as if by habit, then pinched the skin on the crook of his chin. My thumb pressed down, parting his lips. The wafting of poison curled from him. My nose wrinkled. However, nothing could overpower life's breath when provided before the sunrise after one's death. No, whatever had killed him, be it an ailment or toxin in his veins, would vanish as soon as Delphine's vitality entered him.

I lowered my mouth to his in a tender kiss. The life force I'd extracted slithered from me, up my throat and into him. As I withdrew, a flutter coiled in my belly. My brow knitted, but the fleeting sensation flickered away.

I stepped back. Golden light pulsed through his veins and crawled down his neck, then encompassed his form. The hollows of his cheeks plumped. His graying pallor transformed to olive gold. His once-ravaged body reformed, filling out the once-baggy clothing. Raven hair replaced the speckling of gray. My hand itched to run through his locks, and my lips ached to press against his again. However, that would undo everything. I had no life force within my belly, and my kiss alone was that of death. I shook off this dormant longing from Arianna's exis-tence.

Minutes later, only his soul was left to be beckoned forward. I placed my palm on his heart; a flicker of him lingered, not fully settled into the Great Beyond. His name still eluded me, but his energetic signature matched that of this form.

"Arise," I commanded, and his soul snapped back into his body.

An inhale echoed in the silent room. His chest rose and fell with steady breaths. For a moment, my legs wouldn't move as I drank him in. My heartbeat increased. I forced these irritating reactions away. The overwhelming affection Arianna had had for him still plagued this vessel. I couldn't linger here. No, he would awaken with no recollection of his love. Then he'd head back to Presspin. Then my promise would be fulfilled and this fate mark would leave my wrist.

Before being seen, I exited the morgue. As I stepped onto the silent street, the light of dawn peeked, brightening the sky. As the morning sun rose, I commanded mental shadows upon every single mind Arianna had ever come into contact with. Her existence was blotted out, as if she had never been. As the rays caressed my skin, I stood in the sunshine and smiled. For today started a new era—the rise of Aralia, the goddess of darkness.

EPILOGUE

SILAS

GOOSE BUMPS ROSE ON my flesh, and I shifted on an uncomfortable cot. As I moved, awareness coursed through me. Not a flicker of pain ached in my muscles, nor did my breaths come out as a wheeze. Had Xavier done it? Had he procured the elixir of life? My eyes flew open, taking in the cold stone cellar. Whispers of light curled in from a window toward the top of the wall, washing over a table filled with medical tools. Confused, I stood. To my relief, my legs held my weight with ease. I glanced about the room, taking in the devoid space. Where was Xavier? Where was I? Needing answers before I found a way out of this basement, I ambled to the desk, trying to remember what had led me here.

I stared at the unsettling devices strewn about, but nothing seemed familiar. Uneasy, I took a steadying breath and recalled the last events before I'd slipped into unconsciousness. Xavier and I had been on the path between Krella and Hallowhaven when we were stopped by an Aralian platoon. They'd been searching for cursed. When they discovered my blight, we'd fought them, but...

My thoughts stretched toward the moment, but a searing pain lanced through my skull. I pushed my palm to my forehead. Only a single moment pressed forward—I'd kept crawling, reaching for something important. A knot formed in my throat, and I swallowed it, confused by this swell of anguish. However, beyond that moment was only darkness. My teeth gritted in frustration. The high fever had likely caused the gaps in my memories. I must have battled the Aralians with the very final flickers of my power before passing out. However, something grazed the recesses of my mind, a soft touch like a light feather.

My fingers grabbed the ledge, as if anchoring myself would steady my jumbled brain. A sense of foreboding settled. Had Xavier stashed me with some Hallowhaven doctor? Was that what this place was? Given my healed state, I could only assume that Xavier had succeeded. Yet why wasn't he here?

The floorboards creaked overhead, then a pair of footsteps echoed down the steps behind me. Unease settled on my skin, and power coiled in my palm, ready to strike a blow if I needed to escape.

An unfamiliar voice cut through my ruminations. "He's down here. An Aralian dropped him off last night. She told me to fetch you in the morning."

"A disciple brought him here?" Xavier asked.

A wash of relief loosened my tight shoulders at his familiar tone. Despite my uncertainty about my father's methods, he'd proven himself an ally. He'd ventured to Presspin after hearing of my illness. Then he'd whisked me to Hallowhaven, placing himself in danger with the disciples searching for those like me. Given my current state, he somehow had provided me the elixir of life as promised. These actions placed him in a more favorable light.

The pulsing darkness in my palm diminished just as Xavier and an elderly man stepped onto the landing and froze. The gentleman's face paled, as if he'd seen a ghost. He swayed on his feet. His eyes rolled back into his head. Xavier lunged forward and caught him before his skull smacked against the stone steps.

My brow knitted. "Did you jab him with a tranquilizer?"

Xavier leaned the man against the wall. As he stood, shock coated his expression, though it quickly smoothed into a look of elation. He sprinted to me and wrapped me in a hug. I blinked, but my stony heart had softened on our travels. I returned his embrace.

"My boy. You...you were dead. The elixir, it was a trap. Poison. But you're alive. I don't know how, but you're alive." He withdrew, and his fingers trembled as they cupped my face. "I don't care how this miracle happened. All that matters is you're alive." His Adam's apple bobbed. "Now we—"

"You, you unholy monster!" the man screamed. He lifted a finger at me.

Xavier's countenance transformed from shocked elation to cold resolve. He spun and plucked a dagger from his coat. He flicked the blade. It sailed and pierced the man's neck. The elderly gentleman's features twisted in horror. His fingers dug at the hilt, but before he could withdraw it, he slumped.

"Why did you do that?" I hissed.

"Because he would likely scream in the streets about some resurrected lord, drawing attention to you." Xavier walked to the deceased, plucked the blade from his throat, and wiped it on his shirt. "When I came down here, we thought you'd perished. Needless to say the dead resurrecting would draw the attention not only of the townsfolk but of the Aralians."

I opened my mouth to argue but snapped it shut. Dead? My lips pulled into a tight line, but a gnawing sensation tugged in my gut.

"You're in a morgue. The undertaker summoned me to retrieve your body, and well…" He turned and gestured to me. He shivered, as if the realization that something unnatural had occurred here was giving him pause. He took a breath and smoothed his composure. "We'll have to leave at once. His wife left for the market, but she'll likely return." He strode past me and to the table. He tugged at some drawers and pulled out a journal. The ripping of paper punctuated the air. "Excellent. No trace of us now. We'll get you to the safe house, and then we can figure out how you're alive."

I peered down at my nightshirt and gestured to my half-dressed form. "Oh yes, this will be very inconspicuous."

He huffed a sigh. "Fine, I'll find you some clothes."

He retreated up the stairs.

A beat passed, and that strange sensation coiled along my skin. I shook it off. I could ruminate over my resurrection later. As I headed for the steps, I took in the man. Though I didn't care for dispatching the innocent, Xavier was correct; he likely would have revealed not only my presence but drawn attention to the blight I'd kept hidden. Needing to be freed from this place, I exited the cellar.

At the top of the stairs sat a quaint kitchen painted in a bright buttercream. My nose wrinkled at the overly chipper color for a morgue. A few paces ahead was a table for two with a plate of bacon and eggs upon it. To my right lay a woodstove with a kettle boiling atop. Its whistle punctuated the air. I removed it from the stove and placed it on the counter, stopping the infernal noise.

"These should work," Xavier said from the threshold.

As I pivoted to him, he thrust a stack of clothing and a pair of boots forward.

Without a word, I exited the dining space and opened a door in the corridor, which led into a cramped bathing chamber. As I stripped out of the nightshirt, my gaze dipped over my body. The lean muscle I'd lost over the winter had returned, as if I'd never suffered from the wasting sickness. I paused. I'd never born the mask as my uncle. How had I contracted the ailment? Again, that dark hole burrowed into my brain, causing me to flinch.

My fingers dragged through my hair and settled on my nape. My eyes shifted to the mirror above the porcelain basin as I studied my features, which were no longer hollowed and gaunt. I'd been livid when Xavier arrived in Hallowhaven, but he'd saved my life. However, hadn't he said that the elixir had been laced with poison?

My curse flared, as if it were trying to speak, but I suppressed whatever bubbled internally. No, the blight needn't further confuse me. Quickly, I pulled on the too-short trousers. Then

I yanked the tunic on. The fabric tugged against my shoulders and barely covered my stomach. Finally, I slipped into the boots a size too small with a groan. Dressed, I searched for Xavier.

"Xavier?" I stepped into the kitchen, but he wasn't there. I pressed through the hall and toward the entrance, where he lingered. He clutched a letter, perusing the contents.

My lips pulled into a thin line, and I approached. "What is it?"

His pallor blanched. "Something terrible has happened."

He thrust the letter into my hand. Quickly, I read over the missive.

Silas,

It is of the utmost importance that you and Xavier heed my warnings. I have very little time, so I'll only provide you with the most important points.

The good news is that Delphine is dead.

However, the goddess Aralia has risen and will enact her revenge upon this world. I do not know her exact plans. However, her power has not been fully incorporated into the vessel she inhabits. She must be vanquished by the next full moon, or all will be lost.

The Aralians know of the Opposition. Martha and those within the Scarlet Rose are in grave danger. They must disband.

Finally, you must find Naomi Park. She was last seen north of Daviel. She may have returned to Presspin, but I doubt it. Once you locate her, protect her with your life.

My gaze trailed over the letter once, twice, thrice. My mind reeled. Something about the curve of the handwriting felt familiar, yet the writer left no signature. The parchment wrinkled under my fingers' tips, and no seal lay upon the folds. "Who sent this? And who the blasts is Naomi Park?"

Xavier shook his head. "The note was slid under the door. When I peeked out, only townsfolk milled about. It seems we have an ally in the temple. But we can discuss this more at my safe house." His fingers lingered on the knob.

I folded the letter and shoved it into my pocket. My fingers trailed my neck to touch my uncle's onyx ring, as if by habit. I froze at its absence. "Wait. The undertaker must have removed my necklace. It's important."

Before awaiting his answer, I strode back to the cellar, venturing quickly down the steps. As my boots hit the landing, I beelined for the table, searching for the missing heirloom. I yanked the drawers open. To my luck, the chain sat in a small box tucked amongst some papers. My fingers wrapped around the silver strand, but my brain hitched at the two onyx rings laced upon it. One had been my uncle's. However, the other was a woman's.

My fingers traced along the slender band, with the word beloved etched upon it. The curse hissed in my mind so deeply that even I could no longer ignore its protestations.

I closed my eyes, trying to remember this ring and who it might belong to, but a searing sensation pierced my skull. Yet a pang flickered internally, like a thin cord that had been limp now growing taught. It reverberated, as if in time with my heartbeat.

My mate, my blight growled; the pressure of the words curled throughout my being.

I flinched, the bone-deep understanding coiling within me with such a resonance that my muscles tensed.

My mate, it screamed again as I stared at the dainty warded piece. My pulse climbed, and the whisper of a kiss lingered, as if a ghost had brushed my lips.

"Gods above, Silas, we can't wait all morning. What are you doing?" Xavier called from the stairwell.

My hand balled into a fist, encompassing the rings. I longed to leave for Presspin, but something in my gut tugged, like an ancient knowing. Something was missing from me, like a piece of my soul had been extracted, leaving a gaping hole not only within me but in my memories. Resolve coated me, and the blight settled in this joint understanding.

Though I knew not who she was, one thing was for certain: this jewelry belonged to my beloved, my mate. No matter what, I would find her.

APPENDIX

CHARACTER GUIDE:

ARIANNA (PARK) BELMONT – Lady Belmont – Married to Silas Belmont, sister to Naomi Park.

Silas Belmont – Lord Belmont – Overseer of Presspin, married to Arianna Belmont, sister to Beatrix Belmont.

Beatrix Belmont (Archer) – Sister to Lord Belmont, Married to Duncan Archer.

Duncan Archer – Husband to Beatrix Belmont.

Naomi Park – Sister to Arianna Park and herbalist apprentice to Brielle Fairchild.

Brielle Fairchild – Presspin herbalist, previous casual paramour to Lord Belmont, friend to Arianna Belmont and Naomi Park, soul mate to Wren and in a relationship with Mateo Reed.

Vincent Gallager – Steward to Belmont Manor, friend to Mateo Reed and Silas Belmont, harbors not so secret crush on Beatrix Belmont.

Mateo Reed – Paramour to Brielle Fairchild, militia member and friend to Vincent Gallager.

Peter Hargrave – Adoptive grandfather to Silas and Beatrix Belmont, General of Presspin militia, owner of the inn south of the Presspin boarder, married to Agnes Hargrave.

Mrs. (Maggie) Potter – House manager for Belmont Manor, maternal figure for all those within Belmont Manor.

Kaine Darkmont – Leader of the Huntsmen. Previously lived in Presspin. The young man who attacked Silas, was injured and fled Presspin during Silas's adolescents.

Xavier Veronin – Biological father to Beatrix & Silas Belmont, Councilmember to the High Council in Hallowhaven, paramour to Delphine, co-creator of the Opposition.

Robin – Member of the Opposition.

Martha – Owner of the Scarlet Rose, Ex-Aralian Disciple, leader and co-creator of the Opposition.

Wolf – Cursed Ward to Xavier Veronin, under the care of Martha within the Scarlet Rose.

Yulia – The Oracle, ability to see flashes of the future, blessed with eternal life.

Delphine – High Disciple, and leader of the Aralians.

Wren – Soulmate to Brielle Fairchild, cursed woman.

Aralia – Goddess of Darkness.

Cassius – God of Light.

Word Guide

Aralians – The religious sect under Delphine's control who worship's Aralia. The majority believe that Aralia is the Goddess of Light and not of Darkness.

Wasting Sickness – An ailment contracted from the overuse of the cursed power and/or the draining of cursed power. Exhibits in symptoms similar to tuberculous, until the person succumbs. Same alignment that Uncle Oliver contracted and perished from.

Yulia's Tonic – Made from flowers grown from a prick of her blood. Extremely potent and will amplify a person's life force but will cause it to burn to quickly, like an epic adrenaline boost, but whoever imbibes will die unless paired with the elixir of life to restore vitality.

The Opposition – Group of Ex-Disciples and cursed that oppose the Aralian's rule.

The Realm Between Realms – Aralia's prison world where souls that are between life and death cross from the mortal world to the Great Beyond.

Lacrima – A magical stone that is enchanted and stores cursed power.

Elixir of Life – A cure all remedy drained from the cursed. It uses the properties of the blessing from the God of Life, Cassius to revitalize mortals.

Delphine's Thirteen Noble Elite – Delphine's inner circle that know the truth, that Aralia is the Goddess of Darkness.

ACKNOWLEDGEMENT

Dear Reader,

What a ride this novel has been! When I was talking with my chaos gremlin, Tia, about this book, her daughter gave the perfect descriptor as to my feelings as I wrote Claiming the Curse—*if I can't be happy, no one can be happy.* Which is an accurate depiction of the ebb and flow of depression I suffered from during the last year while rewriting and editing this novel. Between moving states in 2023, starting a new business with my husband, and navigating old wounds associated with small-town life, I struggled. A lot of my internal world is depicted through Arianna's grief, isolation, and feelings of unworthiness. Though Claiming the Curse ended on a gruesome cliffhanger, there is a spark of hope. Much like the light cresting through—it's always the darkest before the dawn. Though our tale is not complete, I'm happy to report that I've been walking with more joy and purpose with each passing day. So thank you for coming on this emotionally challenging journey with me, for walking with me and sharing a fraction of the pain I've carried. Please remember, if you are struggling with your inner darkness, there's always hope. In my journey, I've been blessed to be surrounded by so many caring and kind individuals. Which perfectly leads me to the much-needed acknowledgements to those who've circled around me over the past two years.

Thank you to the editing team, who made this a success. A huge shout-out to Brittany Mack, my developmental editor with Conquest Publishing, KT Wishert my line editor, Beth Lawton with VB Edits my copy editor and Sage Editorial for my proofreading. Thank you to V.H. Faolon for the sensitivity reading and notes. Plus, a round of applause to my beta readers: April, KT, and Kamy, for reading through the novel and offering me their stellar notes. I can't forget to thank my epic street team for all their help in promoting not only this book but all my projects. Thank you to my chaos gremlin, Tia, for reminding me to balance caring for myself while writing. This book wouldn't have been possible without the help of every one of you.

In my personal life, a huge shout-out goes to my besties Alyssa, Haley and Kristen. Thank you for listening to my multiple versions of book two, including the OG where Naomi and her love interest completely took over. Thank you for attending events, listening to my read-throughs, plot holes, and all the things. Also, shout out to my author buddies Sabrina, Sloan, & Ashley. Thank you so much for checking in on me when I went silent. Also, this book wouldn't have been complete without the gamification of my edits, so thank you to Love & Deepspace and specifically the study/work timers that kept me on task. I can't forget my lovely family. Thank you to my kids for reminding me of the importance of taking breaks, as well as my husband for wrangling our children out of the house when my deadlines were nipping at my heels this summer.

Finally, as we mourn the passing of Mateo, know a part of him will live on. I am extremely excited to continue the series. The next couple to be explored is likely going to be Beatrix X Vincent as they navigate their forced proximity in Belmont Manor, in a loose, ugly duckling retelling (Vicent's ugly duckling origin story). After the unfolding of our friends to lovers, I will explore Naomi's story, a red riding hood retelling with the recently introduced Wolf. Once those threads are set, the final story will be released as we delve into the villain Aralia's rule and Silas's search for his lost beloved in our epic finale.

Again, thank you so much to everyone who took a chance on my book, who took a chance on me. Your support, encouragement and care have meant more than you truly know.

ABOUT THE AUTHOR

Chelle Cypress is a voracious reader, mother, wife and anime enthusiast. As a child, Chelle dreamed of becoming a published author. Through hard work, many late nights, and copious amounts of coffee, she has finally achieved her dream of sharing the stories of her heart with the world. Chelle infuses her writing with themes from classic literature, regency romances, and fantasy. She enjoys blending the contents together in a novel that she hopes speaks to the hearts of her readers. Chelle has used writing as a therapeutic outlet which has helped her maintain her sobriety (7/30/21).

Follow me on
Tiktok: @chellecypressbooks
Instagram: @chellecypressbooks
Threads: @chellecypressbooks

MORE BOOKS COMING SOON

ARALIAN SERIES

VINCENT X BEATRIX NOVELLA – Ugly Duckling Reimagined (Winter 2026)

Naomi x Wolf Story – Red Riding Hood Reimagined (2027)

Epic Finale – (TBD)

DEMI GOD DUOLOGY

Seduced by the Summer King novella - Beauty & The Beast x Mid-Summer Nights Dream Vibes – (Summer 2026)

Winter King Spin Off - (TBD)